KAIROS

ULYSSE MALASSAGNE

:01

First Second
New York

First Second

English translation by Anne and Owen Smith
English translation copyright © 2020 by Roaring Brook Press

Published by First Second
First Second is an imprint of Roaring Brook Press,
a division of Holtzbrinck Publishing Holdings Limited Partnership
120 Broadway, New York, NY 10271

Don't miss your next favorite book from First Second! For the latest updates go to
firstsecondnewsletter.com and sign up for our enewsletter.

Library of Congress Control Number: 2019930670
ISBN: 978-1-250-20961-0

Our books may be purchased in bulk for promotional, educational, or business use.
Please contact your local bookseller or the Macmillan Corporate and Premium Sales Department at
(800) 221-7945 ext. 5442 or by email at MacmillanSpecialMarkets@macmillan.com.

FIRST

EDITION

Originally published in French under the title *Kairos-Intégrale*
© ANKAMA EDITIONS 2015, by Ulysse Malassagne
First American edition 2020

American edition edited by Mark Siegel and Tim Stout
Cover design by Andrew Arnold
Interior book design by Rob Steen
Printed in China

1 3 5 7 9 10 8 6 4 2

PART ONE

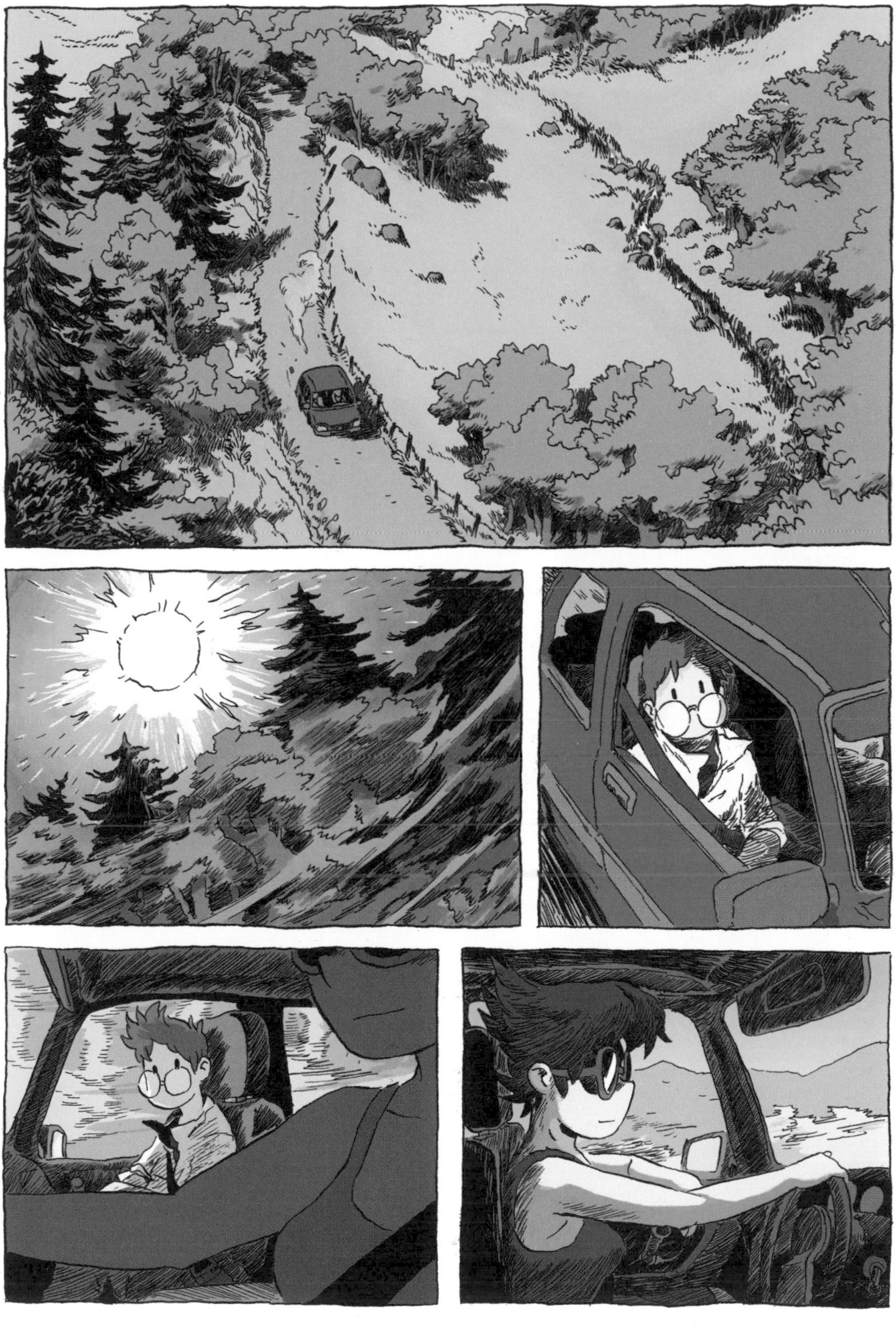

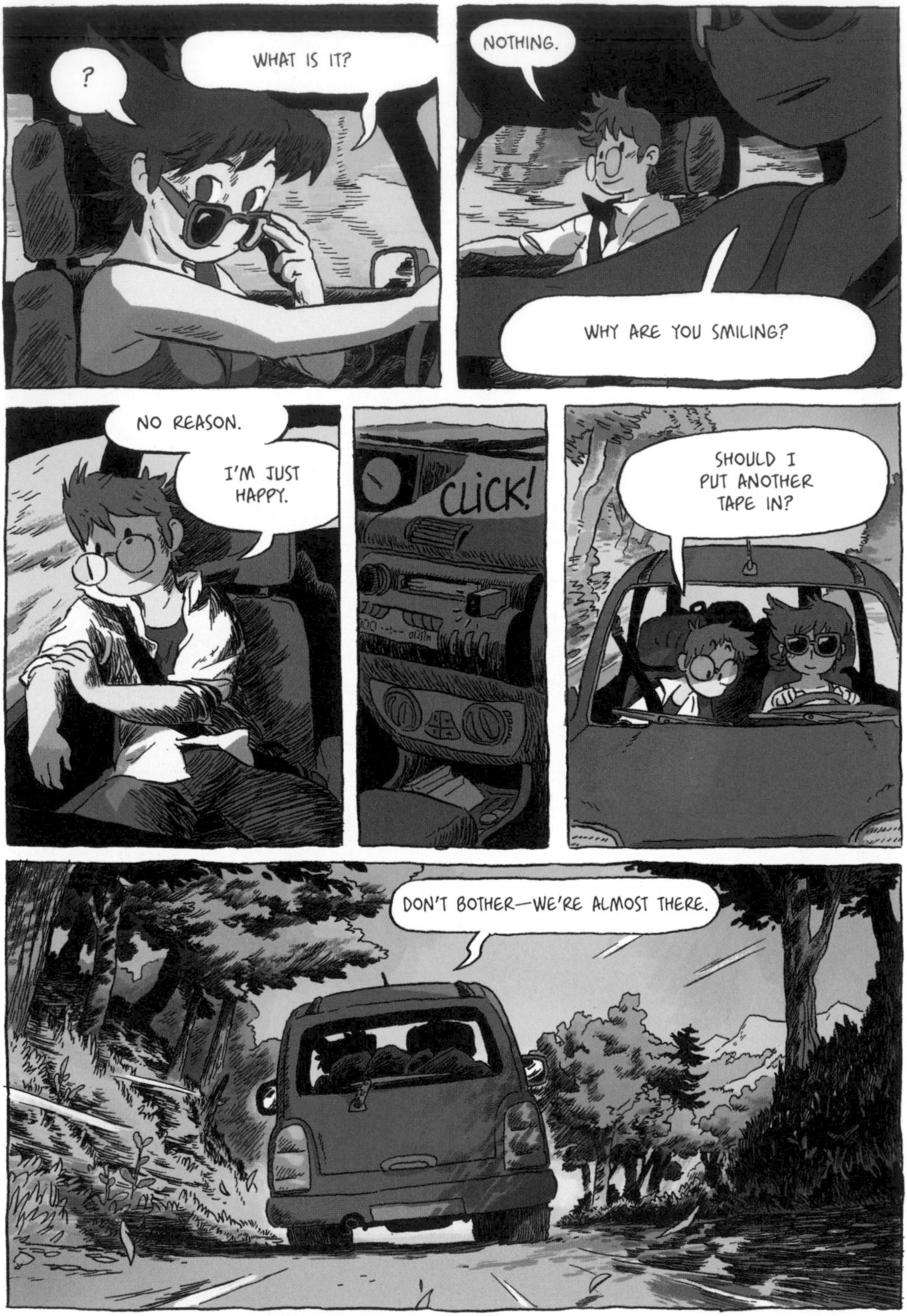
?
WHAT IS IT?
NOTHING.
WHY ARE YOU SMILING?
NO REASON.
I'M JUST HAPPY.
CLICK!
SHOULD I PUT ANOTHER TAPE IN?
DON'T BOTHER—WE'RE ALMOST THERE.

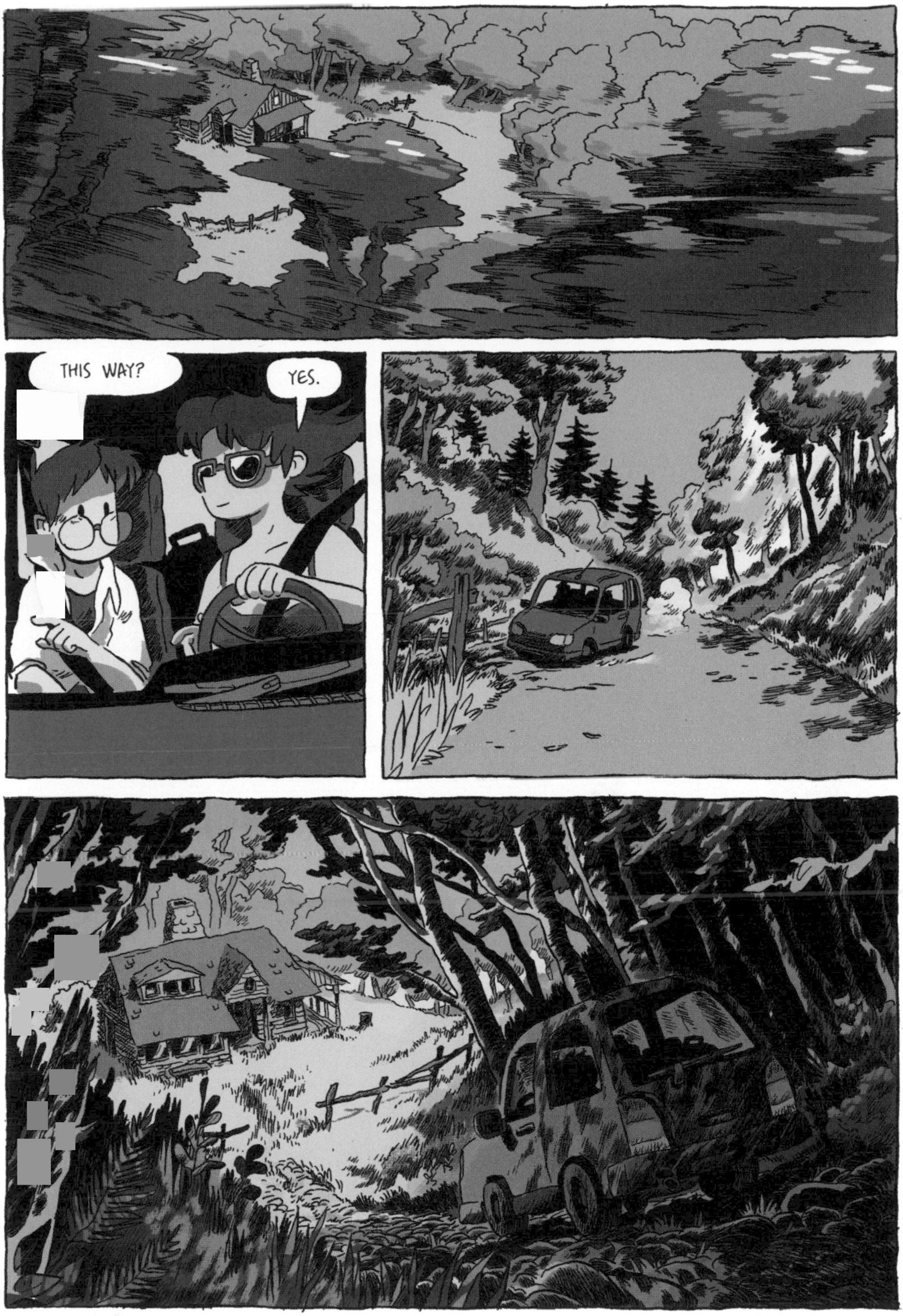
THIS WAY?
YES.

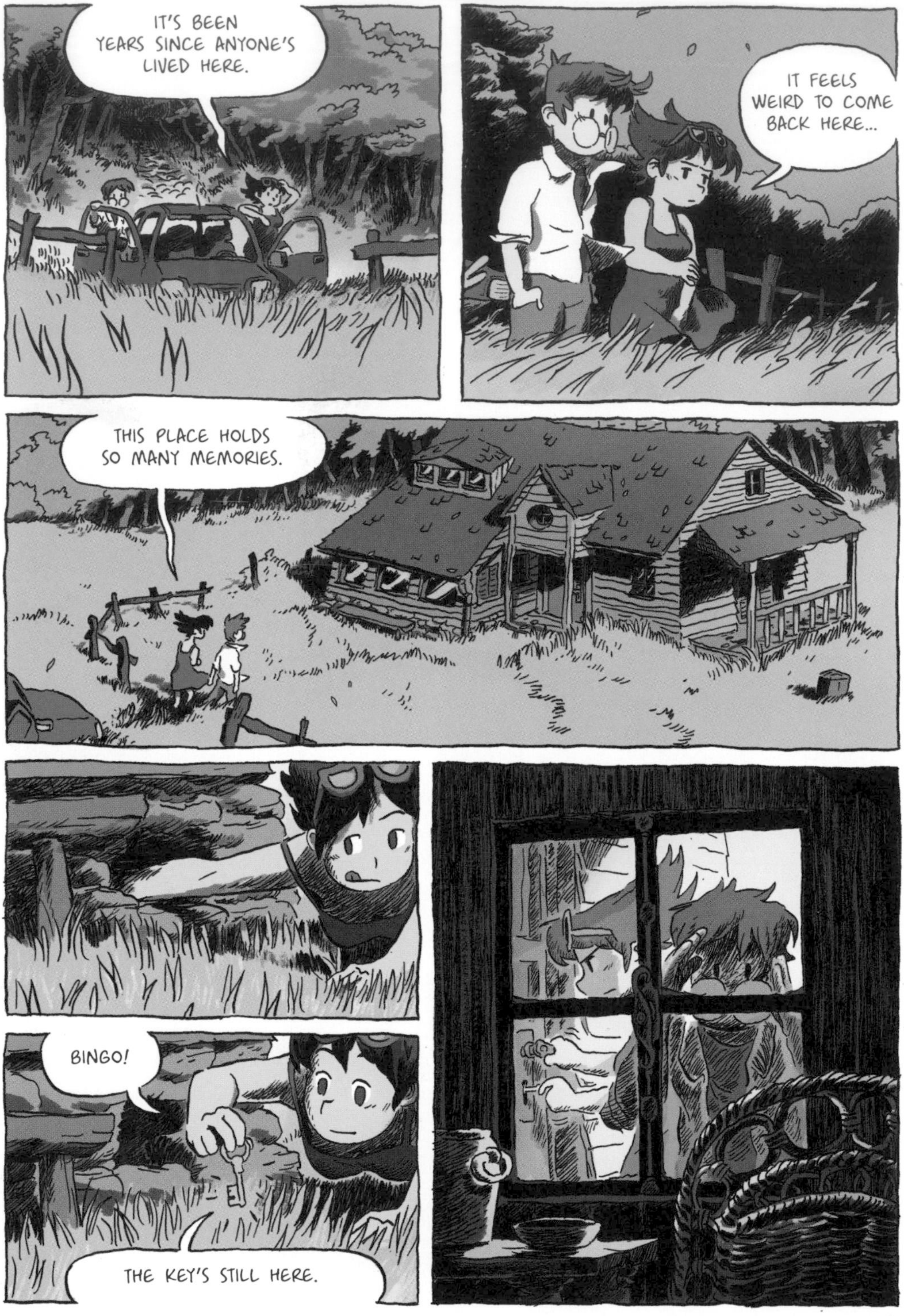
IT'S BEEN YEARS SINCE ANYONE'S LIVED HERE.
IT FEELS WEIRD TO COME BACK HERE...
THIS PLACE HOLDS SO MANY MEMORIES.
BINGO!
THE KEY'S STILL HERE.

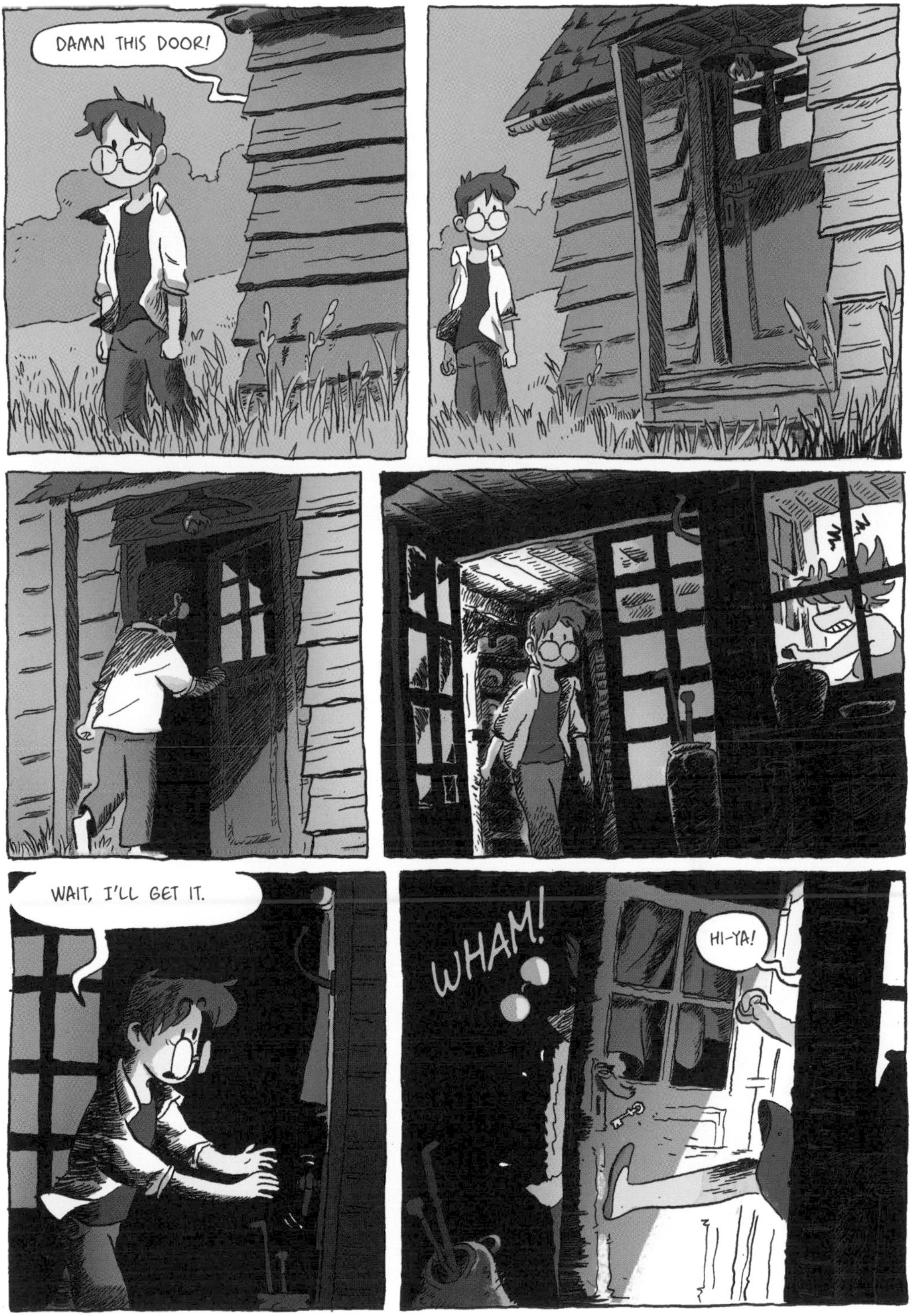
DAMN THIS DOOR!
WAIT, I'LL GET IT.
WHAM!
HI-YA!

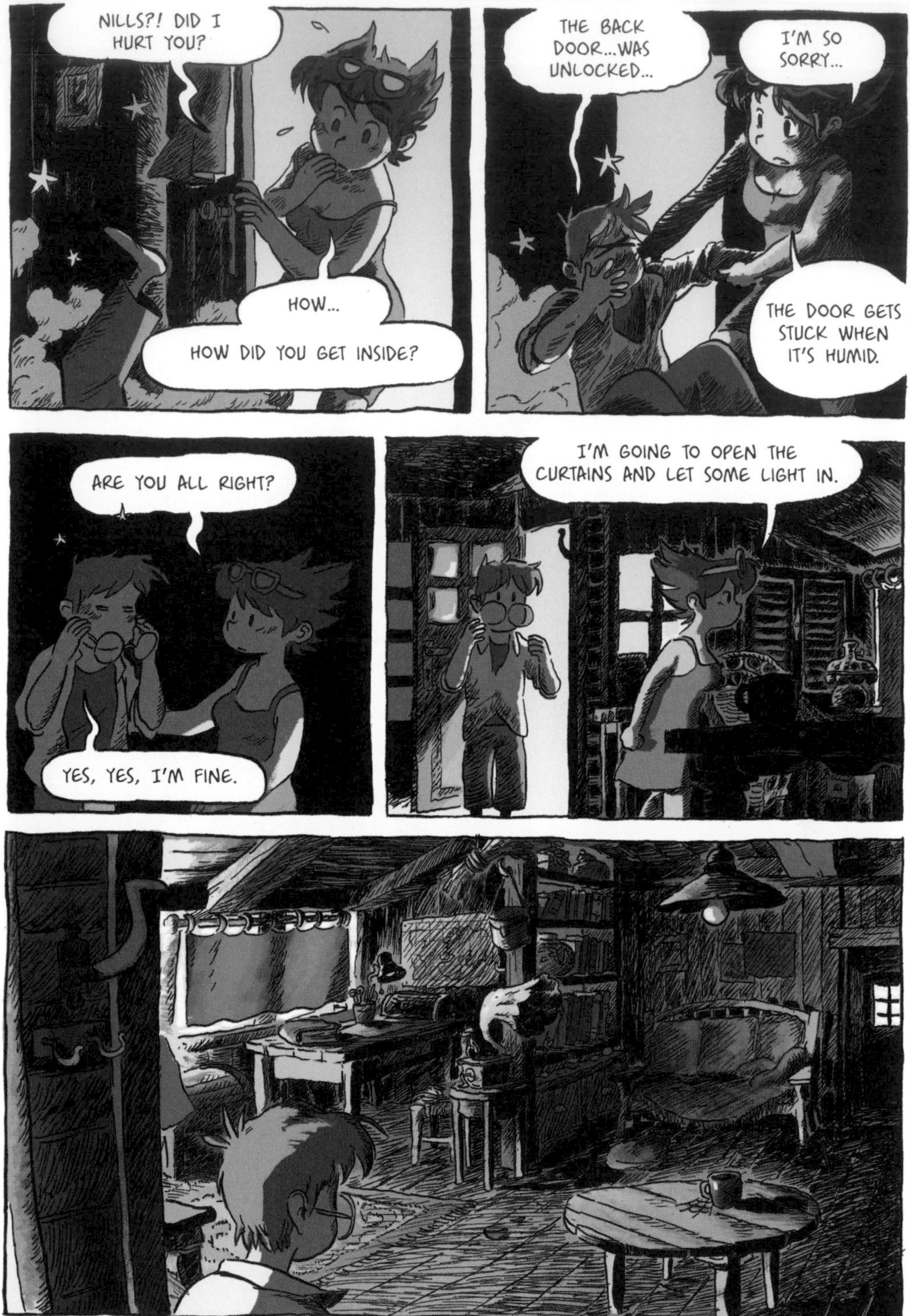

NILLS?! DID I HURT YOU?
HOW...
HOW DID YOU GET INSIDE?
THE BACK DOOR...WAS UNLOCKED...
I'M SO SORRY...
THE DOOR GETS STUCK WHEN IT'S HUMID.
ARE YOU ALL RIGHT?
YES, YES, I'M FINE.
I'M GOING TO OPEN THE CURTAINS AND LET SOME LIGHT IN.

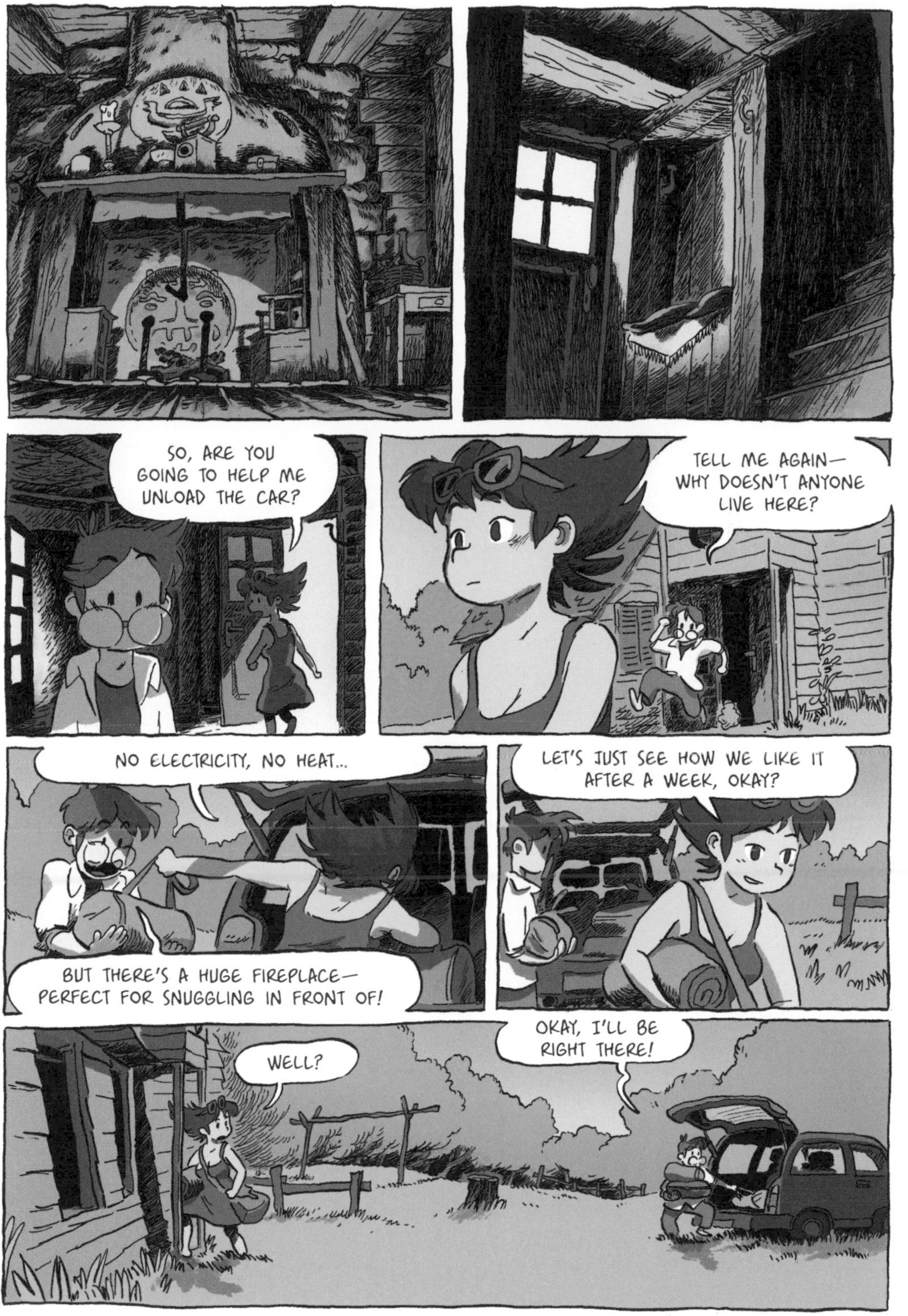
SO, ARE YOU GOING TO HELP ME UNLOAD THE CAR?
TELL ME AGAIN— WHY DOESN'T ANYONE LIVE HERE?
NO ELECTRICITY, NO HEAT...
BUT THERE'S A HUGE FIREPLACE— PERFECT FOR SNUGGLING IN FRONT OF!
LET'S JUST SEE HOW WE LIKE IT AFTER A WEEK, OKAY?
WELL?
OKAY, I'LL BE RIGHT THERE!

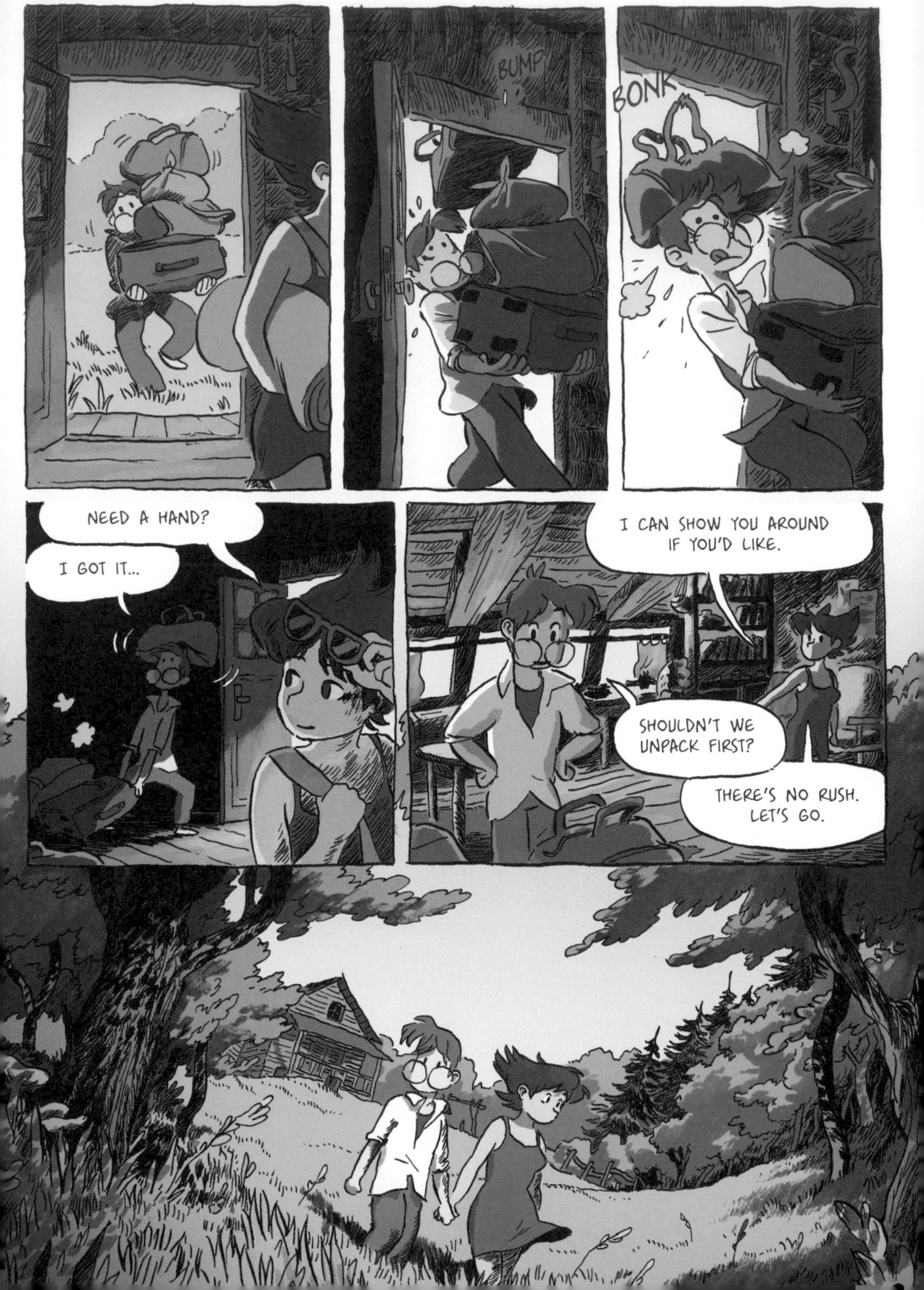
BUMP
BONK
NEED A HAND?
I GOT IT...
I CAN SHOW YOU AROUND IF YOU'D LIKE.
SHOULDN'T WE UNPACK FIRST?
THERE'S NO RUSH. LET'S GO.

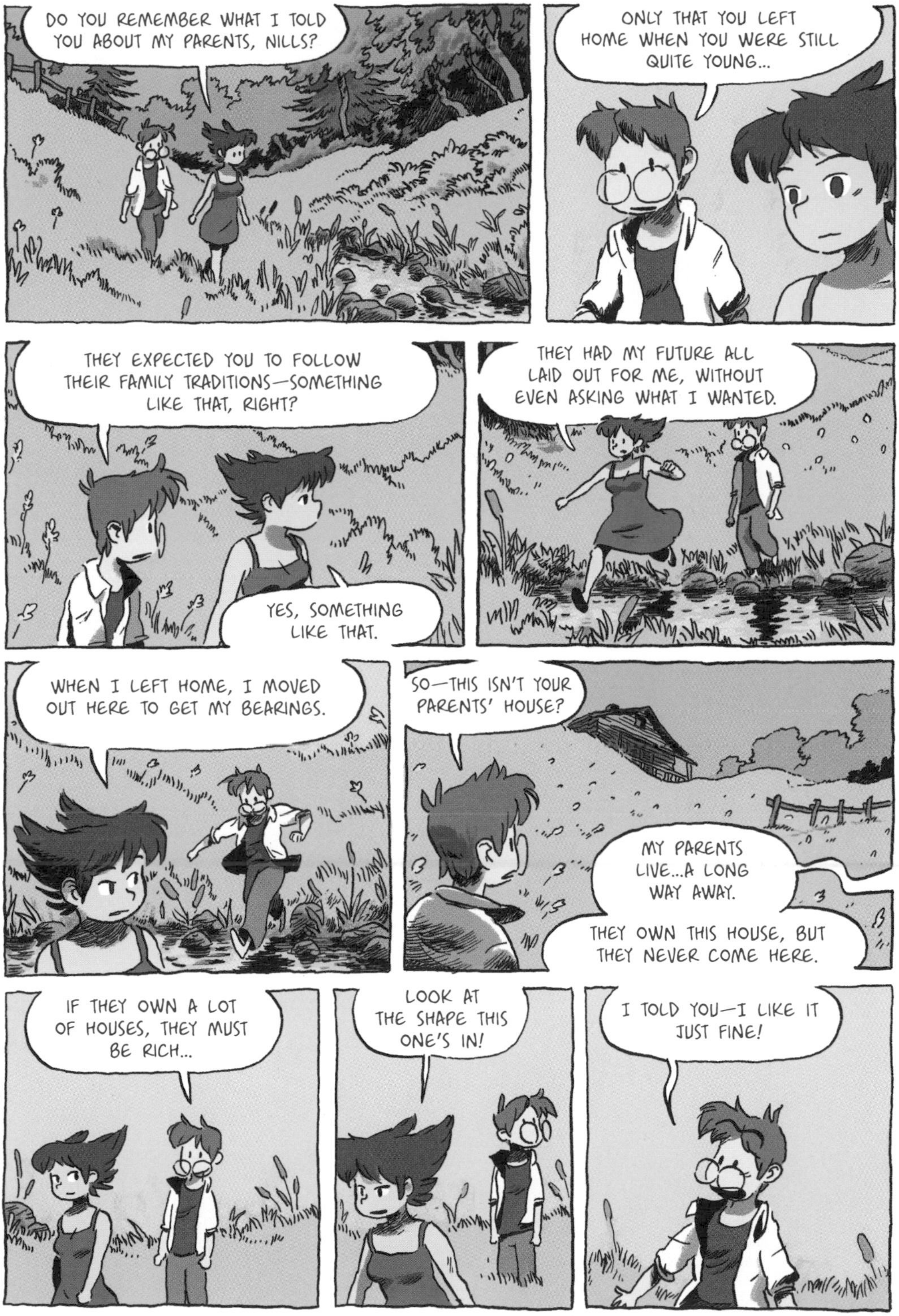
DO YOU REMEMBER WHAT I TOLD YOU ABOUT MY PARENTS, NILLS?
ONLY THAT YOU LEFT HOME WHEN YOU WERE STILL QUITE YOUNG...
THEY EXPECTED YOU TO FOLLOW THEIR FAMILY TRADITIONS—SOMETHING LIKE THAT, RIGHT?
YES, SOMETHING LIKE THAT.
THEY HAD MY FUTURE ALL LAID OUT FOR ME, WITHOUT EVEN ASKING WHAT I WANTED.
WHEN I LEFT HOME, I MOVED OUT HERE TO GET MY BEARINGS.
SO—THIS ISN'T YOUR PARENTS' HOUSE?
MY PARENTS LIVE...A LONG WAY AWAY.
THEY OWN THIS HOUSE, BUT THEY NEVER COME HERE.
IF THEY OWN A LOT OF HOUSES, THEY MUST BE RICH...
LOOK AT THE SHAPE THIS ONE'S IN!
I TOLD YOU—I LIKE IT JUST FINE!

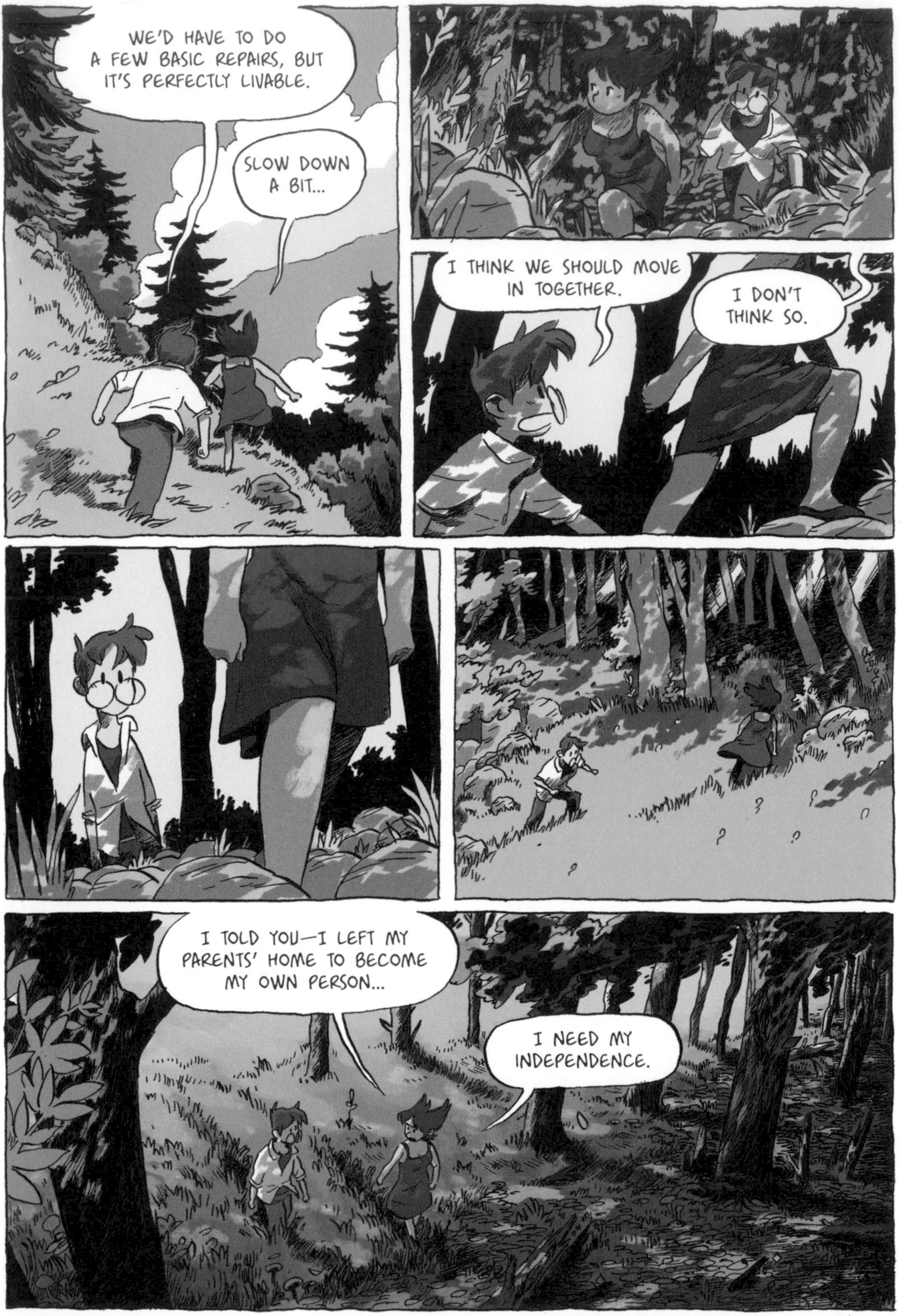
WE'D HAVE TO DO A FEW BASIC REPAIRS, BUT IT'S PERFECTLY LIVABLE.
SLOW DOWN A BIT...
I THINK WE SHOULD MOVE IN TOGETHER.
I DON'T THINK SO.
I TOLD YOU—I LEFT MY PARENTS' HOME TO BECOME MY OWN PERSON...
I NEED MY INDEPENDENCE.

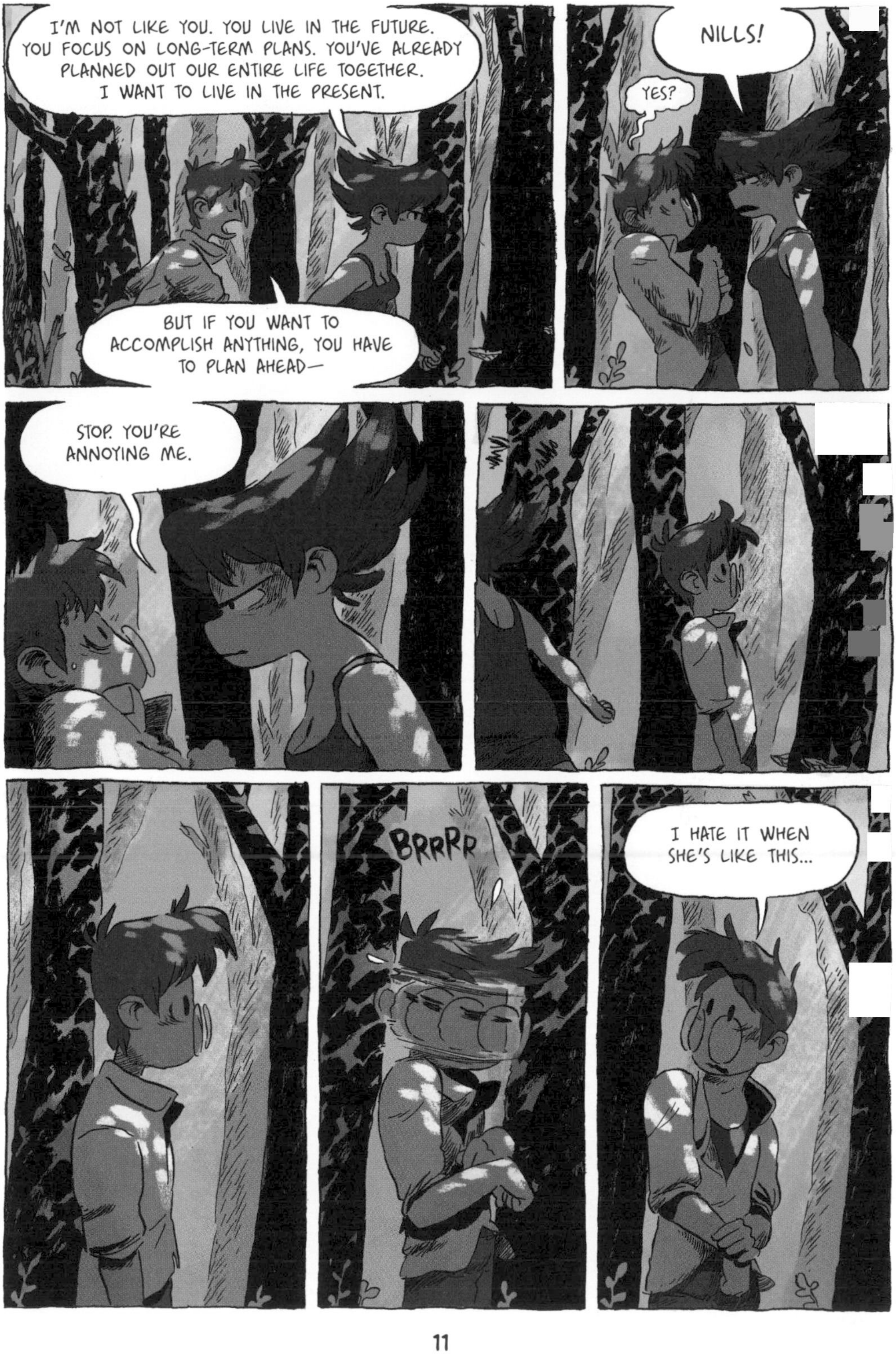

I'M NOT LIKE YOU. YOU LIVE IN THE FUTURE. YOU FOCUS ON LONG-TERM PLANS. YOU'VE ALREADY PLANNED OUT OUR ENTIRE LIFE TOGETHER. I WANT TO LIVE IN THE PRESENT.
BUT IF YOU WANT TO ACCOMPLISH ANYTHING, YOU HAVE TO PLAN AHEAD—
NILLS!
YES?
STOP. YOU'RE ANNOYING ME.
BRRRR
I HATE IT WHEN SHE'S LIKE THIS...

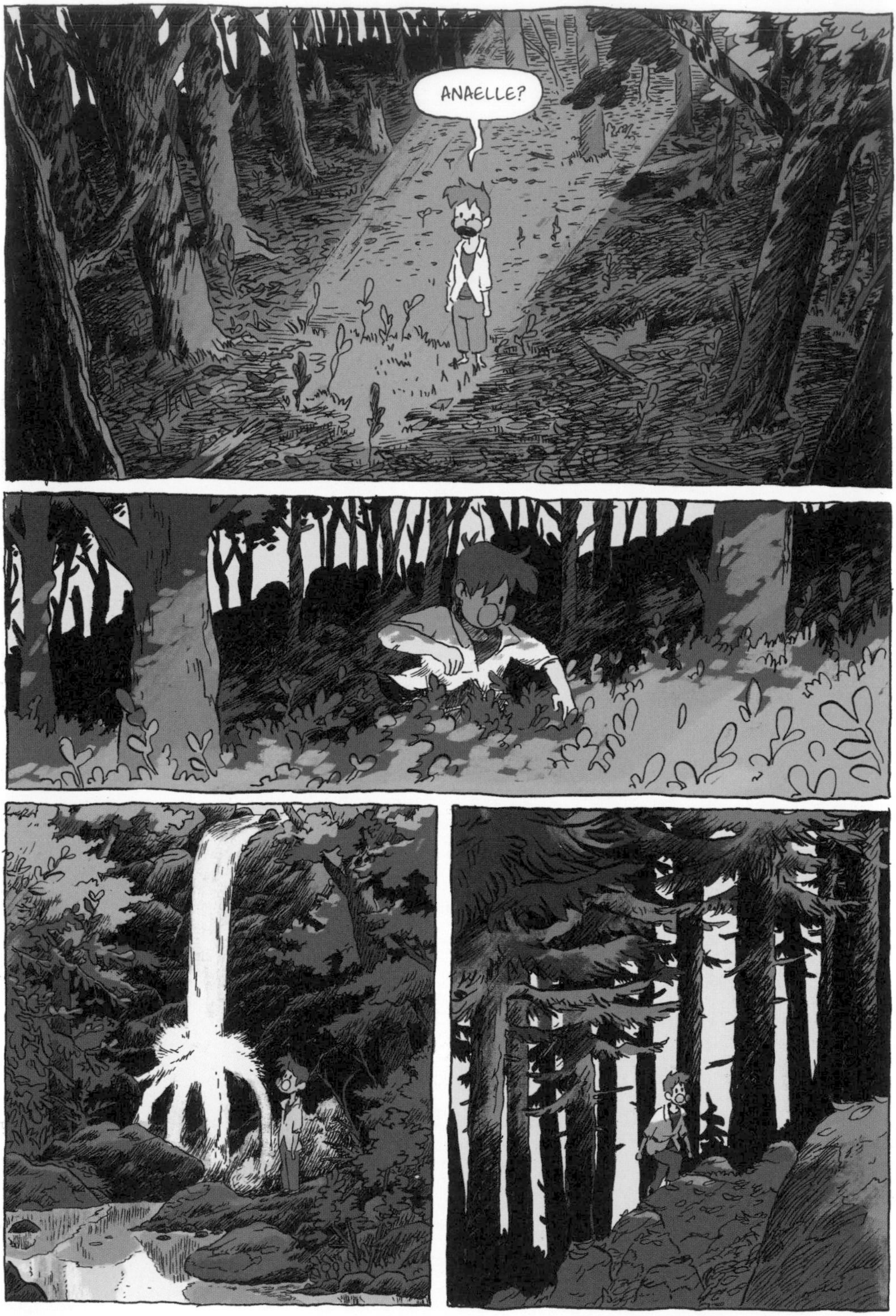
ANAELLE?

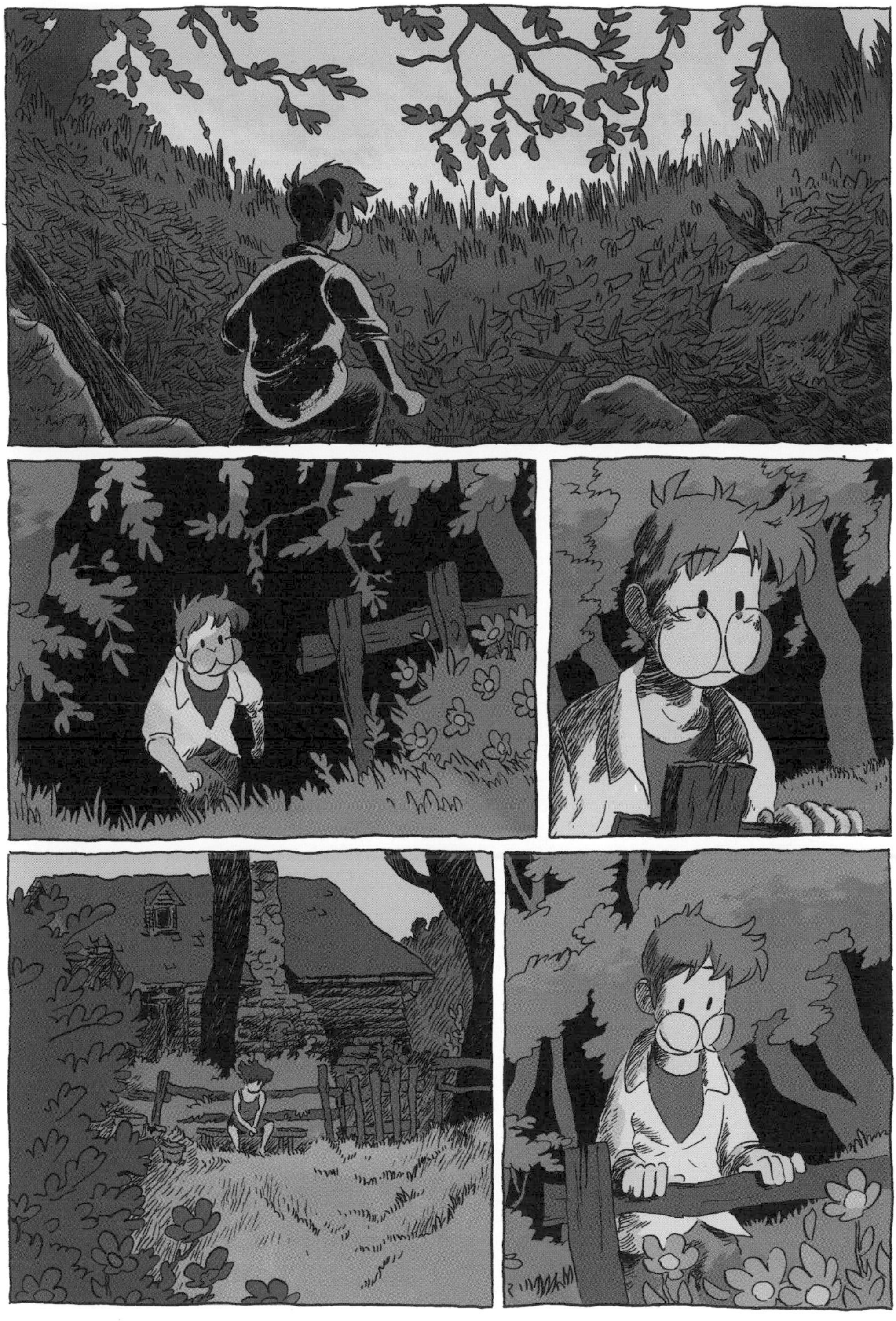

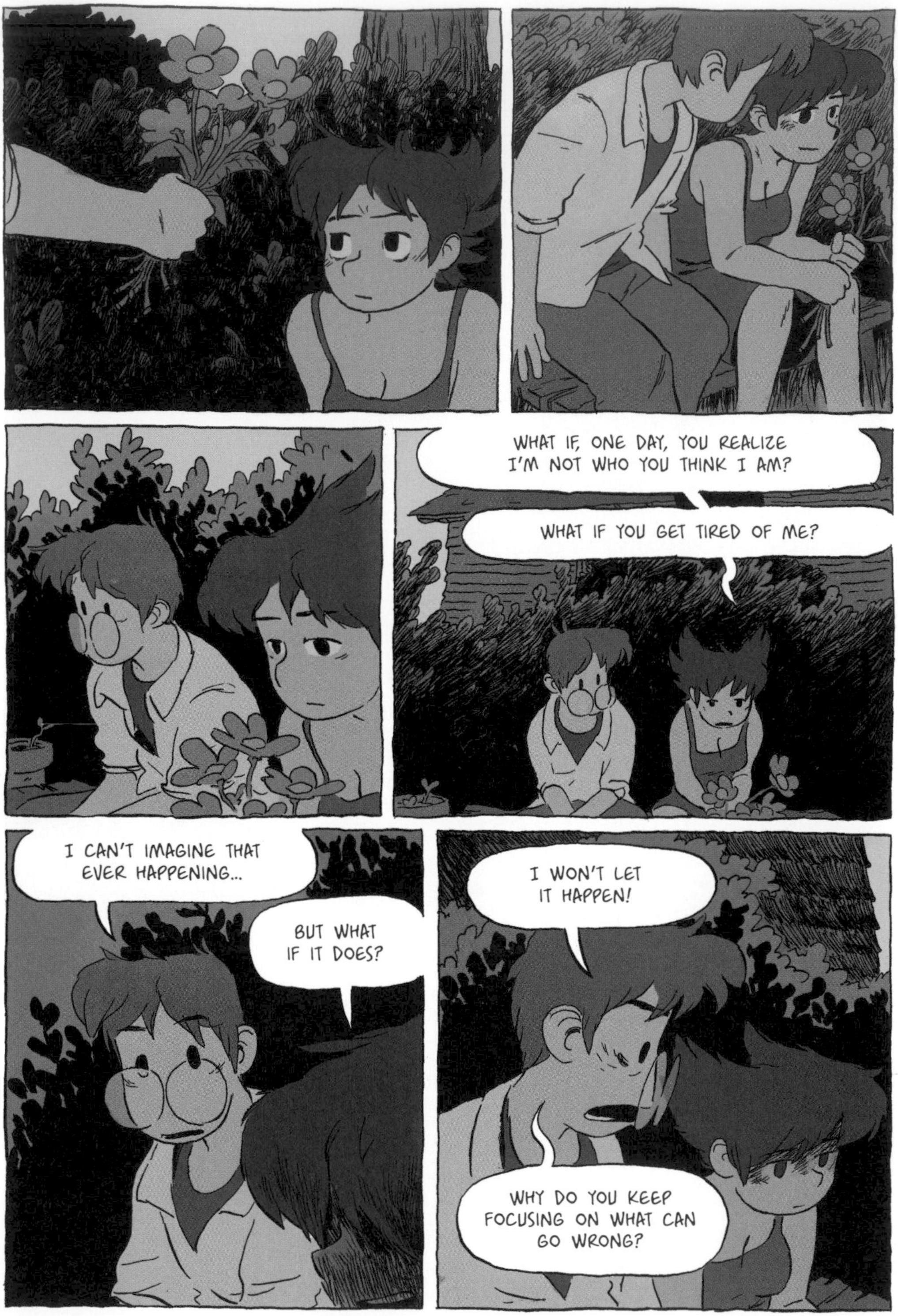
WHAT IF, ONE DAY, YOU REALIZE I'M NOT WHO YOU THINK I AM?
WHAT IF YOU GET TIRED OF ME?
I CAN'T IMAGINE THAT EVER HAPPENING...
BUT WHAT IF IT DOES?
I WON'T LET IT HAPPEN!
WHY DO YOU KEEP FOCUSING ON WHAT CAN GO WRONG?

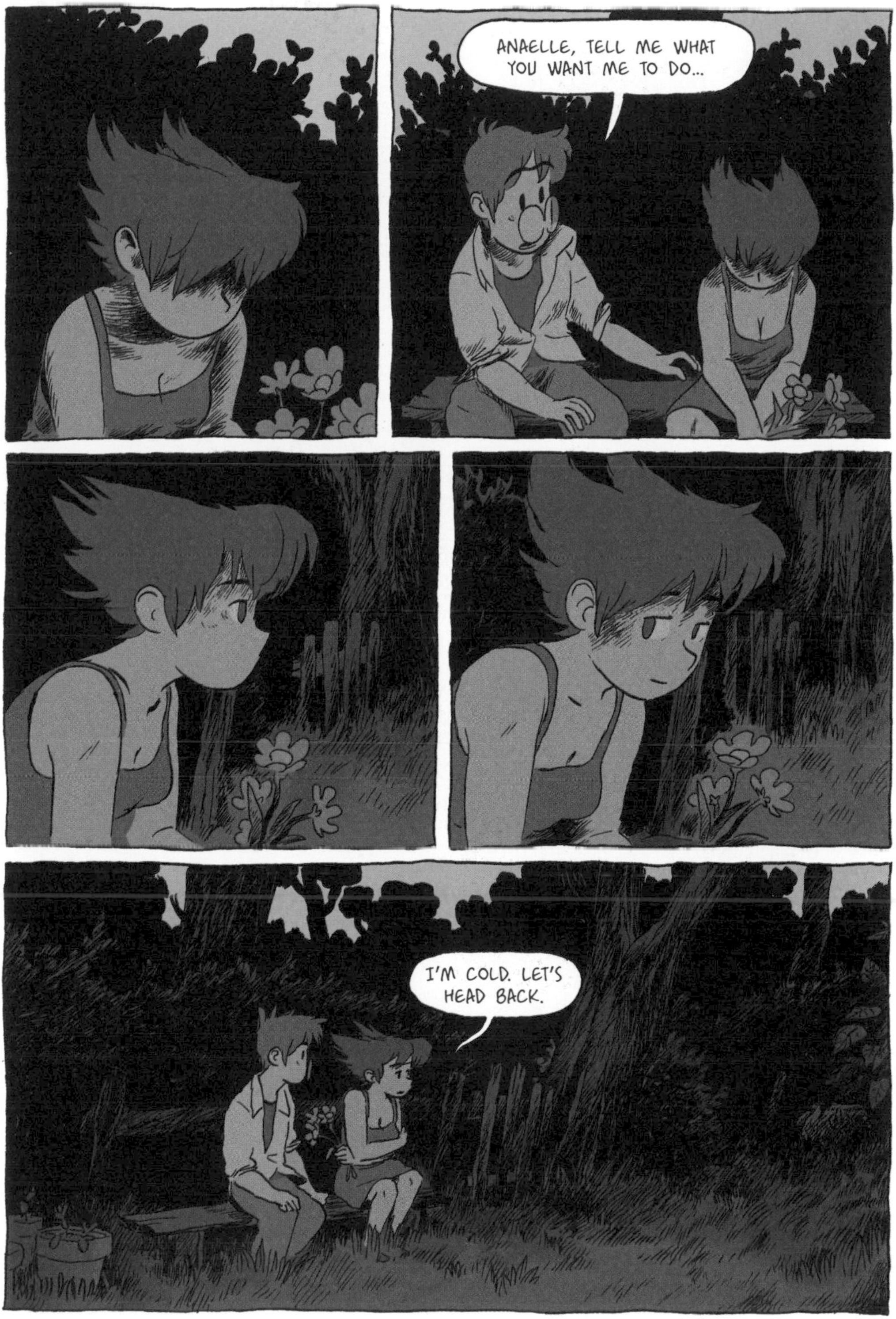
ANAELLE, TELL ME WHAT YOU WANT ME TO DO...
I'M COLD. LET'S HEAD BACK.

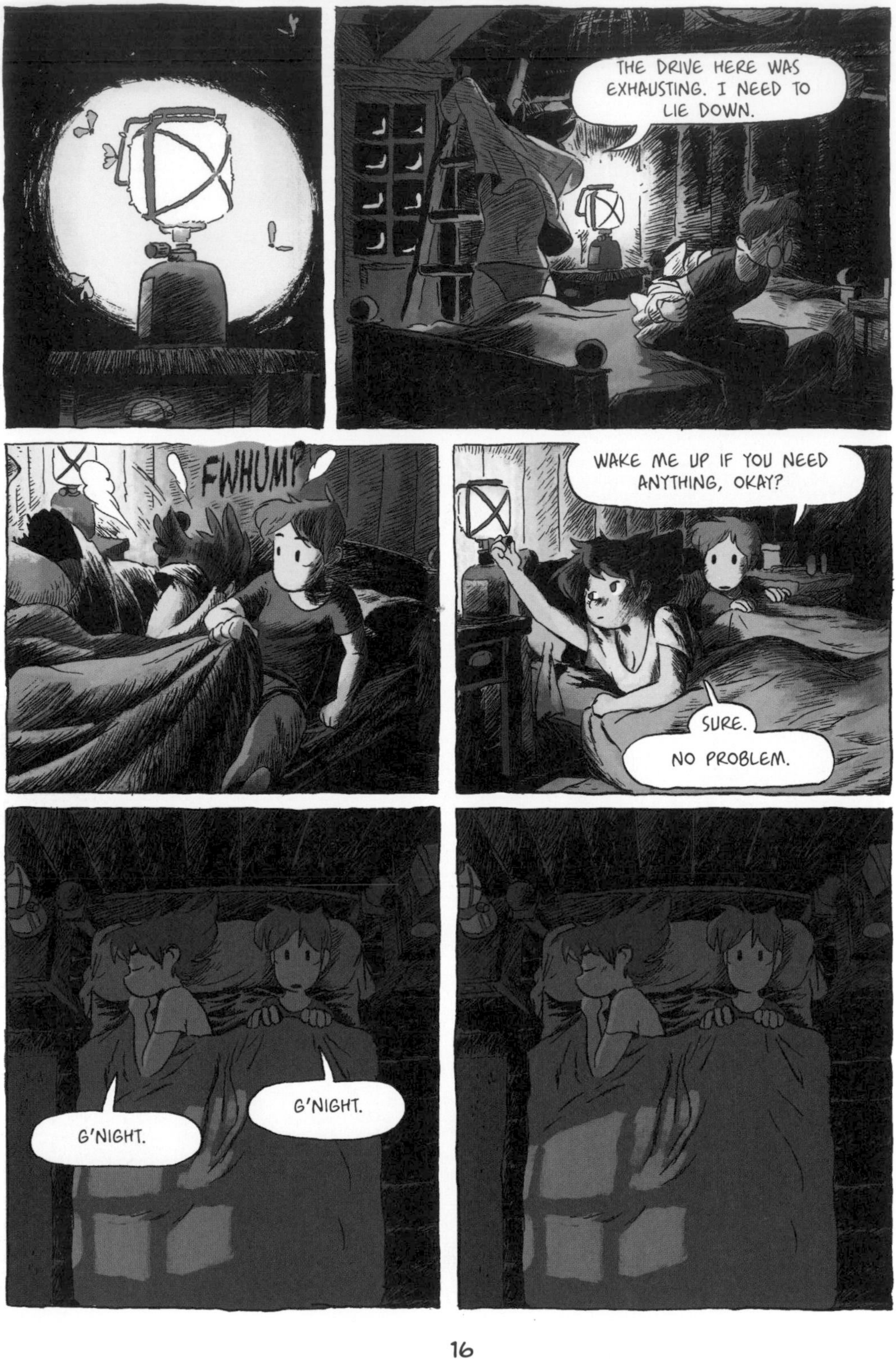

THE DRIVE HERE WAS EXHAUSTING. I NEED TO LIE DOWN.
FWHUMP
WAKE ME UP IF YOU NEED ANYTHING, OKAY?
SURE.
NO PROBLEM.
G'NIGHT.
G'NIGHT.

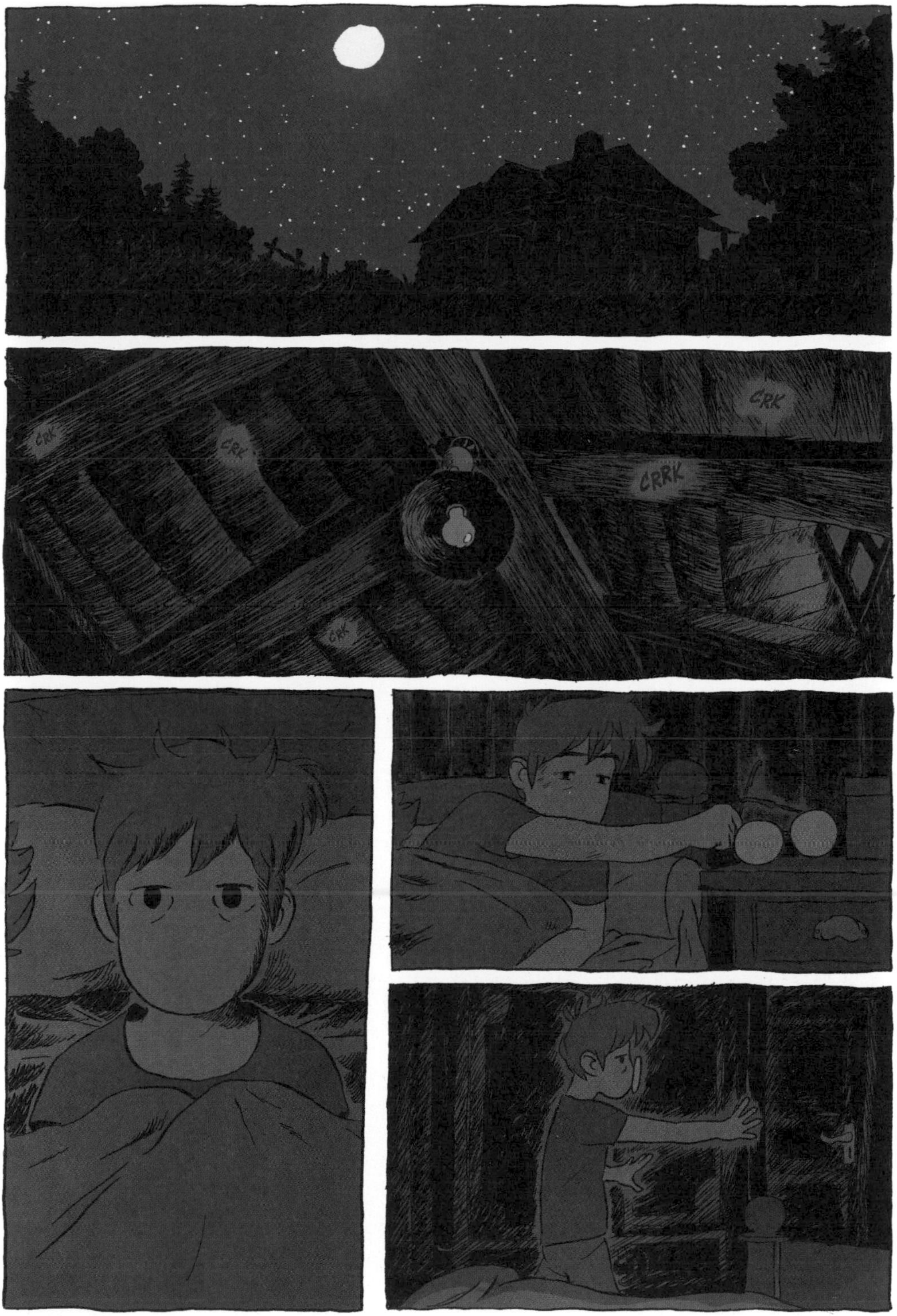
CRK
CRK
CRK
CRRK
CRK

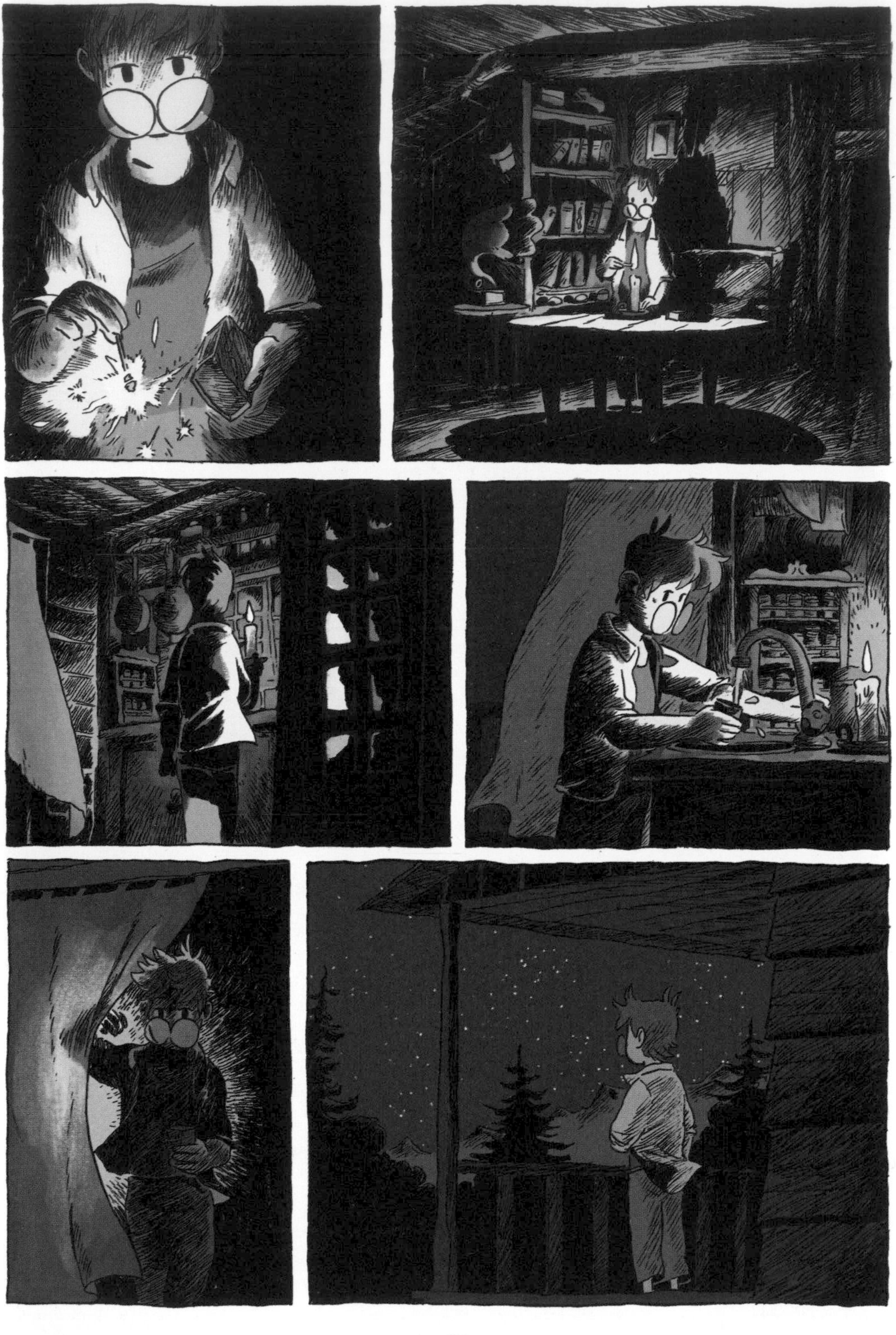

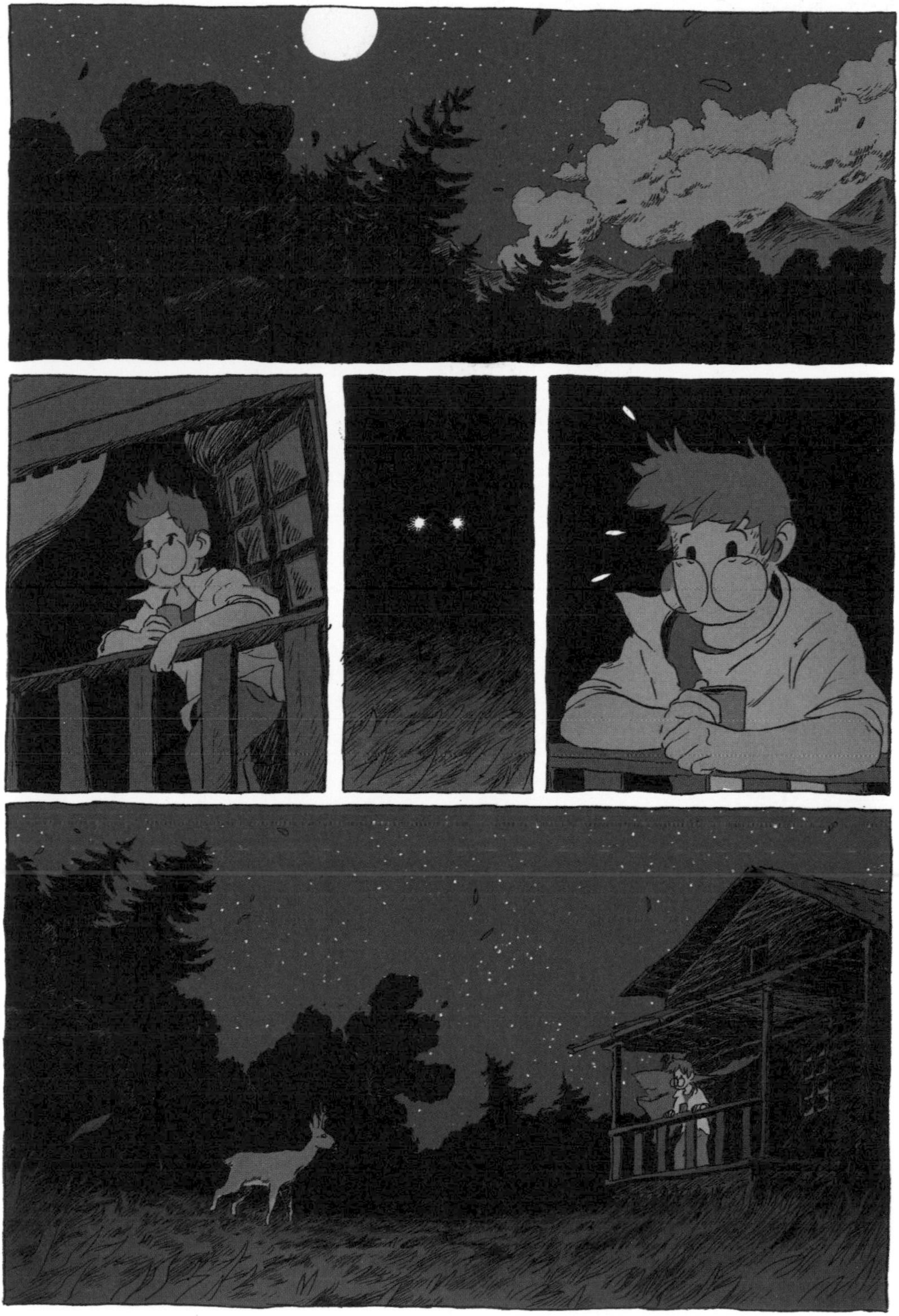

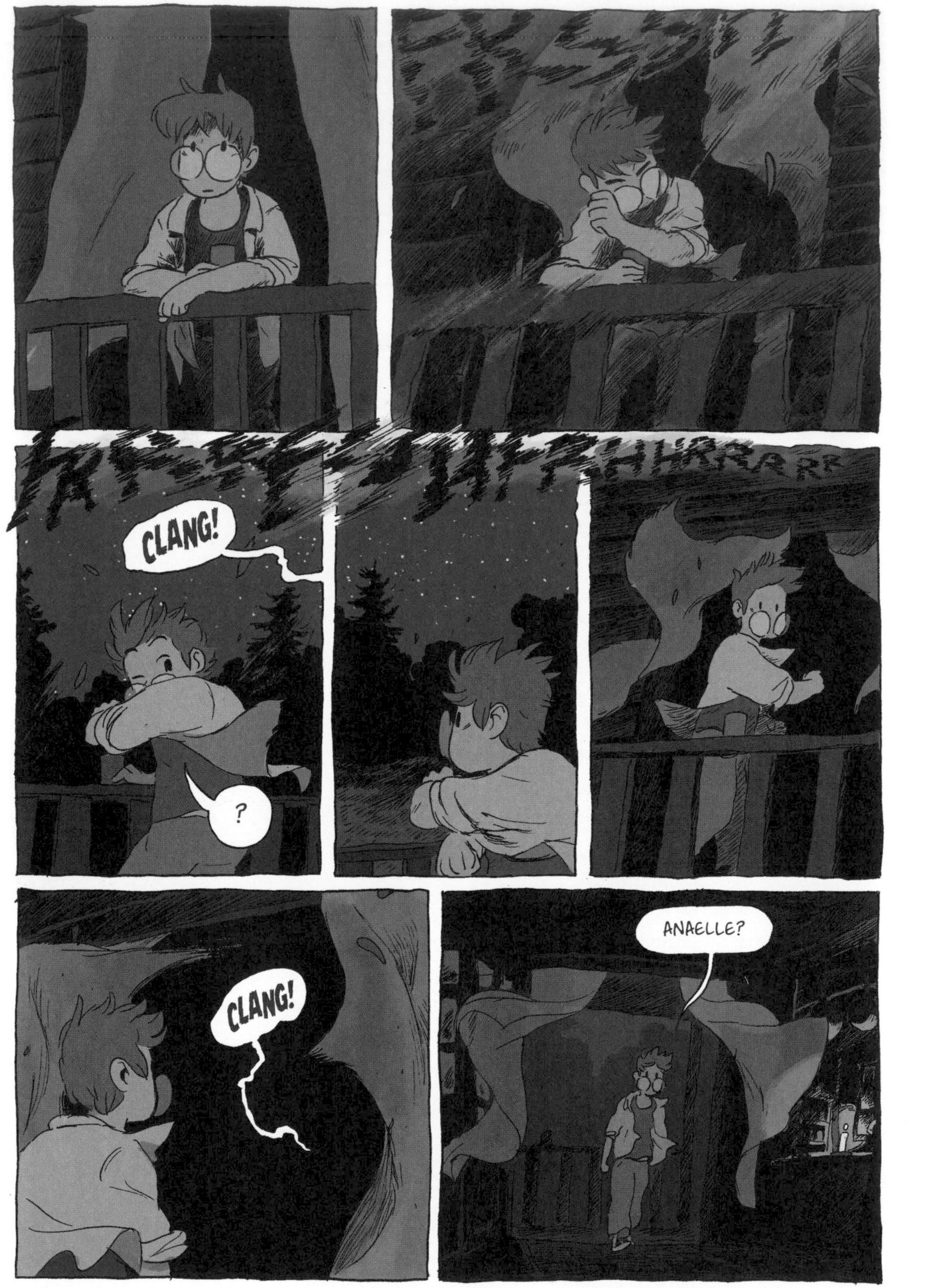
CLANG!
?
CLANG!
ANAELLE?

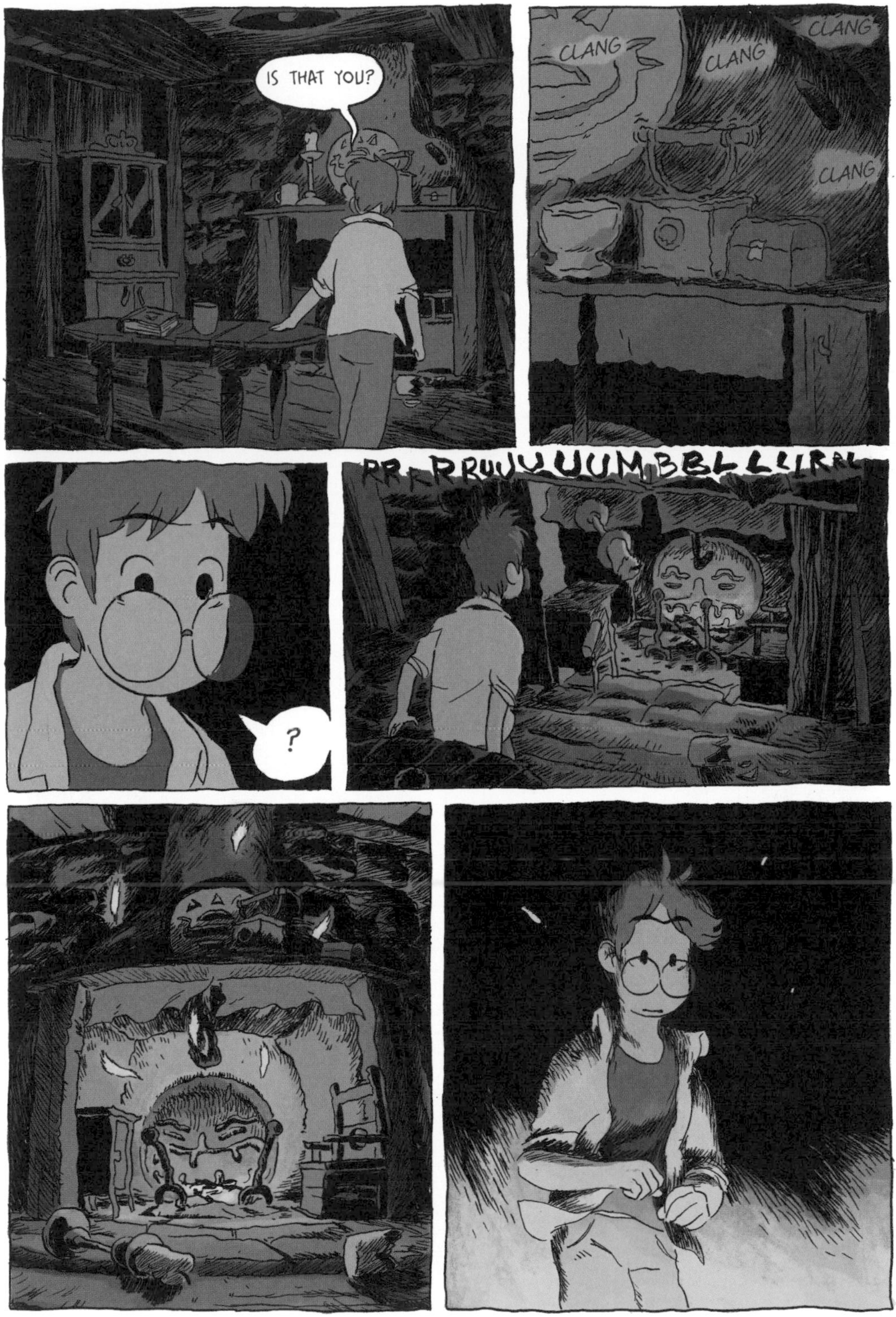
IS THAT YOU?
CLANG
CLANG
CLANG
CLANG
?
RRRRUUUUUMBBLLLLRRL

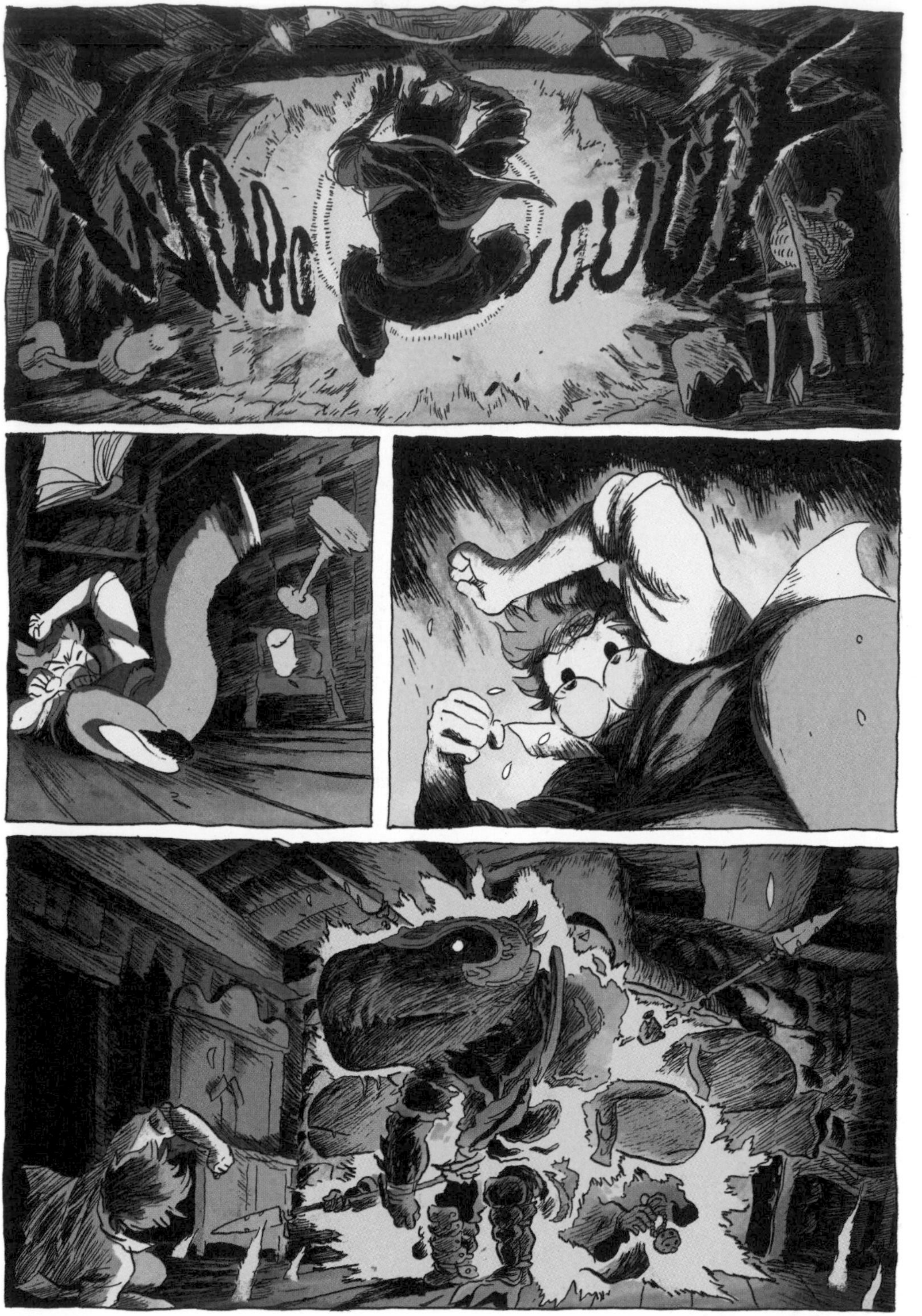

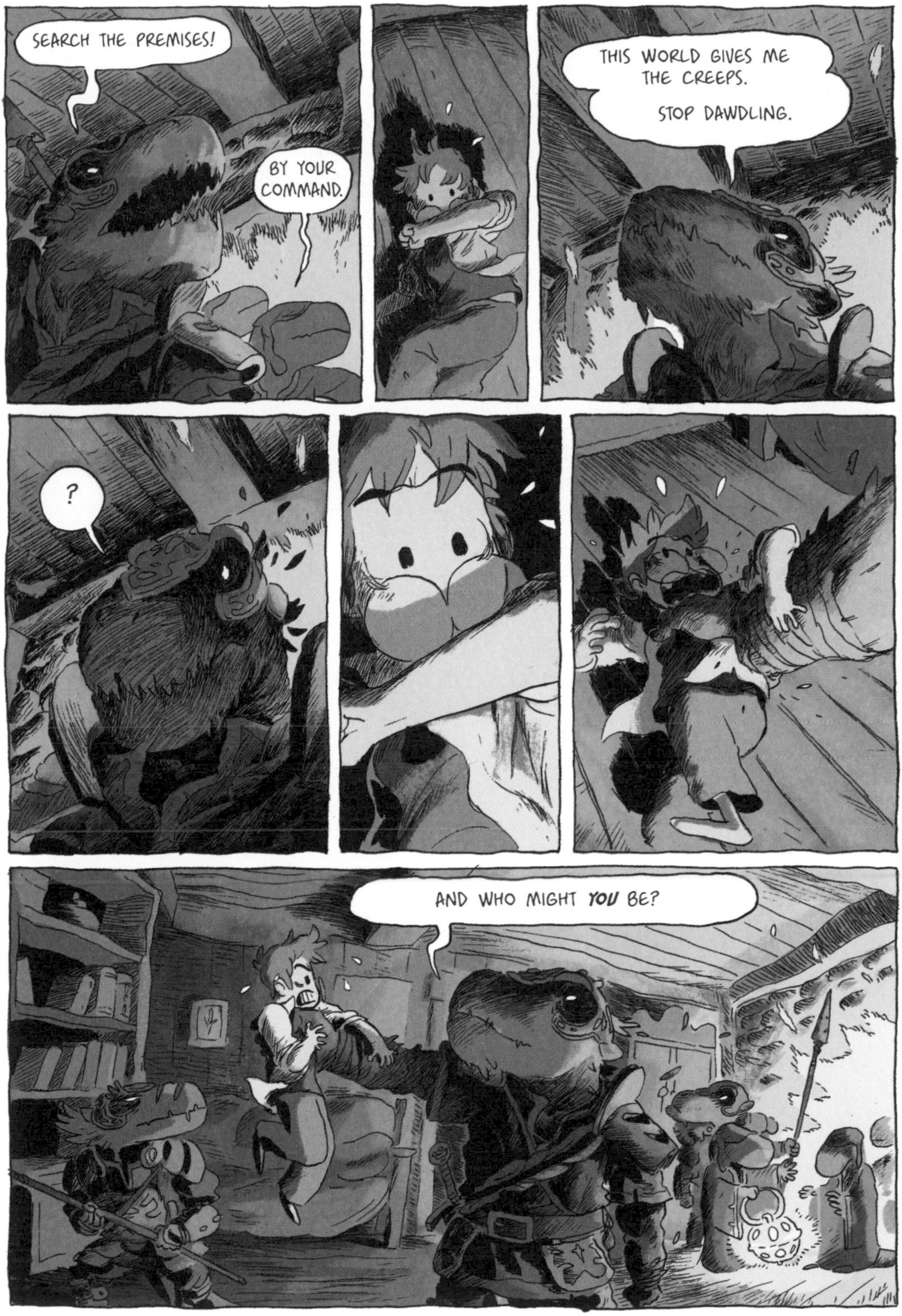
SEARCH THE PREMISES!
BY YOUR COMMAND.
THIS WORLD GIVES ME THE CREEPS.
STOP DAWDLING.
?
AND WHO MIGHT *YOU* BE?

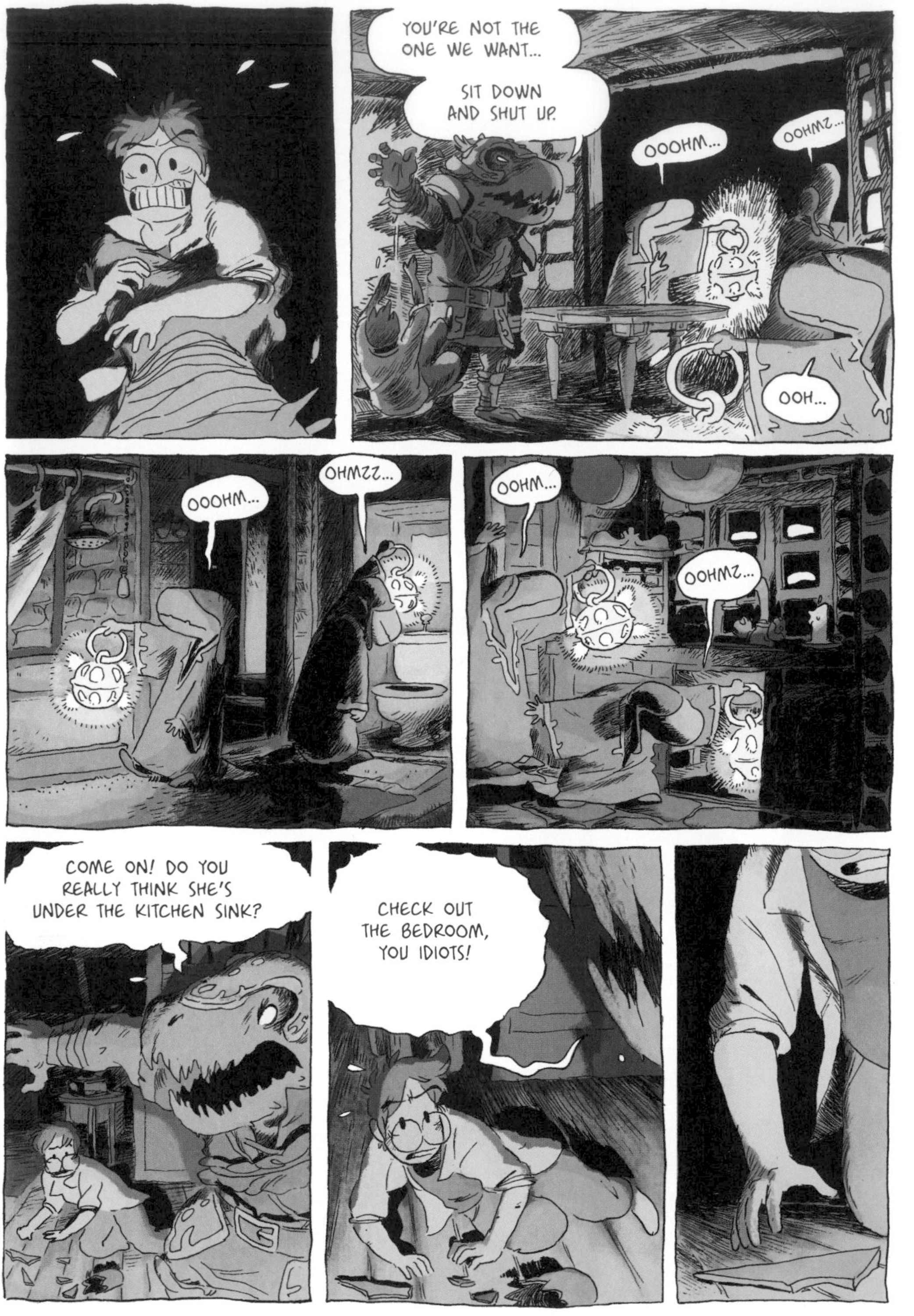
YOU'RE NOT THE ONE WE WANT...
SIT DOWN AND SHUT UP.
OOOHM...
OOHMZ...
OOH...
OOOHM...
OHMZZ...
OOHM...
OOHMZ...
COME ON! DO YOU REALLY THINK SHE'S UNDER THE KITCHEN SINK?
CHECK OUT THE BEDROOM, YOU IDIOTS!

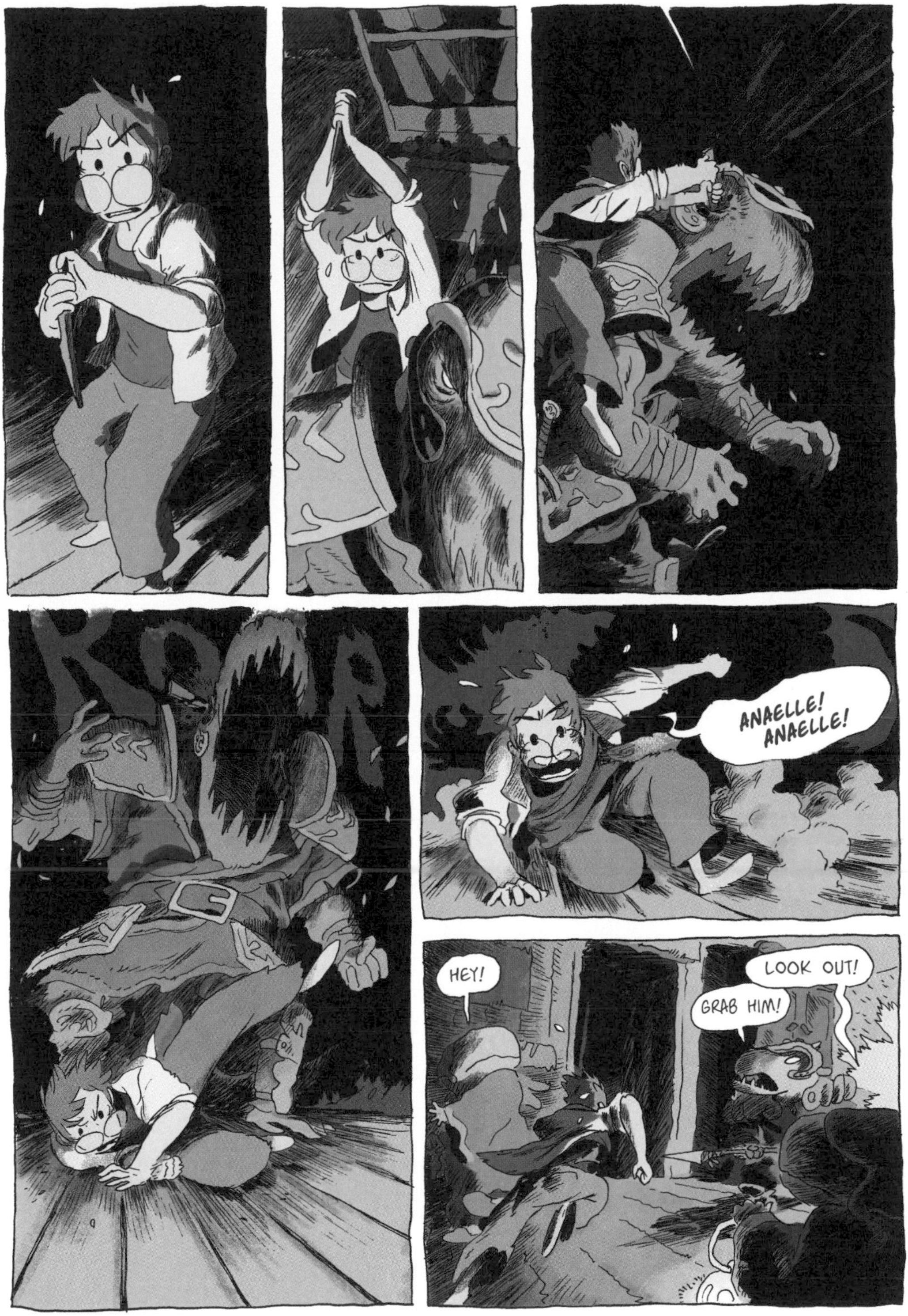
ANAELLE! ANAELLE!
HEY!
LOOK OUT!
GRAB HIM!

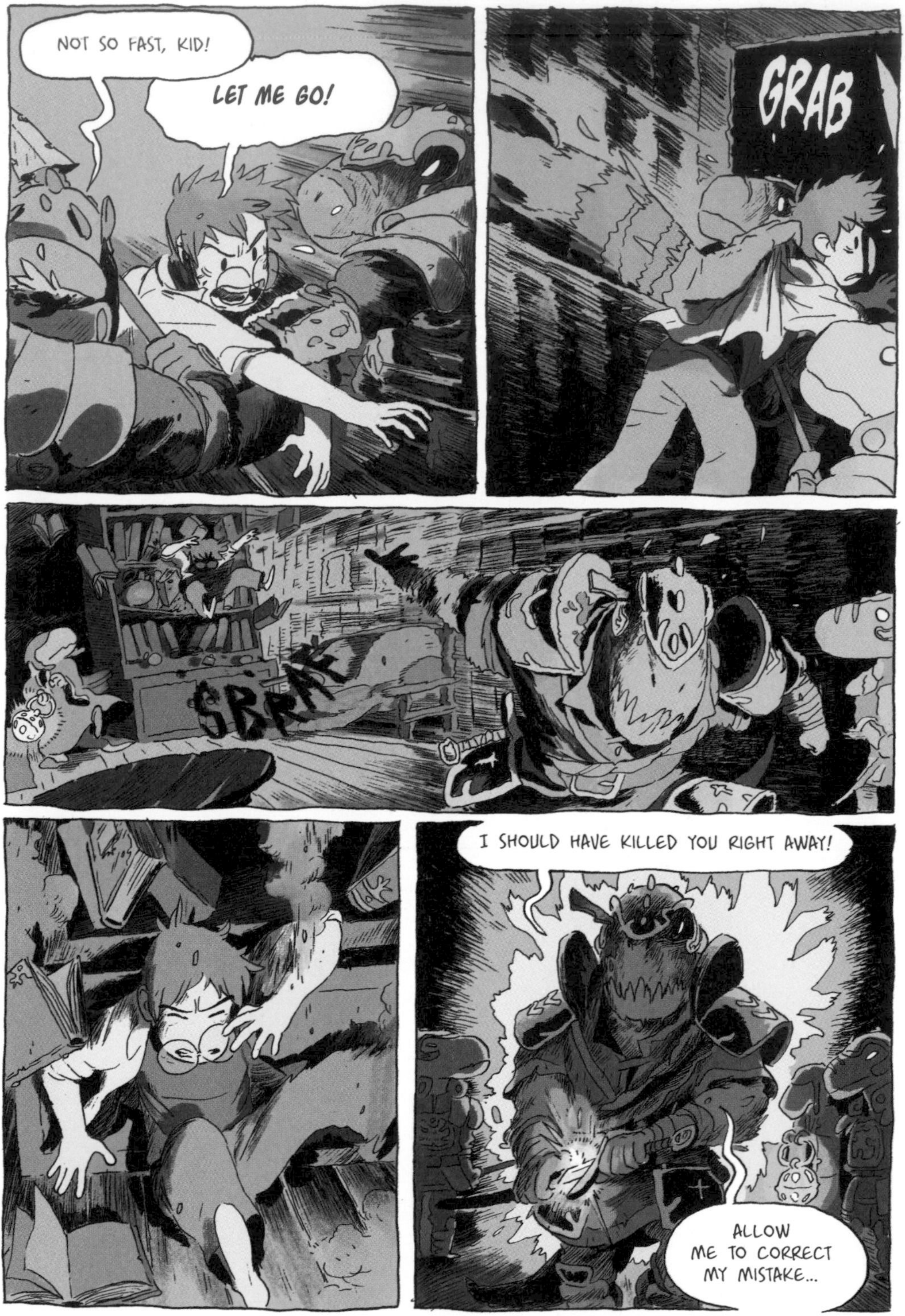

NOT SO FAST, KID!
LET ME GO!
GRAB
SBRAK
I SHOULD HAVE KILLED YOU RIGHT AWAY!
ALLOW ME TO CORRECT MY MISTAKE...

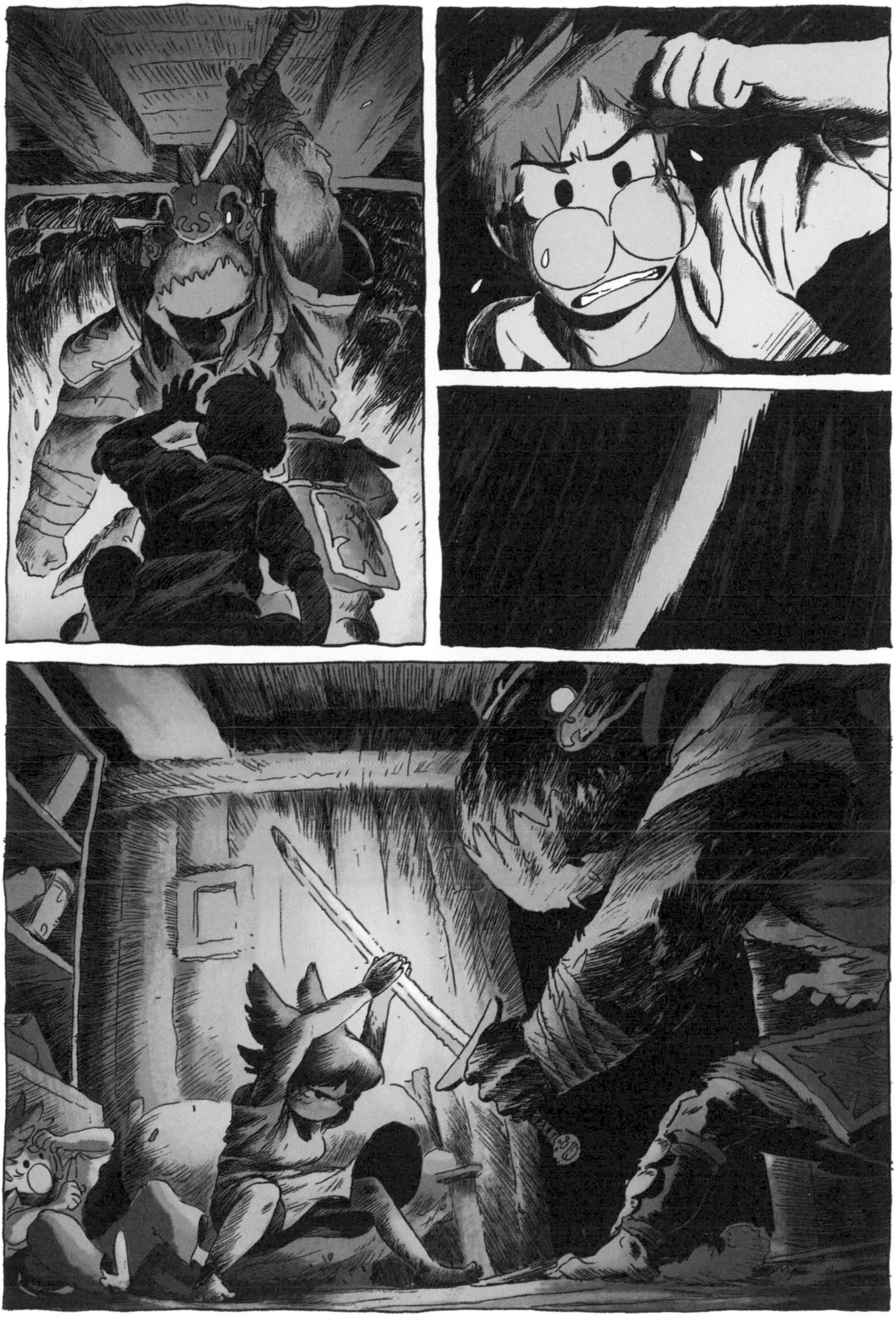

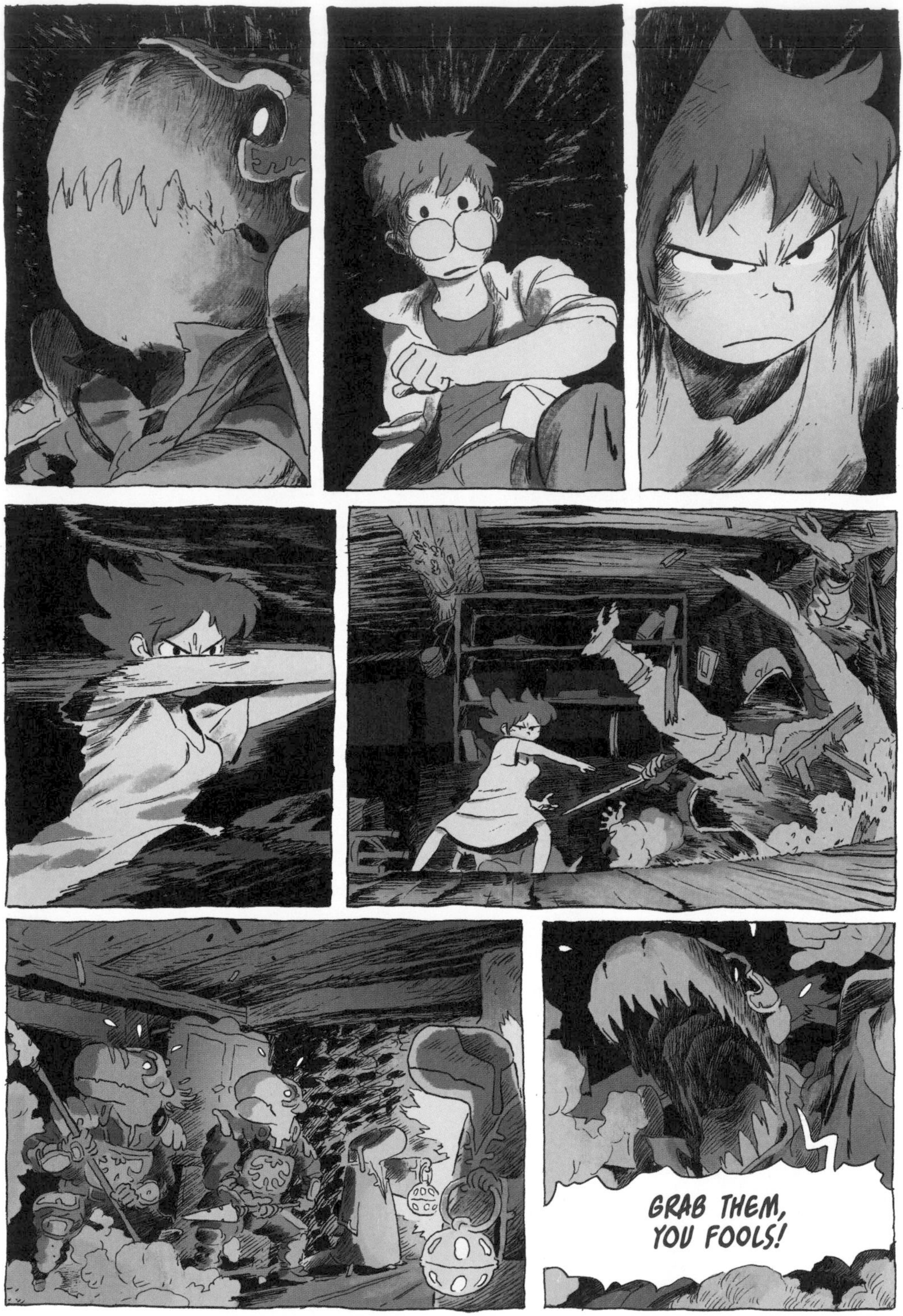
GRAB THEM,
YOU FOOLS!

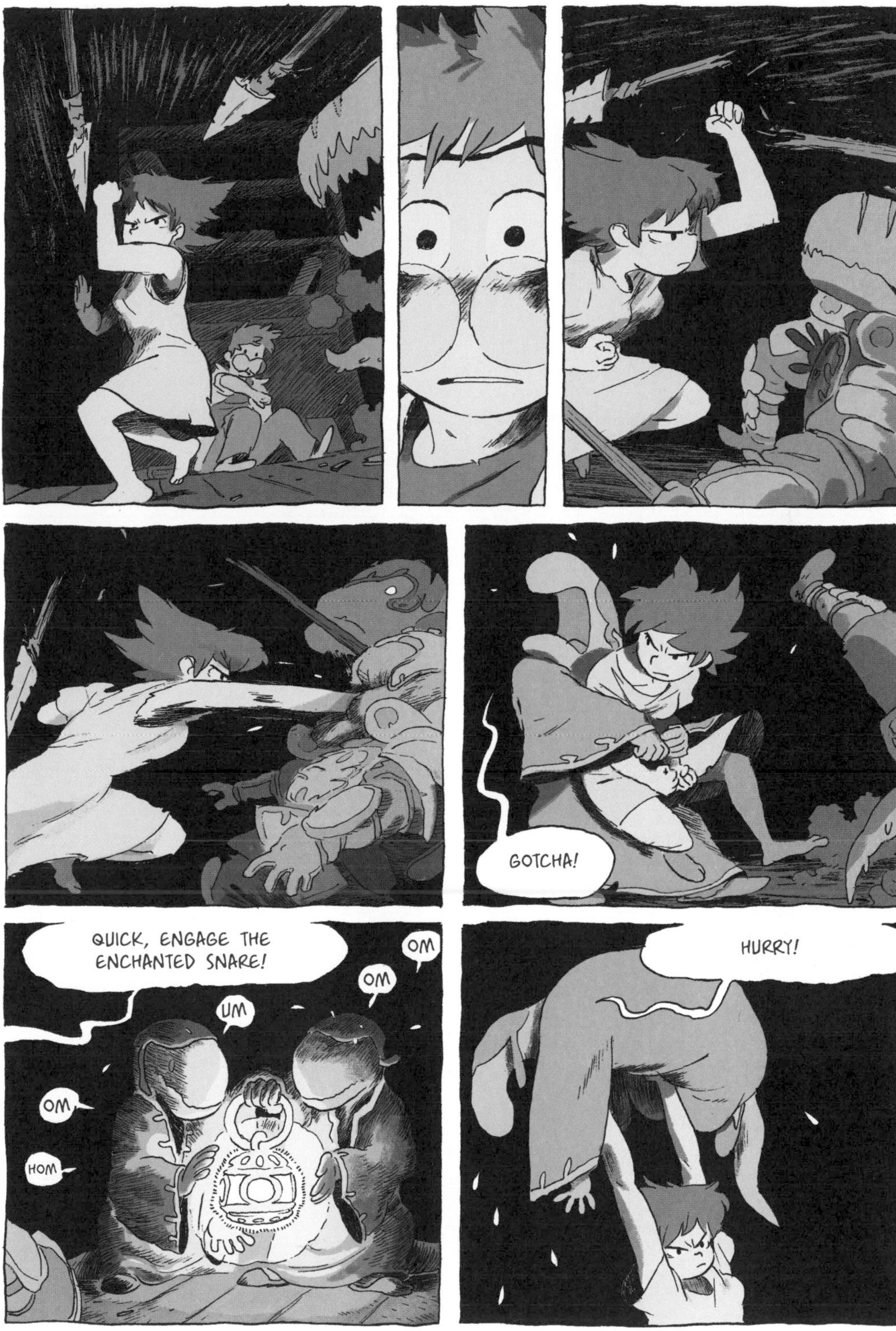
GOTCHA!
QUICK, ENGAGE THE ENCHANTED SNARE!
OM
OM
UM
OM
HOM
HURRY!

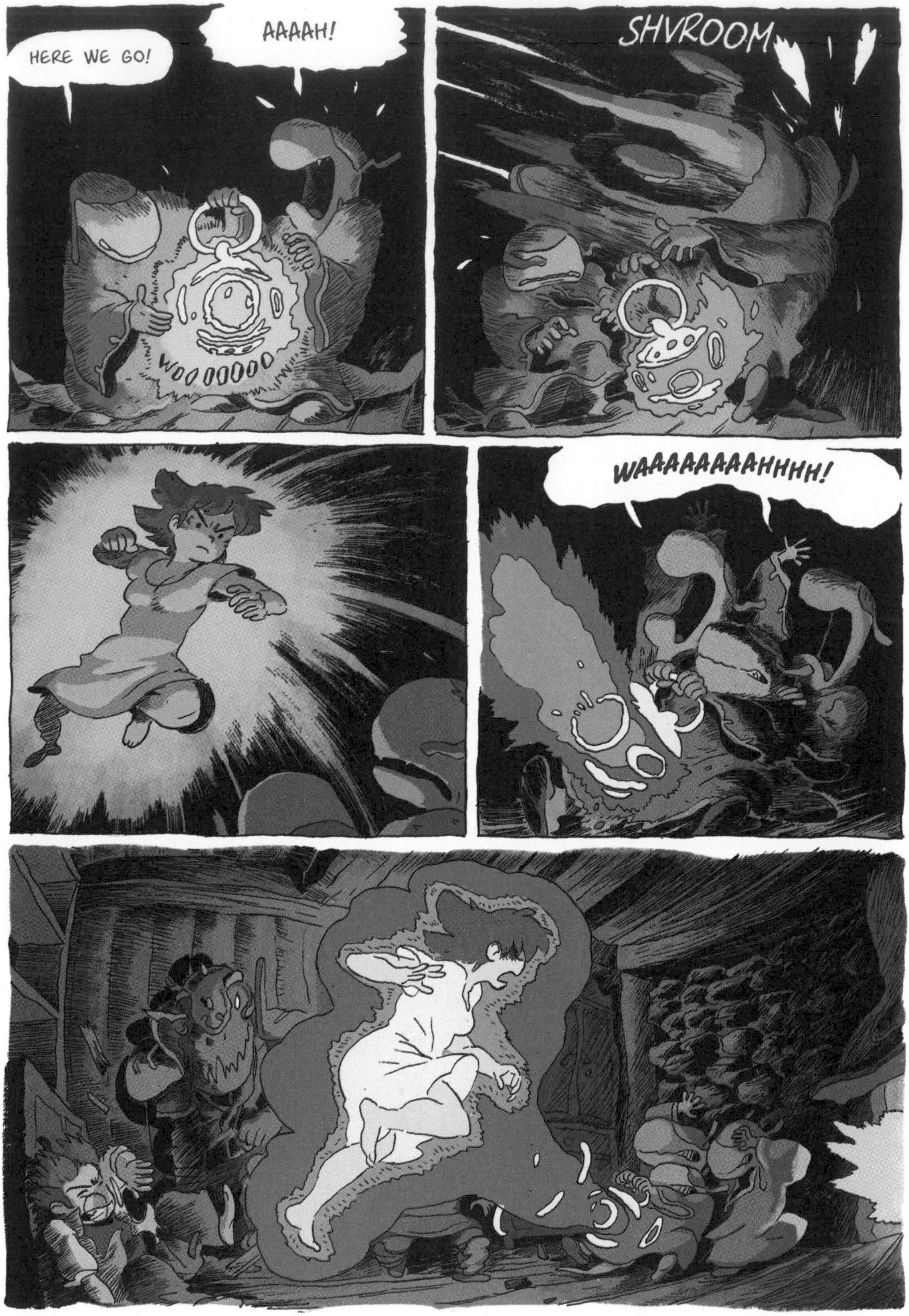
HERE WE GO!
AAAAH!
WOOOOOOO
SHVROOM
WAAAAAAAAHHHH!

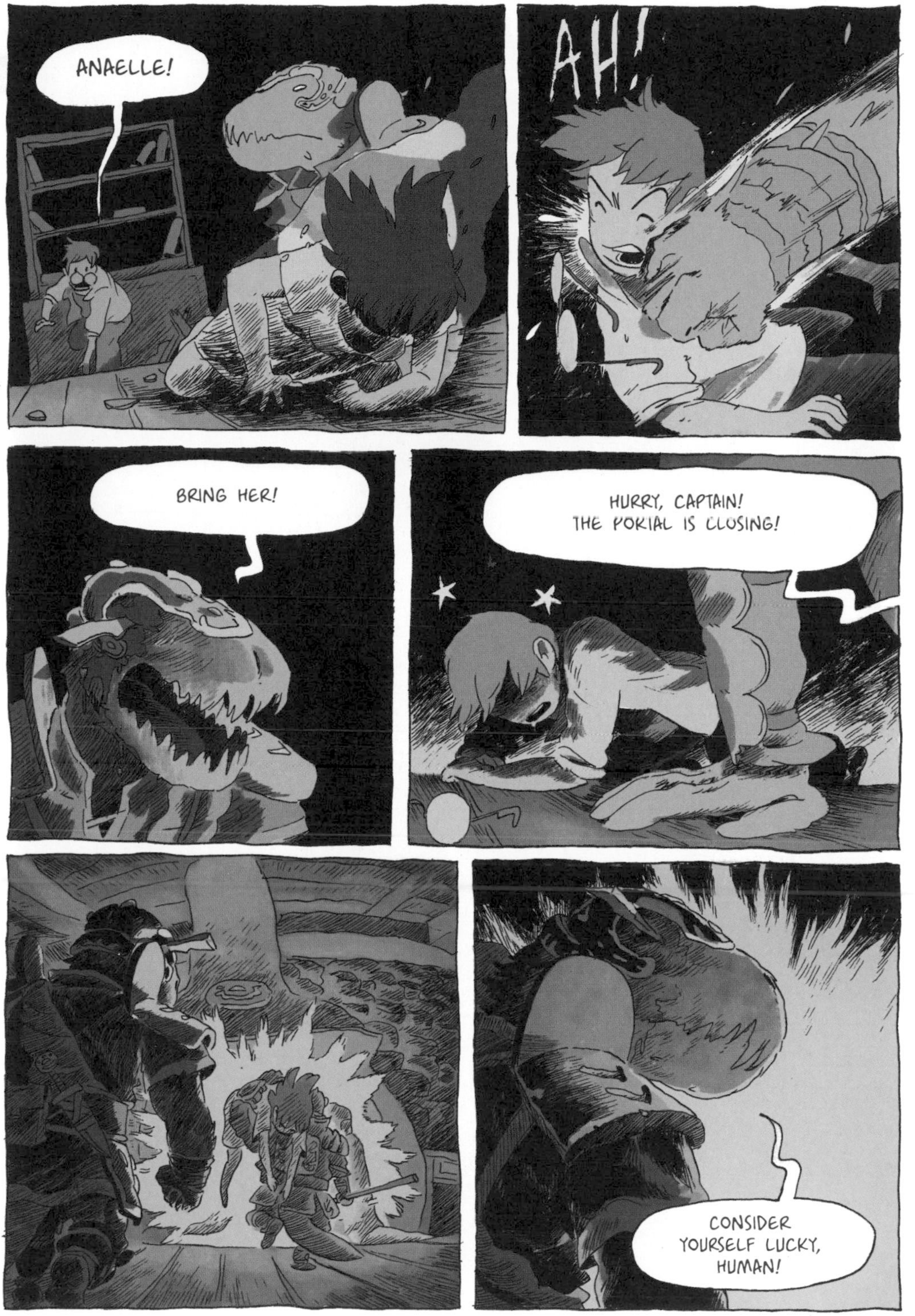
ANAELLE!
AH!
BRING HER!
HURRY, CAPTAIN!
THE PORTAL IS CLOSING!
CONSIDER
YOURSELF LUCKY,
HUMAN!

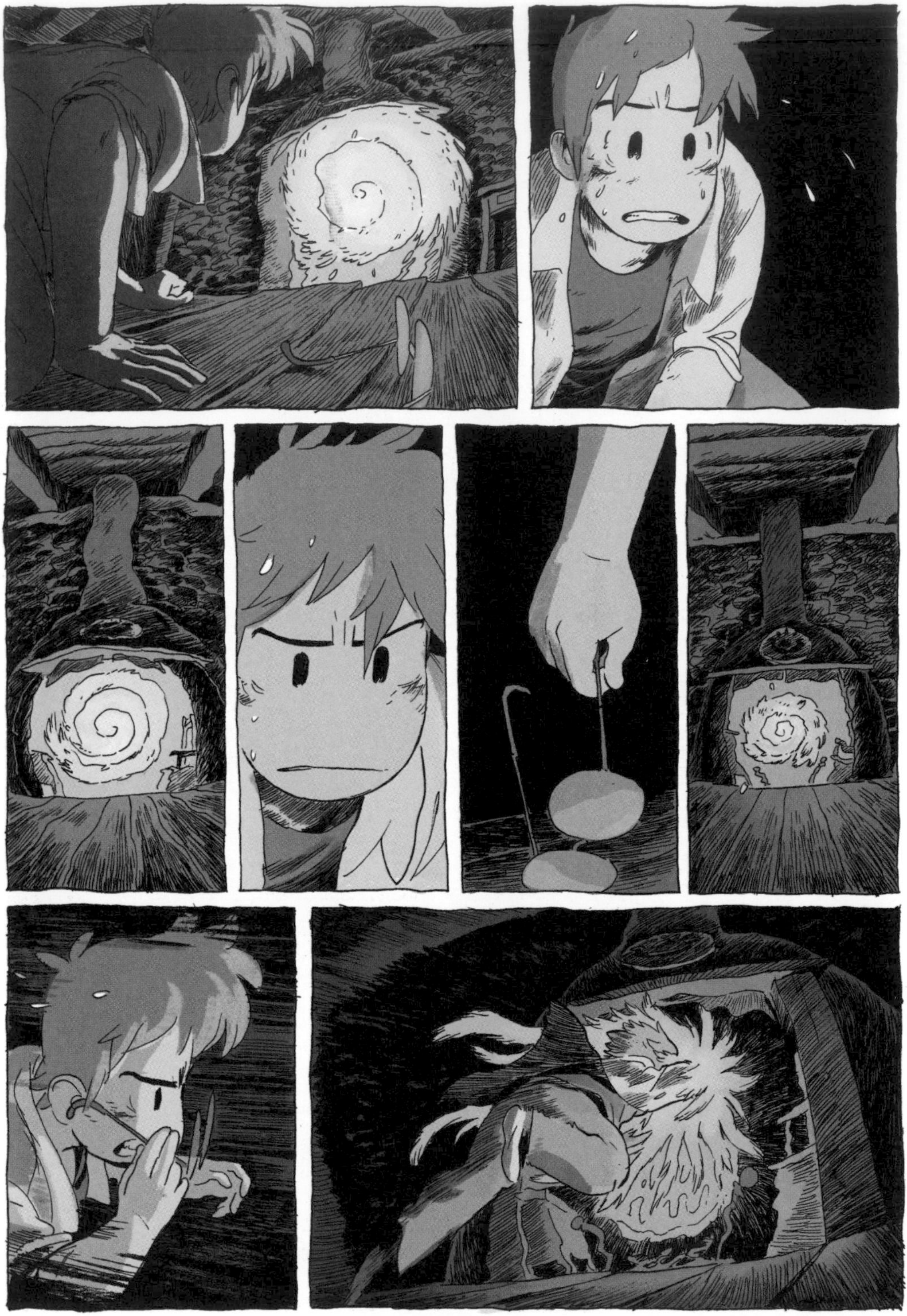

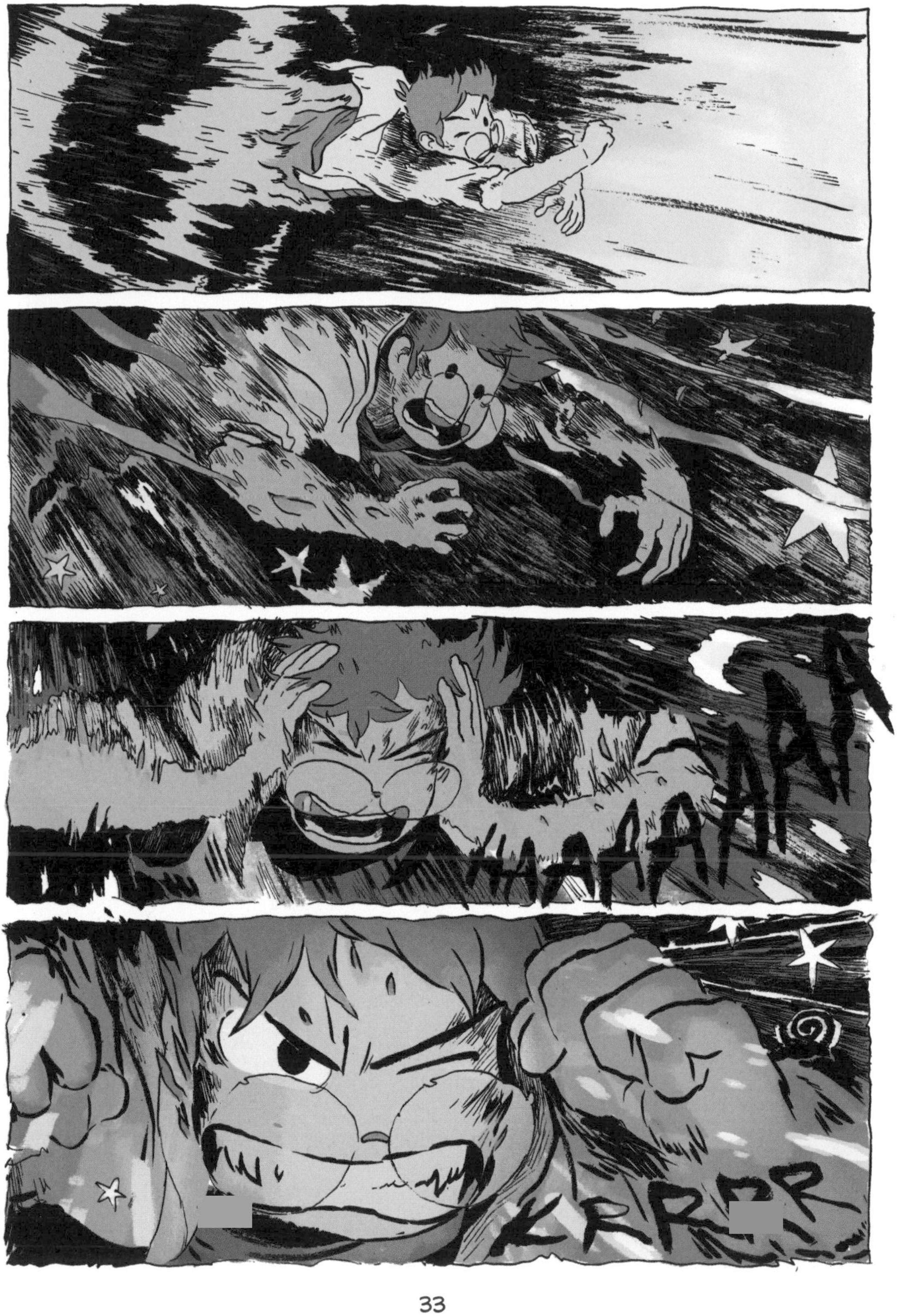
HAAAAAPP!
KRRRR

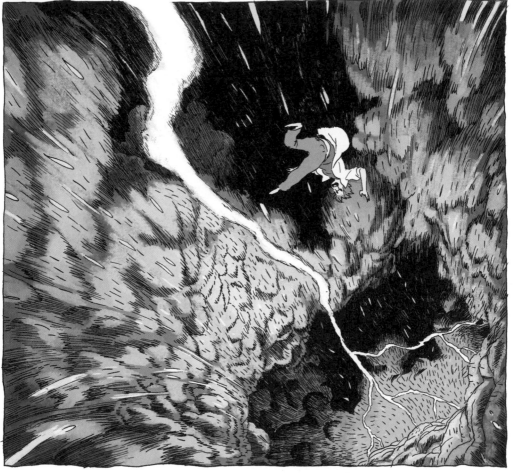

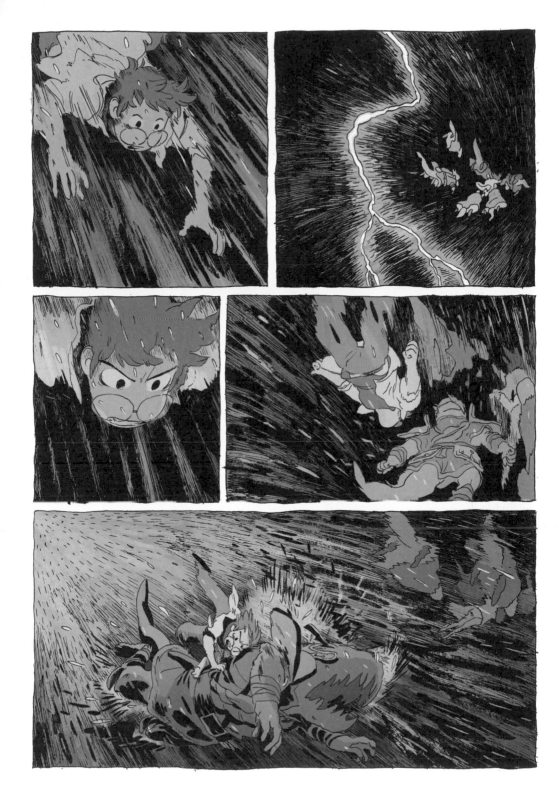

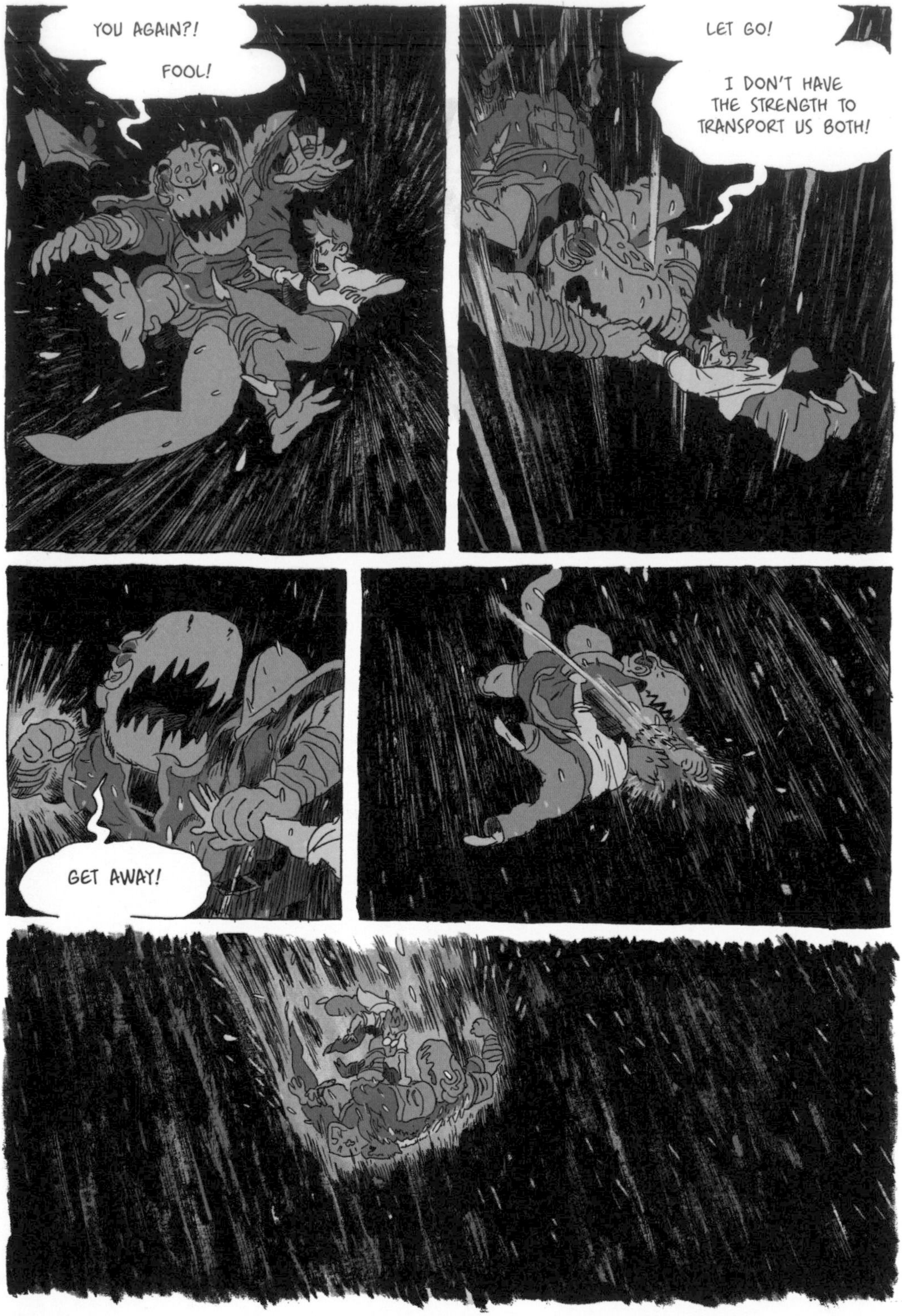
YOU AGAIN?!
FOOL!
LET GO!
I DON'T HAVE THE STRENGTH TO TRANSPORT US BOTH!
GET AWAY!

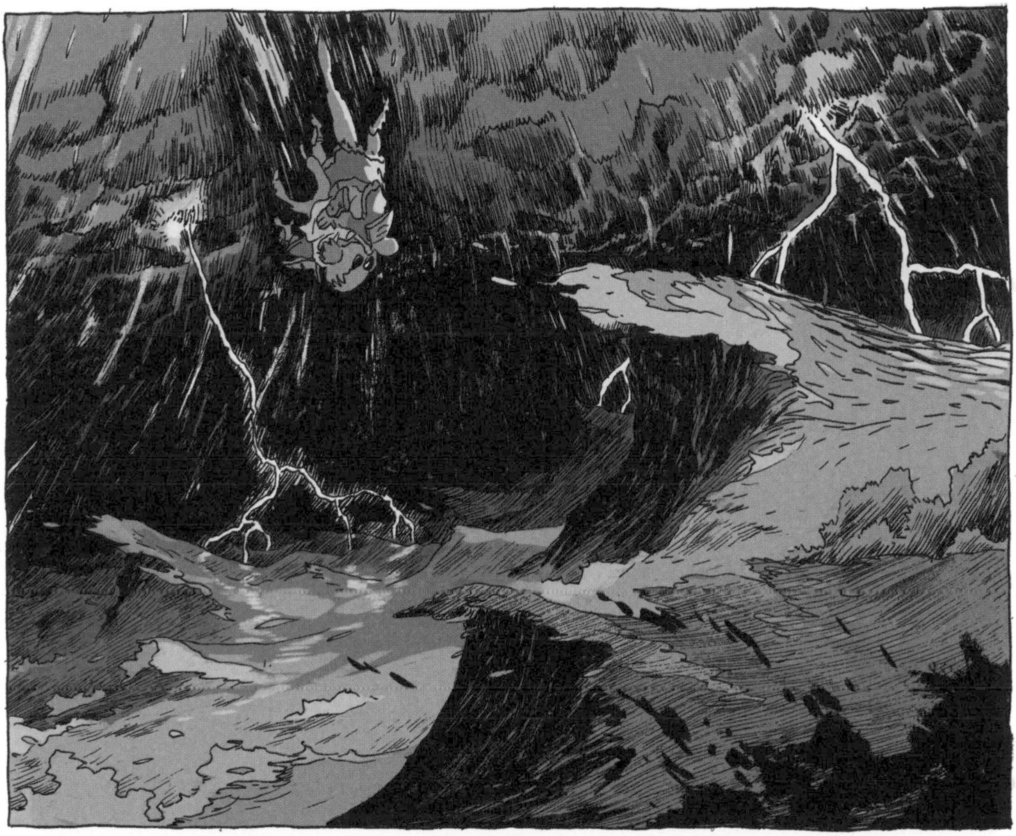

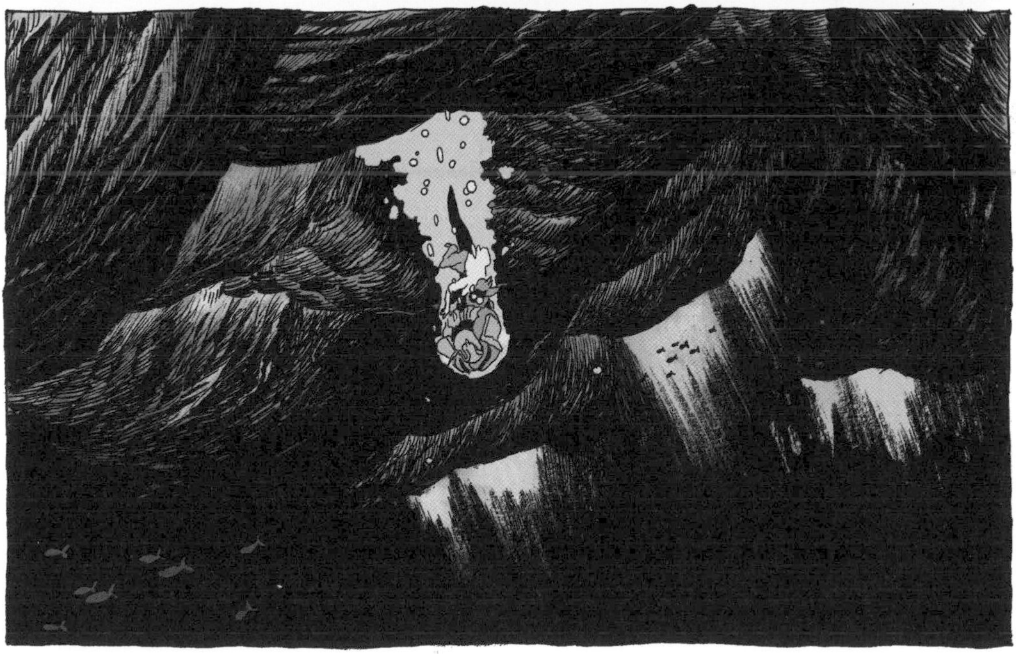

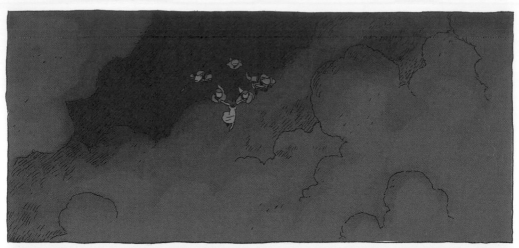

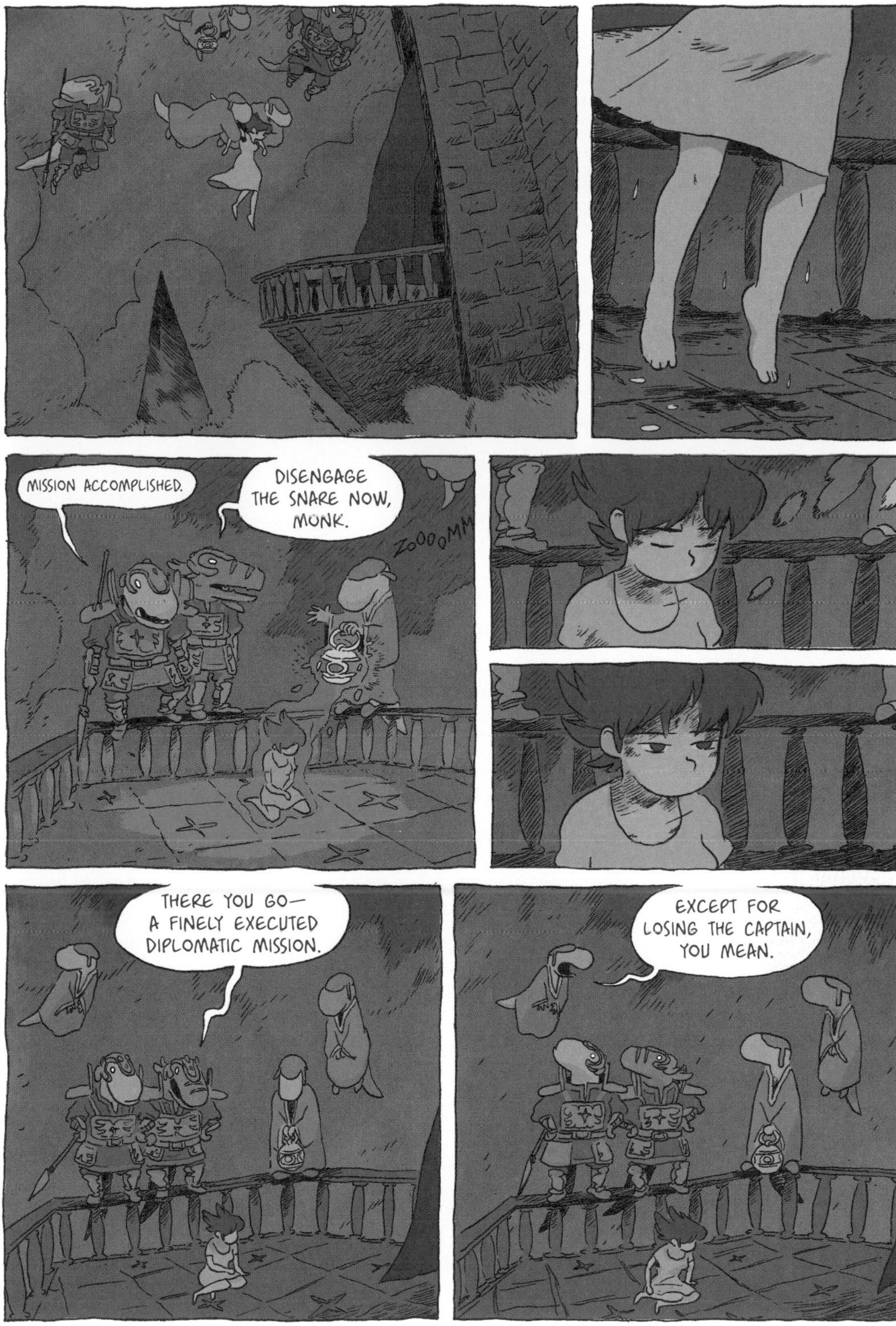
MISSION ACCOMPLISHED.
DISENGAGE THE SNARE NOW, MONK.
ZOOOOMM
THERE YOU GO— A FINELY EXECUTED DIPLOMATIC MISSION.
EXCEPT FOR LOSING THE CAPTAIN, YOU MEAN.

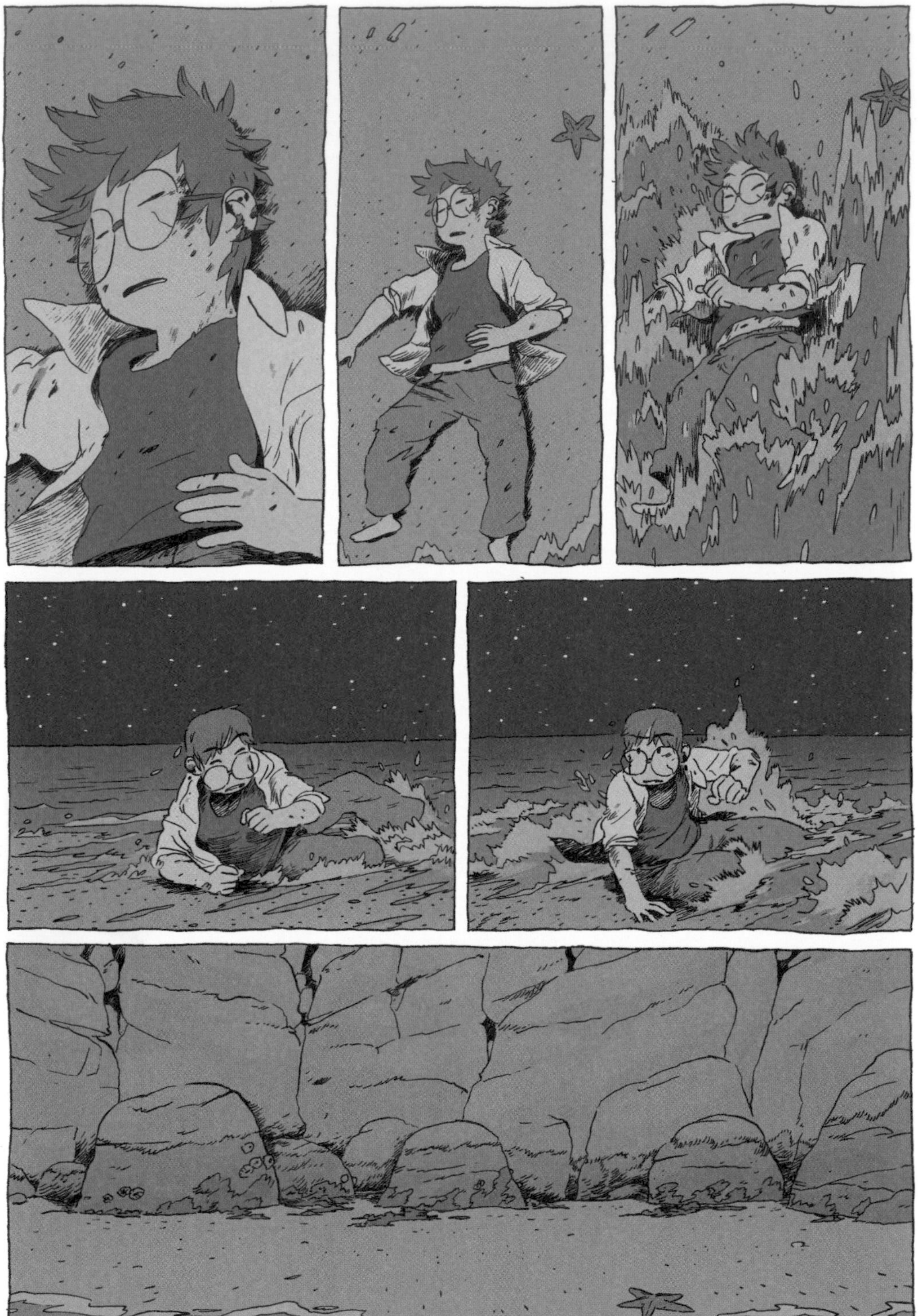

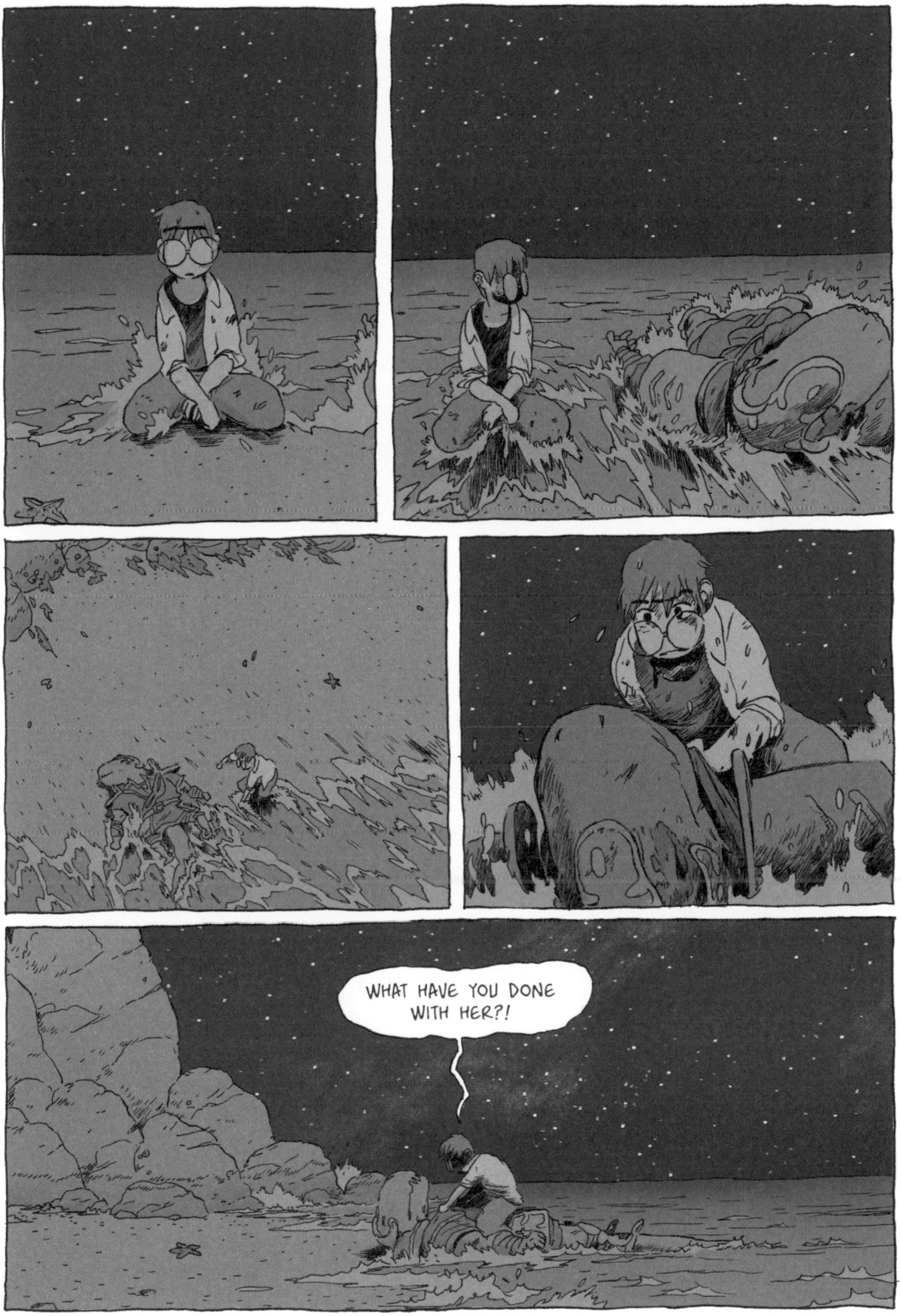
WHAT HAVE YOU DONE WITH HER?!

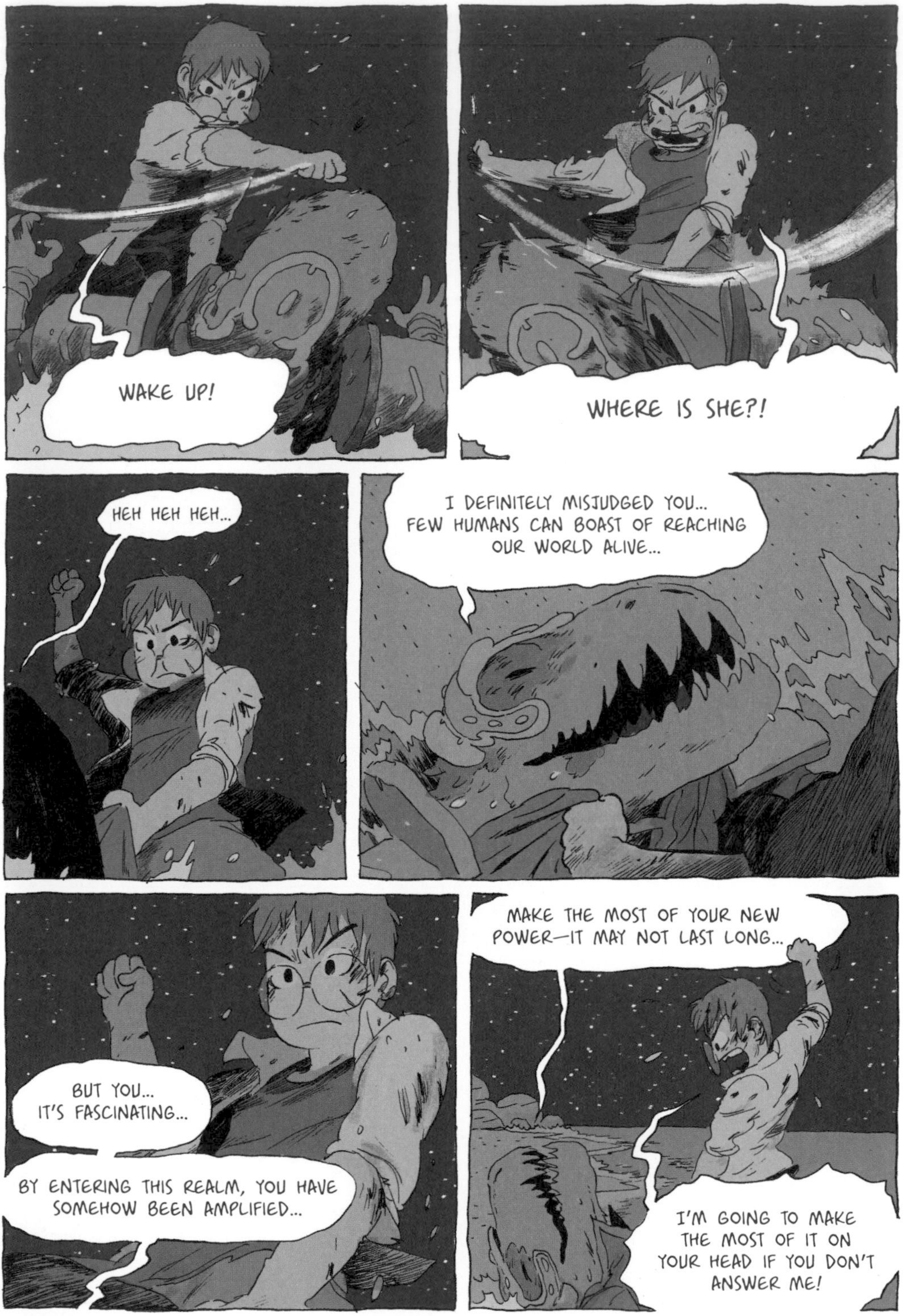
WAKE UP!
WHERE IS SHE?!
HEH HEH HEH...
I DEFINITELY MISJUDGED YOU... FEW HUMANS CAN BOAST OF REACHING OUR WORLD ALIVE...
BUT YOU... IT'S FASCINATING...
BY ENTERING THIS REALM, YOU HAVE SOMEHOW BEEN AMPLIFIED...
MAKE THE MOST OF YOUR NEW POWER—IT MAY NOT LAST LONG...
I'M GOING TO MAKE THE MOST OF IT ON YOUR HEAD IF YOU DON'T ANSWER ME!

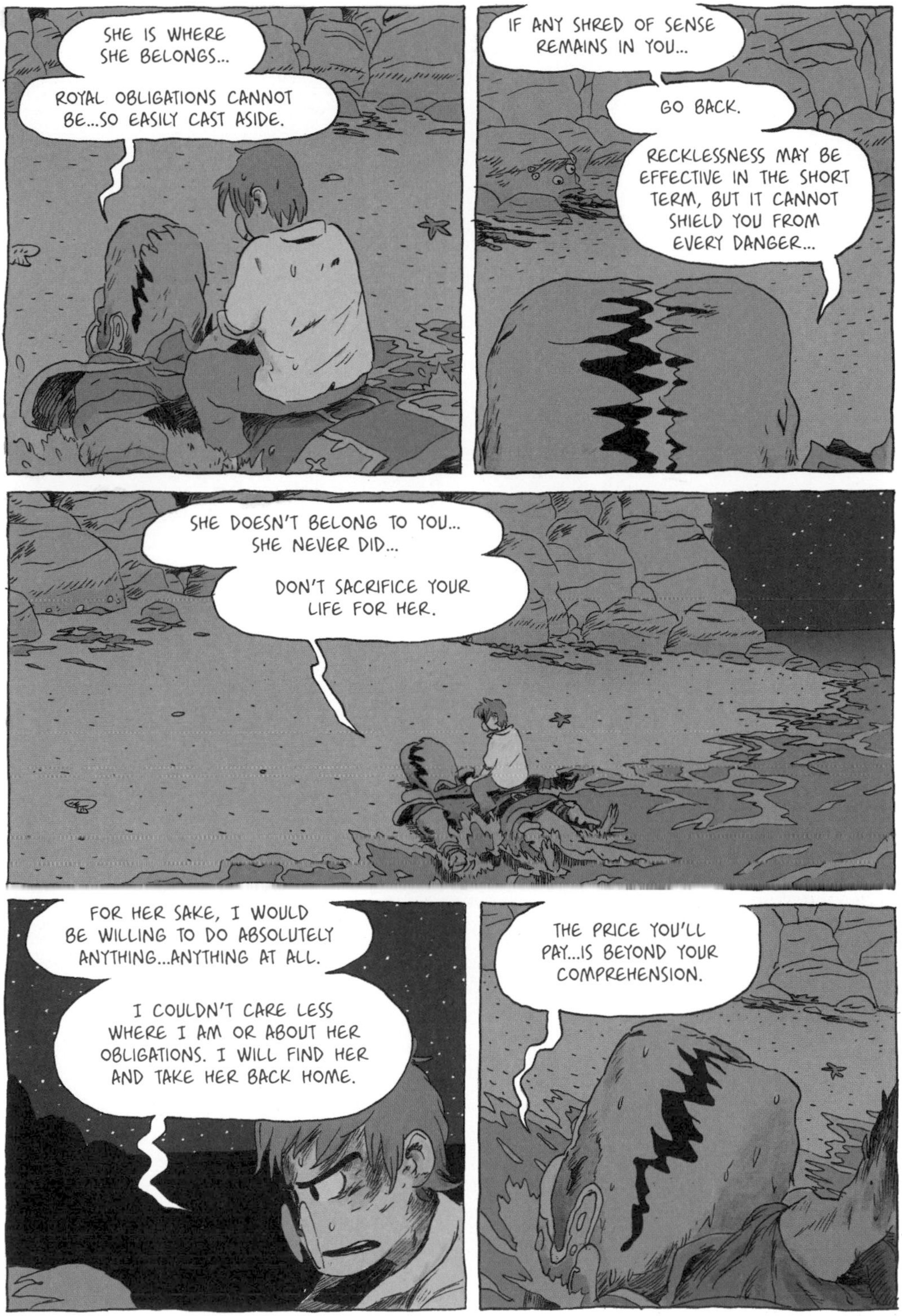
SHE IS WHERE SHE BELONGS...
ROYAL OBLIGATIONS CANNOT BE...SO EASILY CAST ASIDE.
IF ANY SHRED OF SENSE REMAINS IN YOU...
GO BACK.
RECKLESSNESS MAY BE EFFECTIVE IN THE SHORT TERM, BUT IT CANNOT SHIELD YOU FROM EVERY DANGER...
SHE DOESN'T BELONG TO YOU... SHE NEVER DID...
DON'T SACRIFICE YOUR LIFE FOR HER.
FOR HER SAKE, I WOULD BE WILLING TO DO ABSOLUTELY ANYTHING...ANYTHING AT ALL.
I COULDN'T CARE LESS WHERE I AM OR ABOUT HER OBLIGATIONS. I WILL FIND HER AND TAKE HER BACK HOME.
THE PRICE YOU'LL PAY...IS BEYOND YOUR COMPREHENSION.

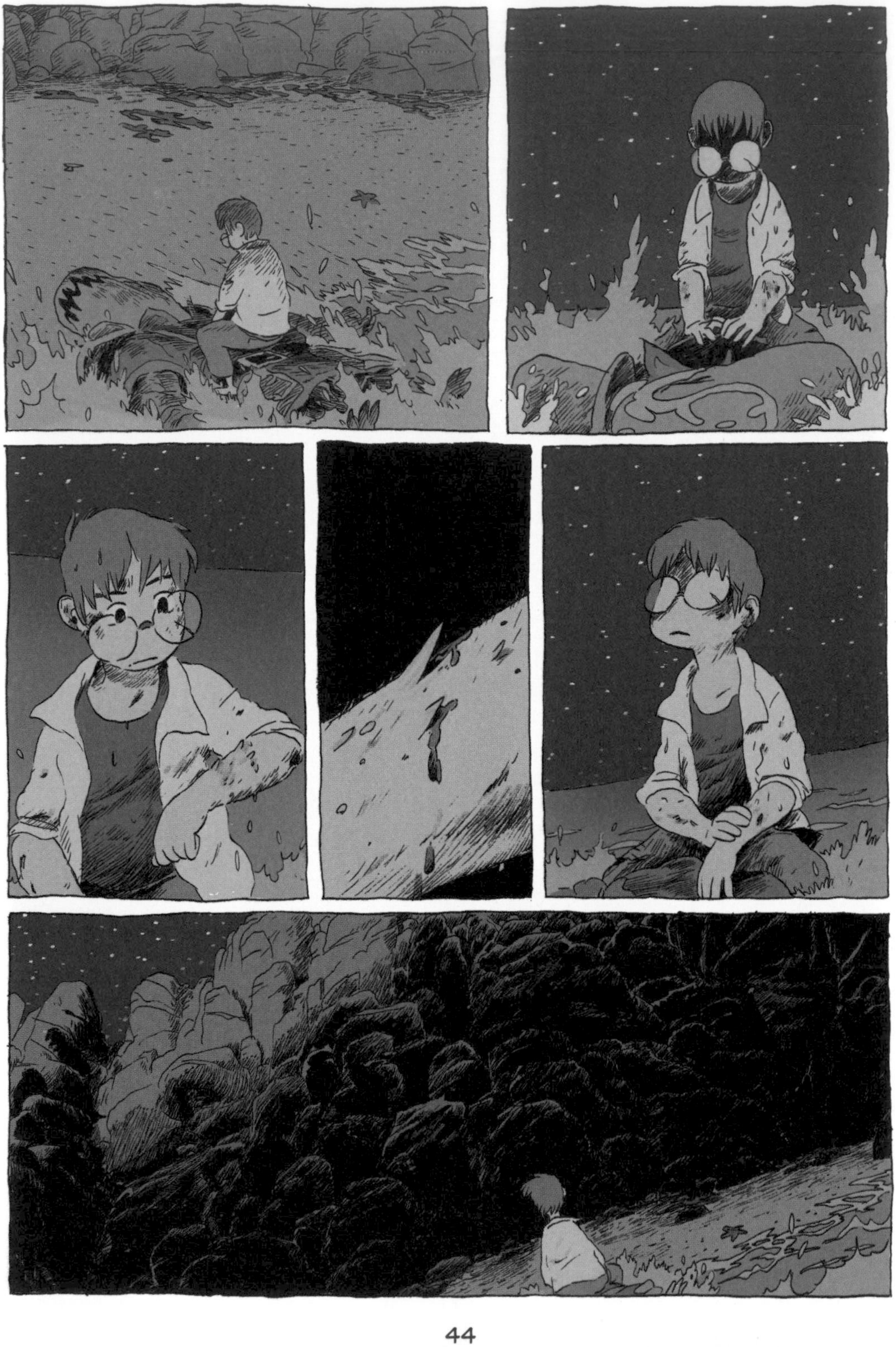

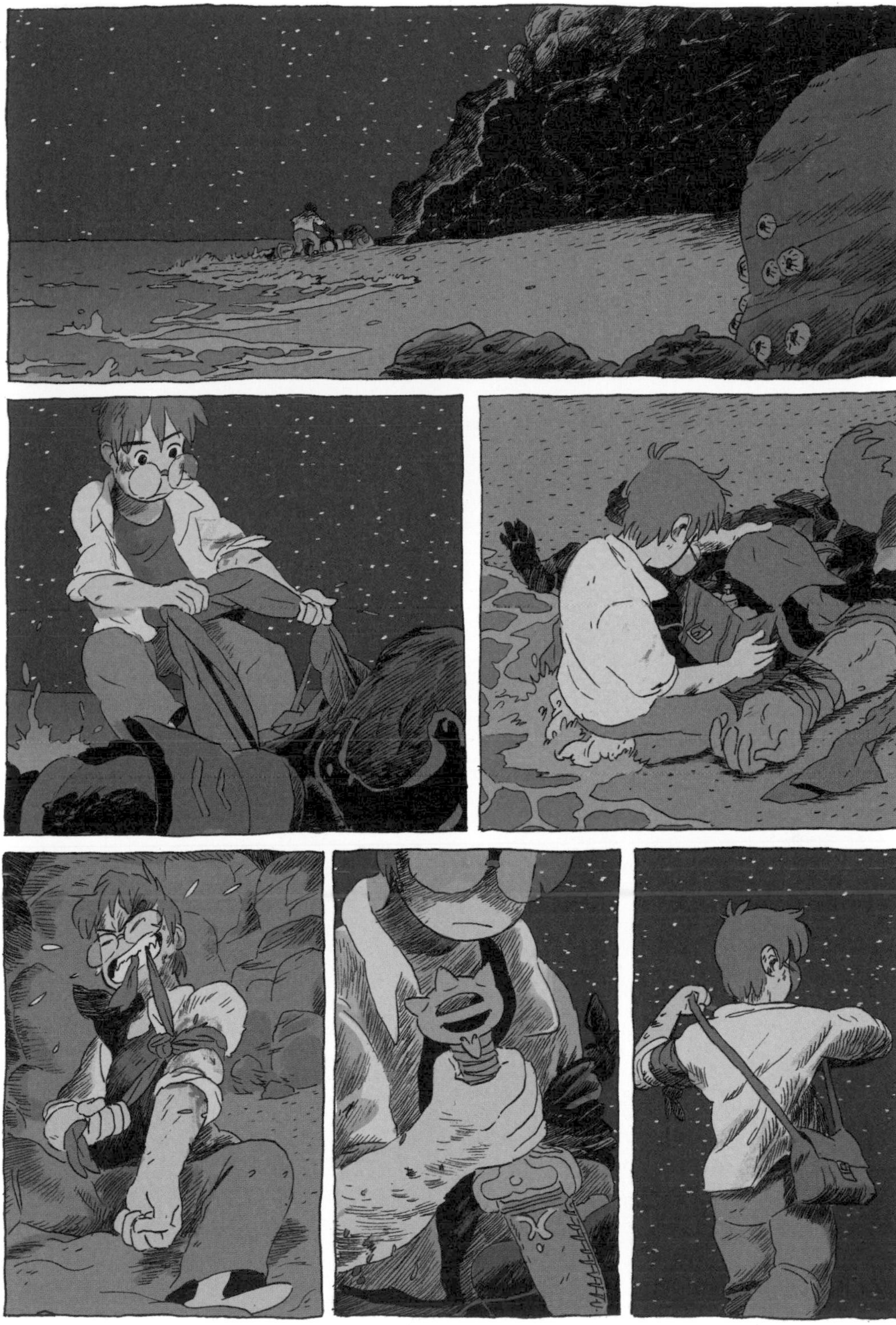

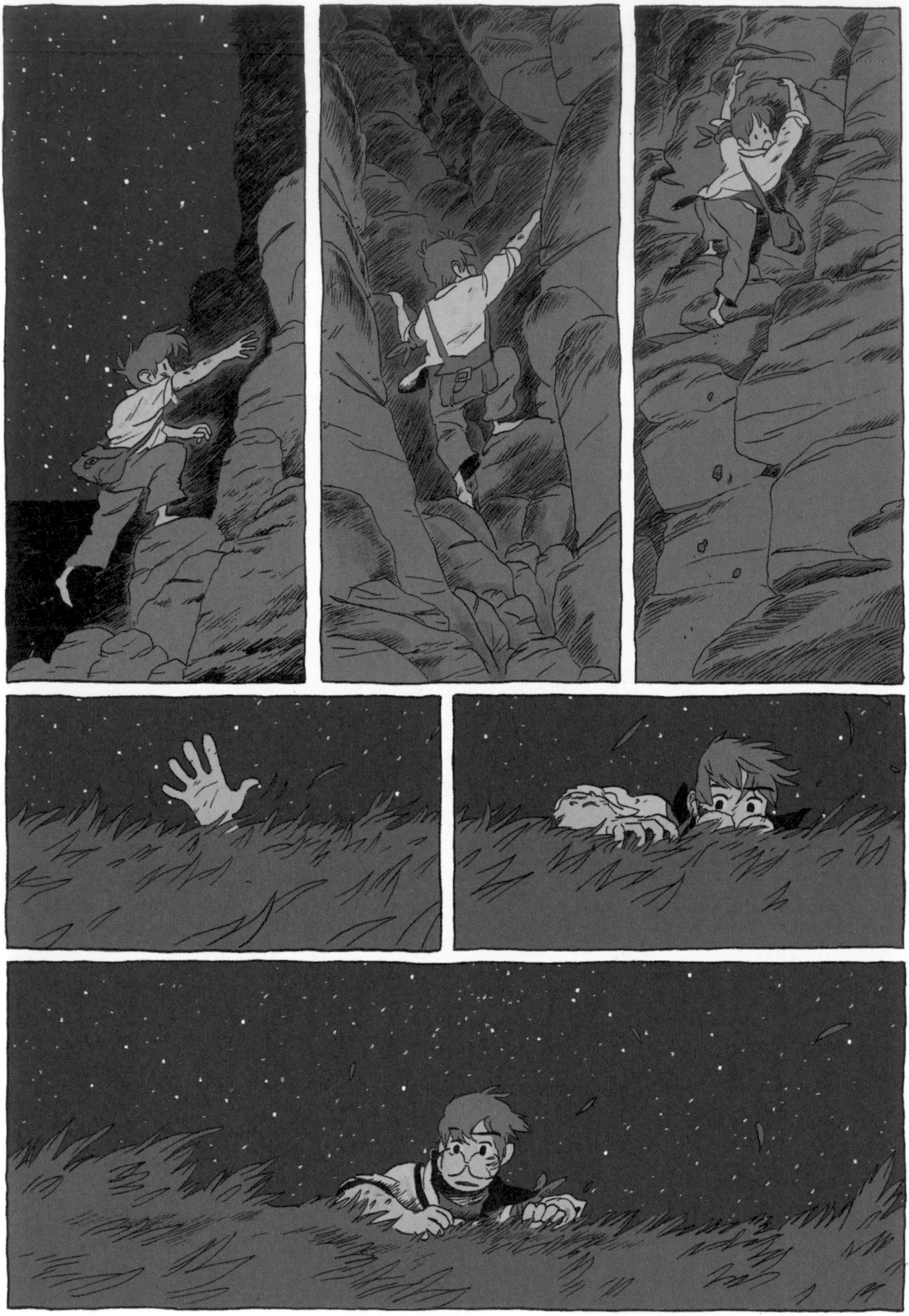

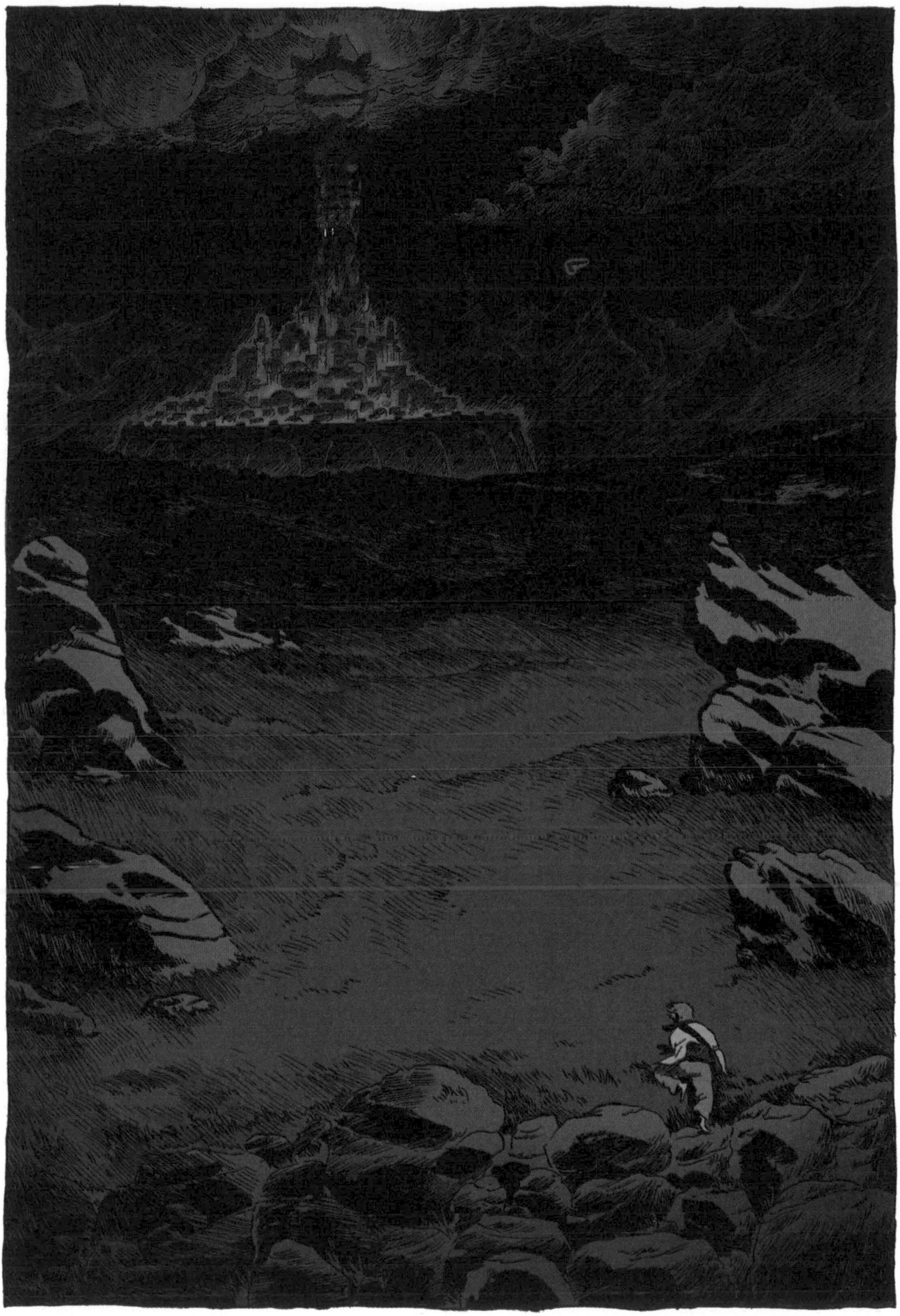

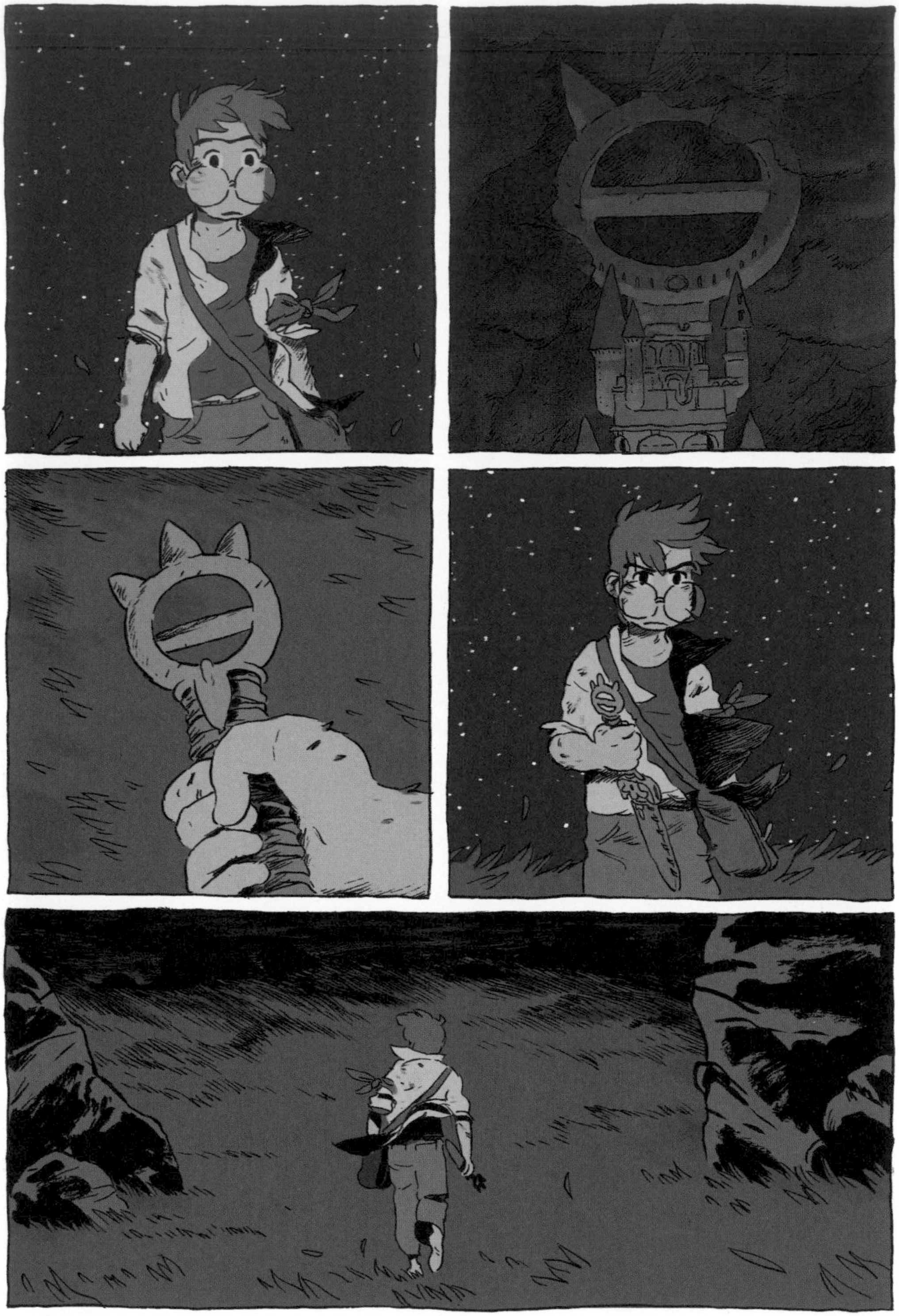

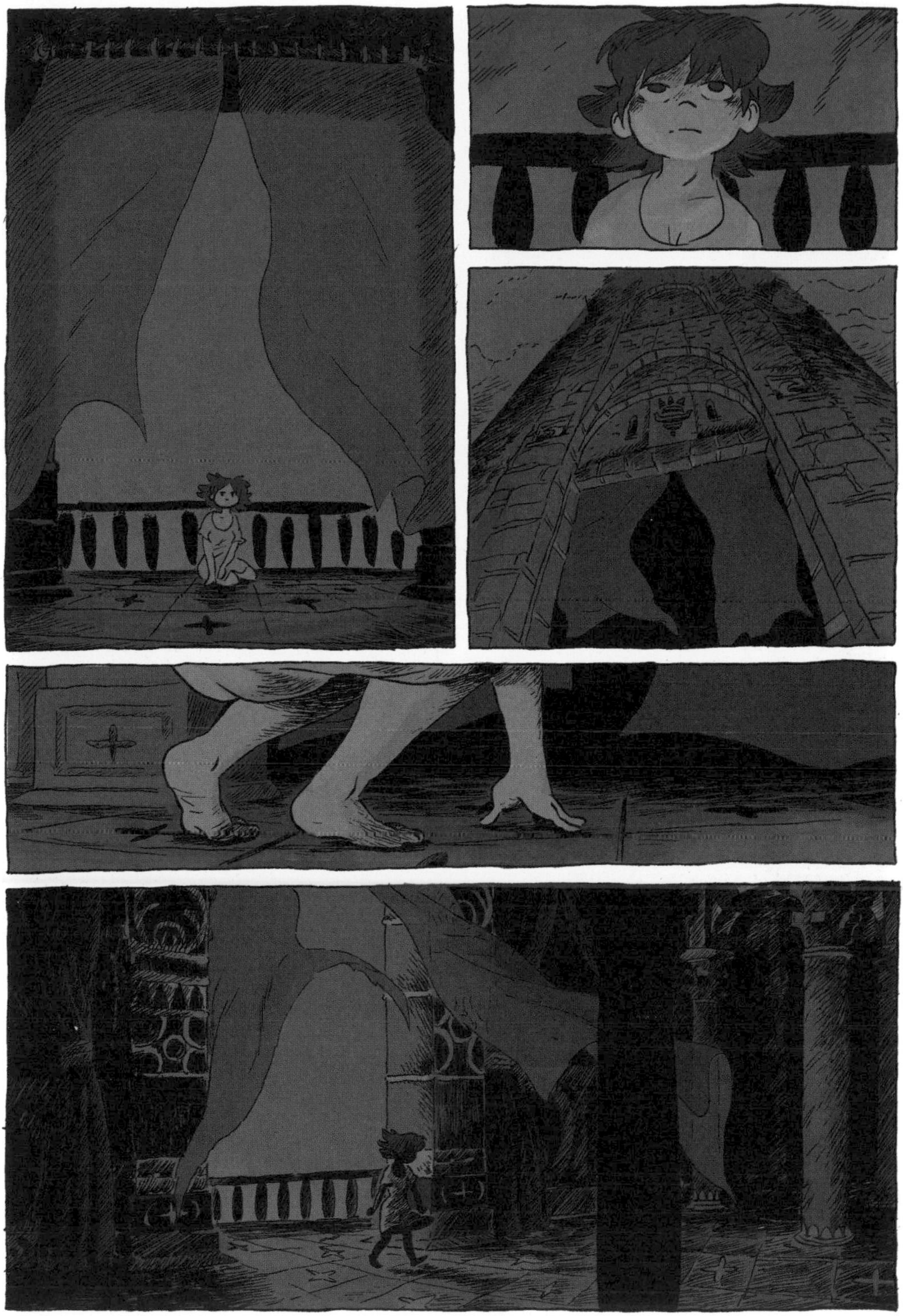

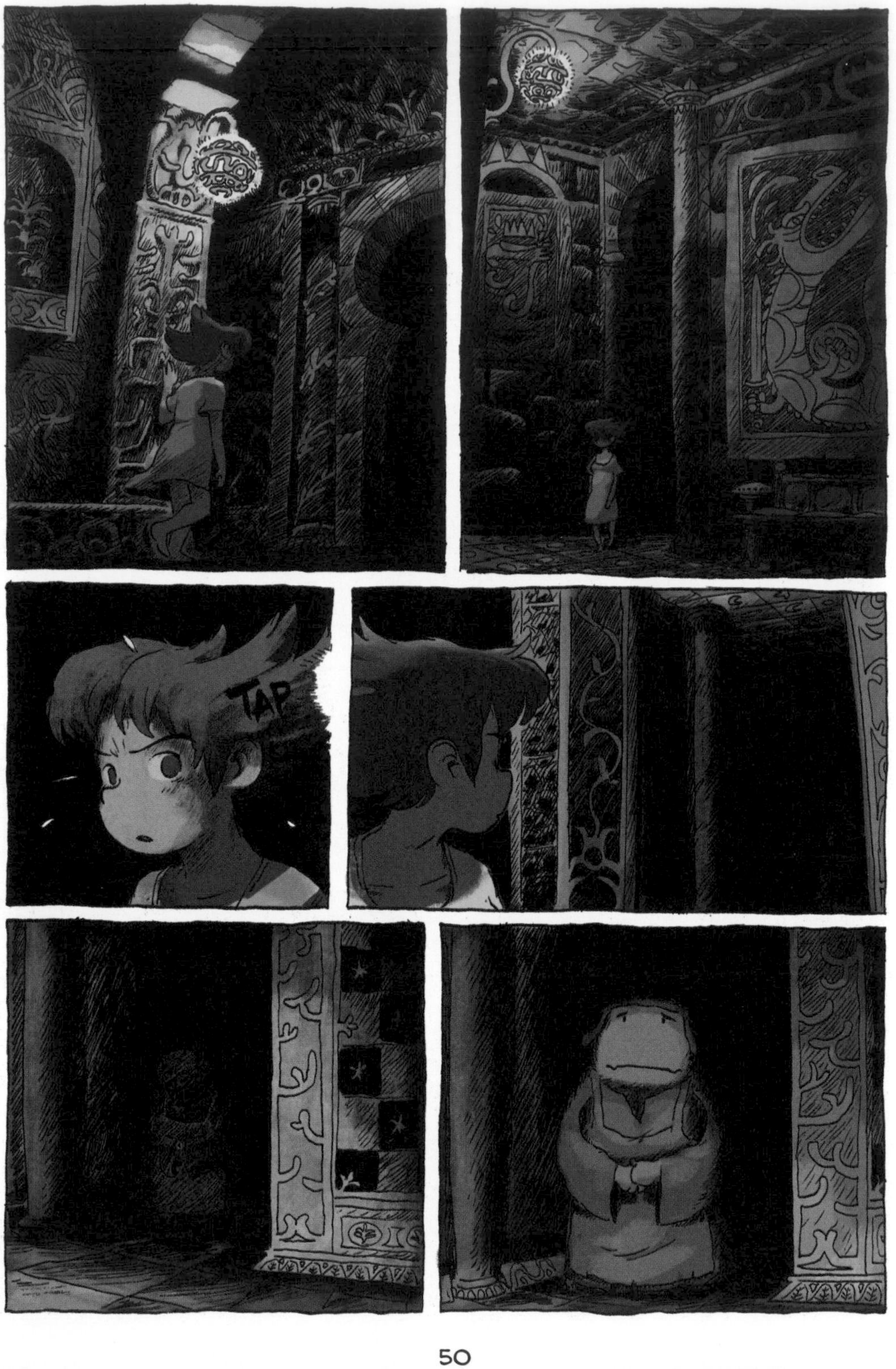
TAP

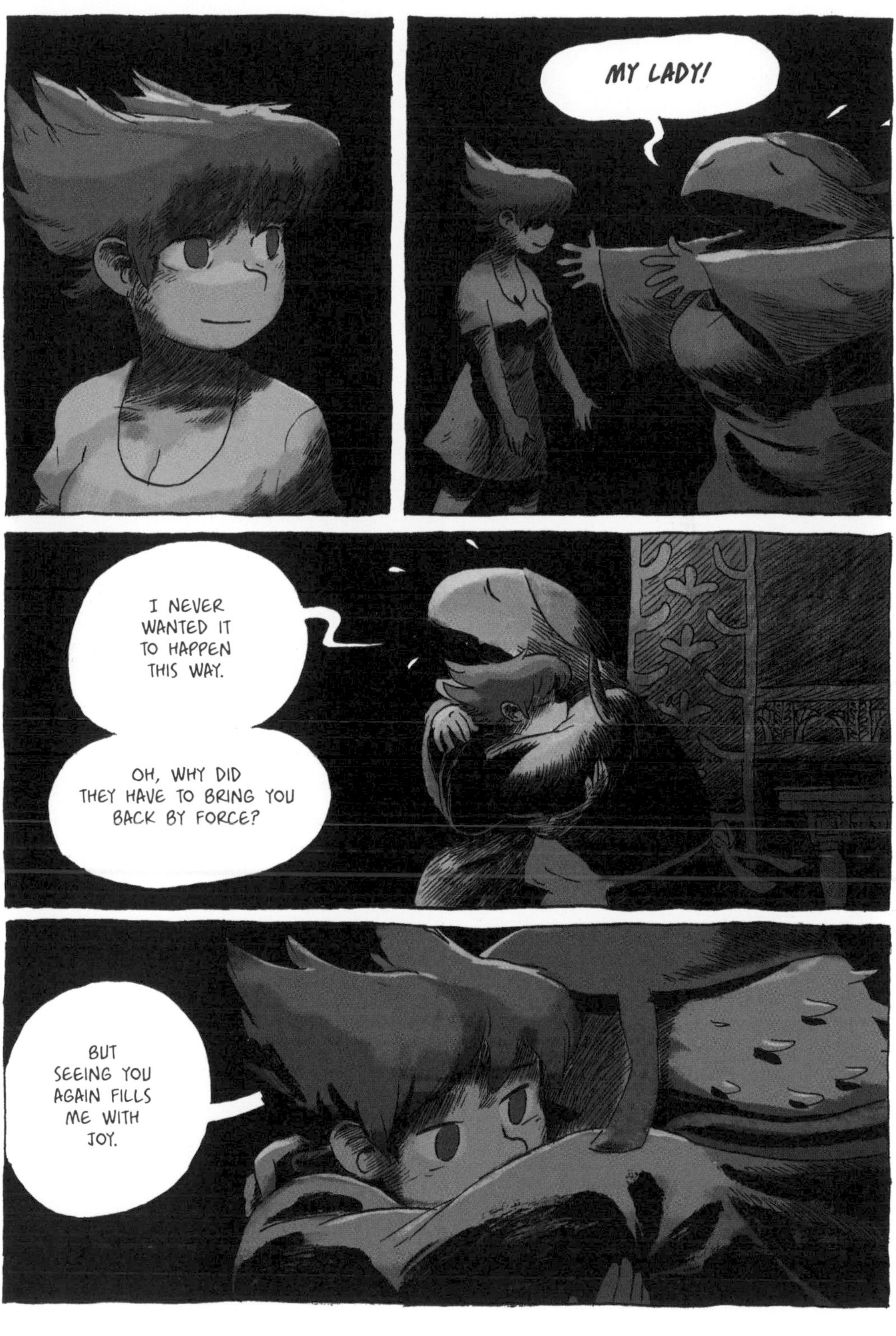
MY LADY!
I NEVER WANTED IT TO HAPPEN THIS WAY.
OH, WHY DID THEY HAVE TO BRING YOU BACK BY FORCE?
BUT SEEING YOU AGAIN FILLS ME WITH JOY.

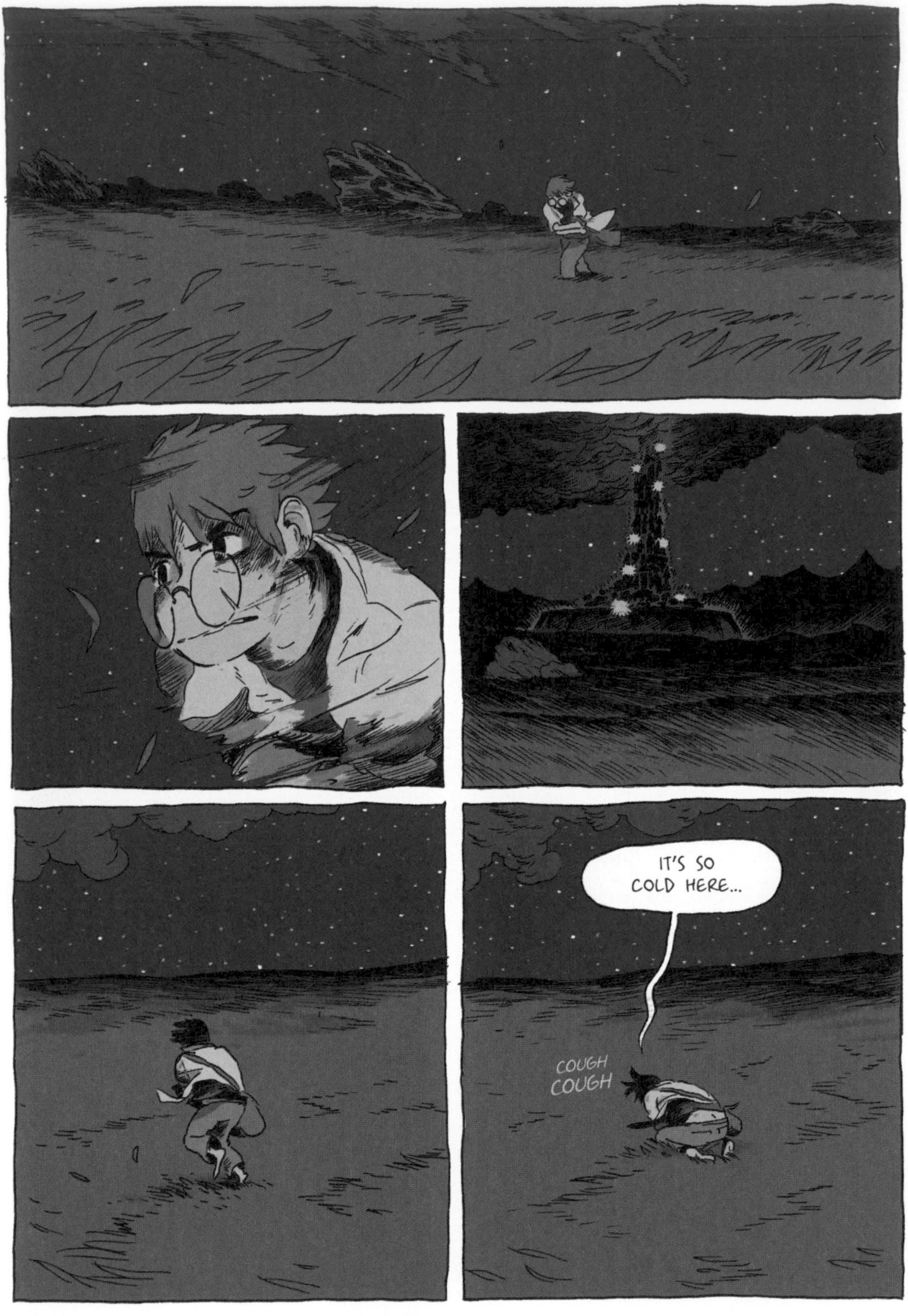
IT'S SO COLD HERE...
COUGH COUGH

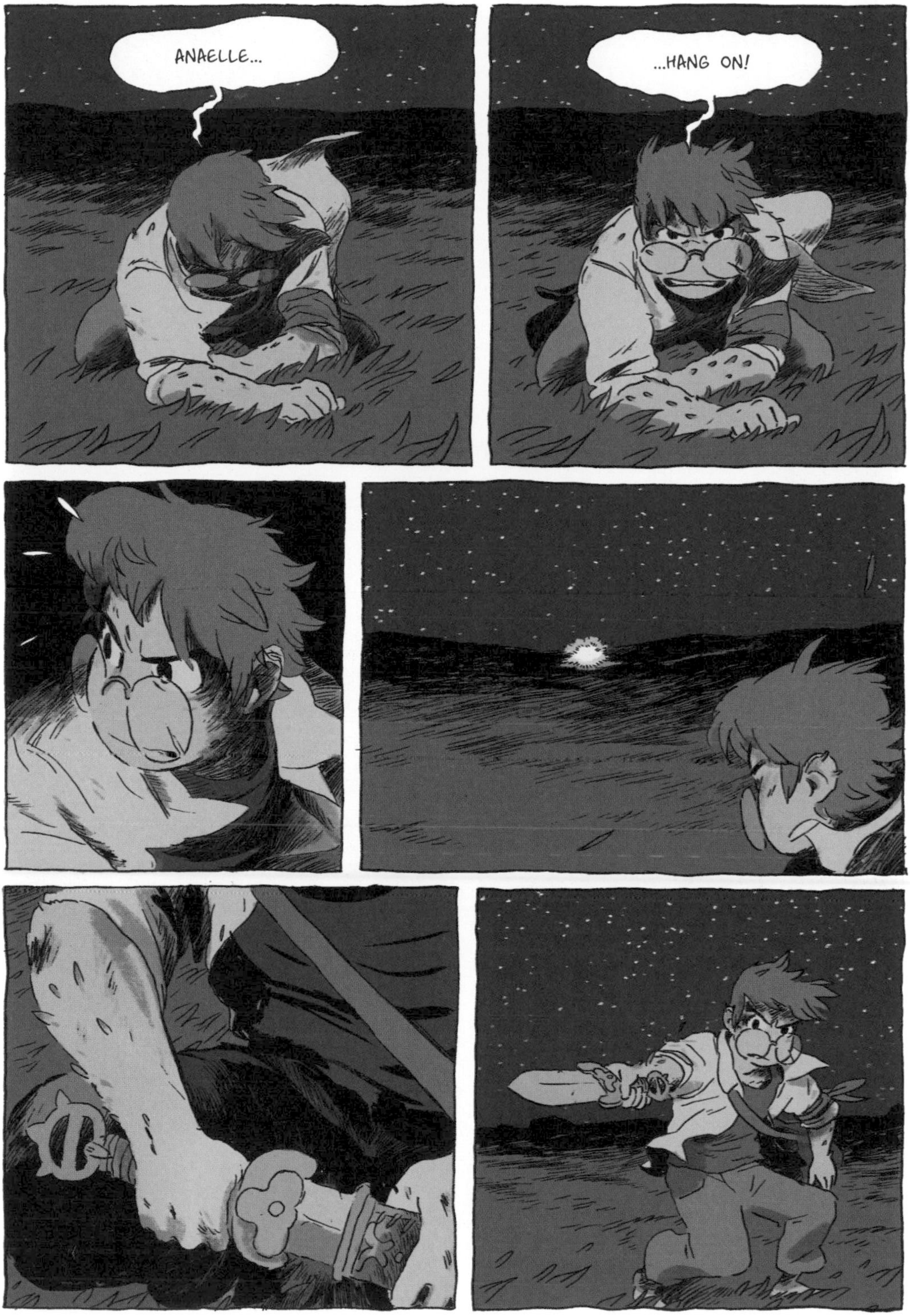
ANAELLE...
...HANG ON!

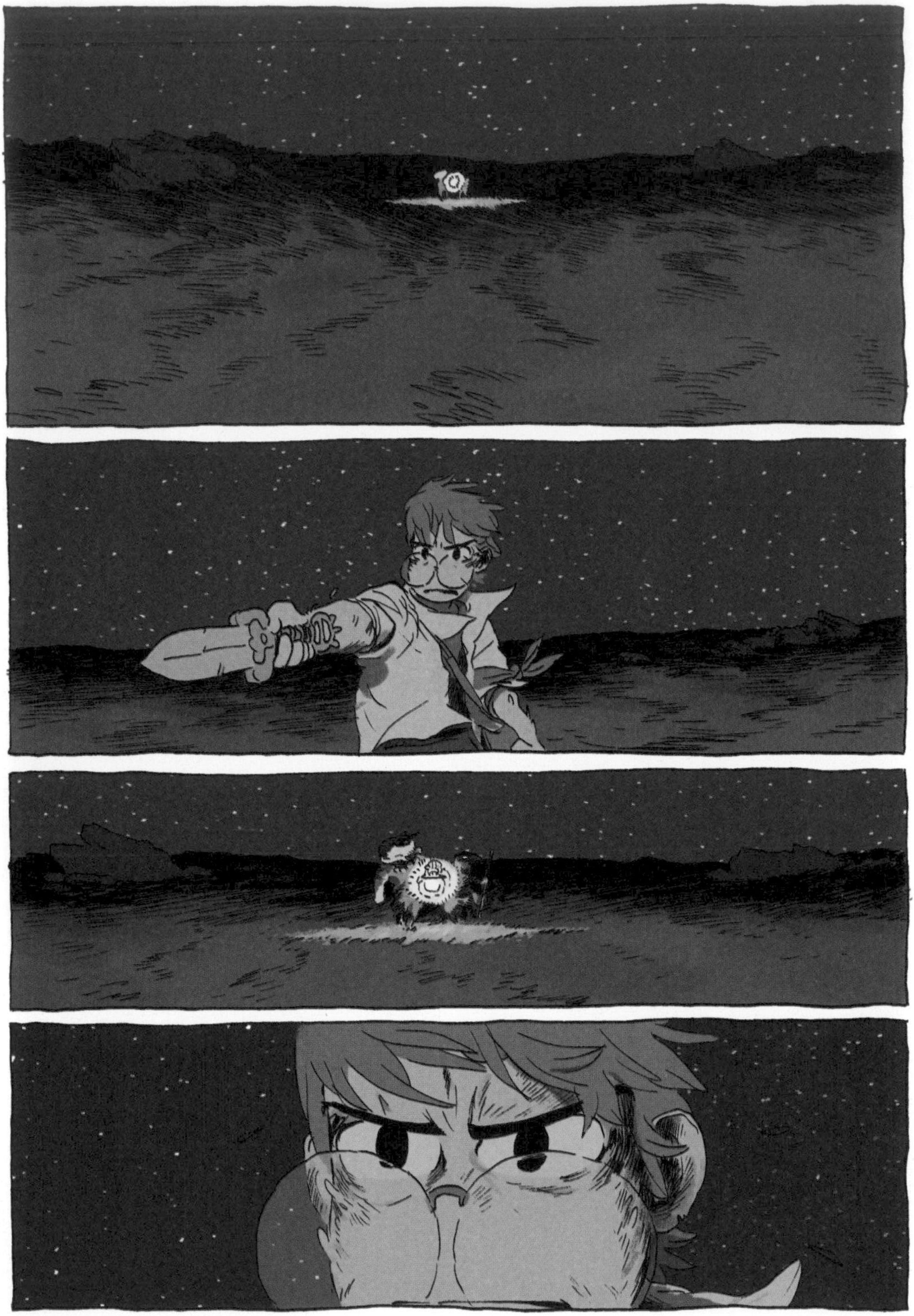

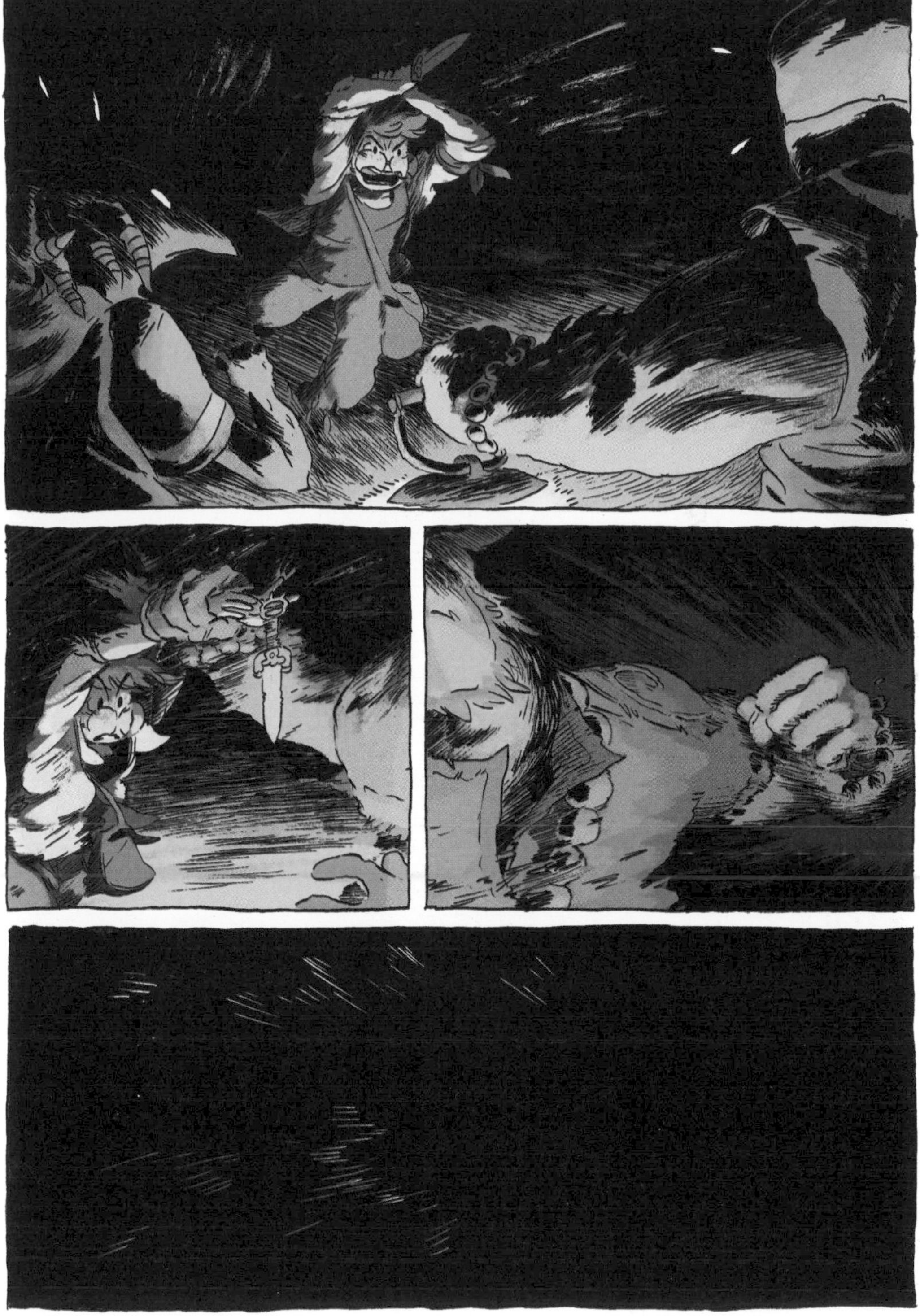

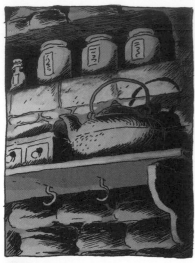

EVERYONE IS STILL ASLEEP.

LET ME MAKE YOU A CUP OF HERBAL TEA AND THEN YOU CAN REST. YOUR MOTHER WILL SEE YOU TOMORROW.

YOU CAN SIT HERE, MY LADY...

WE'VE MISSED YOU SO MUCH!

I MISSED YOU, TOO...

WHEN I LEFT, MY ONLY REGRET WAS LEAVING YOU BEHIND.

BAH! WHAT WOULD HAVE BECOME OF ME IN THE WORLD OF HUMANS? I'M JUST AN OLD SERVING WOMAN.

YOU'RE SO MUCH MORE THAN THAT TO ME.

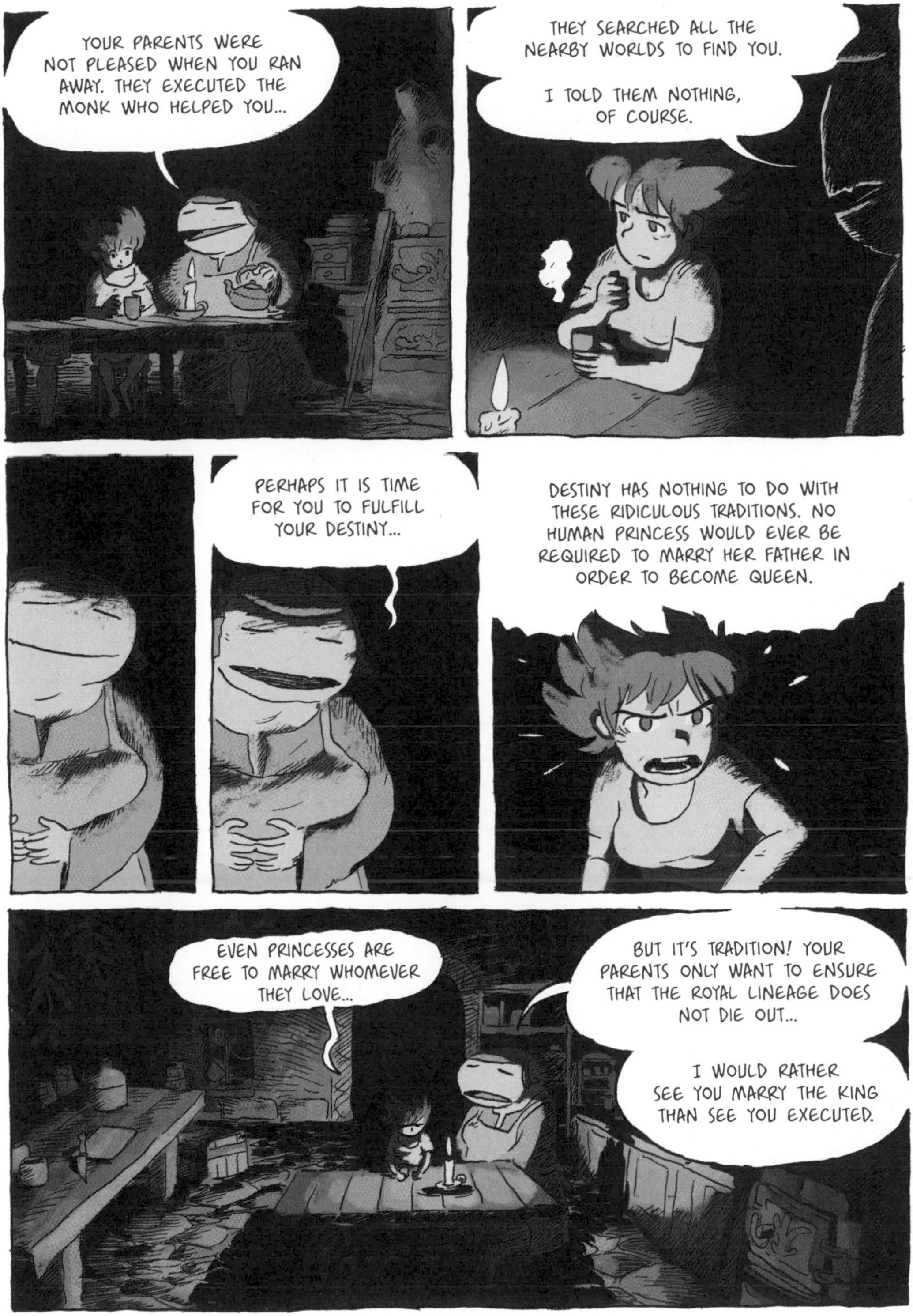
YOUR PARENTS WERE NOT PLEASED WHEN YOU RAN AWAY. THEY EXECUTED THE MONK WHO HELPED YOU...
THEY SEARCHED ALL THE NEARBY WORLDS TO FIND YOU.
I TOLD THEM NOTHING, OF COURSE.
PERHAPS IT IS TIME FOR YOU TO FULFILL YOUR DESTINY...
DESTINY HAS NOTHING TO DO WITH THESE RIDICULOUS TRADITIONS. NO HUMAN PRINCESS WOULD EVER BE REQUIRED TO MARRY HER FATHER IN ORDER TO BECOME QUEEN.
EVEN PRINCESSES ARE FREE TO MARRY WHOMEVER THEY LOVE...
BUT IT'S TRADITION! YOUR PARENTS ONLY WANT TO ENSURE THAT THE ROYAL LINEAGE DOES NOT DIE OUT...
I WOULD RATHER SEE YOU MARRY THE KING THAN SEE YOU EXECUTED.

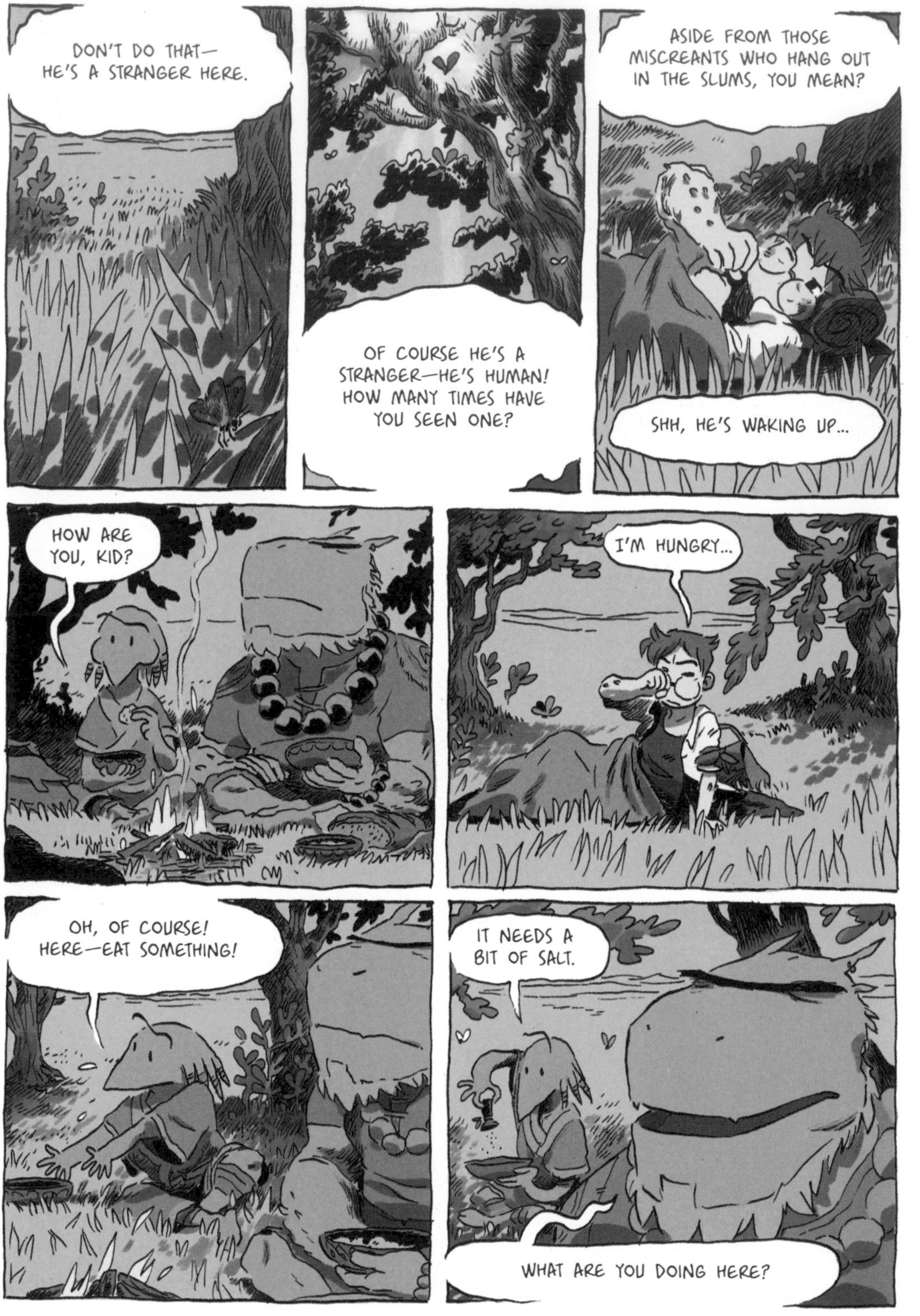
DON'T DO THAT—
HE'S A STRANGER HERE.
OF COURSE HE'S A STRANGER—HE'S HUMAN! HOW MANY TIMES HAVE YOU SEEN ONE?
ASIDE FROM THOSE MISCREANTS WHO HANG OUT IN THE SLUMS, YOU MEAN?
SHH, HE'S WAKING UP...
HOW ARE YOU, KID?
I'M HUNGRY...
OH, OF COURSE! HERE—EAT SOMETHING!
IT NEEDS A BIT OF SALT.
WHAT ARE YOU DOING HERE?

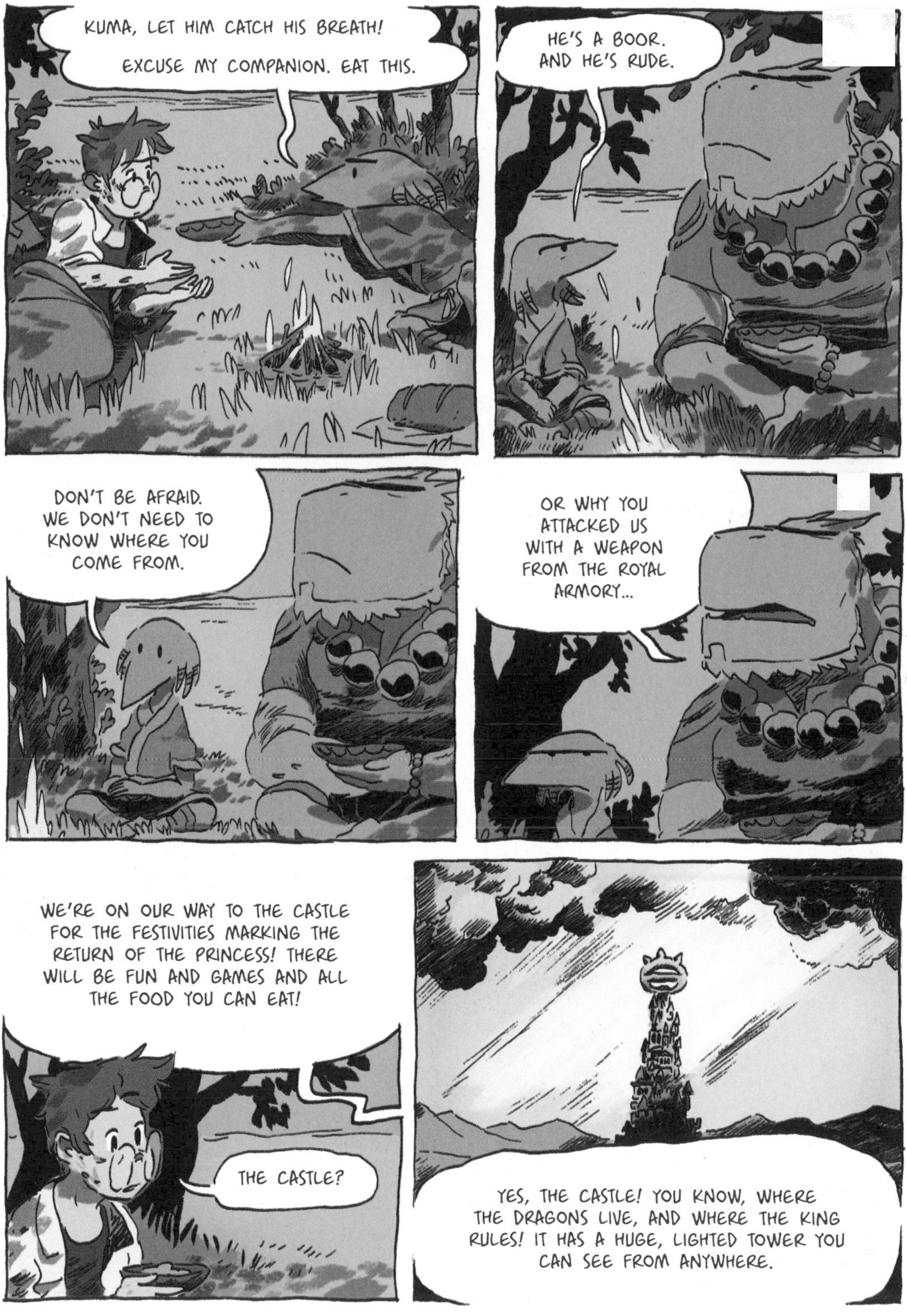
KUMA, LET HIM CATCH HIS BREATH!
EXCUSE MY COMPANION. EAT THIS.
HE'S A BOOR. AND HE'S RUDE.
DON'T BE AFRAID. WE DON'T NEED TO KNOW WHERE YOU COME FROM.
OR WHY YOU ATTACKED US WITH A WEAPON FROM THE ROYAL ARMORY...
WE'RE ON OUR WAY TO THE CASTLE FOR THE FESTIVITIES MARKING THE RETURN OF THE PRINCESS! THERE WILL BE FUN AND GAMES AND ALL THE FOOD YOU CAN EAT!
THE CASTLE?
YES, THE CASTLE! YOU KNOW, WHERE THE DRAGONS LIVE, AND WHERE THE KING RULES! IT HAS A HUGE, LIGHTED TOWER YOU CAN SEE FROM ANYWHERE.

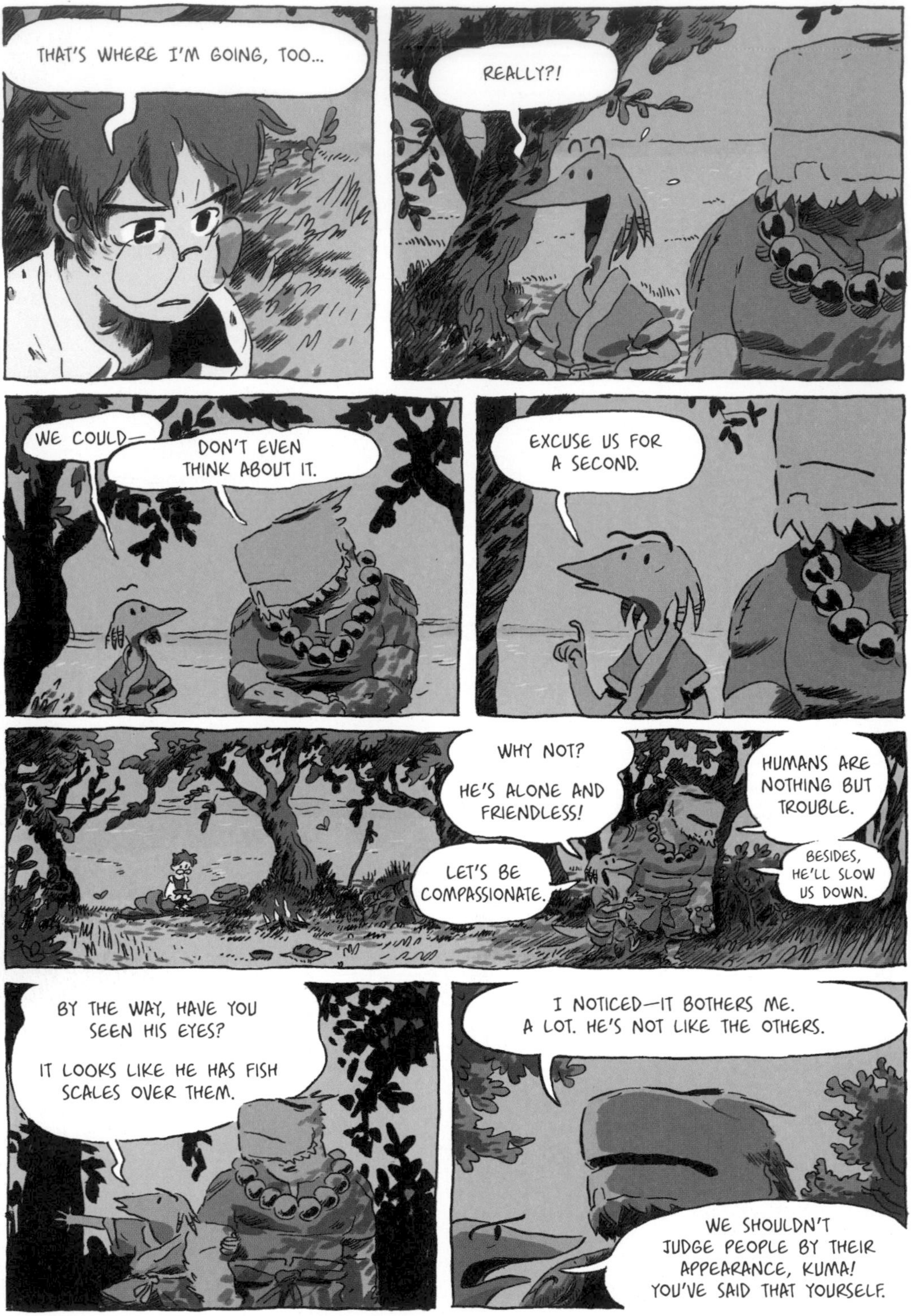

THAT'S WHERE I'M GOING, TOO...
REALLY?!
WE COULD—
DON'T EVEN THINK ABOUT IT.
EXCUSE US FOR A SECOND.
WHY NOT?
HE'S ALONE AND FRIENDLESS!
LET'S BE COMPASSIONATE.
HUMANS ARE NOTHING BUT TROUBLE.
BESIDES, HE'LL SLOW US DOWN.
BY THE WAY, HAVE YOU SEEN HIS EYES?
IT LOOKS LIKE HE HAS FISH SCALES OVER THEM.
I NOTICED—IT BOTHERS ME. A LOT. HE'S NOT LIKE THE OTHERS.
WE SHOULDN'T JUDGE PEOPLE BY THEIR APPEARANCE, KUMA! YOU'VE SAID THAT YOURSELF.

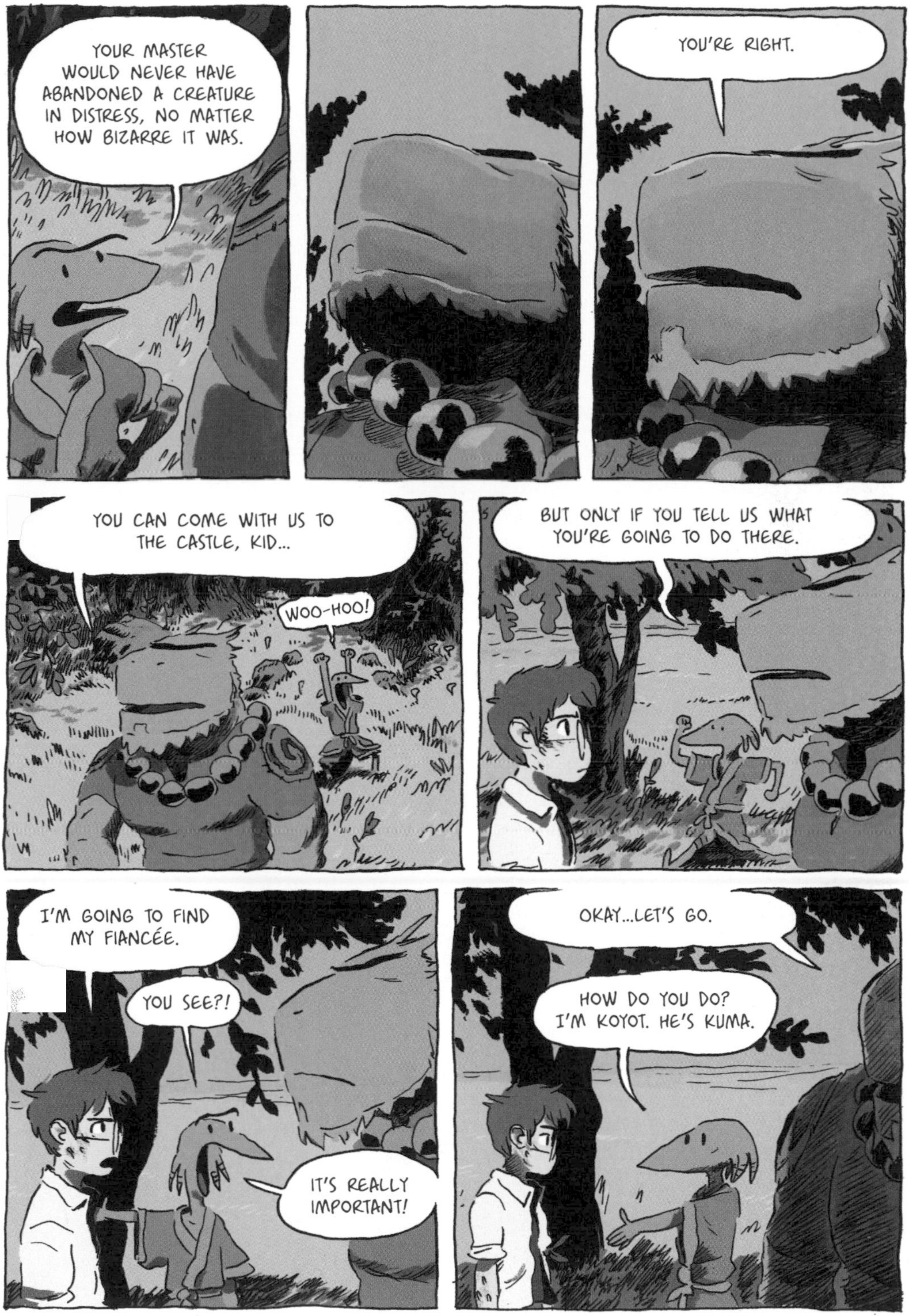
YOUR MASTER WOULD NEVER HAVE ABANDONED A CREATURE IN DISTRESS, NO MATTER HOW BIZARRE IT WAS.
YOU'RE RIGHT.
YOU CAN COME WITH US TO THE CASTLE, KID...
WOO-HOO!
BUT ONLY IF YOU TELL US WHAT YOU'RE GOING TO DO THERE.
I'M GOING TO FIND MY FIANCÉE.
YOU SEE?!
IT'S REALLY IMPORTANT!
OKAY...LET'S GO.
HOW DO YOU DO? I'M KOYOT. HE'S KUMA.

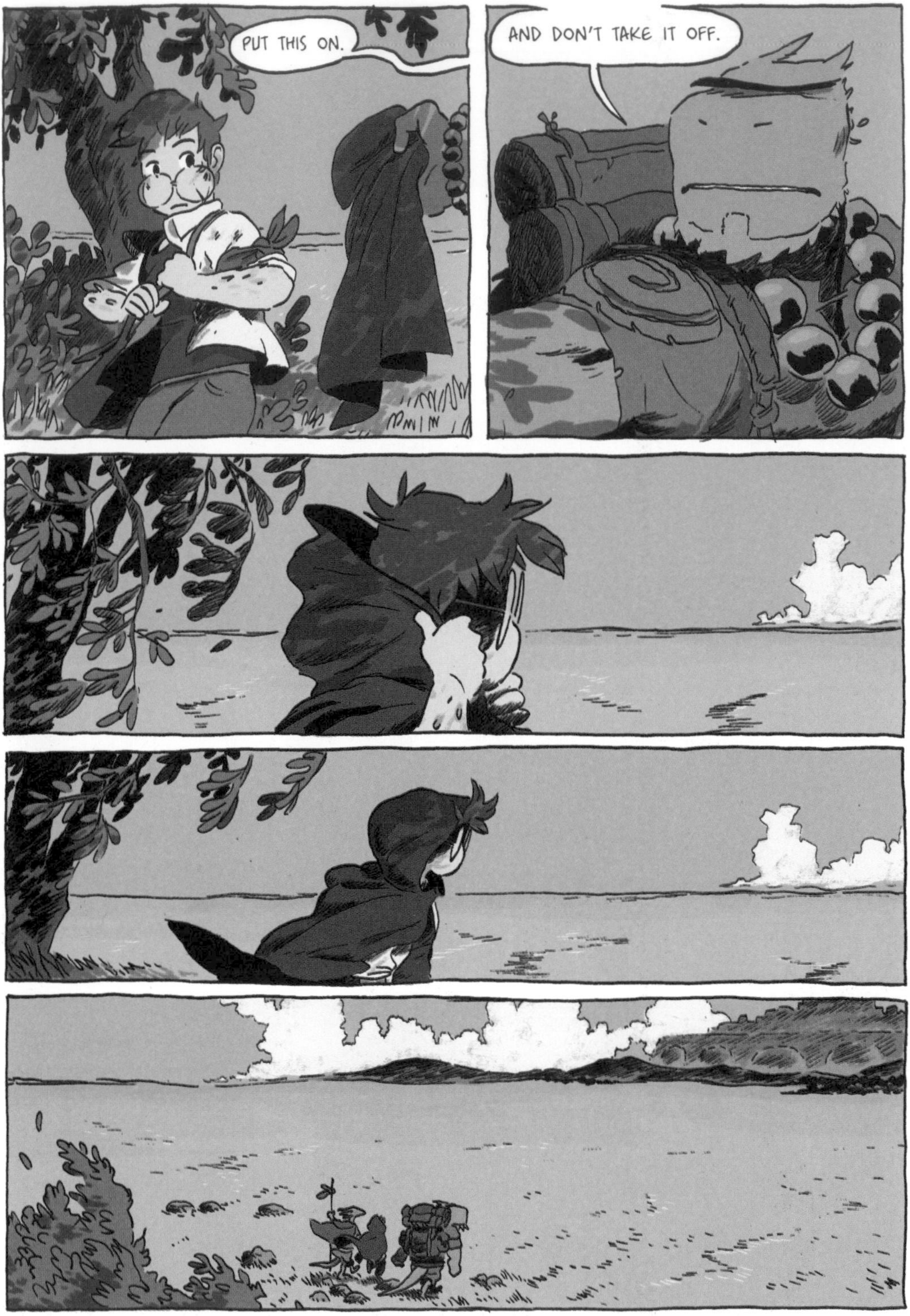
PUT THIS ON.
AND DON'T TAKE IT OFF.

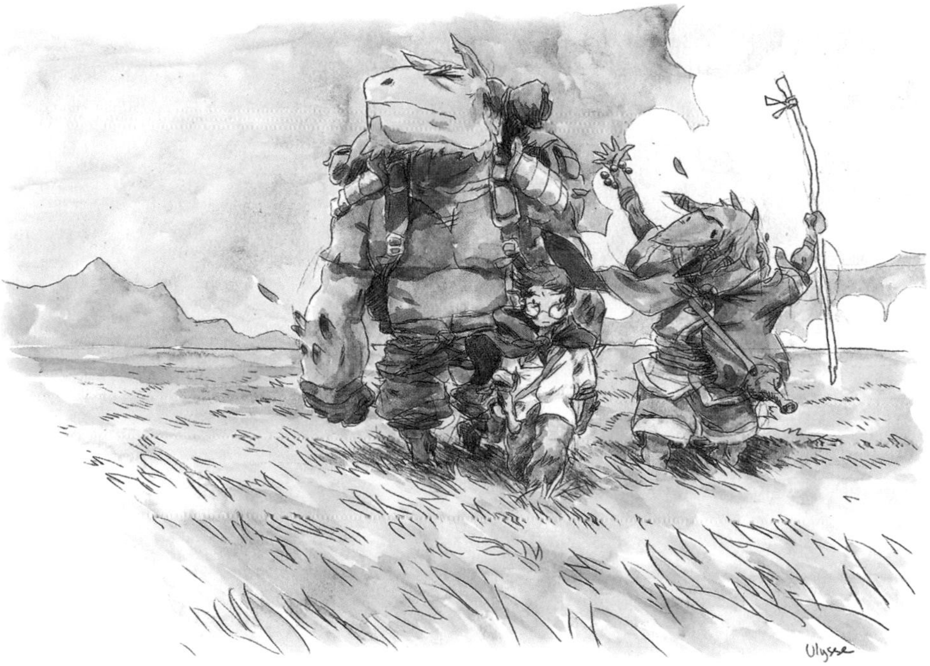
Ulysse

PART TWO

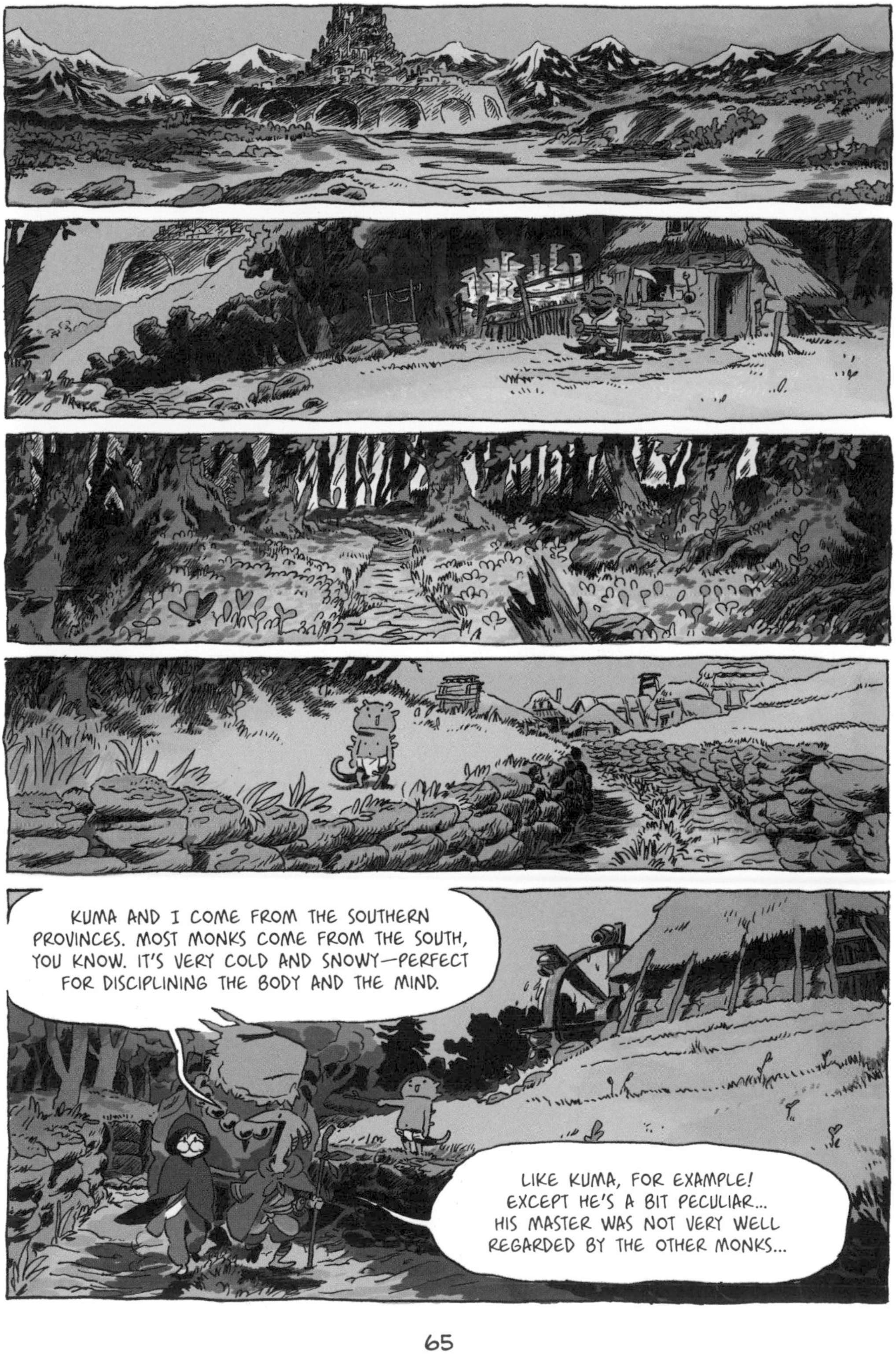

KUMA AND I COME FROM THE SOUTHERN PROVINCES. MOST MONKS COME FROM THE SOUTH, YOU KNOW. IT'S VERY COLD AND SNOWY—PERFECT FOR DISCIPLINING THE BODY AND THE MIND.
LIKE KUMA, FOR EXAMPLE! EXCEPT HE'S A BIT PECULIAR... HIS MASTER WAS NOT VERY WELL REGARDED BY THE OTHER MONKS...

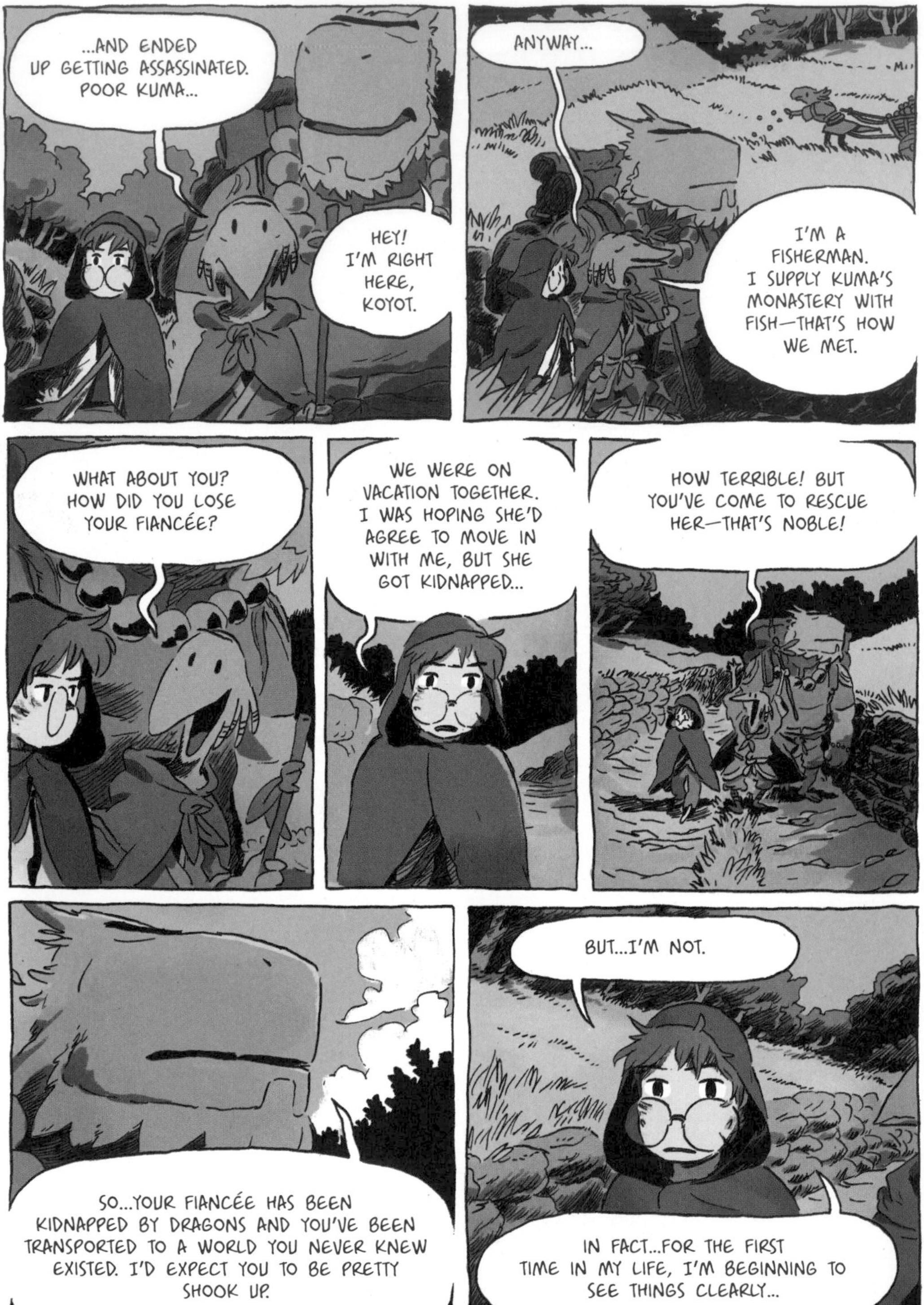
...AND ENDED UP GETTING ASSASSINATED. POOR KUMA...
HEY! I'M RIGHT HERE, KOYOT.
ANYWAY...
I'M A FISHERMAN. I SUPPLY KUMA'S MONASTERY WITH FISH—THAT'S HOW WE MET.
WHAT ABOUT YOU? HOW DID YOU LOSE YOUR FIANCÉE?
WE WERE ON VACATION TOGETHER. I WAS HOPING SHE'D AGREE TO MOVE IN WITH ME, BUT SHE GOT KIDNAPPED...
HOW TERRIBLE! BUT YOU'VE COME TO RESCUE HER—THAT'S NOBLE!
SO...YOUR FIANCÉE HAS BEEN KIDNAPPED BY DRAGONS AND YOU'VE BEEN TRANSPORTED TO A WORLD YOU NEVER KNEW EXISTED. I'D EXPECT YOU TO BE PRETTY SHOOK UP.
BUT...I'M NOT.
IN FACT...FOR THE FIRST TIME IN MY LIFE, I'M BEGINNING TO SEE THINGS CLEARLY...

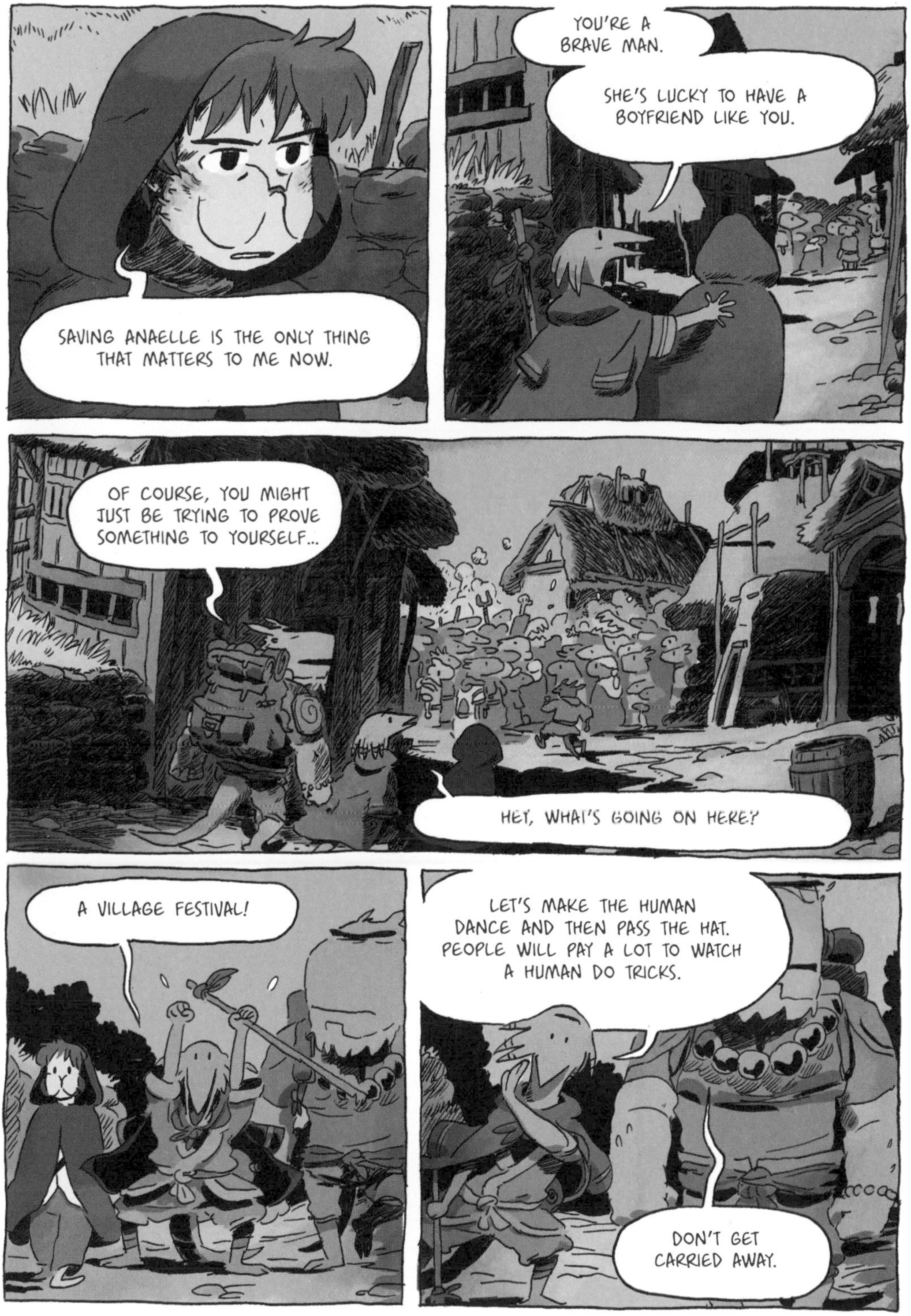

SAVING ANAELLE IS THE ONLY THING THAT MATTERS TO ME NOW.
YOU'RE A BRAVE MAN.
SHE'S LUCKY TO HAVE A BOYFRIEND LIKE YOU.
OF COURSE, YOU MIGHT JUST BE TRYING TO PROVE SOMETHING TO YOURSELF...
HEY, WHAT'S GOING ON HERE?
A VILLAGE FESTIVAL!
LET'S MAKE THE HUMAN DANCE AND THEN PASS THE HAT. PEOPLE WILL PAY A LOT TO WATCH A HUMAN DO TRICKS.
DON'T GET CARRIED AWAY.

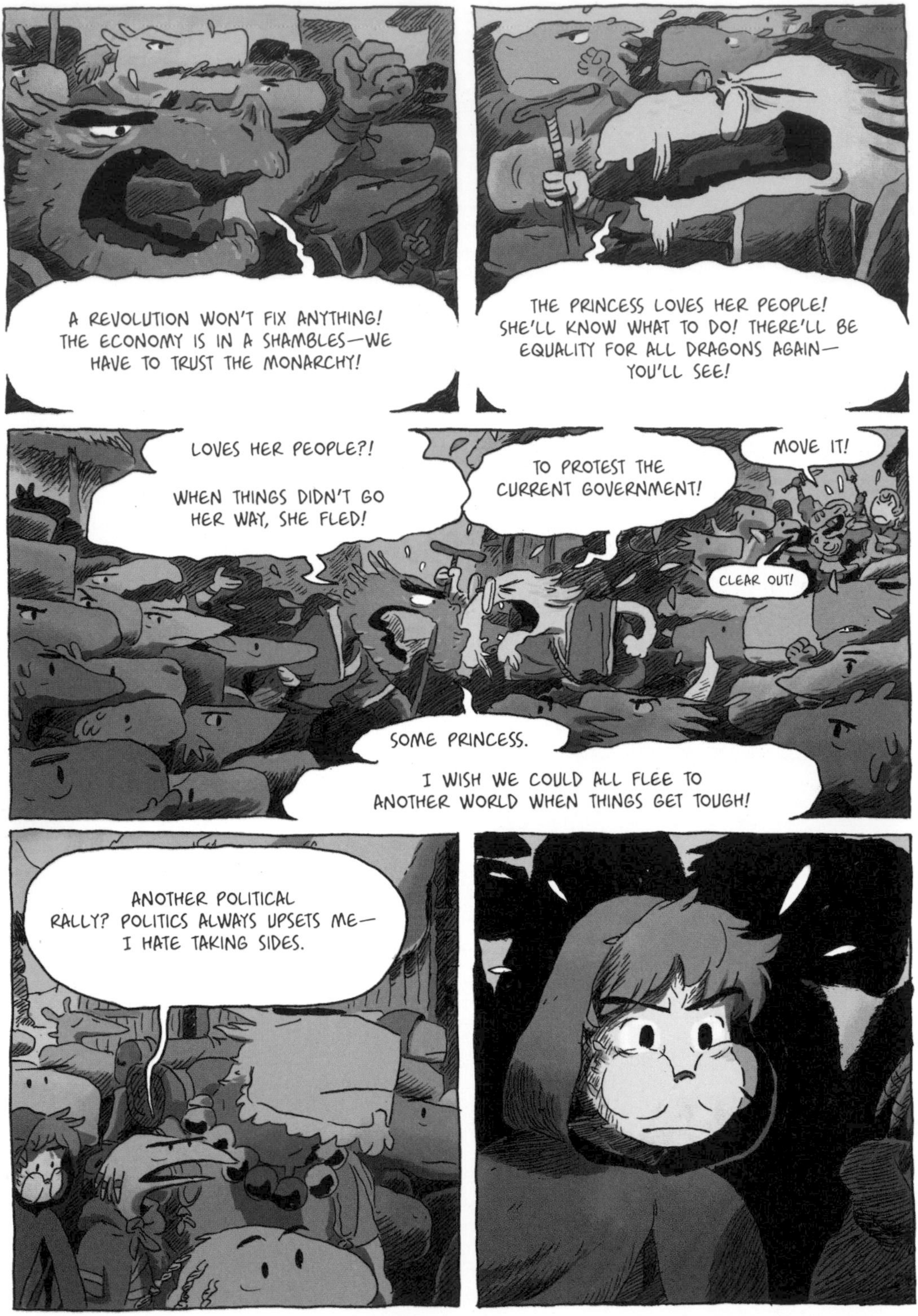
A REVOLUTION WON'T FIX ANYTHING! THE ECONOMY IS IN A SHAMBLES—WE HAVE TO TRUST THE MONARCHY!
THE PRINCESS LOVES HER PEOPLE! SHE'LL KNOW WHAT TO DO! THERE'LL BE EQUALITY FOR ALL DRAGONS AGAIN—YOU'LL SEE!
LOVES HER PEOPLE?!
WHEN THINGS DIDN'T GO HER WAY, SHE FLED!
TO PROTEST THE CURRENT GOVERNMENT!
MOVE IT!
CLEAR OUT!
SOME PRINCESS.
I WISH WE COULD ALL FLEE TO ANOTHER WORLD WHEN THINGS GET TOUGH!
ANOTHER POLITICAL RALLY? POLITICS ALWAYS UPSETS ME—I HATE TAKING SIDES.

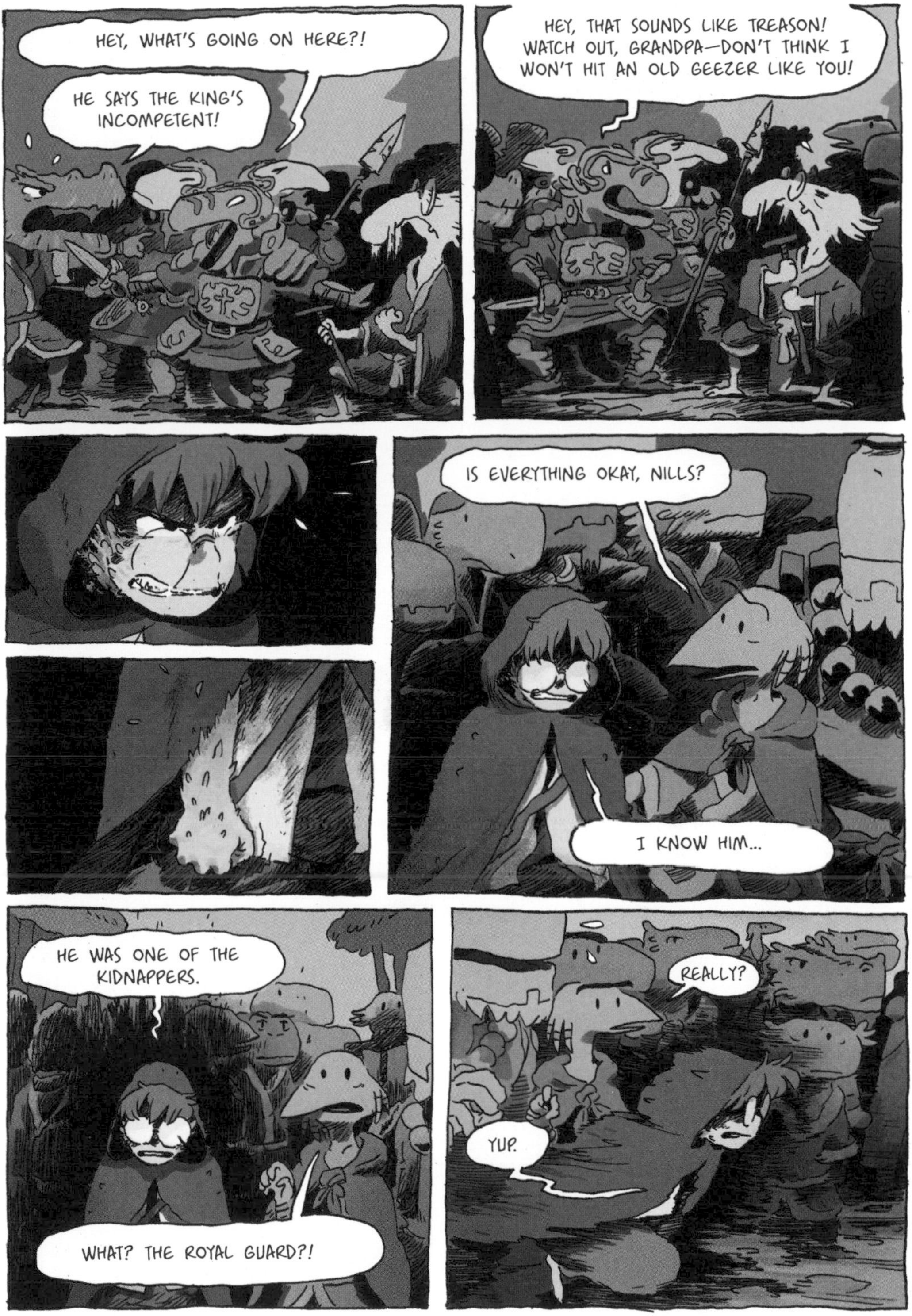
HEY, WHAT'S GOING ON HERE?!
HE SAYS THE KING'S INCOMPETENT!
HEY, THAT SOUNDS LIKE TREASON! WATCH OUT, GRANDPA—DON'T THINK I WON'T HIT AN OLD GEEZER LIKE YOU!
IS EVERYTHING OKAY, NILLS?
I KNOW HIM...
HE WAS ONE OF THE KIDNAPPERS.
WHAT? THE ROYAL GUARD?!
REALLY?
YUP.

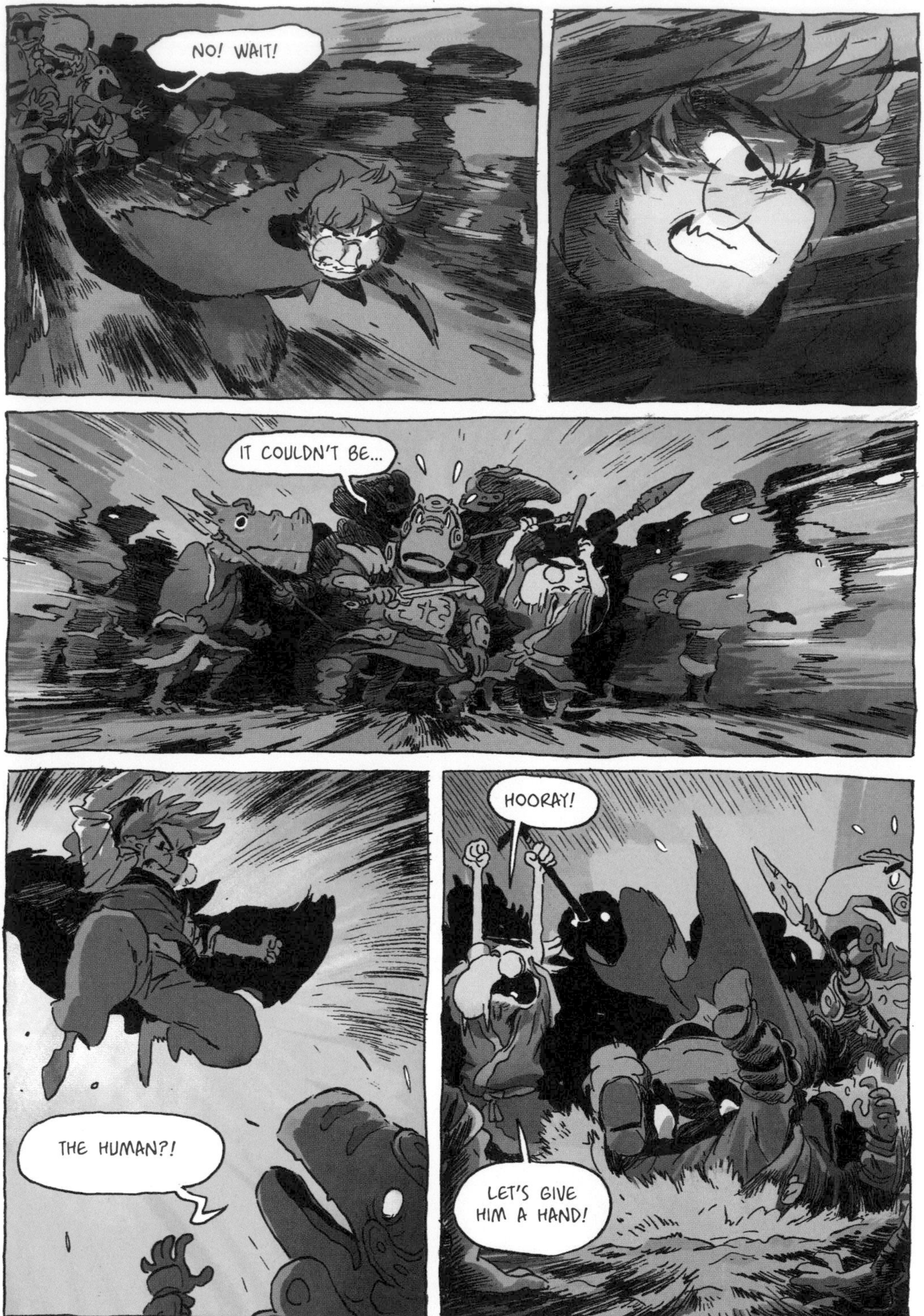
NO! WAIT!
IT COULDN'T BE...
THE HUMAN?!
HOORAY!
LET'S GIVE HIM A HAND!

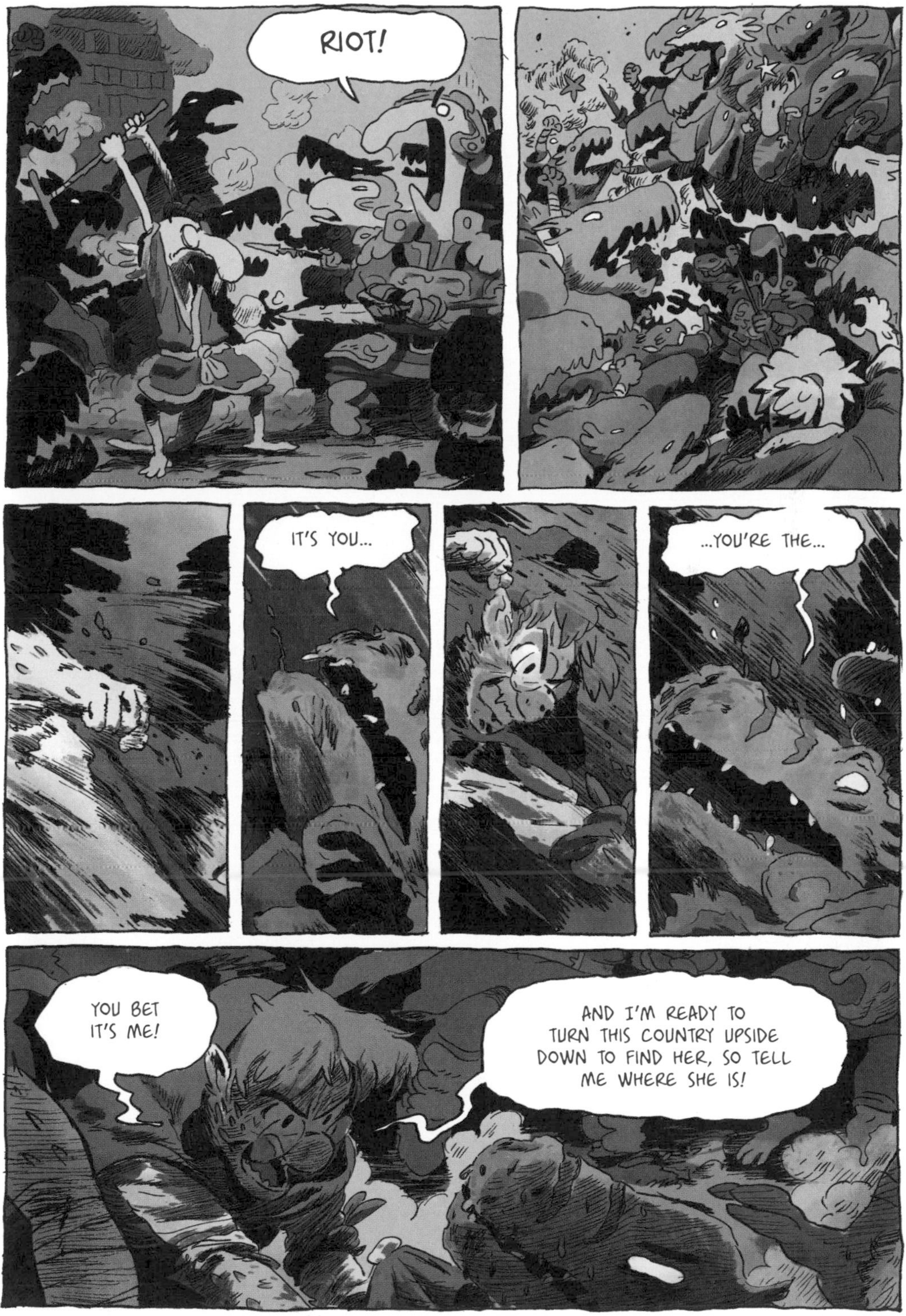
RIOT!
IT'S YOU...
...YOU'RE THE...
YOU BET IT'S ME!
AND I'M READY TO TURN THIS COUNTRY UPSIDE DOWN TO FIND HER, SO TELL ME WHERE SHE IS!

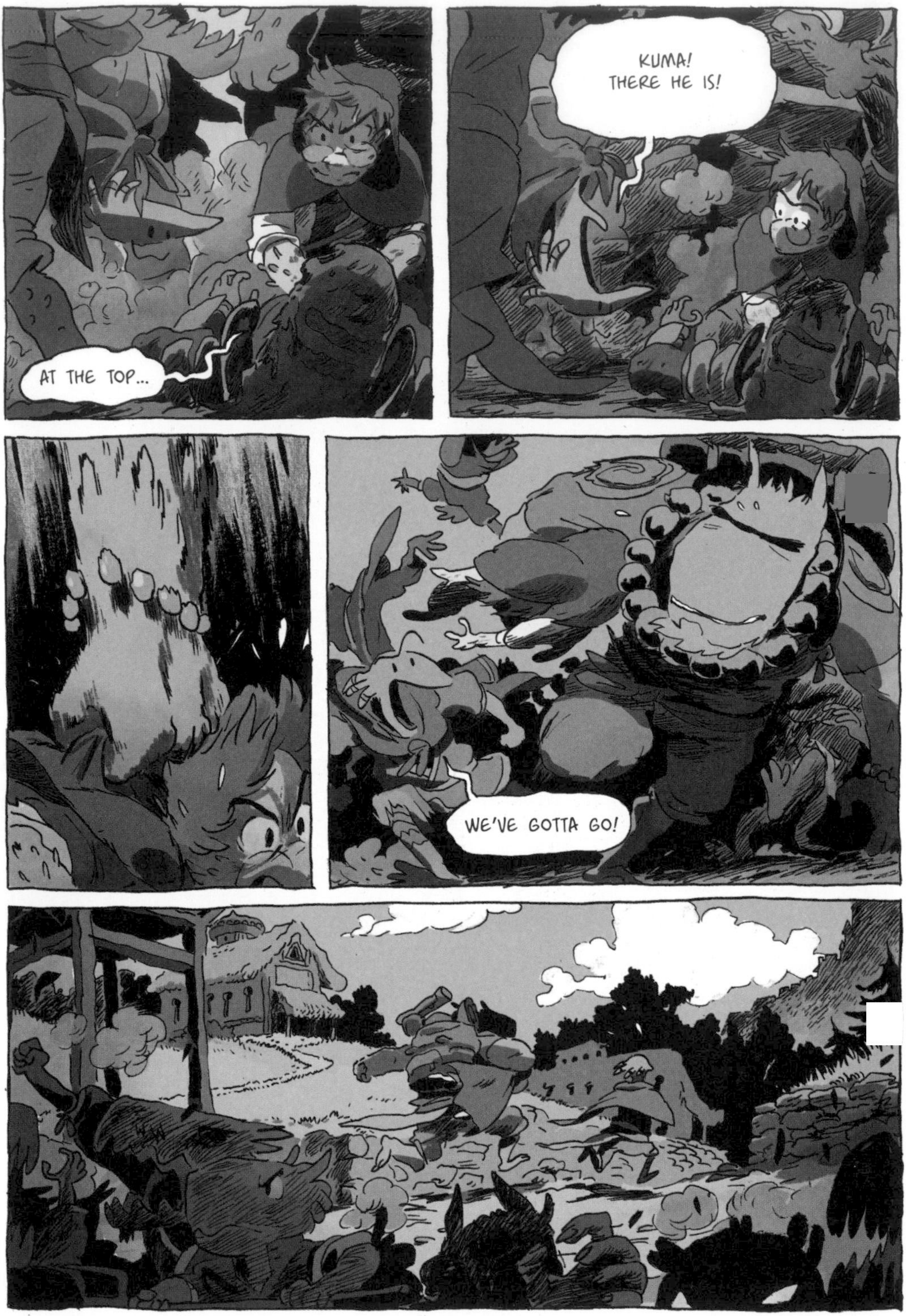
AT THE TOP...
KUMA! THERE HE IS!
WE'VE GOTTA GO!

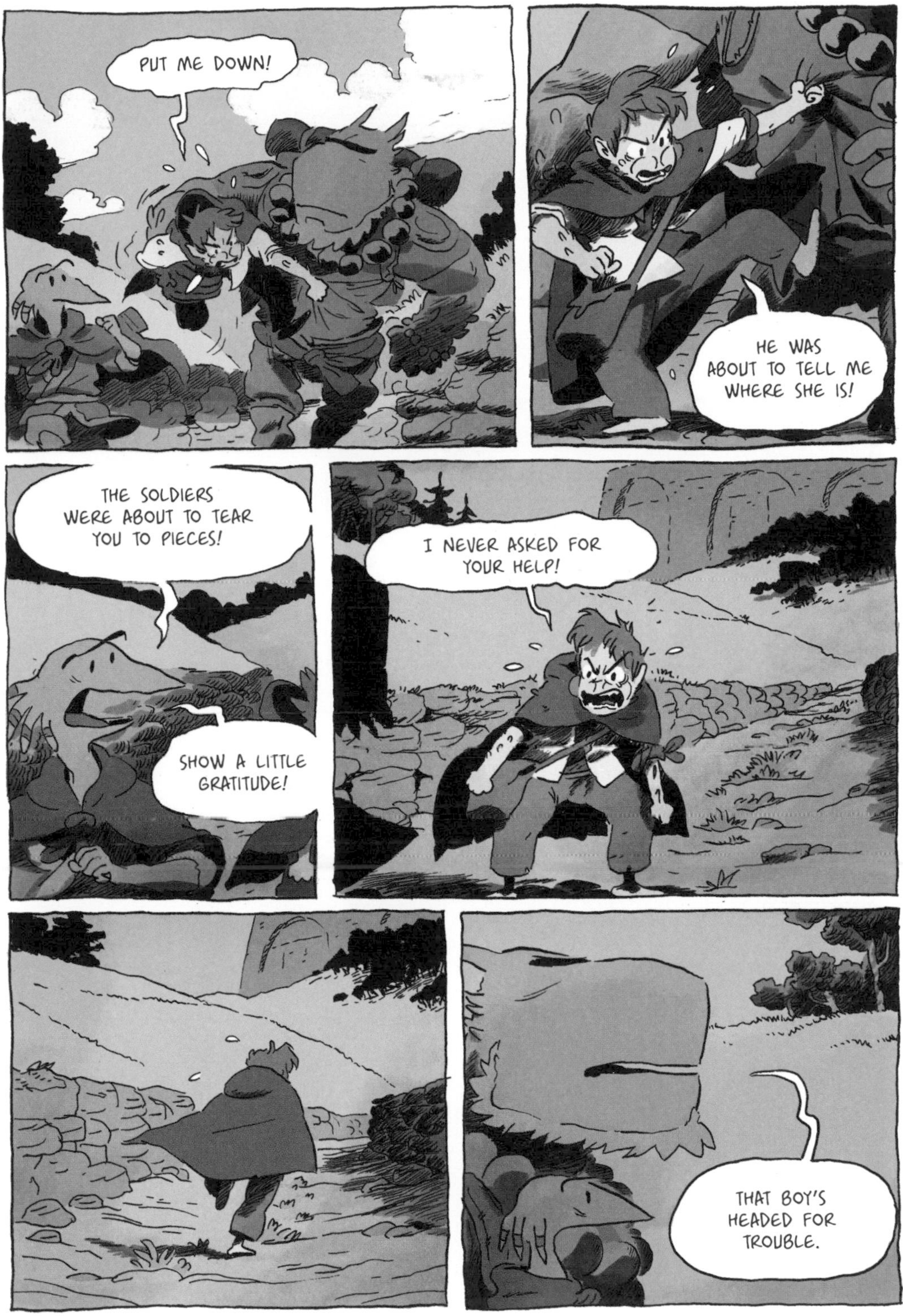
PUT ME DOWN!
HE WAS ABOUT TO TELL ME WHERE SHE IS!
THE SOLDIERS WERE ABOUT TO TEAR YOU TO PIECES!
SHOW A LITTLE GRATITUDE!
I NEVER ASKED FOR YOUR HELP!
THAT BOY'S HEADED FOR TROUBLE.

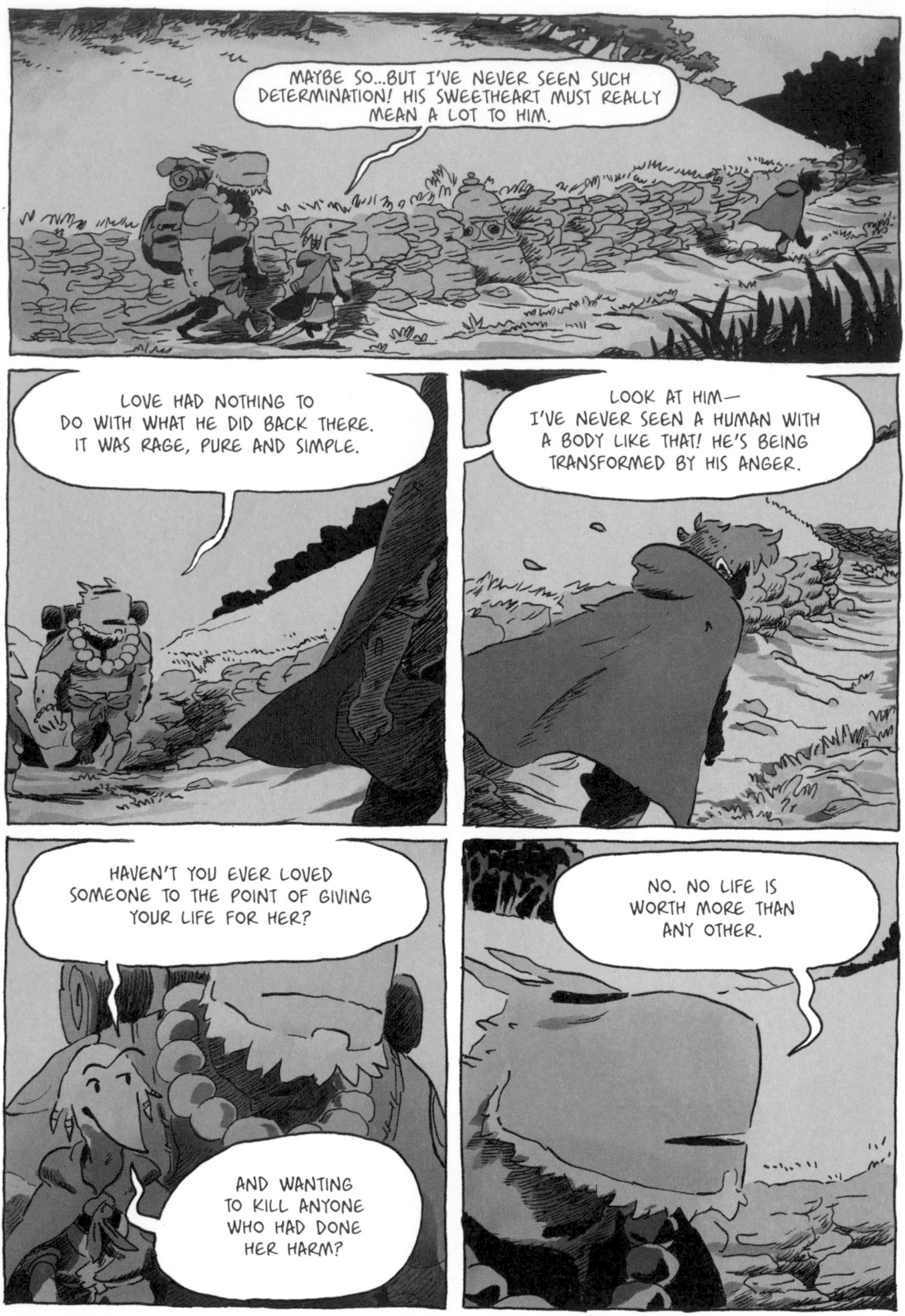
MAYBE SO...BUT I'VE NEVER SEEN SUCH DETERMINATION! HIS SWEETHEART MUST REALLY MEAN A LOT TO HIM.
LOVE HAD NOTHING TO DO WITH WHAT HE DID BACK THERE. IT WAS RAGE, PURE AND SIMPLE.
LOOK AT HIM— I'VE NEVER SEEN A HUMAN WITH A BODY LIKE THAT! HE'S BEING TRANSFORMED BY HIS ANGER.
HAVEN'T YOU EVER LOVED SOMEONE TO THE POINT OF GIVING YOUR LIFE FOR HER?
AND WANTING TO KILL ANYONE WHO HAD DONE HER HARM?
NO. NO LIFE IS WORTH MORE THAN ANY OTHER.

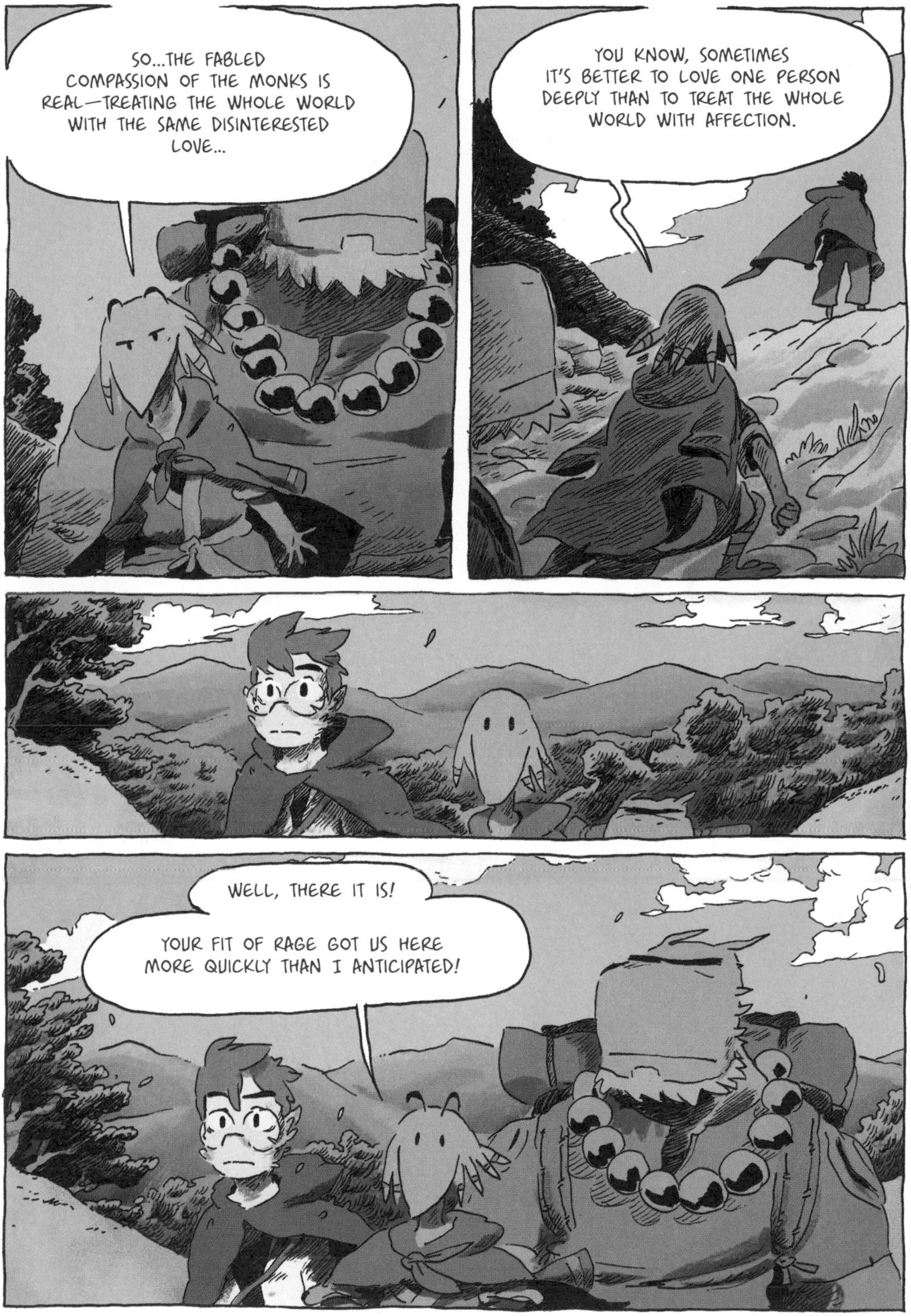
SO...THE FABLED COMPASSION OF THE MONKS IS REAL—TREATING THE WHOLE WORLD WITH THE SAME DISINTERESTED LOVE...
YOU KNOW, SOMETIMES IT'S BETTER TO LOVE ONE PERSON DEEPLY THAN TO TREAT THE WHOLE WORLD WITH AFFECTION.
WELL, THERE IT IS!
YOUR FIT OF RAGE GOT US HERE MORE QUICKLY THAN I ANTICIPATED!

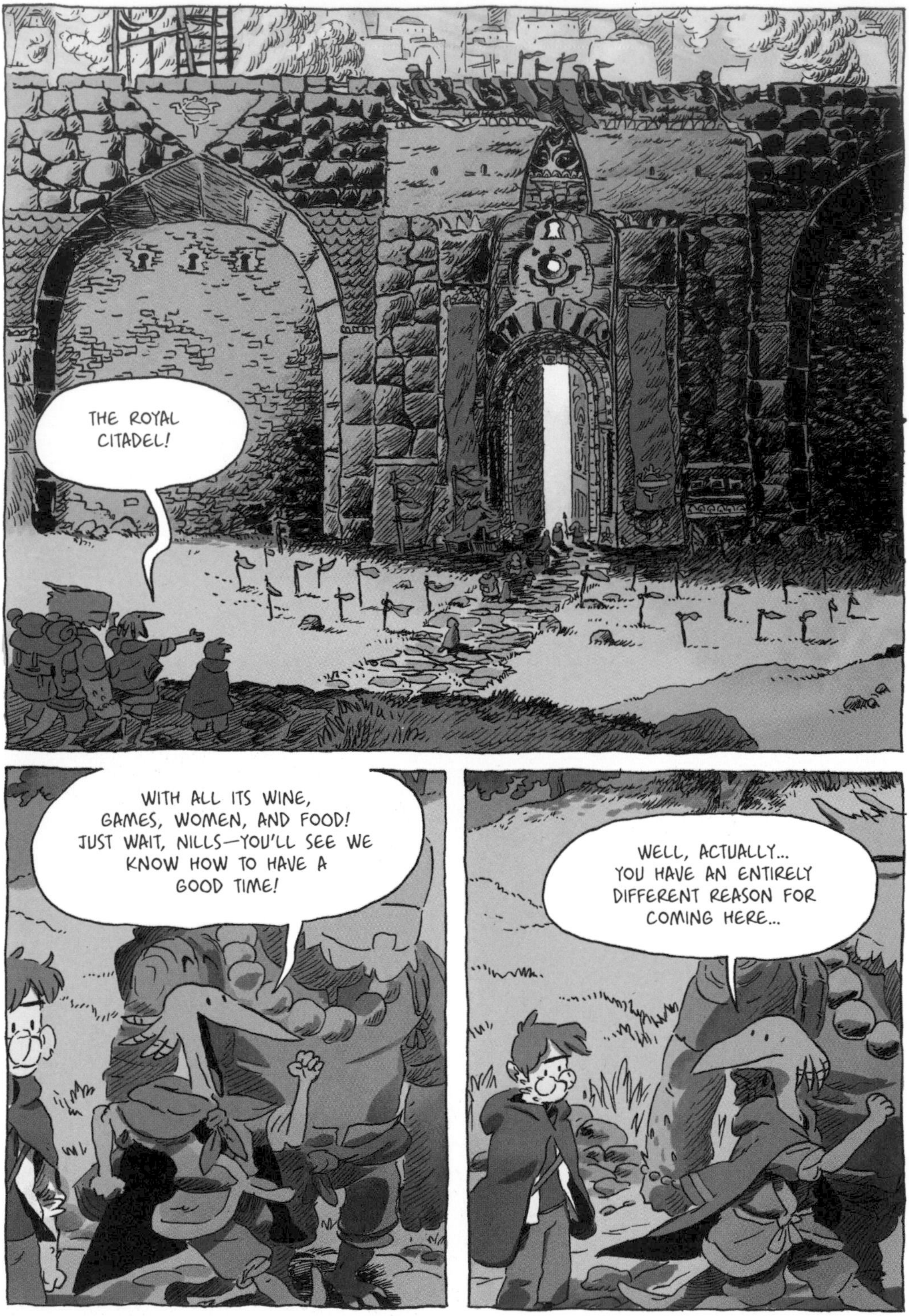
THE ROYAL CITADEL!
WITH ALL ITS WINE, GAMES, WOMEN, AND FOOD! JUST WAIT, NILLS—YOU'LL SEE WE KNOW HOW TO HAVE A GOOD TIME!
WELL, ACTUALLY... YOU HAVE AN ENTIRELY DIFFERENT REASON FOR COMING HERE...

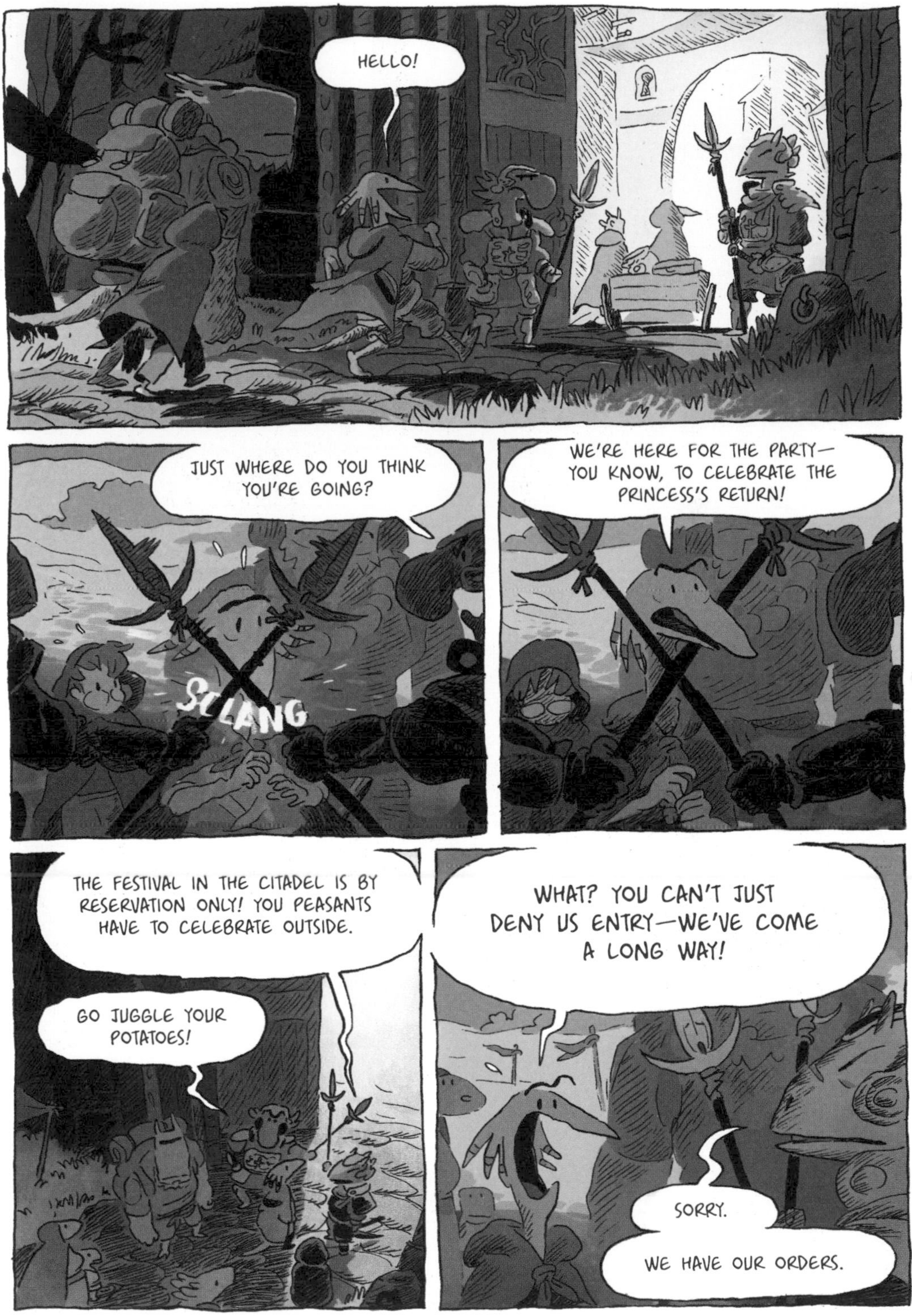
HELLO!
JUST WHERE DO YOU THINK YOU'RE GOING?
SCLANG
WE'RE HERE FOR THE PARTY—YOU KNOW, TO CELEBRATE THE PRINCESS'S RETURN!
THE FESTIVAL IN THE CITADEL IS BY RESERVATION ONLY! YOU PEASANTS HAVE TO CELEBRATE OUTSIDE.
GO JUGGLE YOUR POTATOES!
WHAT? YOU CAN'T JUST DENY US ENTRY—WE'VE COME A LONG WAY!
SORRY.
WE HAVE OUR ORDERS.

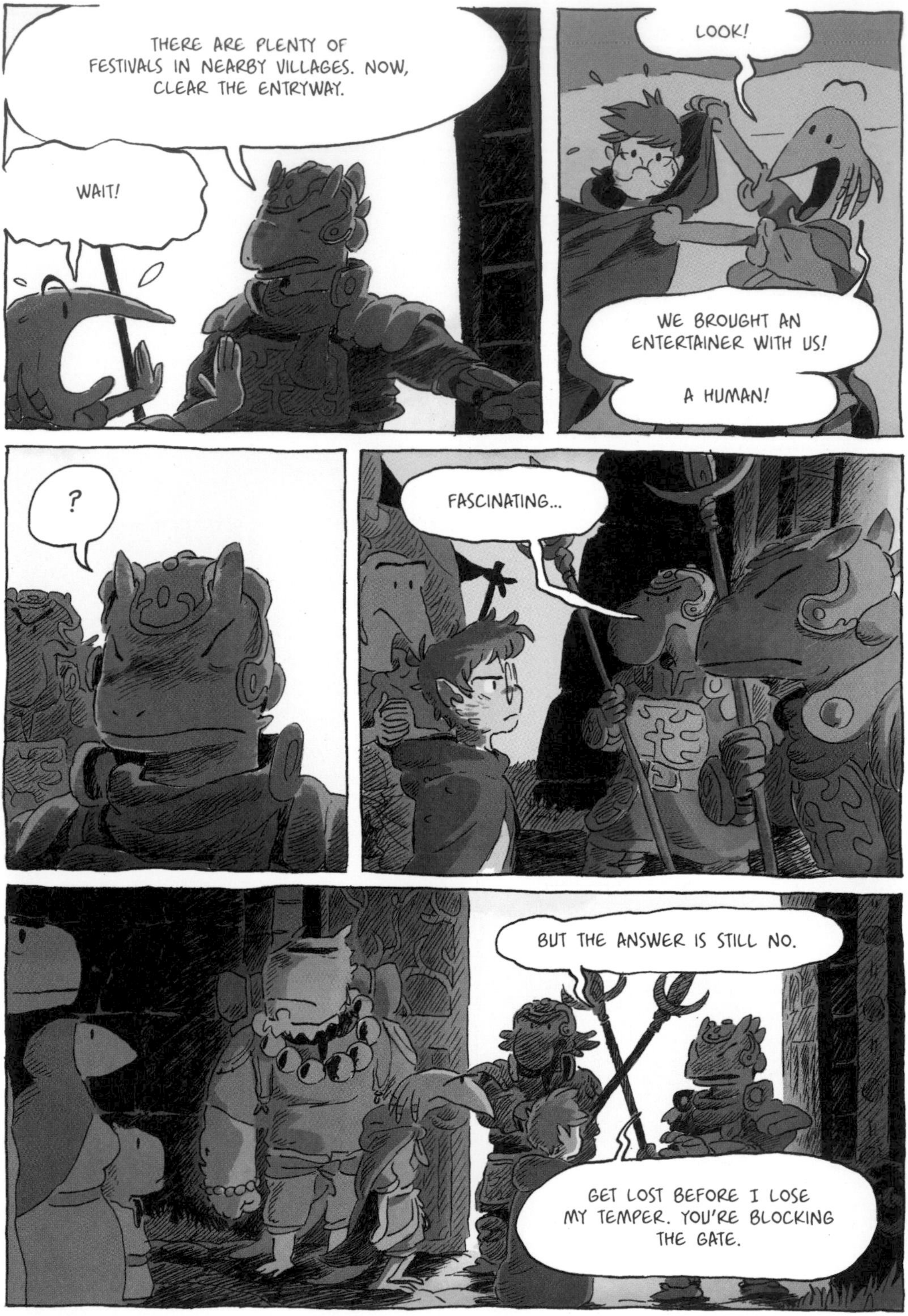

THERE ARE PLENTY OF FESTIVALS IN NEARBY VILLAGES. NOW, CLEAR THE ENTRYWAY.
WAIT!
LOOK!
WE BROUGHT AN ENTERTAINER WITH US!
A HUMAN!
?
FASCINATING...
BUT THE ANSWER IS STILL NO.
GET LOST BEFORE I LOSE MY TEMPER. YOU'RE BLOCKING THE GATE.

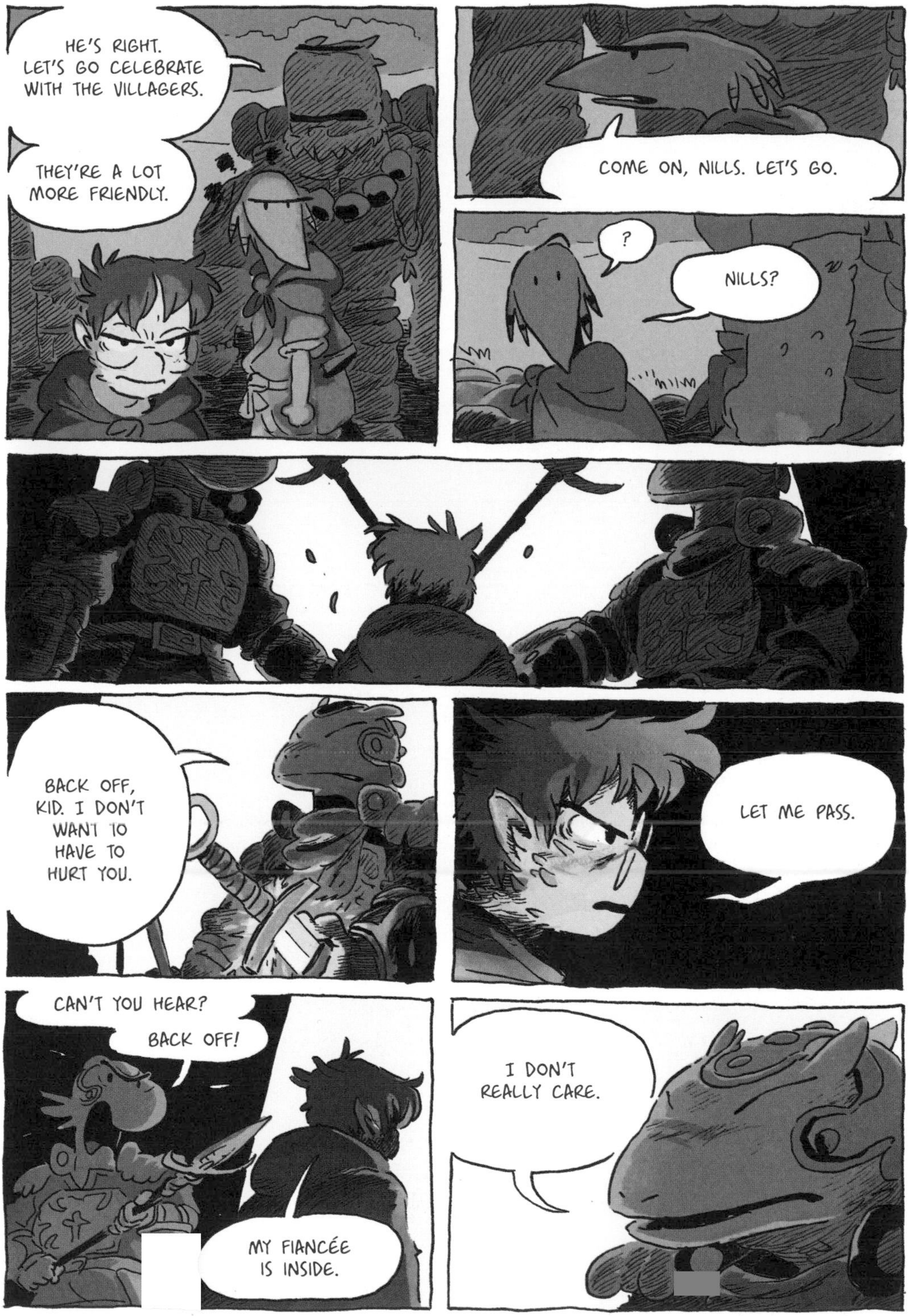
HE'S RIGHT. LET'S GO CELEBRATE WITH THE VILLAGERS.
THEY'RE A LOT MORE FRIENDLY.
COME ON, NILLS. LET'S GO.
?
NILLS?
BACK OFF, KID. I DON'T WANT TO HAVE TO HURT YOU.
LET ME PASS.
CAN'T YOU HEAR?
BACK OFF!
MY FIANCÉE IS INSIDE.
I DON'T REALLY CARE.

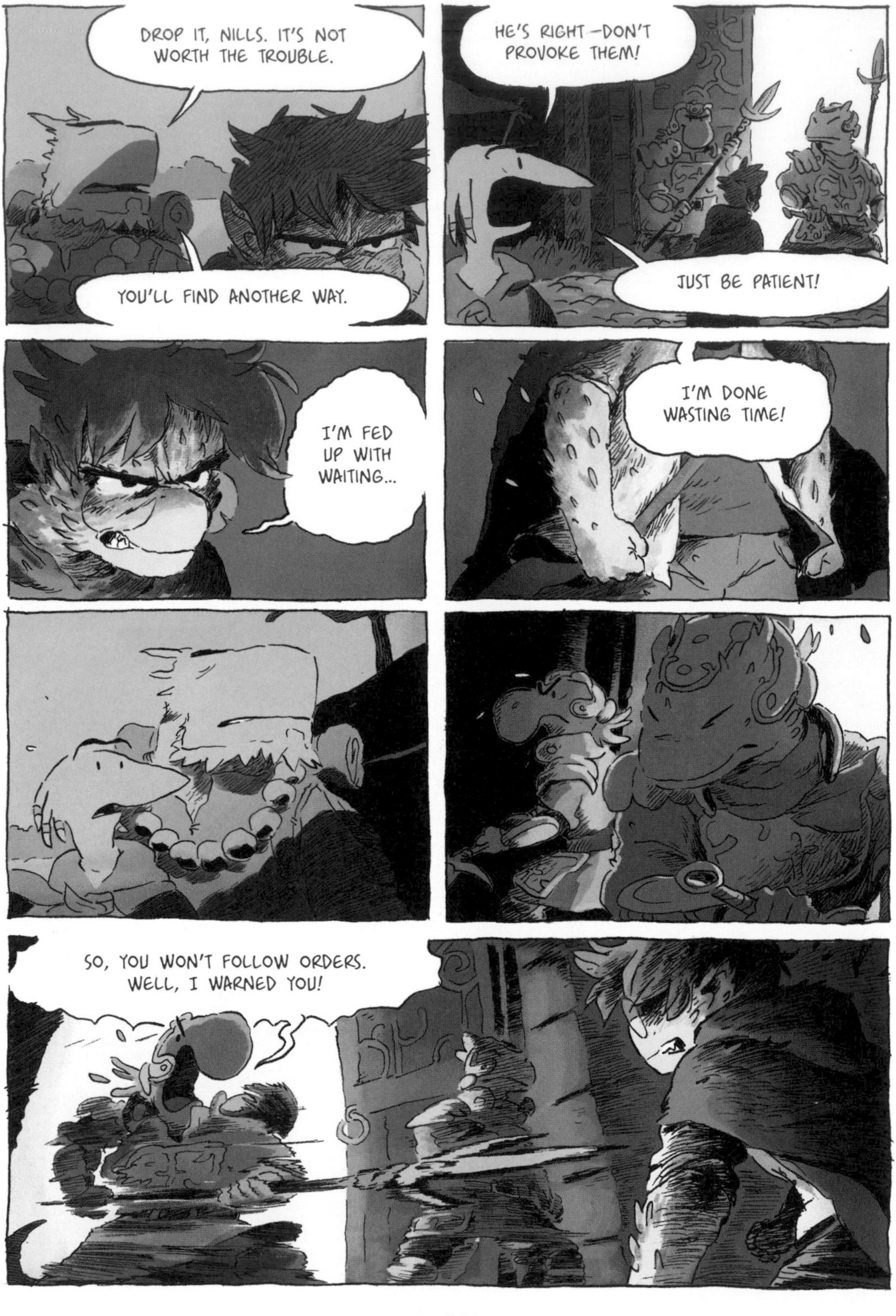
DROP IT, NILLS. IT'S NOT WORTH THE TROUBLE.
YOU'LL FIND ANOTHER WAY.
HE'S RIGHT—DON'T PROVOKE THEM!
JUST BE PATIENT!
I'M FED UP WITH WAITING...
I'M DONE WASTING TIME!
SO, YOU WON'T FOLLOW ORDERS. WELL, I WARNED YOU!

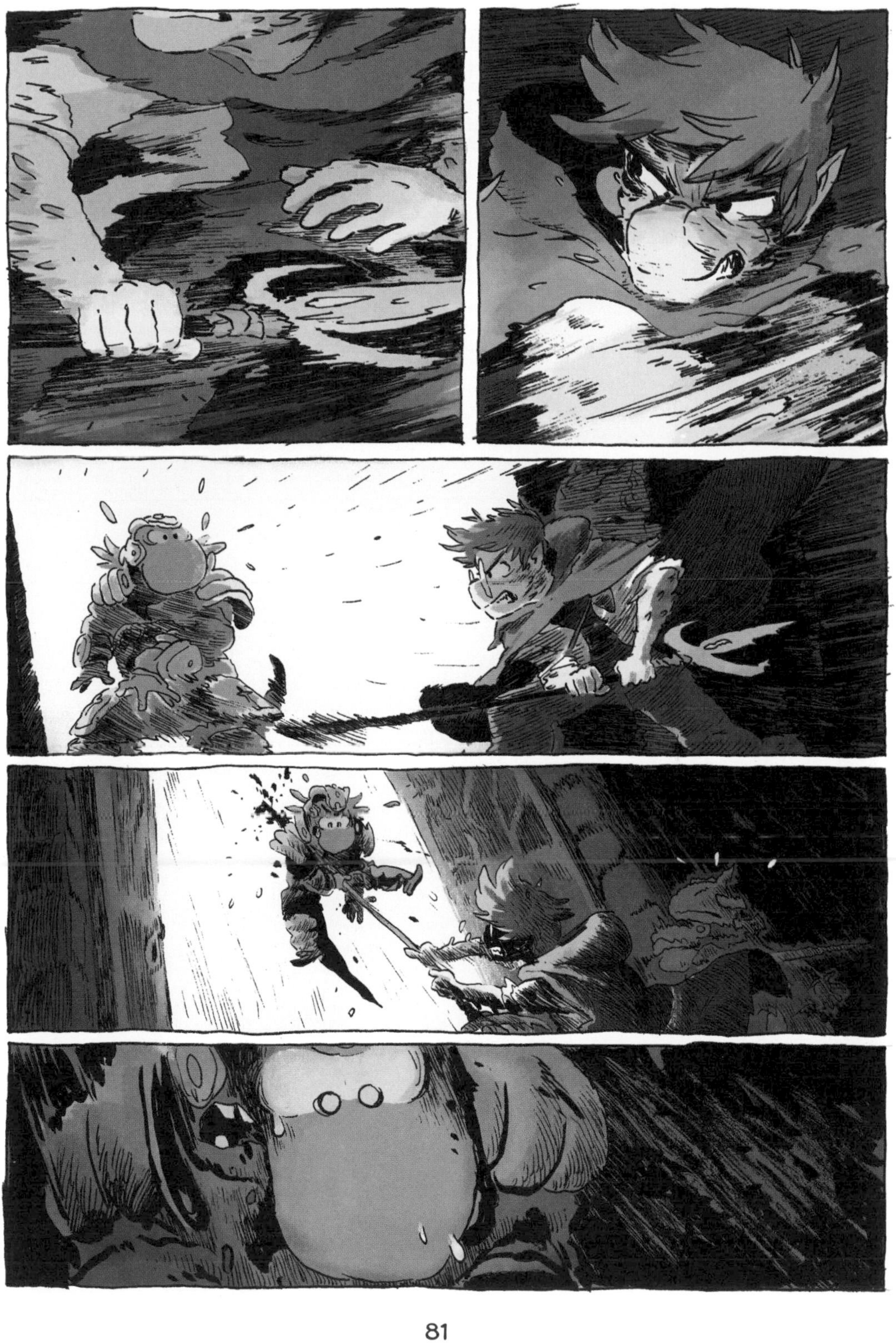

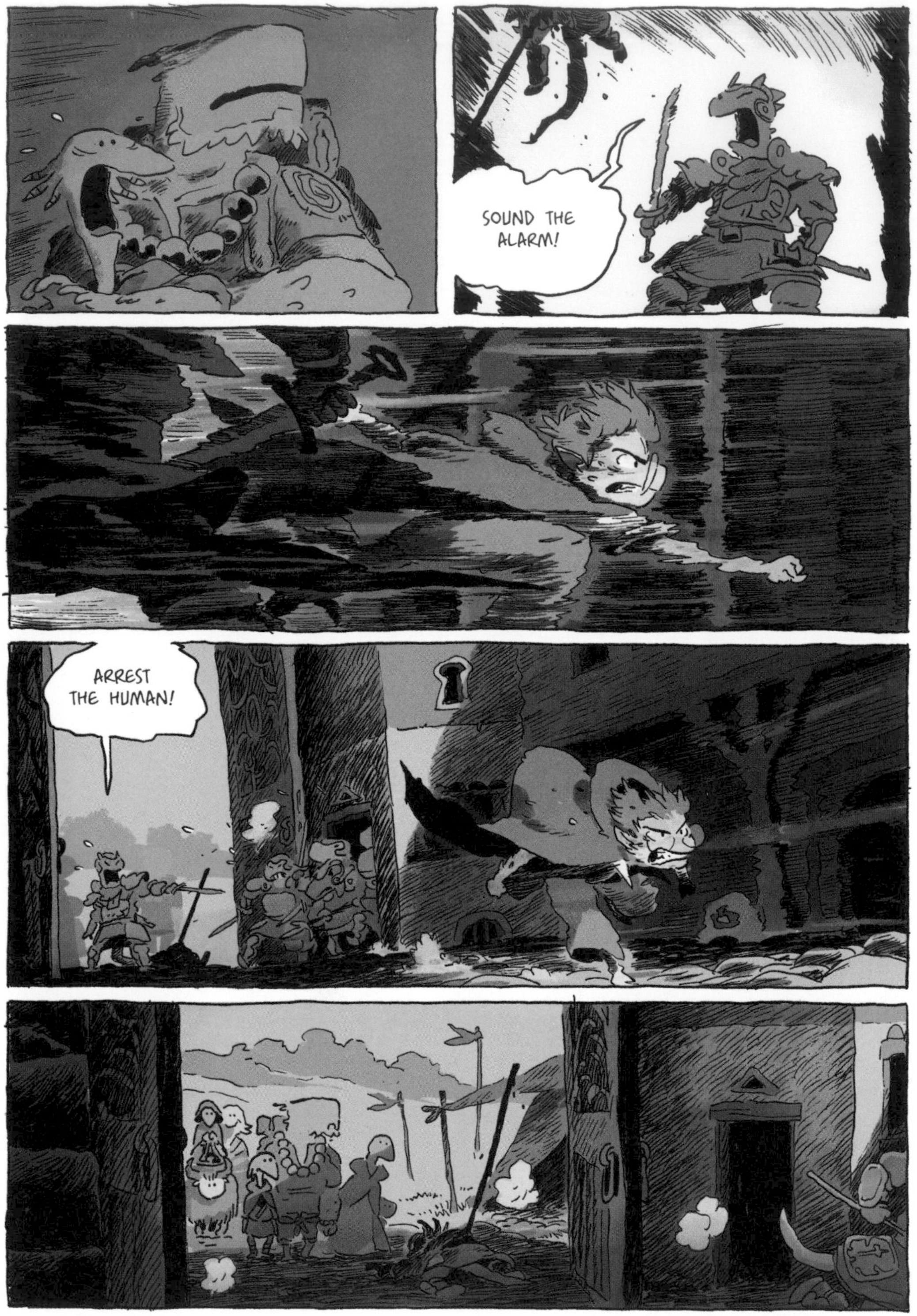
SOUND THE ALARM!
ARREST THE HUMAN!

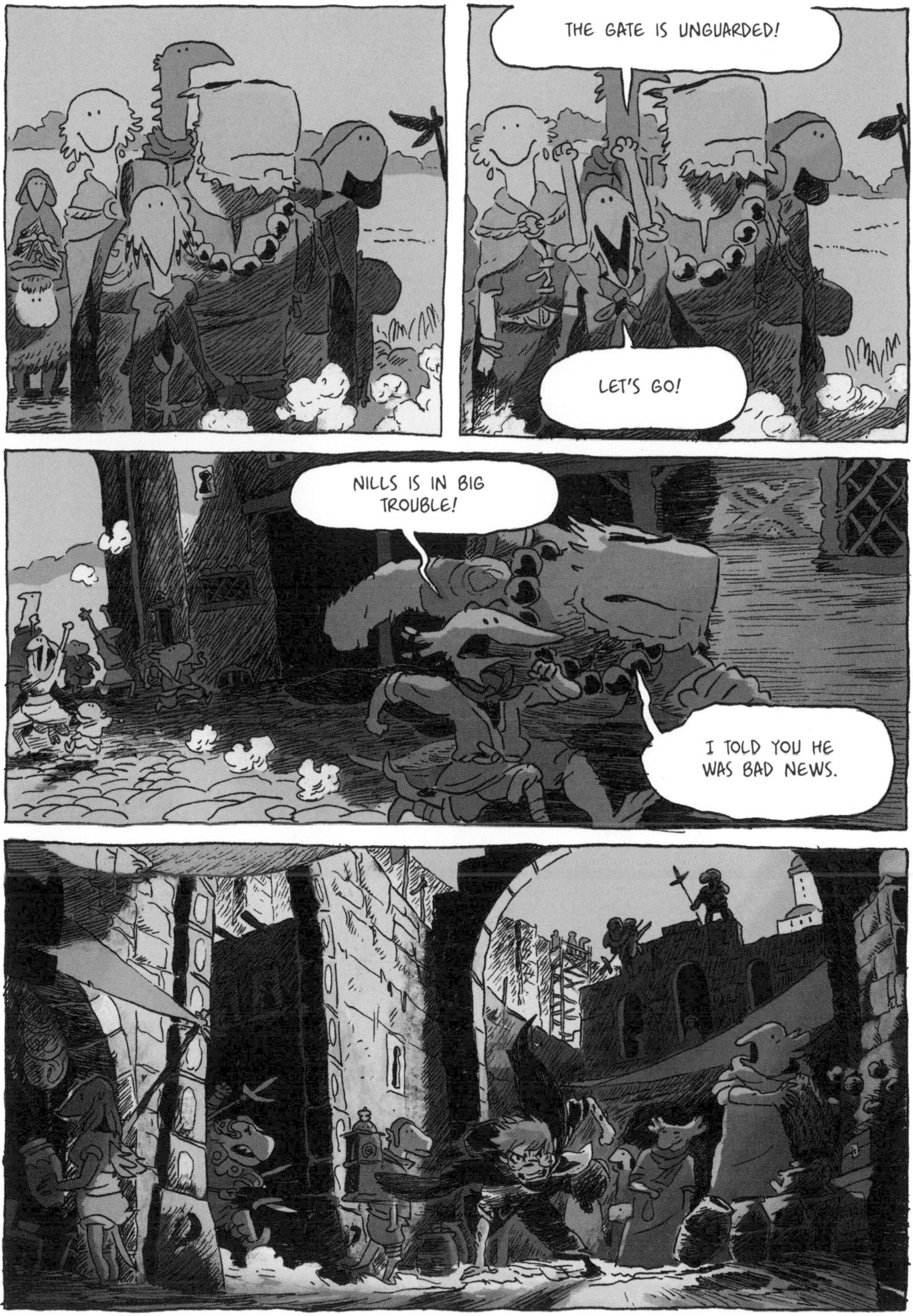
THE GATE IS UNGUARDED!
LET'S GO!
NILLS IS IN BIG TROUBLE!
I TOLD YOU HE WAS BAD NEWS.

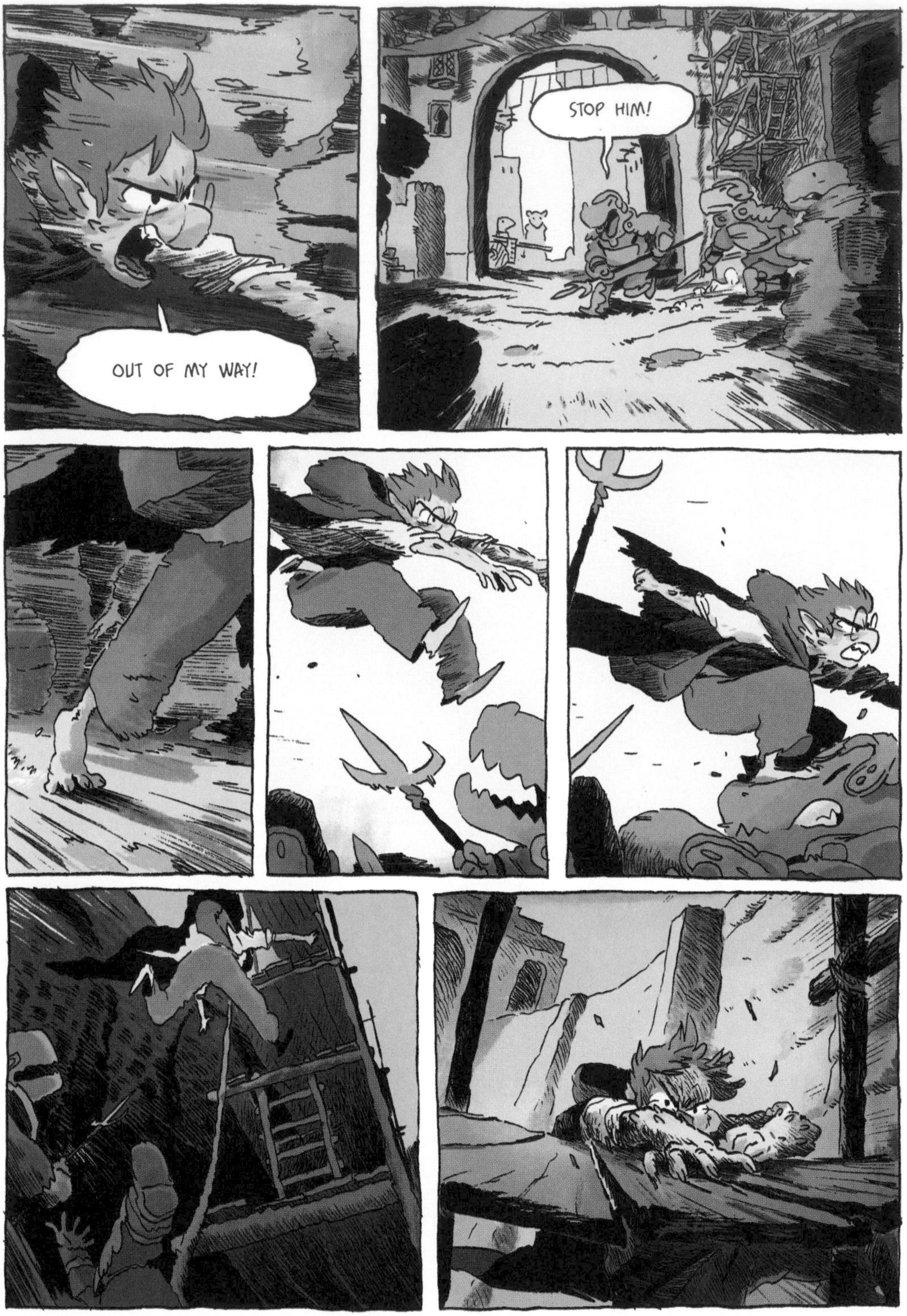
OUT OF MY WAY!
STOP HIM!

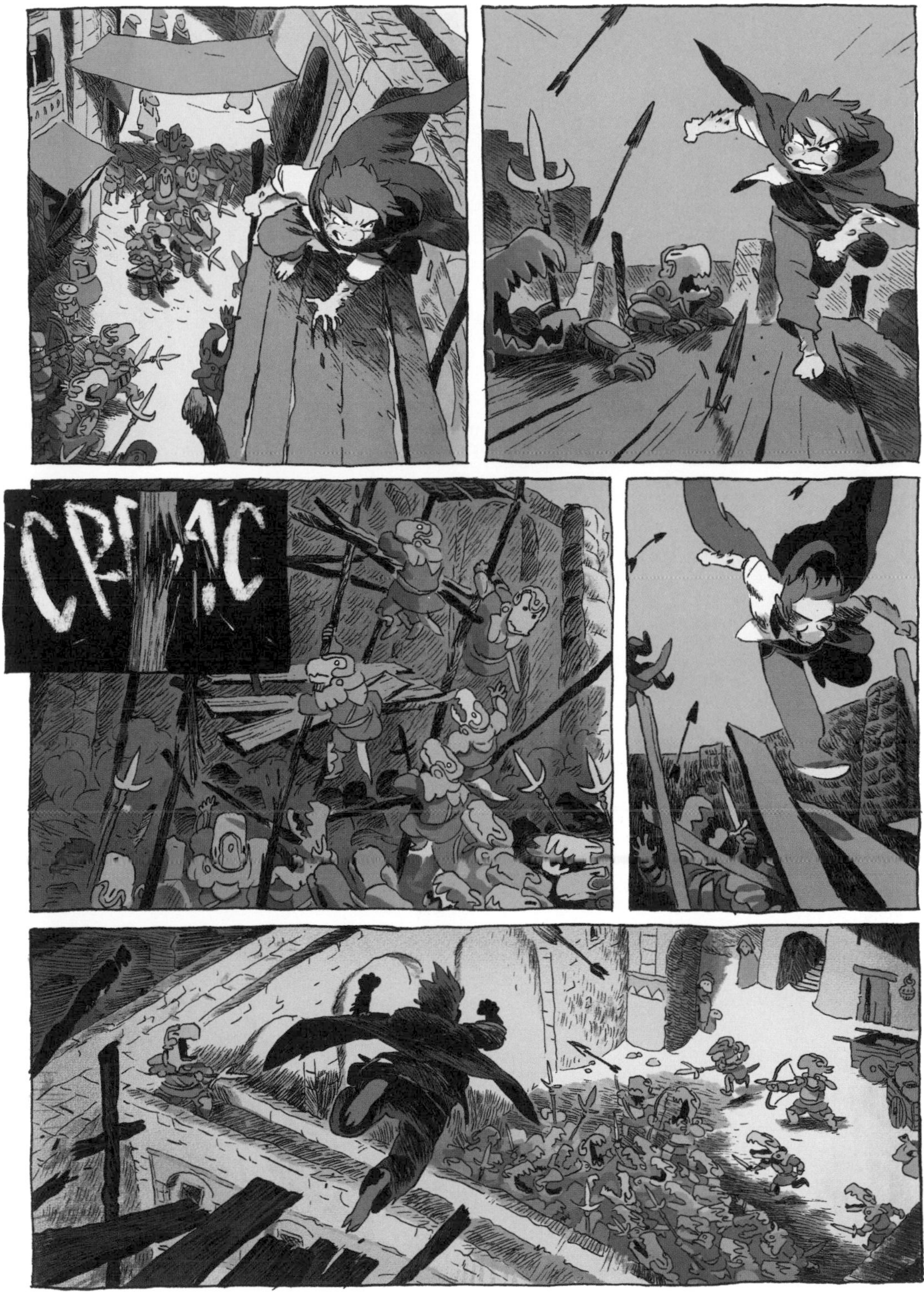

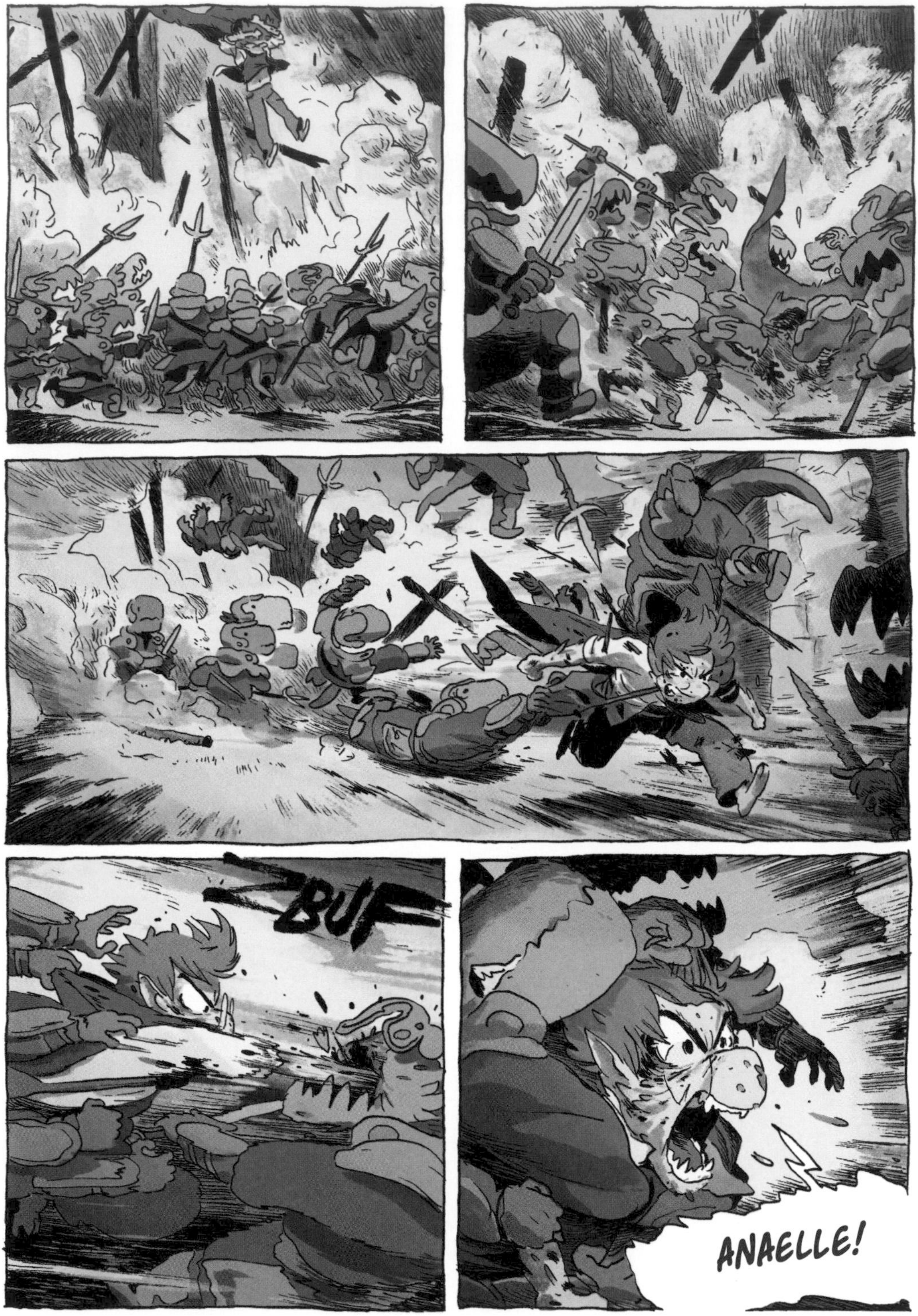
BUF
ANAELLE!

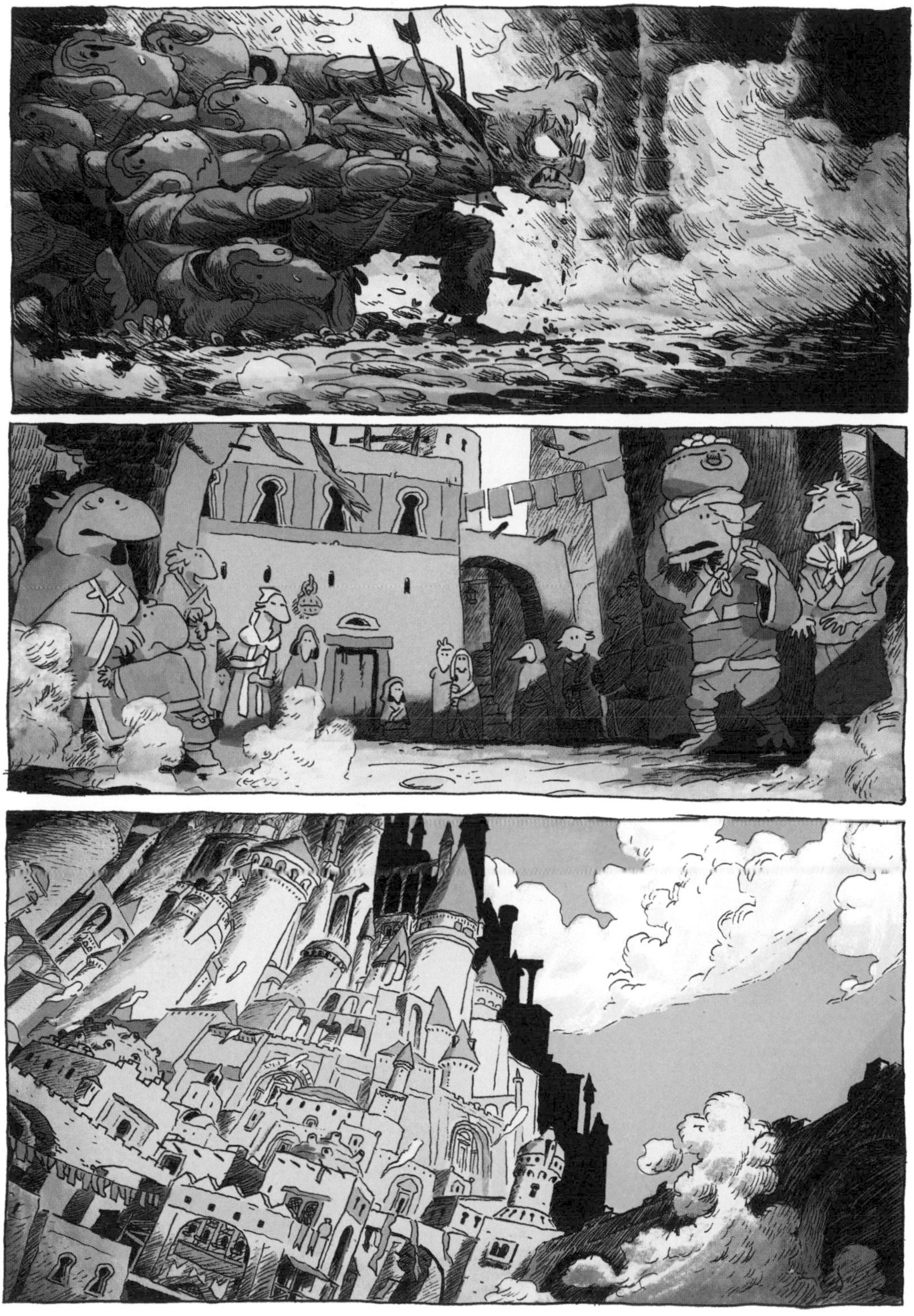

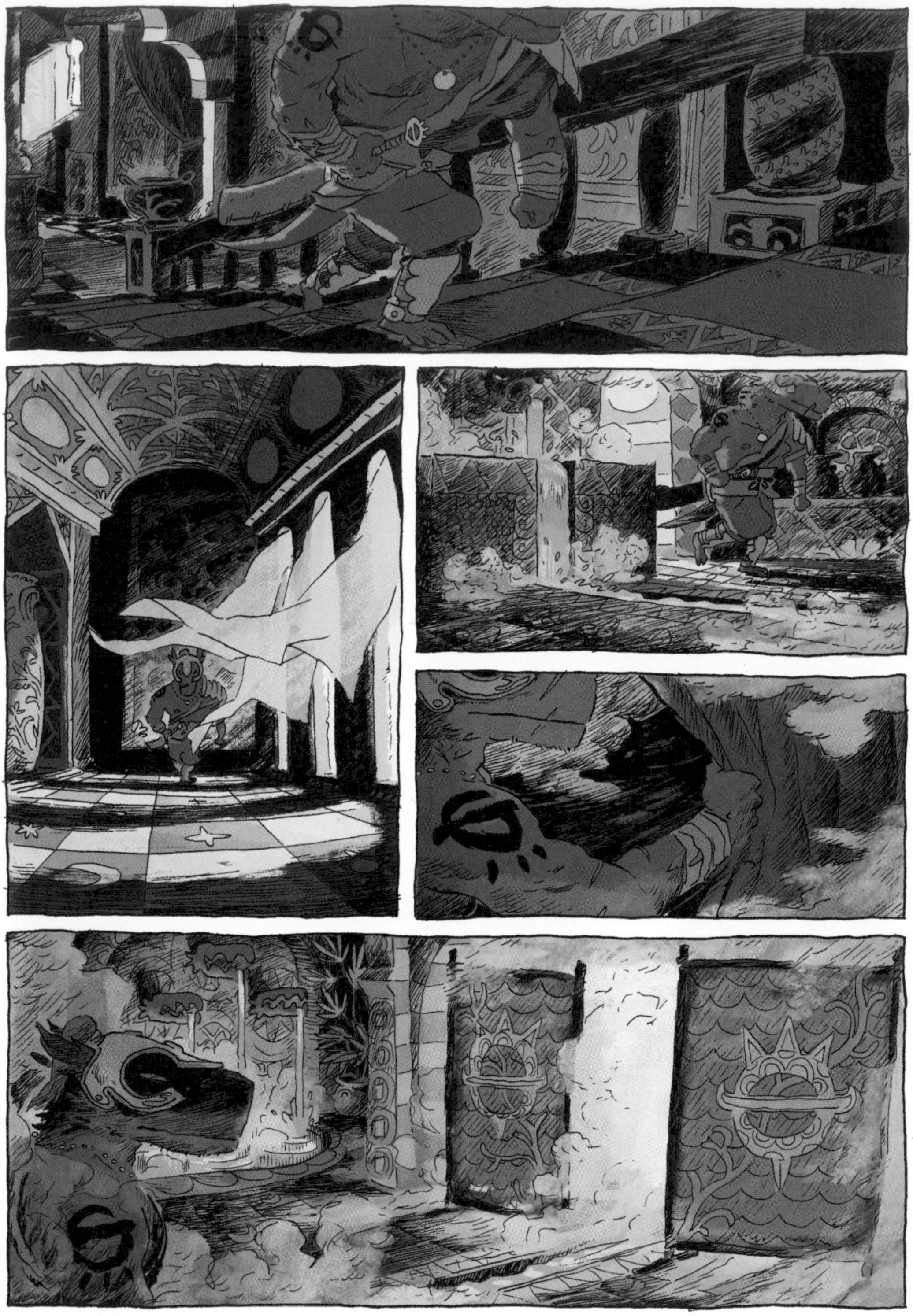

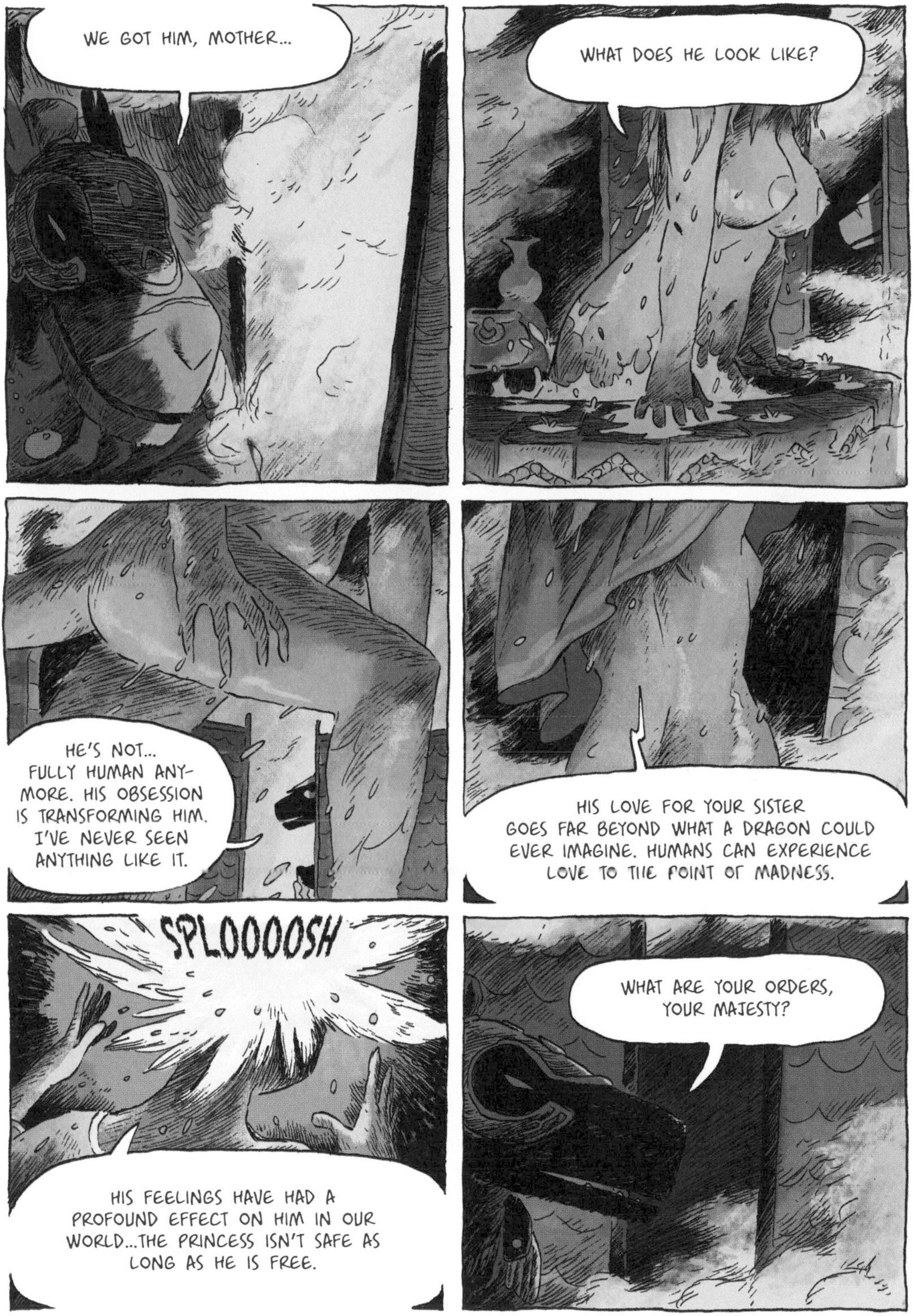
WE GOT HIM, MOTHER...
WHAT DOES HE LOOK LIKE?
HE'S NOT... FULLY HUMAN ANYMORE. HIS OBSESSION IS TRANSFORMING HIM. I'VE NEVER SEEN ANYTHING LIKE IT.
HIS LOVE FOR YOUR SISTER GOES FAR BEYOND WHAT A DRAGON COULD EVER IMAGINE. HUMANS CAN EXPERIENCE LOVE TO THE POINT OF MADNESS.
SPLOOOOSH
HIS FEELINGS HAVE HAD A PROFOUND EFFECT ON HIM IN OUR WORLD...THE PRINCESS ISN'T SAFE AS LONG AS HE IS FREE.
WHAT ARE YOUR ORDERS, YOUR MAJESTY?

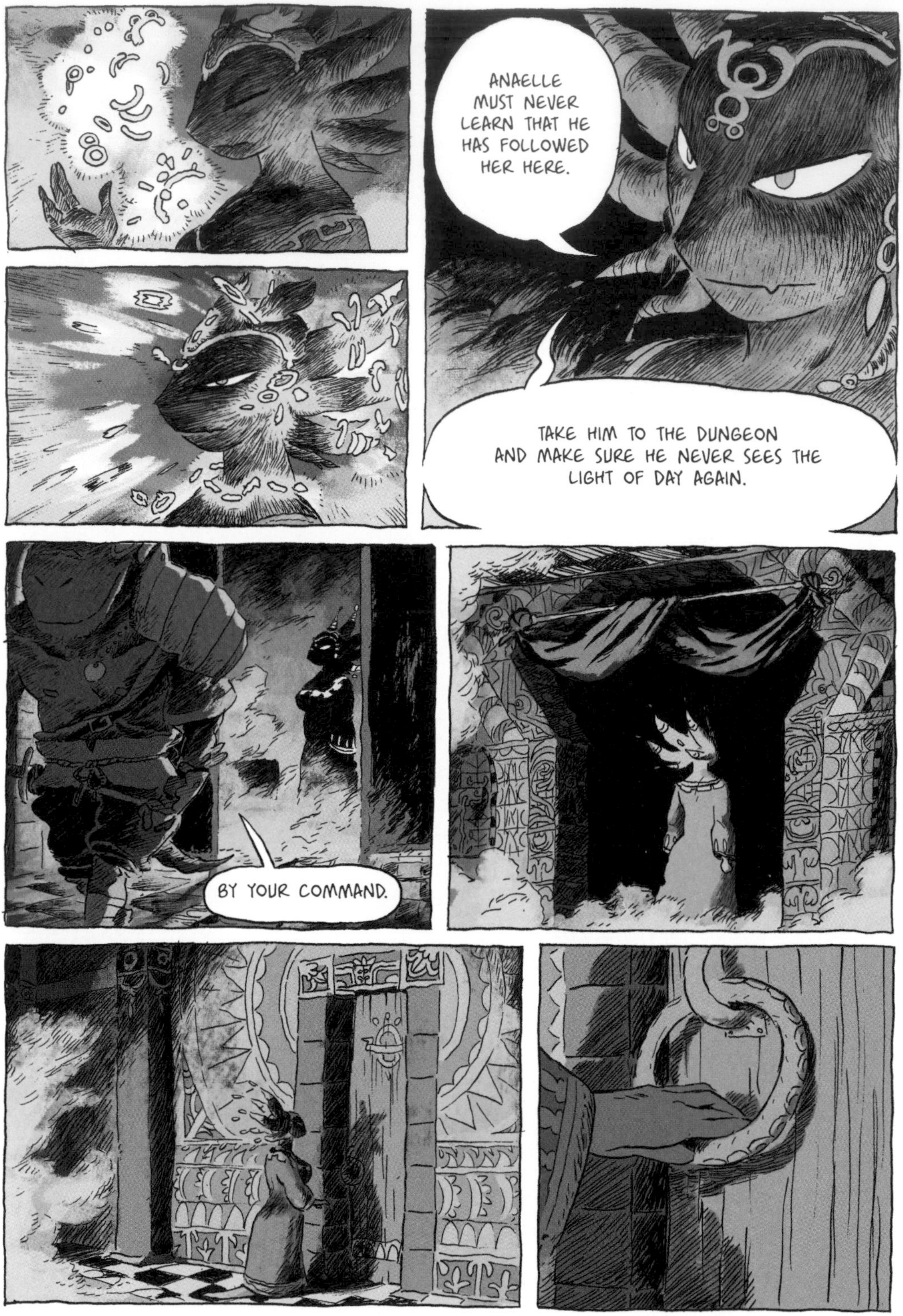
ANAELLE MUST NEVER LEARN THAT HE HAS FOLLOWED HER HERE.
TAKE HIM TO THE DUNGEON AND MAKE SURE HE NEVER SEES THE LIGHT OF DAY AGAIN.
BY YOUR COMMAND.

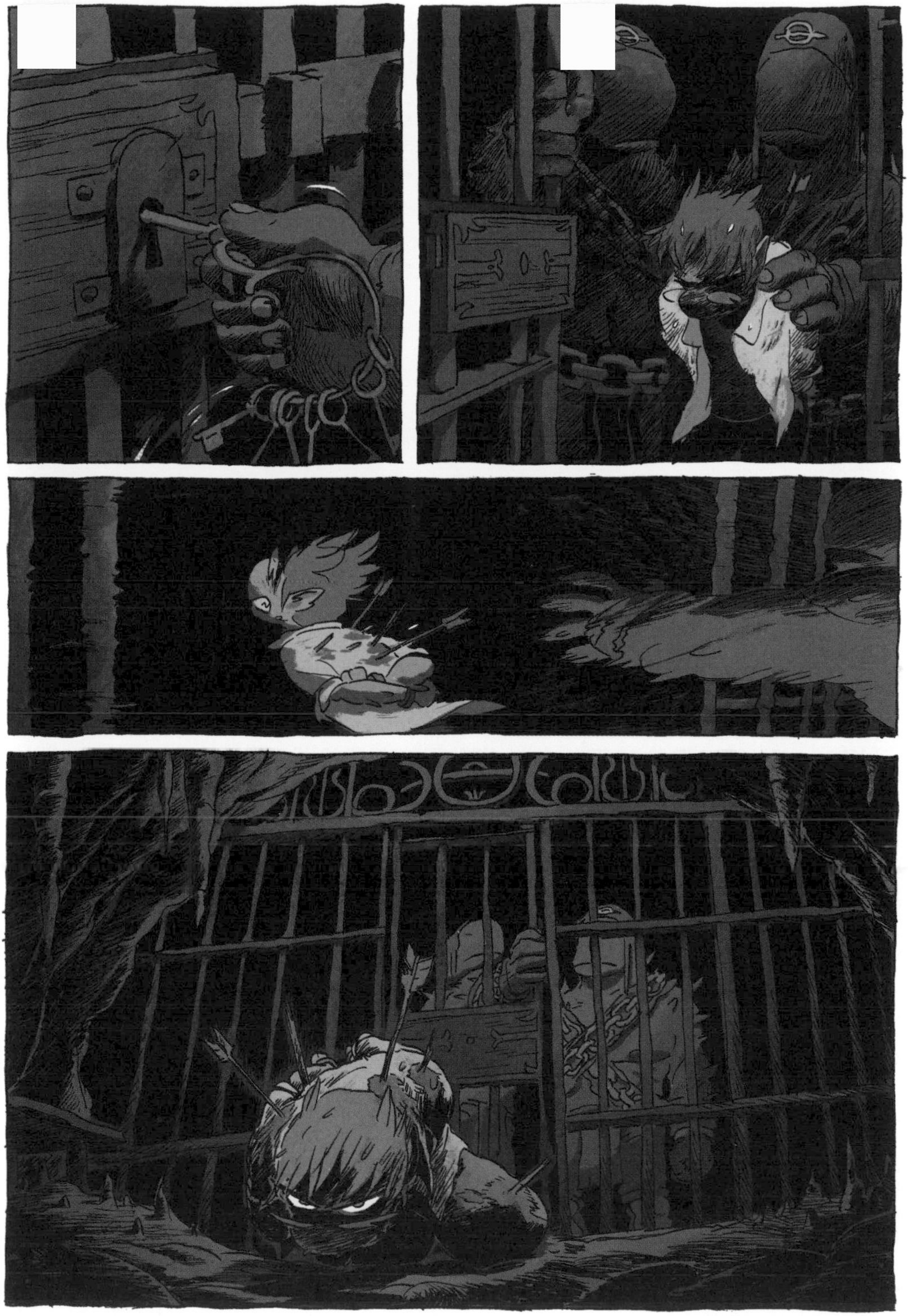

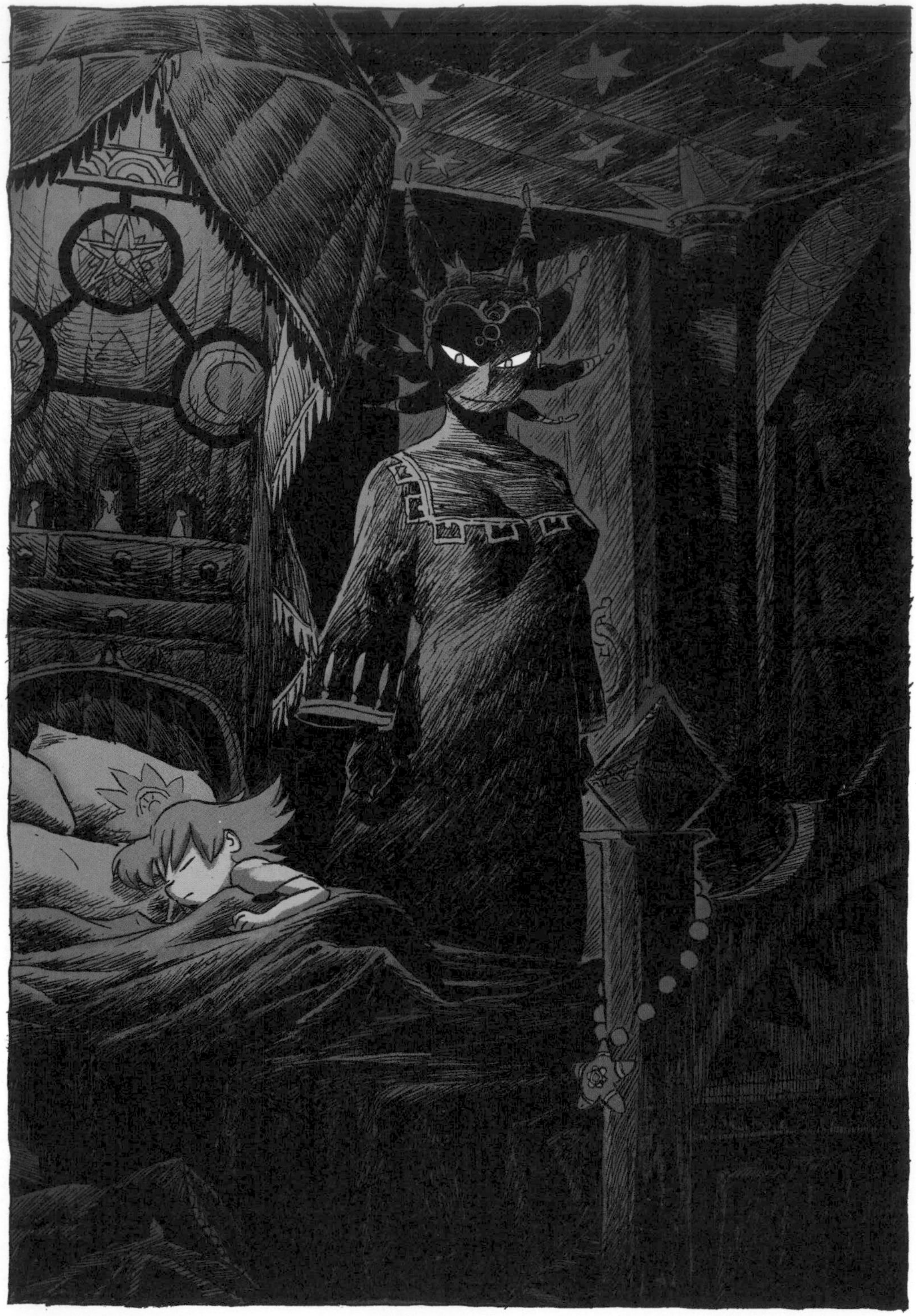

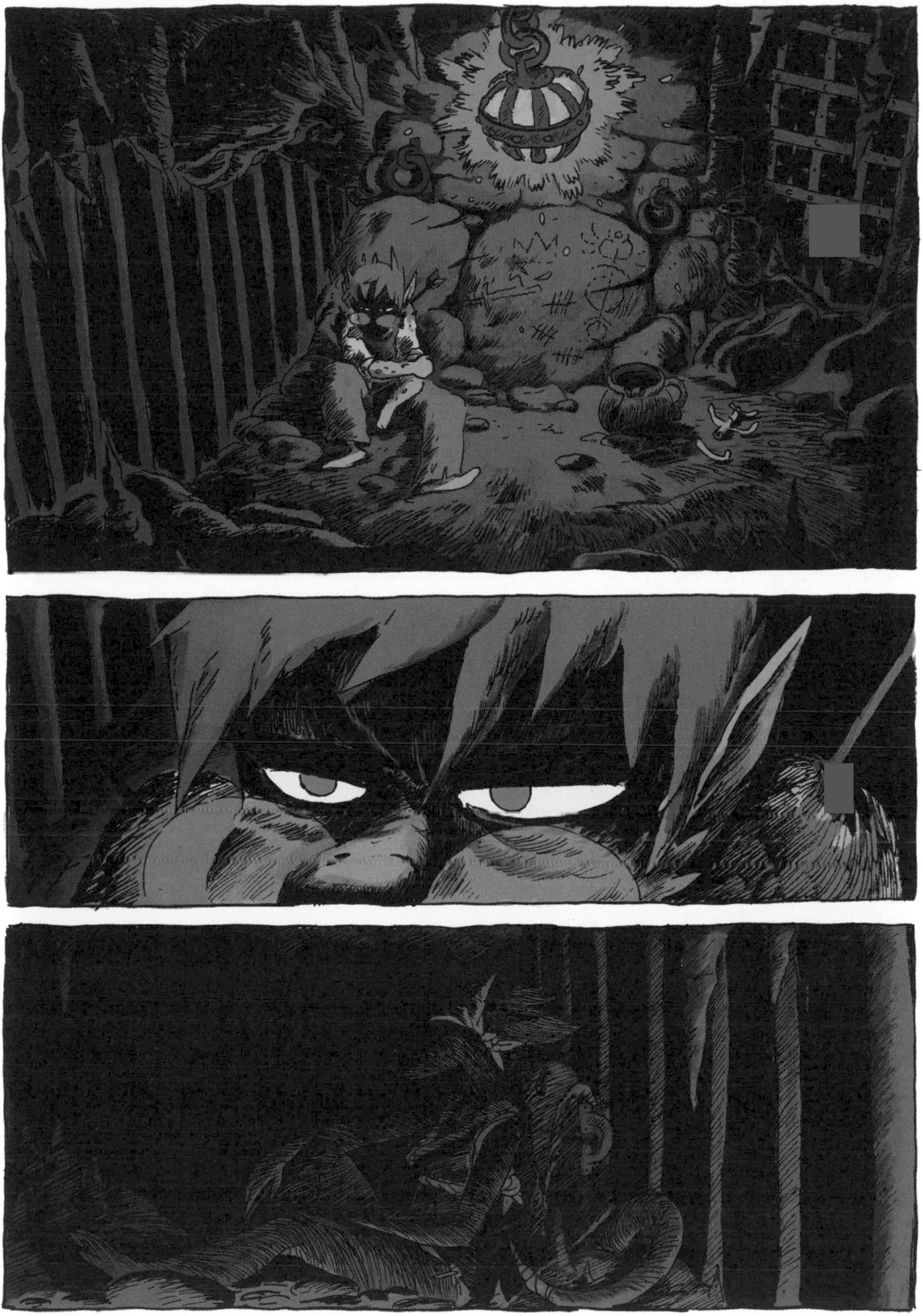

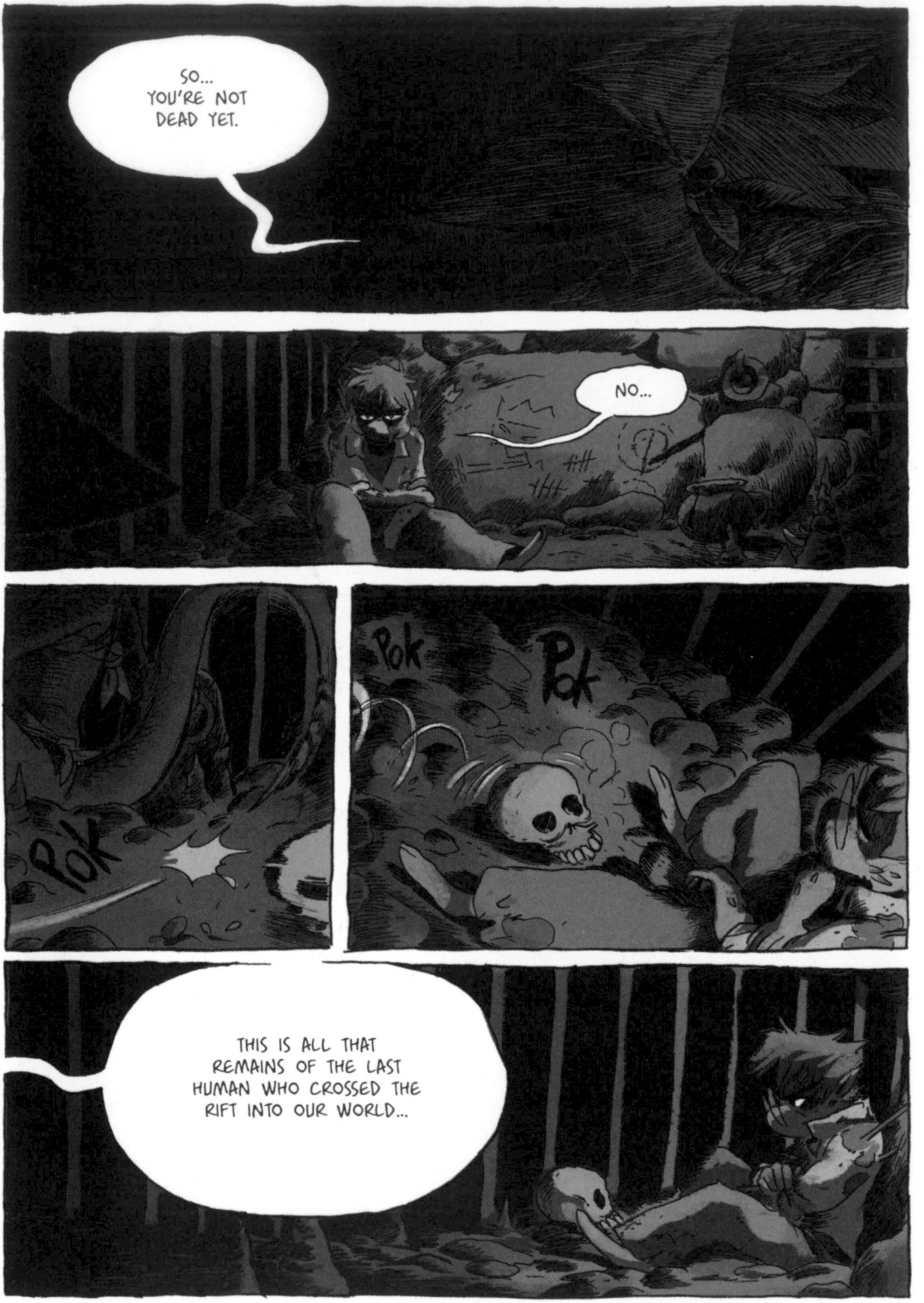

SO... YOU'RE NOT DEAD YET.
NO...
POK
POK
POK
THIS IS ALL THAT REMAINS OF THE LAST HUMAN WHO CROSSED THE RIFT INTO OUR WORLD...

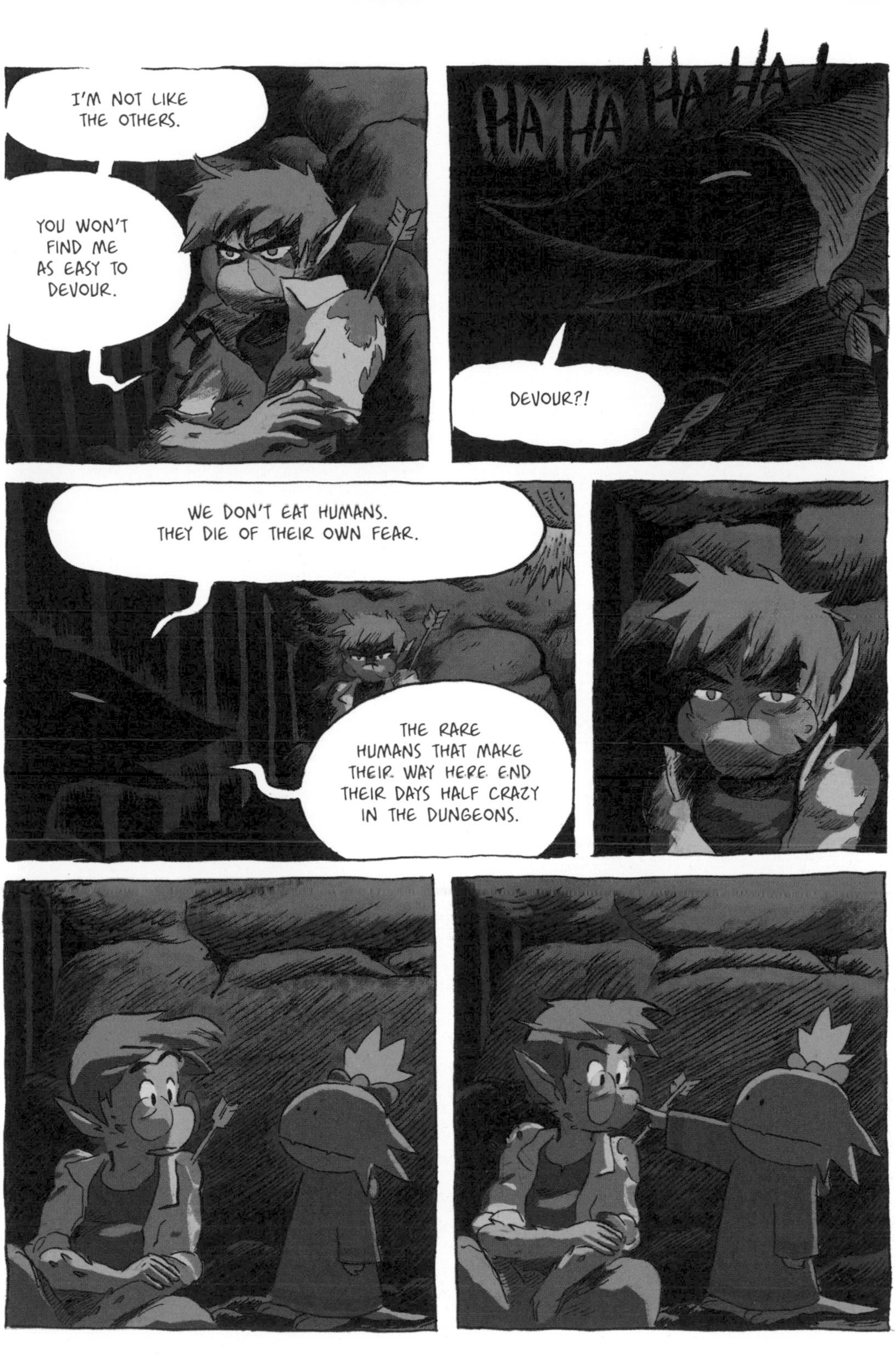
I'M NOT LIKE THE OTHERS.
YOU WON'T FIND ME AS EASY TO DEVOUR.
HA HA HA HA!
DEVOUR?!
WE DON'T EAT HUMANS. THEY DIE OF THEIR OWN FEAR.
THE RARE HUMANS THAT MAKE THEIR WAY HERE END THEIR DAYS HALF CRAZY IN THE DUNGEONS.

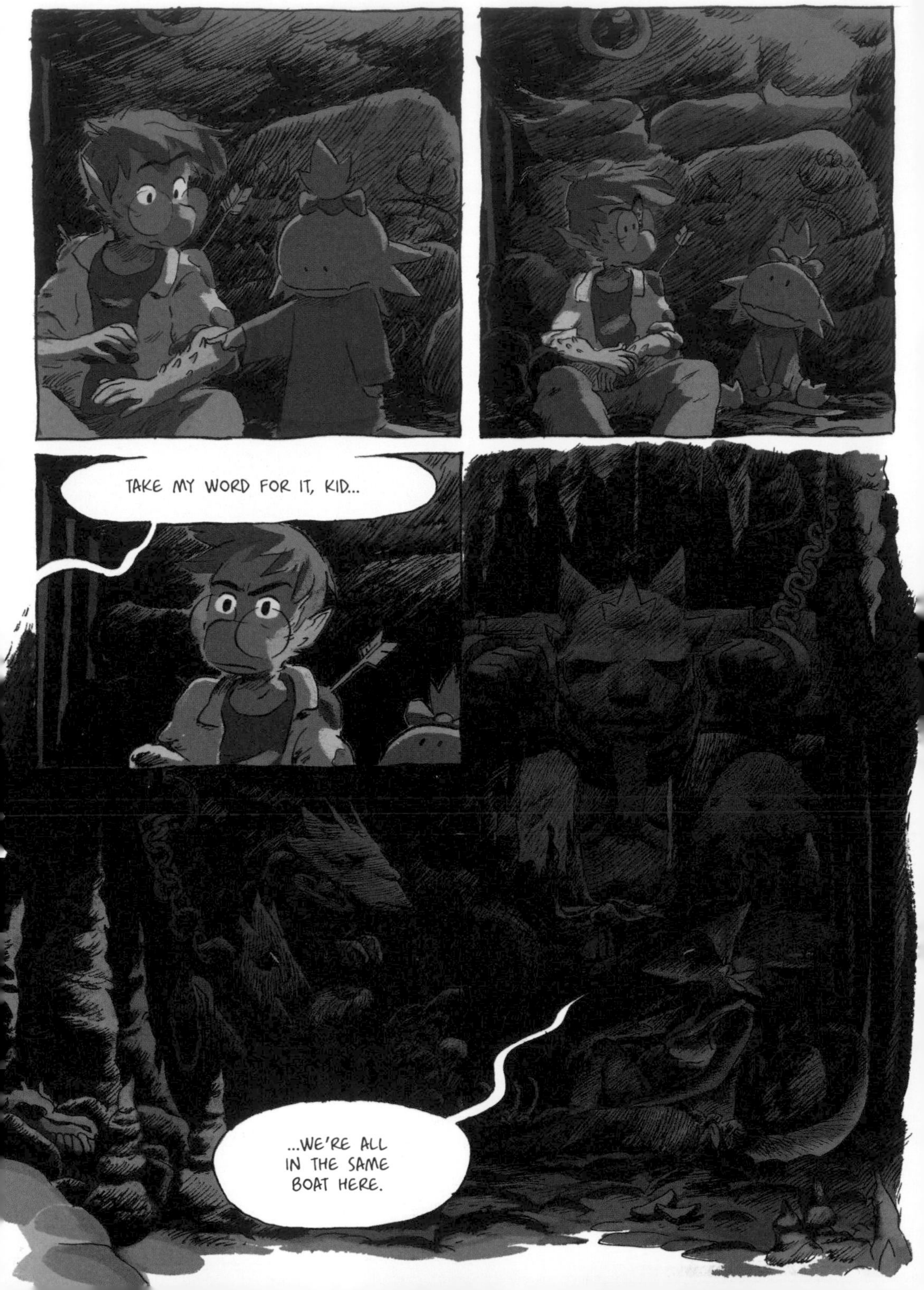
TAKE MY WORD FOR IT, KID...
...WE'RE ALL IN THE SAME BOAT HERE.

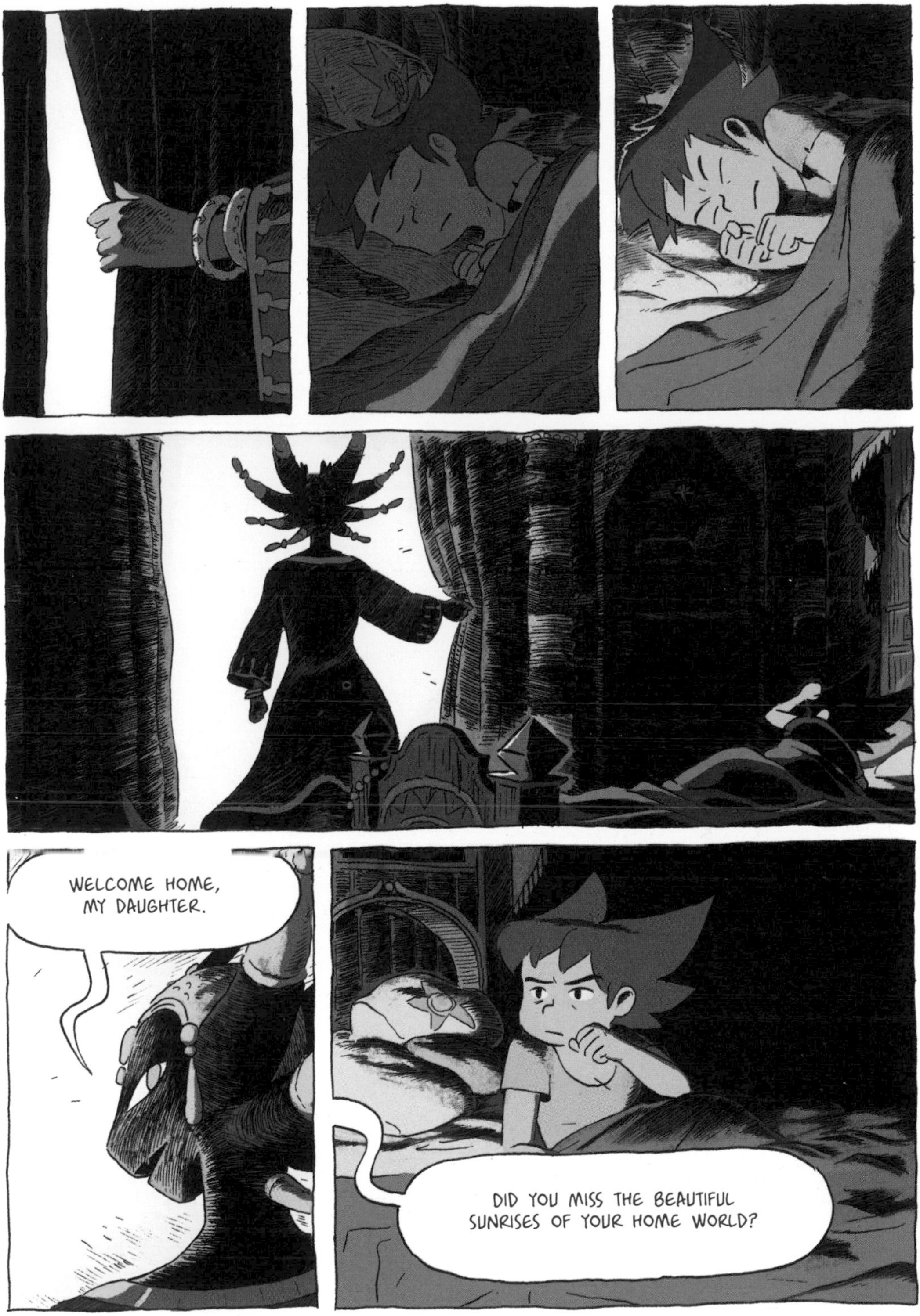
WELCOME HOME, MY DAUGHTER.
DID YOU MISS THE BEAUTIFUL SUNRISES OF YOUR HOME WORLD?

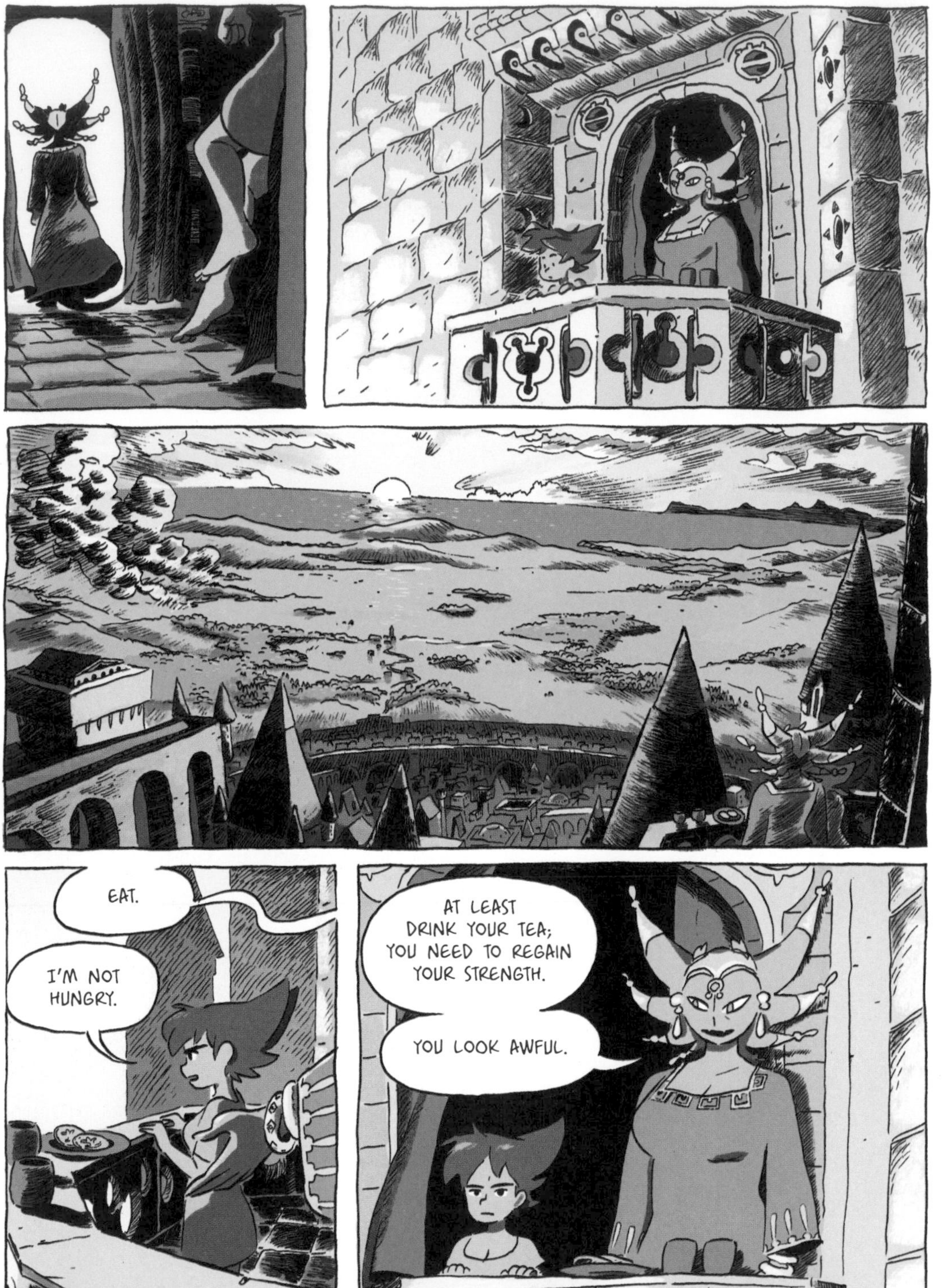
EAT.
I'M NOT HUNGRY.
AT LEAST DRINK YOUR TEA; YOU NEED TO REGAIN YOUR STRENGTH.
YOU LOOK AWFUL.

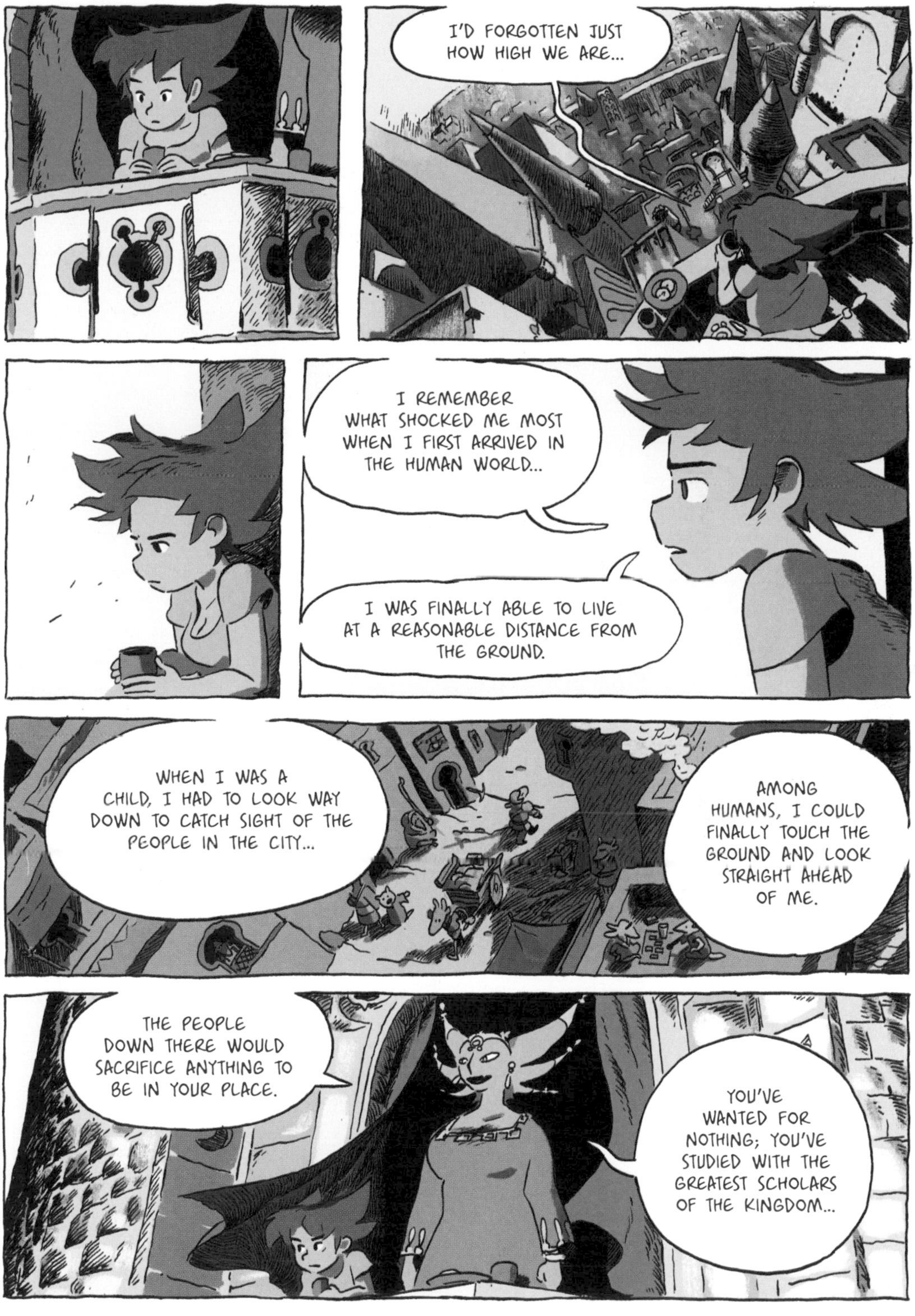
I'D FORGOTTEN JUST HOW HIGH WE ARE...
I REMEMBER WHAT SHOCKED ME MOST WHEN I FIRST ARRIVED IN THE HUMAN WORLD...
I WAS FINALLY ABLE TO LIVE AT A REASONABLE DISTANCE FROM THE GROUND.
WHEN I WAS A CHILD, I HAD TO LOOK WAY DOWN TO CATCH SIGHT OF THE PEOPLE IN THE CITY...
AMONG HUMANS, I COULD FINALLY TOUCH THE GROUND AND LOOK STRAIGHT AHEAD OF ME.
THE PEOPLE DOWN THERE WOULD SACRIFICE ANYTHING TO BE IN YOUR PLACE.
YOU'VE WANTED FOR NOTHING; YOU'VE STUDIED WITH THE GREATEST SCHOLARS OF THE KINGDOM...

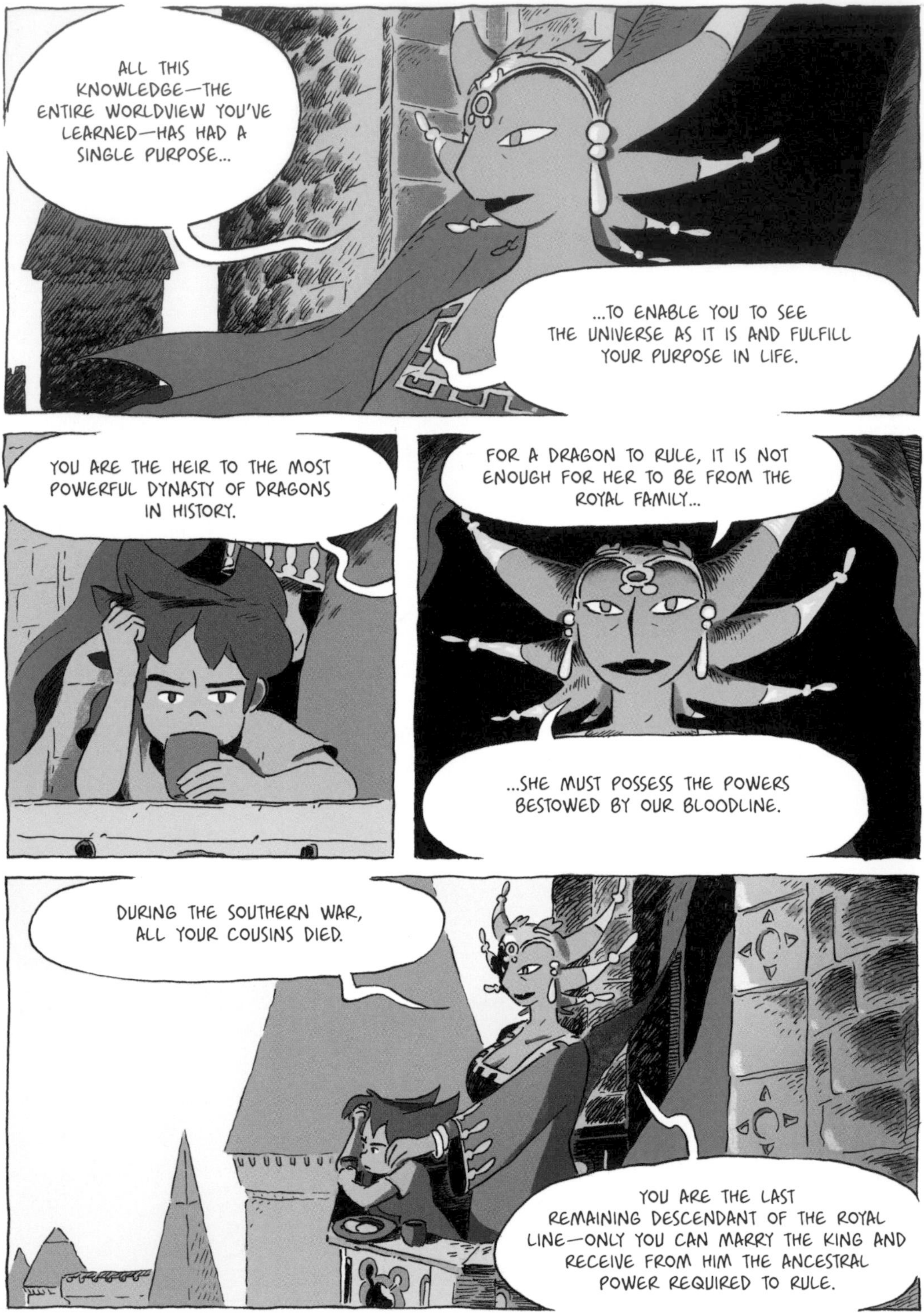
ALL THIS KNOWLEDGE—THE ENTIRE WORLDVIEW YOU'VE LEARNED—HAS HAD A SINGLE PURPOSE...
...TO ENABLE YOU TO SEE THE UNIVERSE AS IT IS AND FULFILL YOUR PURPOSE IN LIFE.
YOU ARE THE HEIR TO THE MOST POWERFUL DYNASTY OF DRAGONS IN HISTORY.
FOR A DRAGON TO RULE, IT IS NOT ENOUGH FOR HER TO BE FROM THE ROYAL FAMILY...
...SHE MUST POSSESS THE POWERS BESTOWED BY OUR BLOODLINE.
DURING THE SOUTHERN WAR, ALL YOUR COUSINS DIED.
YOU ARE THE LAST REMAINING DESCENDANT OF THE ROYAL LINE—ONLY YOU CAN MARRY THE KING AND RECEIVE FROM HIM THE ANCESTRAL POWER REQUIRED TO RULE.

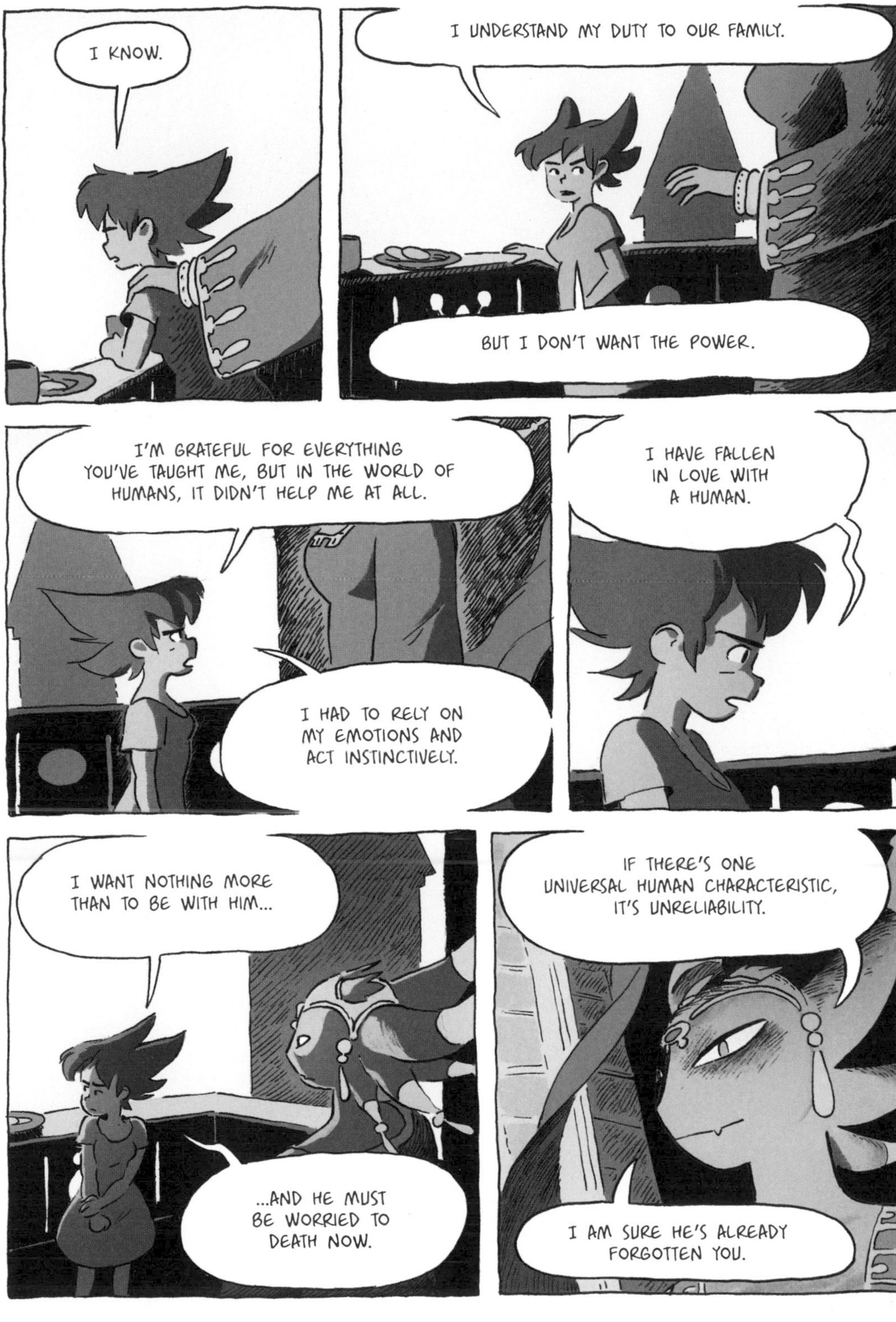
I KNOW.
I UNDERSTAND MY DUTY TO OUR FAMILY.
BUT I DON'T WANT THE POWER.
I'M GRATEFUL FOR EVERYTHING YOU'VE TAUGHT ME, BUT IN THE WORLD OF HUMANS, IT DIDN'T HELP ME AT ALL.
I HAD TO RELY ON MY EMOTIONS AND ACT INSTINCTIVELY.
I HAVE FALLEN IN LOVE WITH A HUMAN.
I WANT NOTHING MORE THAN TO BE WITH HIM...
...AND HE MUST BE WORRIED TO DEATH NOW.
IF THERE'S ONE UNIVERSAL HUMAN CHARACTERISTIC, IT'S UNRELIABILITY.
I AM SURE HE'S ALREADY FORGOTTEN YOU.

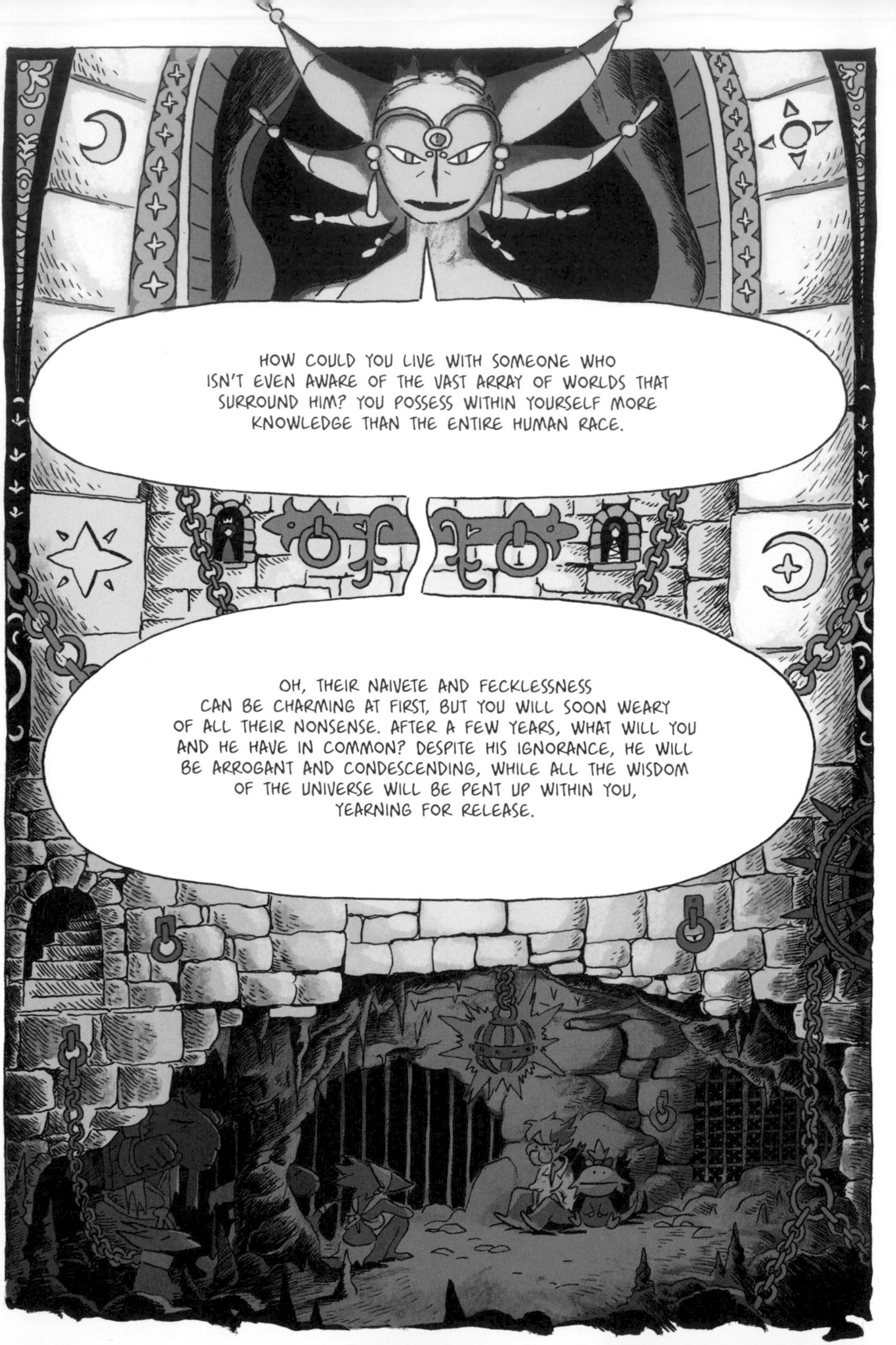
HOW COULD YOU LIVE WITH SOMEONE WHO ISN'T EVEN AWARE OF THE VAST ARRAY OF WORLDS THAT SURROUND HIM? YOU POSSESS WITHIN YOURSELF MORE KNOWLEDGE THAN THE ENTIRE HUMAN RACE.
OH, THEIR NAIVETE AND FECKLESSNESS CAN BE CHARMING AT FIRST, BUT YOU WILL SOON WEARY OF ALL THEIR NONSENSE. AFTER A FEW YEARS, WHAT WILL YOU AND HE HAVE IN COMMON? DESPITE HIS IGNORANCE, HE WILL BE ARROGANT AND CONDESCENDING, WHILE ALL THE WISDOM OF THE UNIVERSE WILL BE PENT UP WITHIN YOU, YEARNING FOR RELEASE.

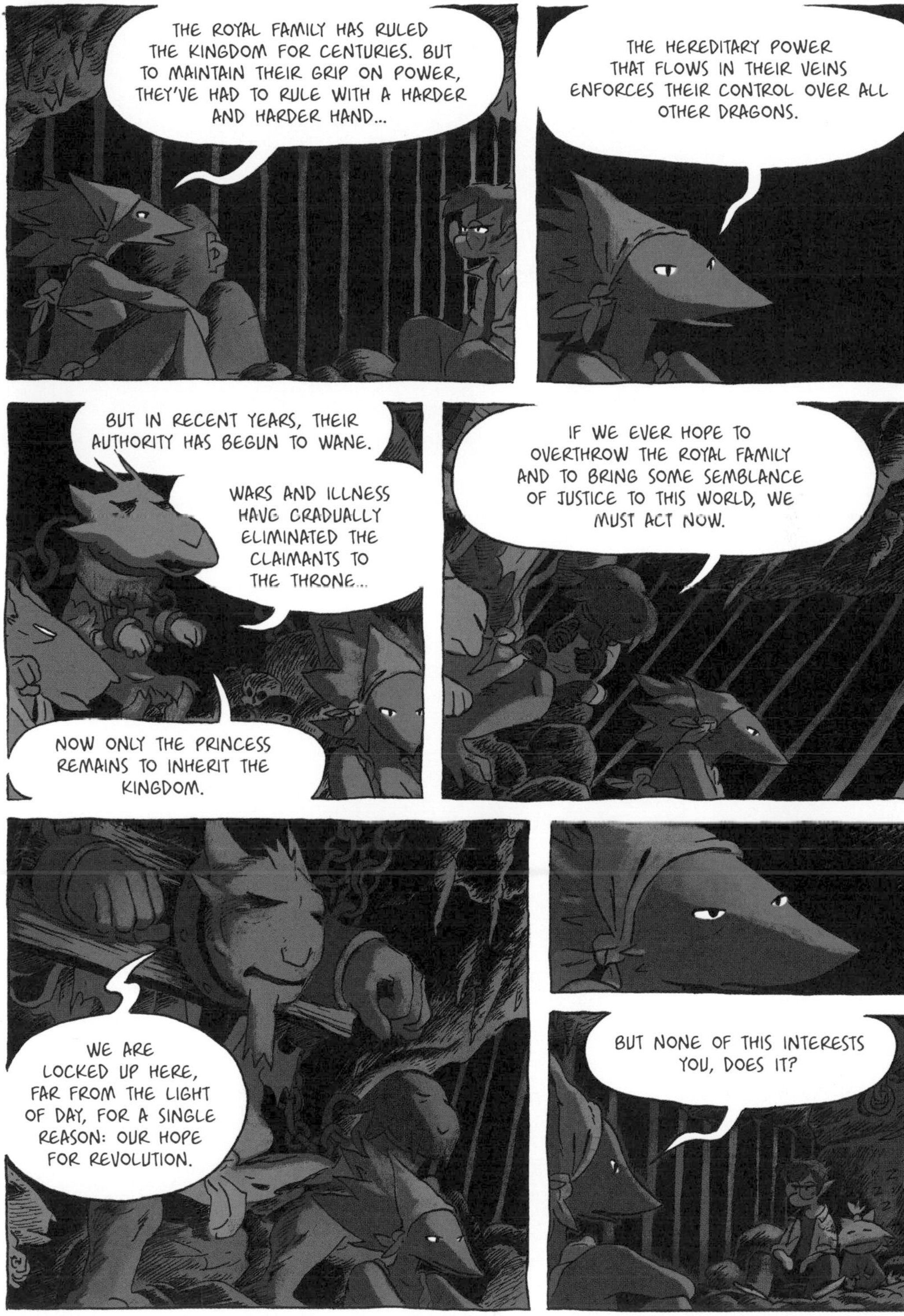
THE ROYAL FAMILY HAS RULED THE KINGDOM FOR CENTURIES. BUT TO MAINTAIN THEIR GRIP ON POWER, THEY'VE HAD TO RULE WITH A HARDER AND HARDER HAND...
THE HEREDITARY POWER THAT FLOWS IN THEIR VEINS ENFORCES THEIR CONTROL OVER ALL OTHER DRAGONS.
BUT IN RECENT YEARS, THEIR AUTHORITY HAS BEGUN TO WANE.
WARS AND ILLNESS HAVE GRADUALLY ELIMINATED THE CLAIMANTS TO THE THRONE...
NOW ONLY THE PRINCESS REMAINS TO INHERIT THE KINGDOM.
IF WE EVER HOPE TO OVERTHROW THE ROYAL FAMILY AND TO BRING SOME SEMBLANCE OF JUSTICE TO THIS WORLD, WE MUST ACT NOW.
WE ARE LOCKED UP HERE, FAR FROM THE LIGHT OF DAY, FOR A SINGLE REASON: OUR HOPE FOR REVOLUTION.
BUT NONE OF THIS INTERESTS YOU, DOES IT?

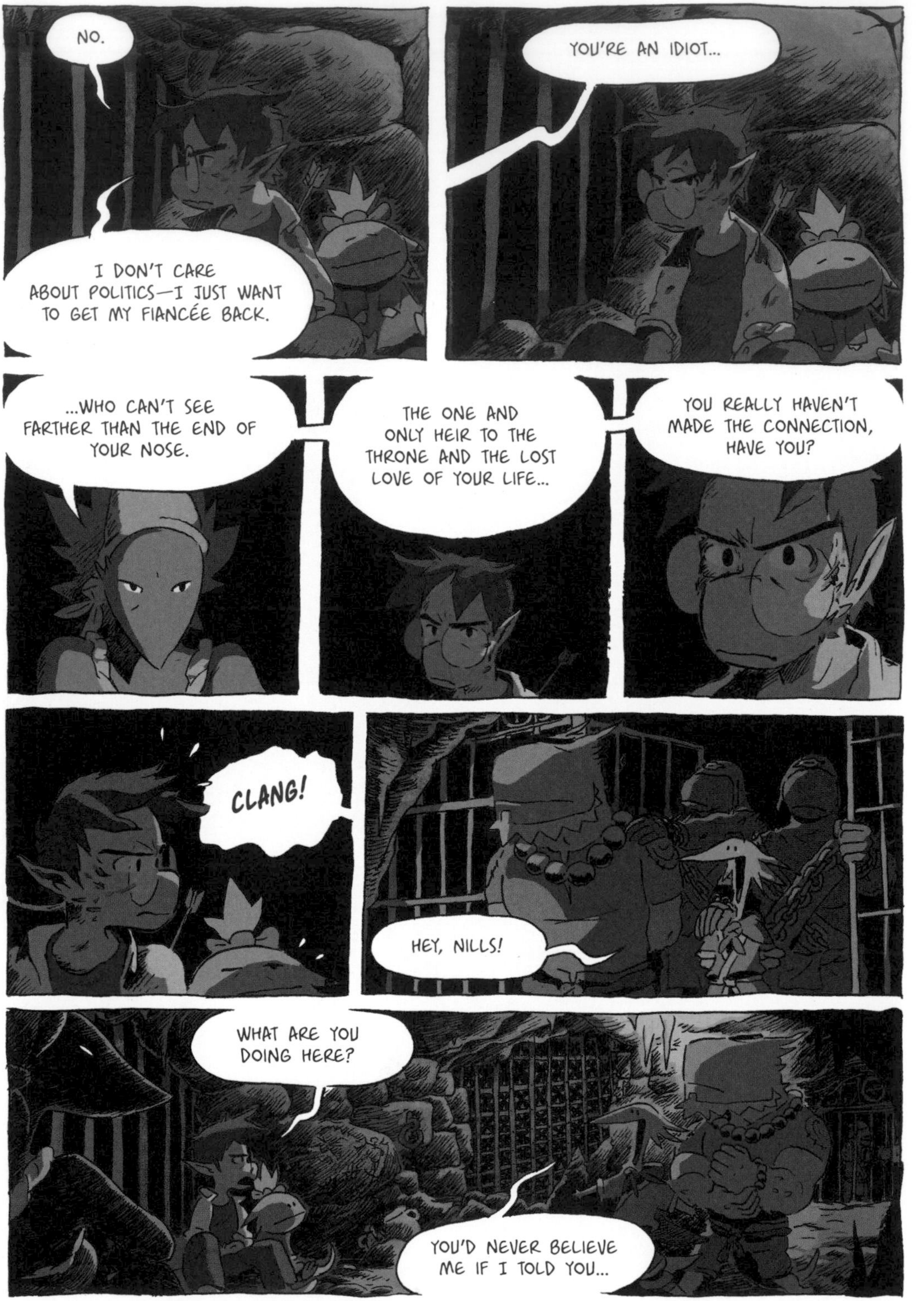
NO.
I DON'T CARE ABOUT POLITICS—I JUST WANT TO GET MY FIANCÉE BACK.
YOU'RE AN IDIOT...
...WHO CAN'T SEE FARTHER THAN THE END OF YOUR NOSE.
THE ONE AND ONLY HEIR TO THE THRONE AND THE LOST LOVE OF YOUR LIFE...
YOU REALLY HAVEN'T MADE THE CONNECTION, HAVE YOU?
CLANG!
HEY, NILLS!
WHAT ARE YOU DOING HERE?
YOU'D NEVER BELIEVE ME IF I TOLD YOU...

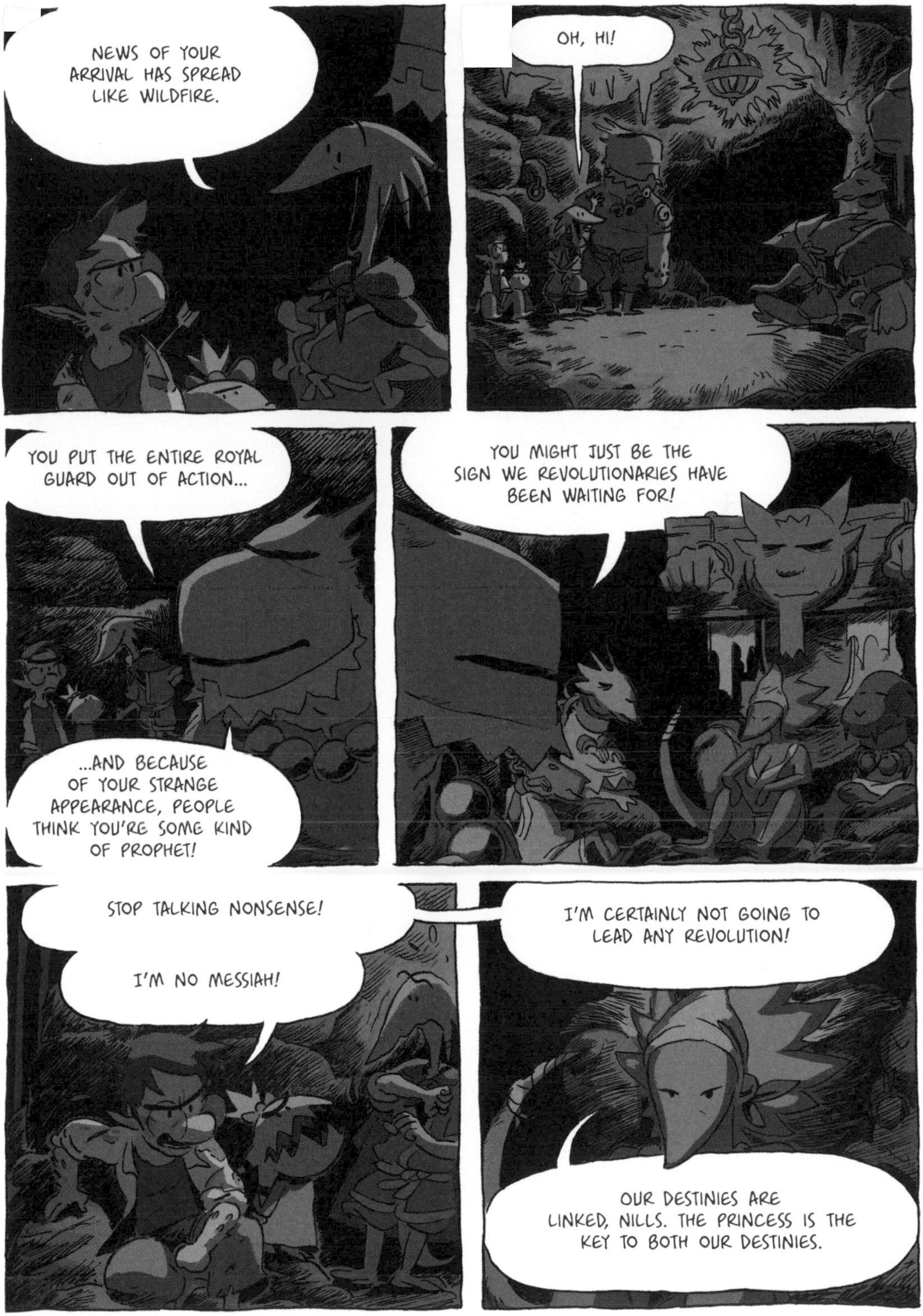
NEWS OF YOUR ARRIVAL HAS SPREAD LIKE WILDFIRE.
OH, HI!
YOU PUT THE ENTIRE ROYAL GUARD OUT OF ACTION...
...AND BECAUSE OF YOUR STRANGE APPEARANCE, PEOPLE THINK YOU'RE SOME KIND OF PROPHET!
YOU MIGHT JUST BE THE SIGN WE REVOLUTIONARIES HAVE BEEN WAITING FOR!
STOP TALKING NONSENSE!
I'M NO MESSIAH!
I'M CERTAINLY NOT GOING TO LEAD ANY REVOLUTION!
OUR DESTINIES ARE LINKED, NILLS. THE PRINCESS IS THE KEY TO BOTH OUR DESTINIES.

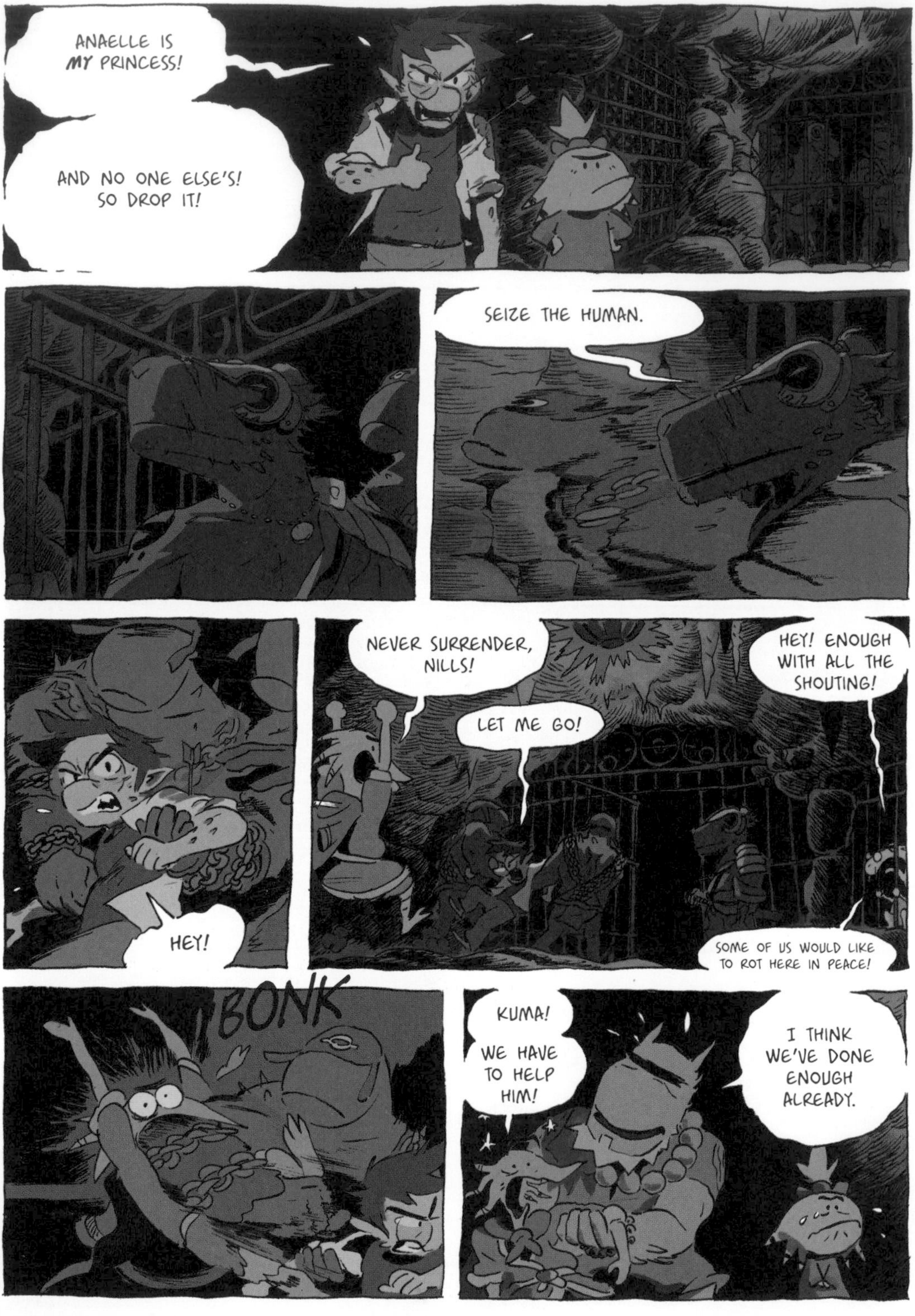
ANAELLE IS MY PRINCESS!
AND NO ONE ELSE'S! SO DROP IT!
SEIZE THE HUMAN.
HEY!
NEVER SURRENDER, NILLS!
LET ME GO!
HEY! ENOUGH WITH ALL THE SHOUTING!
SOME OF US WOULD LIKE TO ROT HERE IN PEACE!
BONK
KUMA!
WE HAVE TO HELP HIM!
I THINK WE'VE DONE ENOUGH ALREADY.

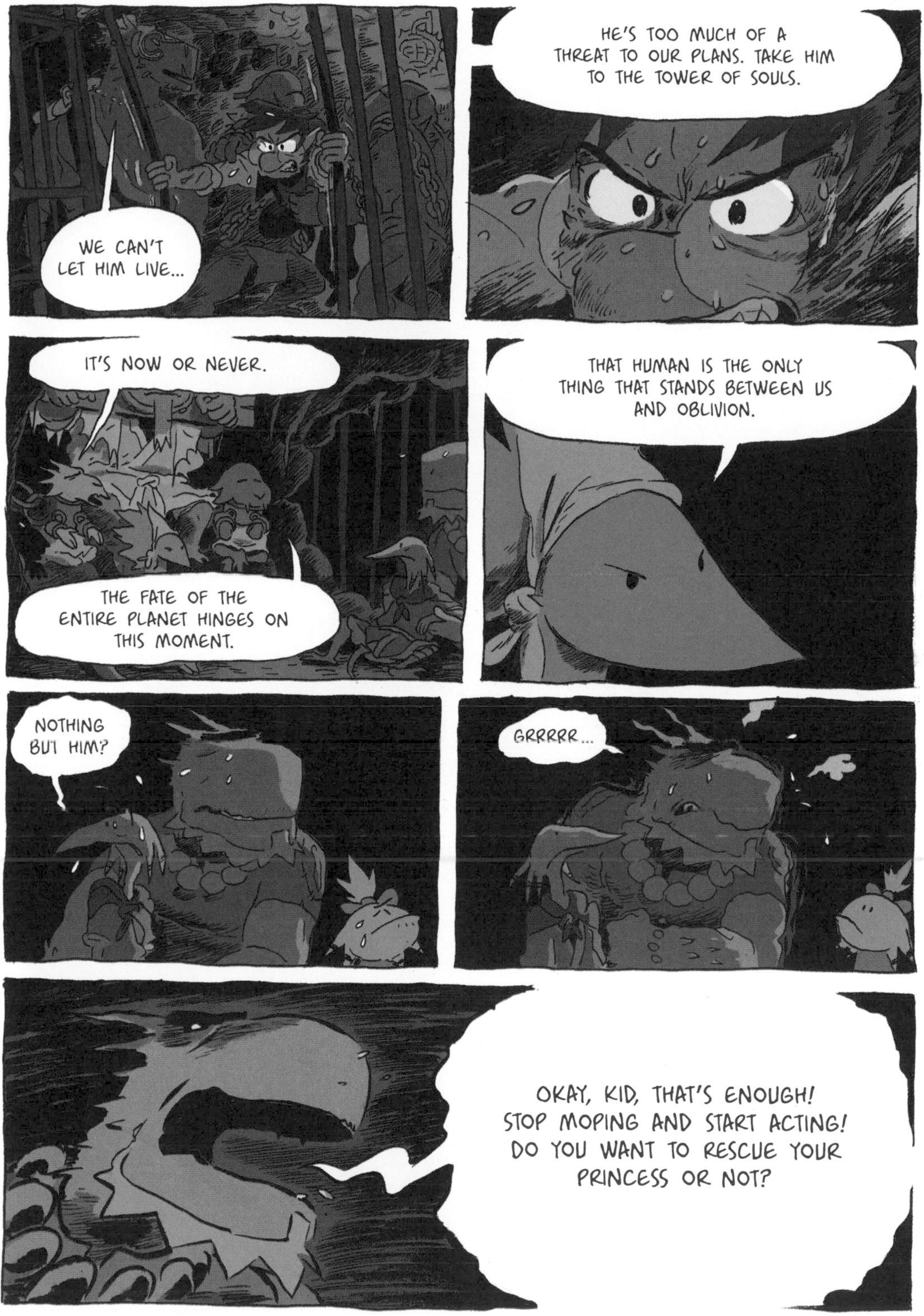
WE CAN'T LET HIM LIVE...
HE'S TOO MUCH OF A THREAT TO OUR PLANS. TAKE HIM TO THE TOWER OF SOULS.
IT'S NOW OR NEVER.
THE FATE OF THE ENTIRE PLANET HINGES ON THIS MOMENT.
THAT HUMAN IS THE ONLY THING THAT STANDS BETWEEN US AND OBLIVION.
NOTHING BUT HIM?
GRRRRR...
OKAY, KID, THAT'S ENOUGH! STOP MOPING AND START ACTING! DO YOU WANT TO RESCUE YOUR PRINCESS OR NOT?

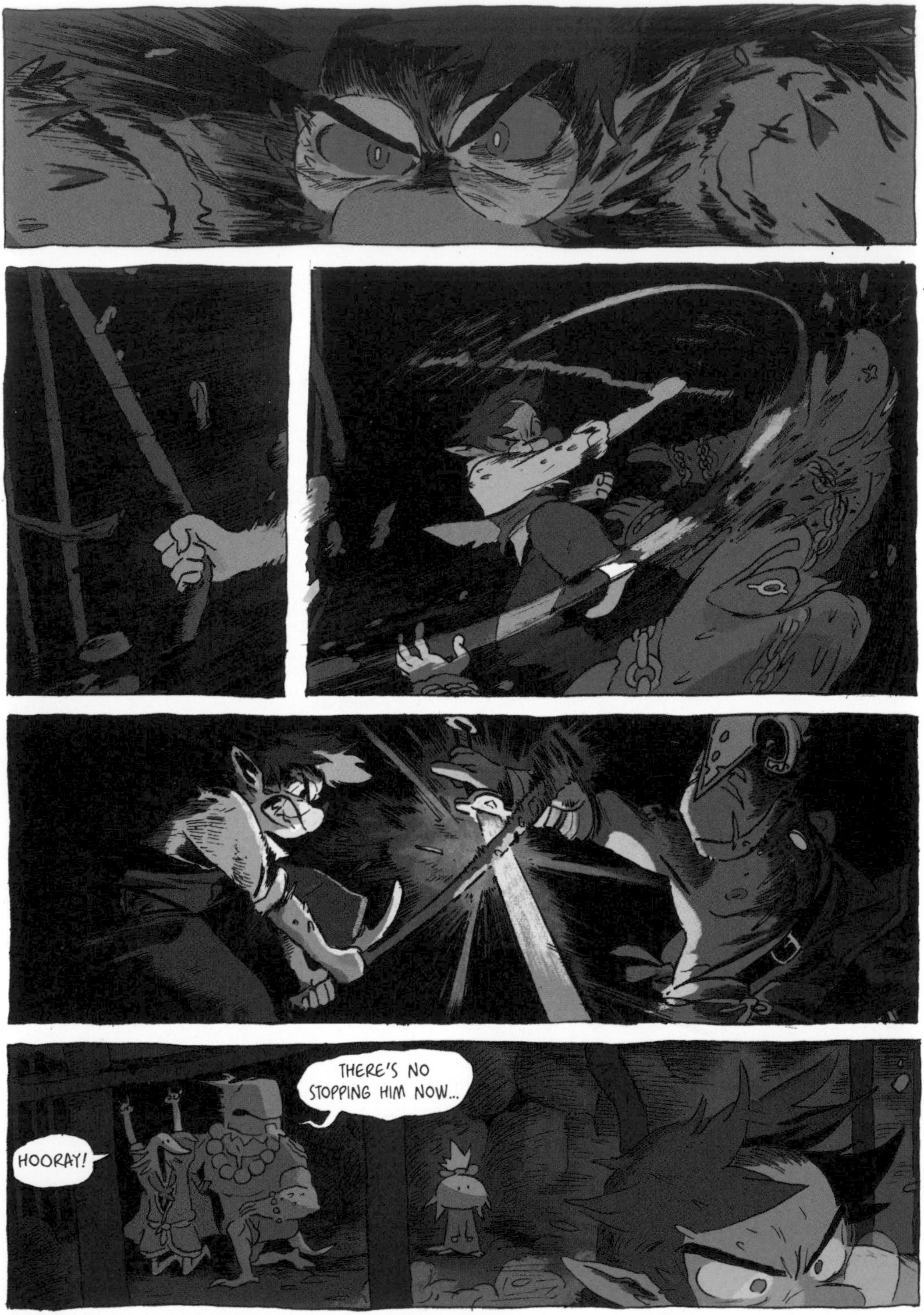

THERE'S NO STOPPING HIM NOW...
HOORAY!

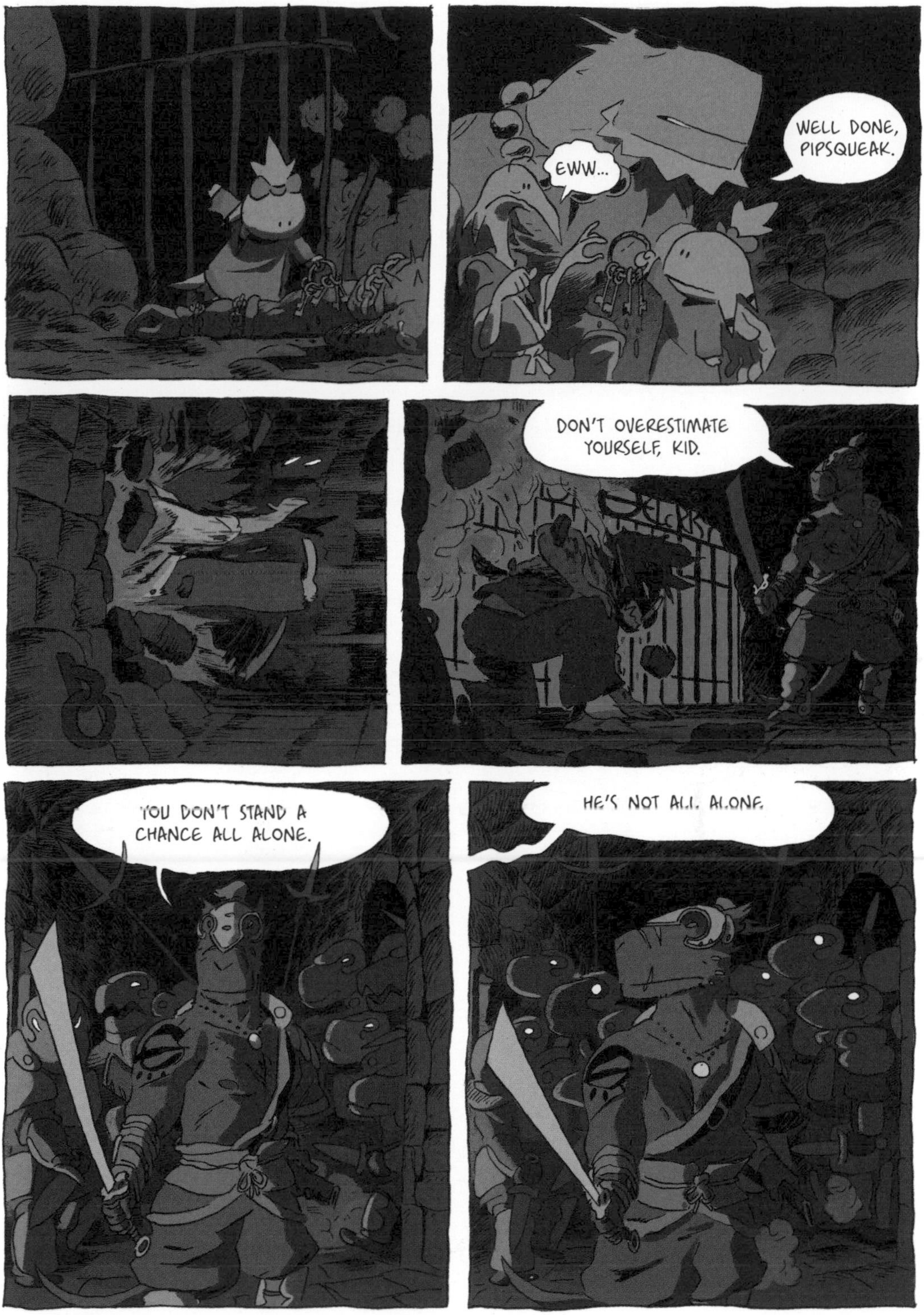
EWW...
WELL DONE, PIPSQUEAK.
DON'T OVERESTIMATE YOURSELF, KID.
YOU DON'T STAND A CHANCE ALL ALONE.
HE'S NOT ALL ALONE.

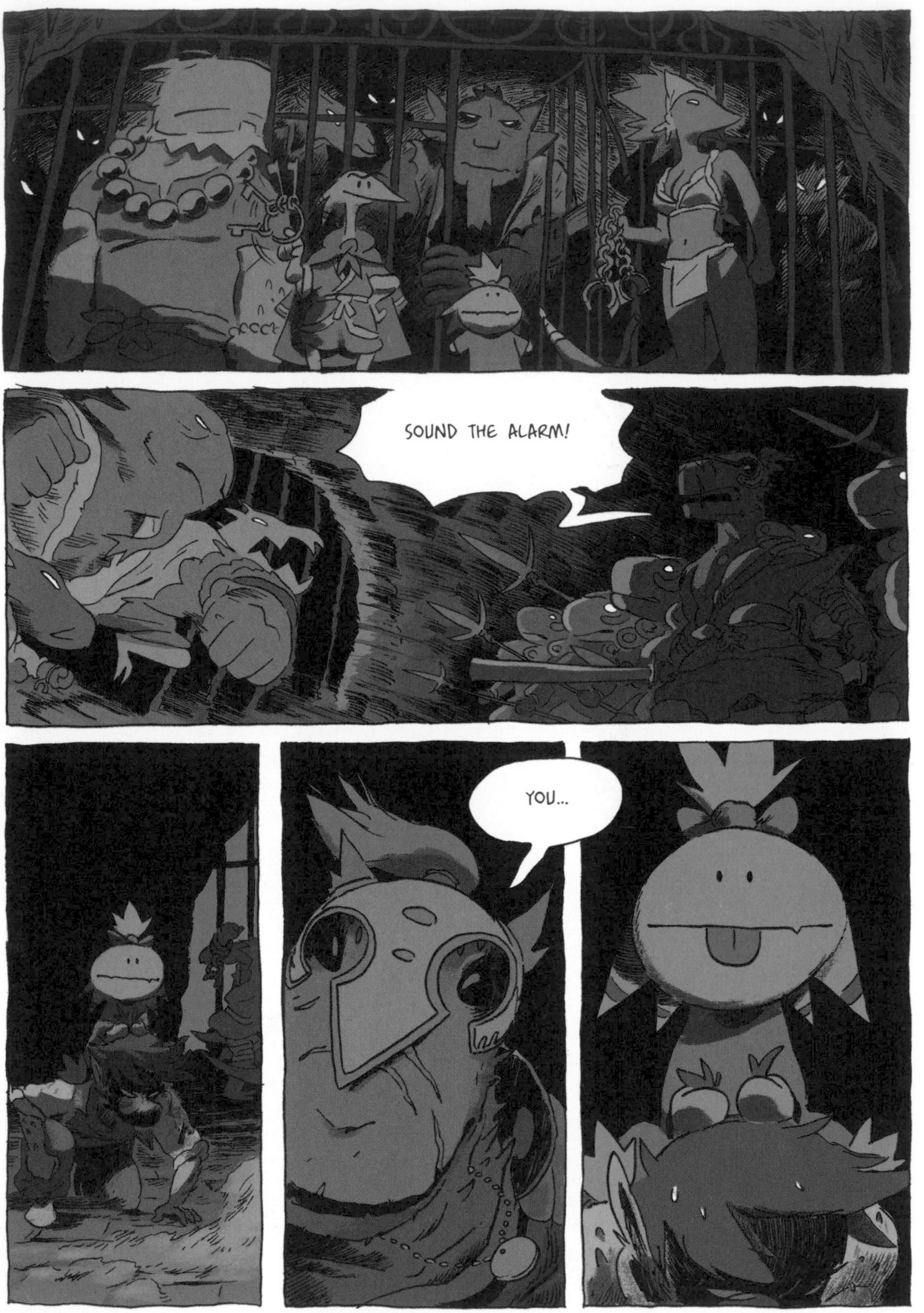
SOUND THE ALARM!
YOU...

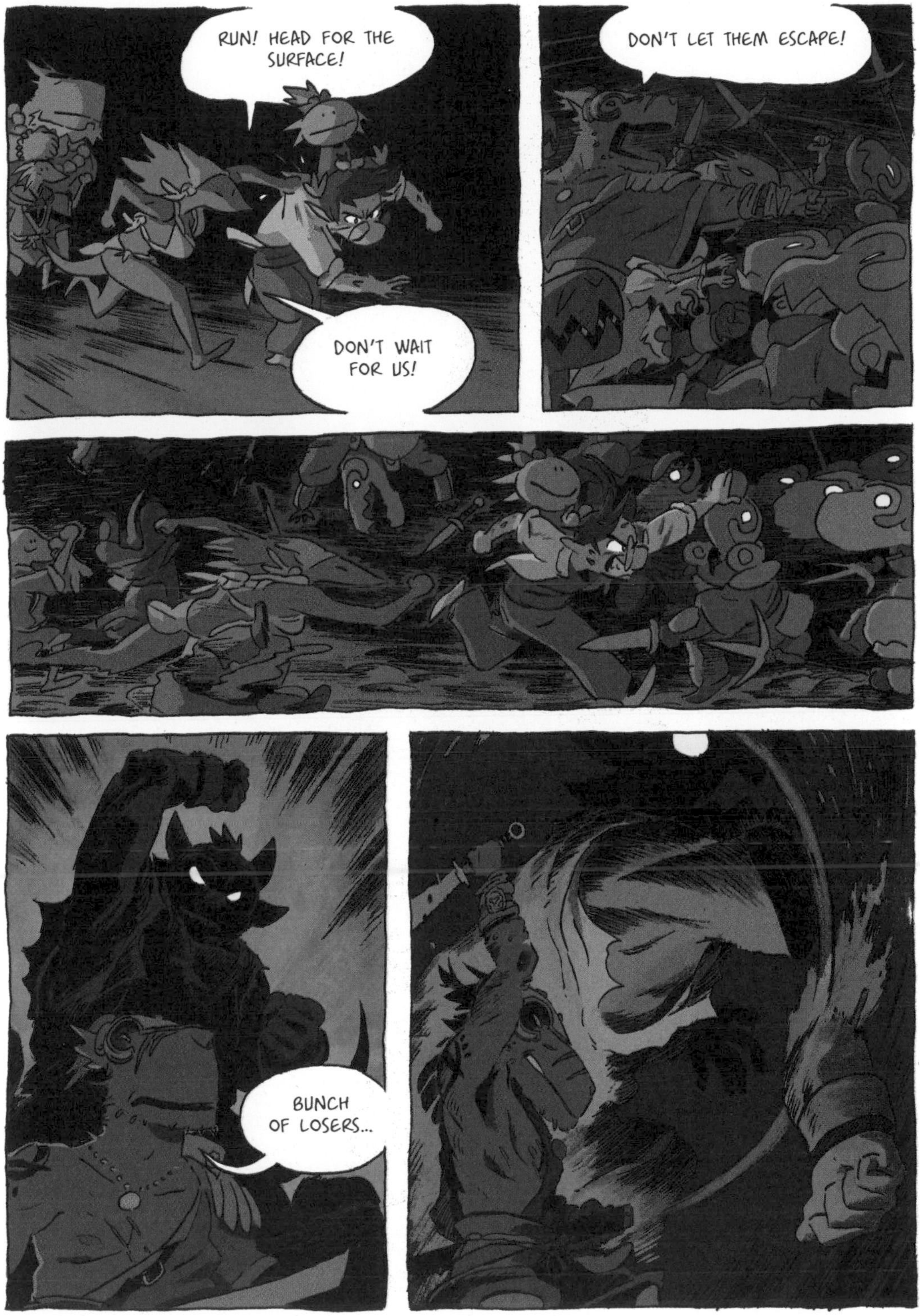
RUN! HEAD FOR THE SURFACE!
DON'T WAIT FOR US!
DON'T LET THEM ESCAPE!
BUNCH OF LOSERS...

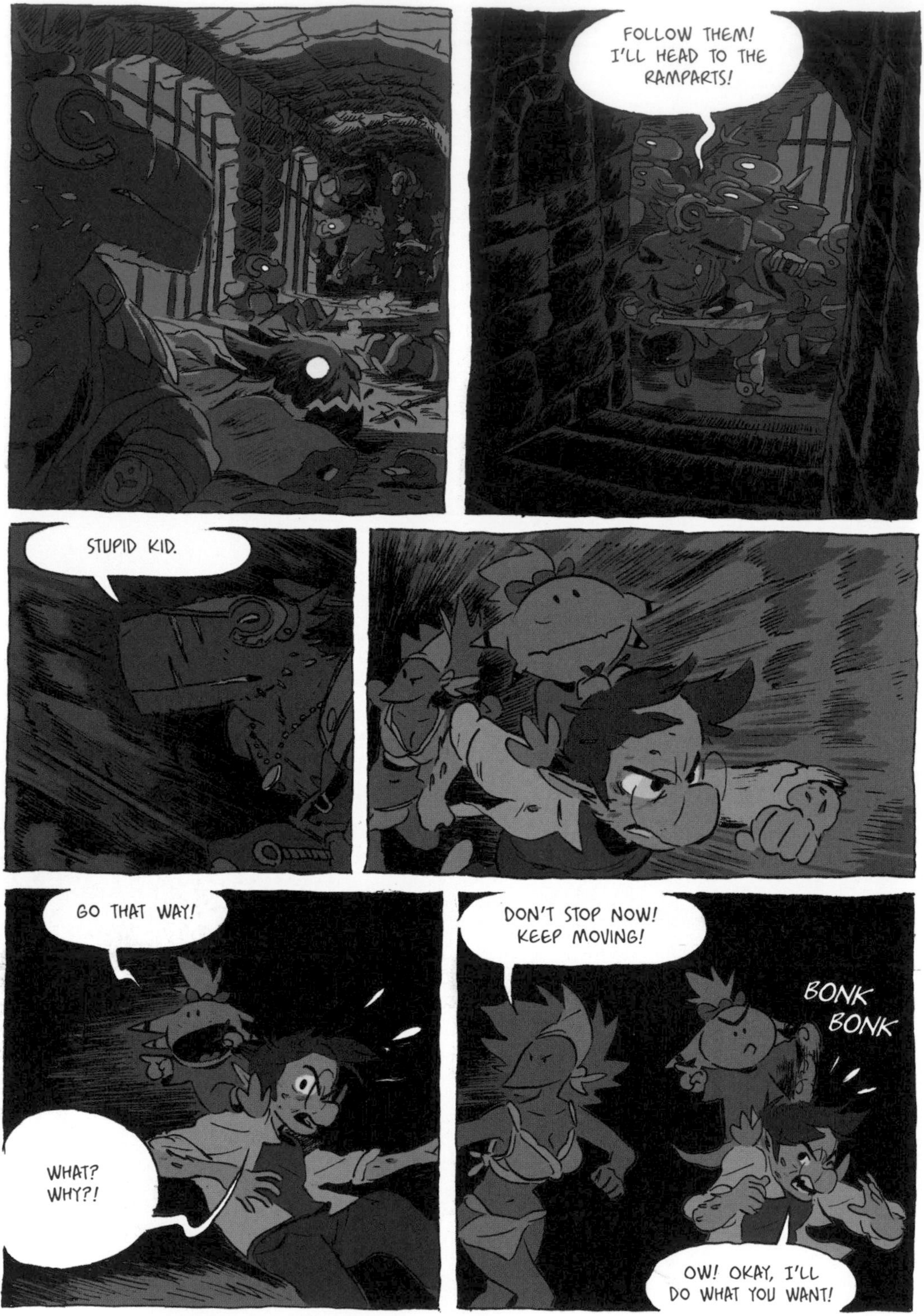
FOLLOW THEM! I'LL HEAD TO THE RAMPARTS!
STUPID KID.
GO THAT WAY!
WHAT? WHY?!
DON'T STOP NOW! KEEP MOVING!
BONK BONK
OW! OKAY, I'LL DO WHAT YOU WANT!

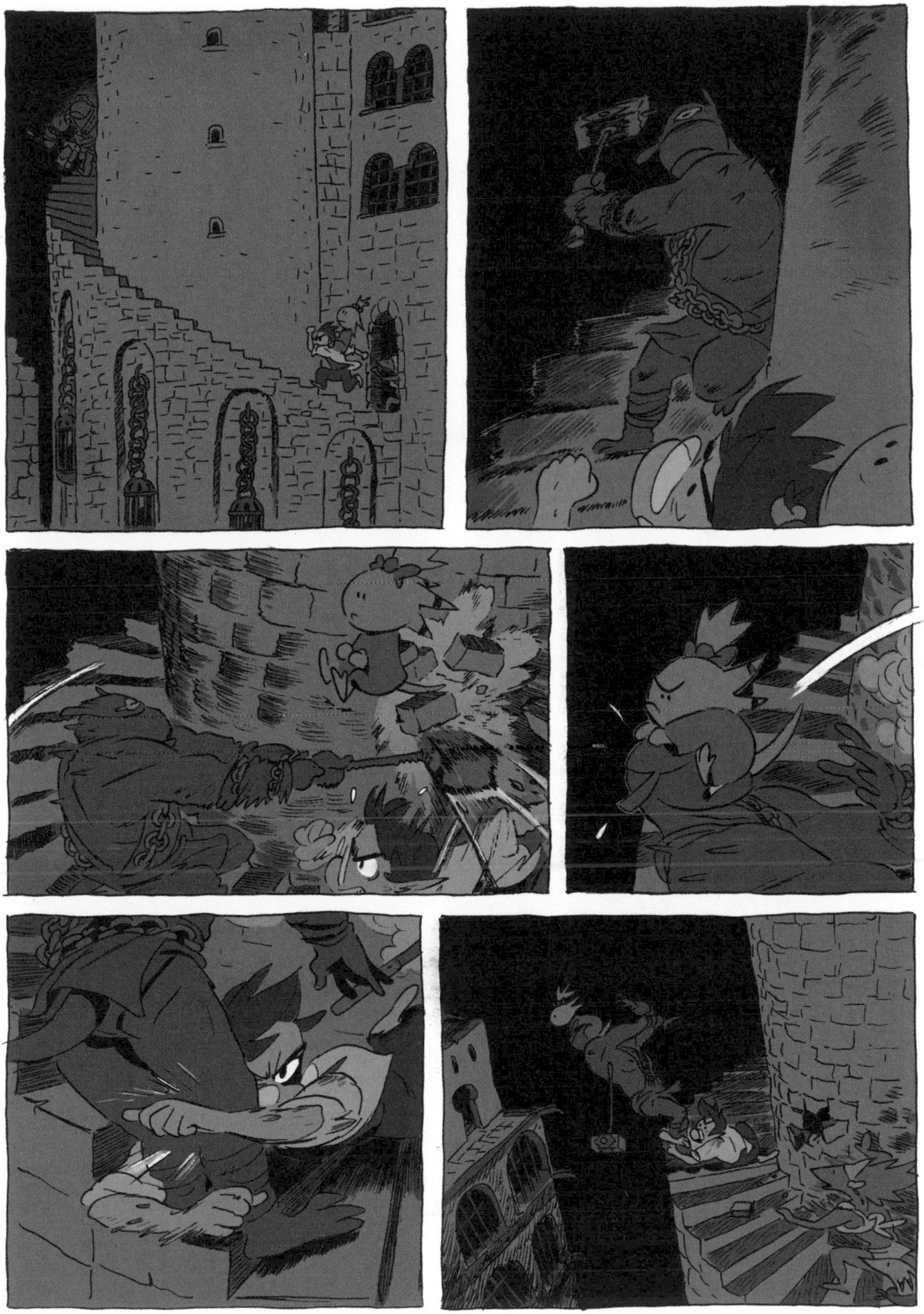

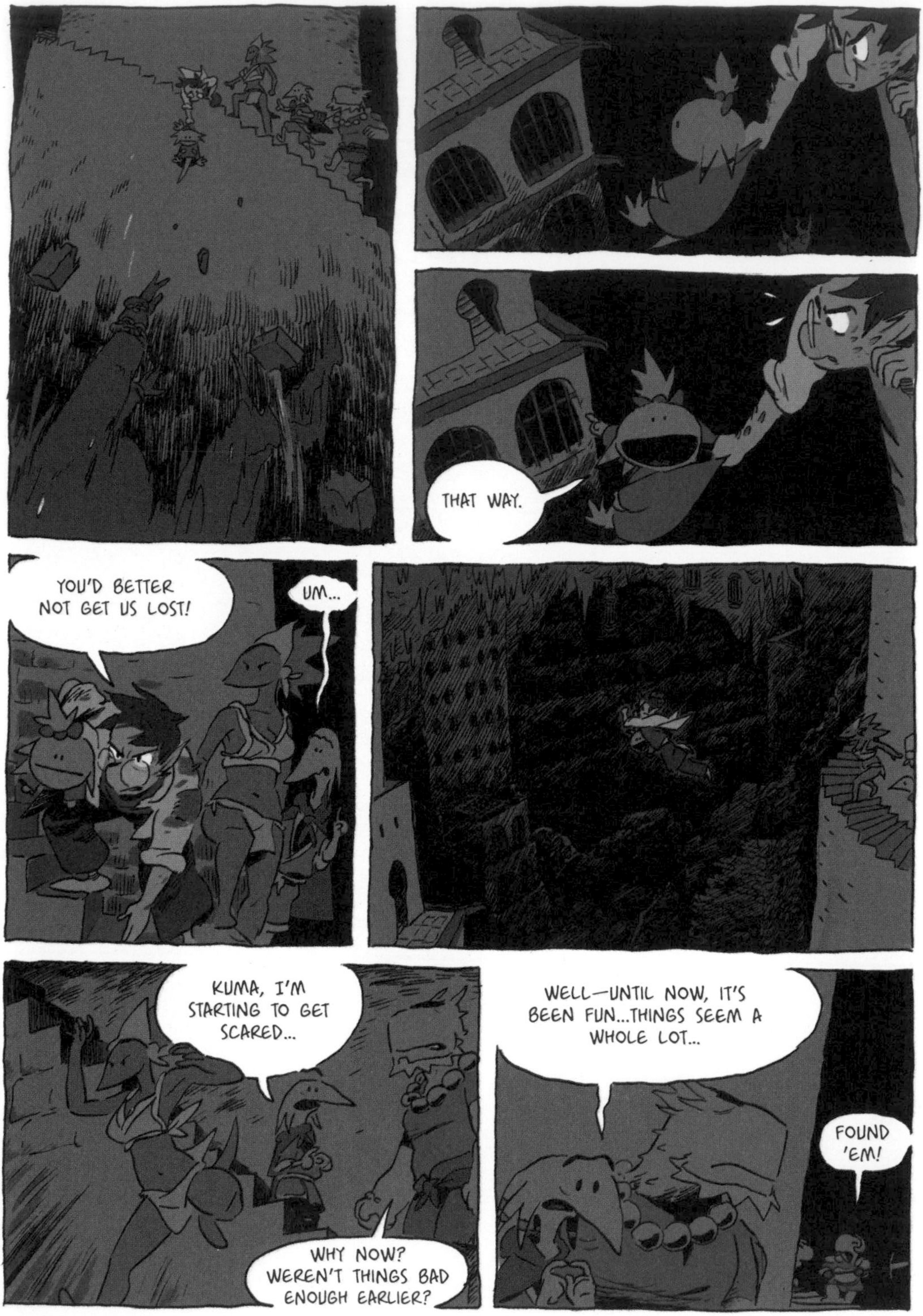
THAT WAY.
YOU'D BETTER NOT GET US LOST!
UM...
KUMA, I'M STARTING TO GET SCARED...
WHY NOW? WEREN'T THINGS BAD ENOUGH EARLIER?
WELL—UNTIL NOW, IT'S BEEN FUN...THINGS SEEM A WHOLE LOT...
FOUND 'EM!

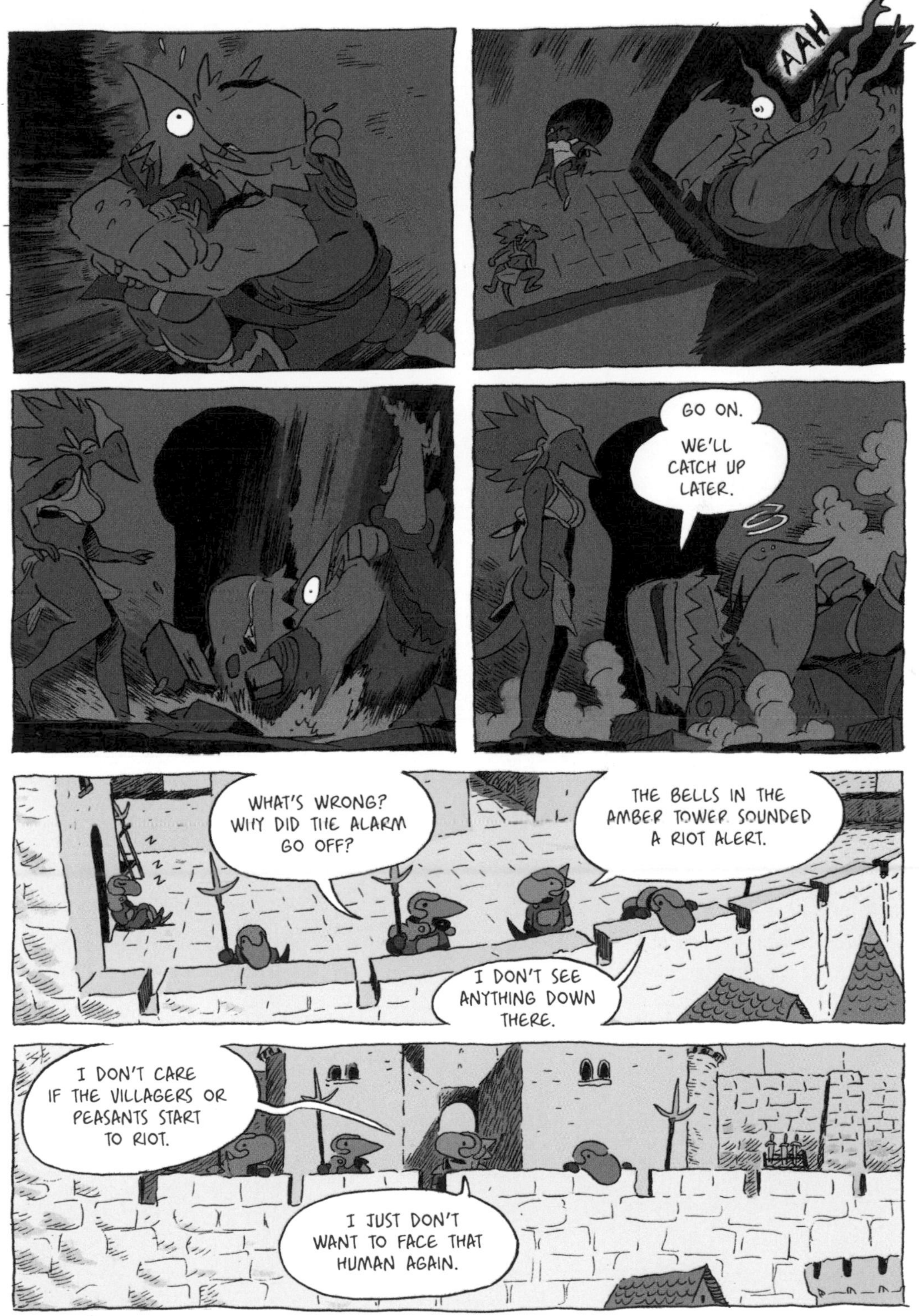
AAH
GO ON.
WE'LL CATCH UP LATER.
WHAT'S WRONG? WHY DID THE ALARM GO OFF?
THE BELLS IN THE AMBER TOWER SOUNDED A RIOT ALERT.
I DON'T SEE ANYTHING DOWN THERE.
I DON'T CARE IF THE VILLAGERS OR PEASANTS START TO RIOT.
I JUST DON'T WANT TO FACE THAT HUMAN AGAIN.

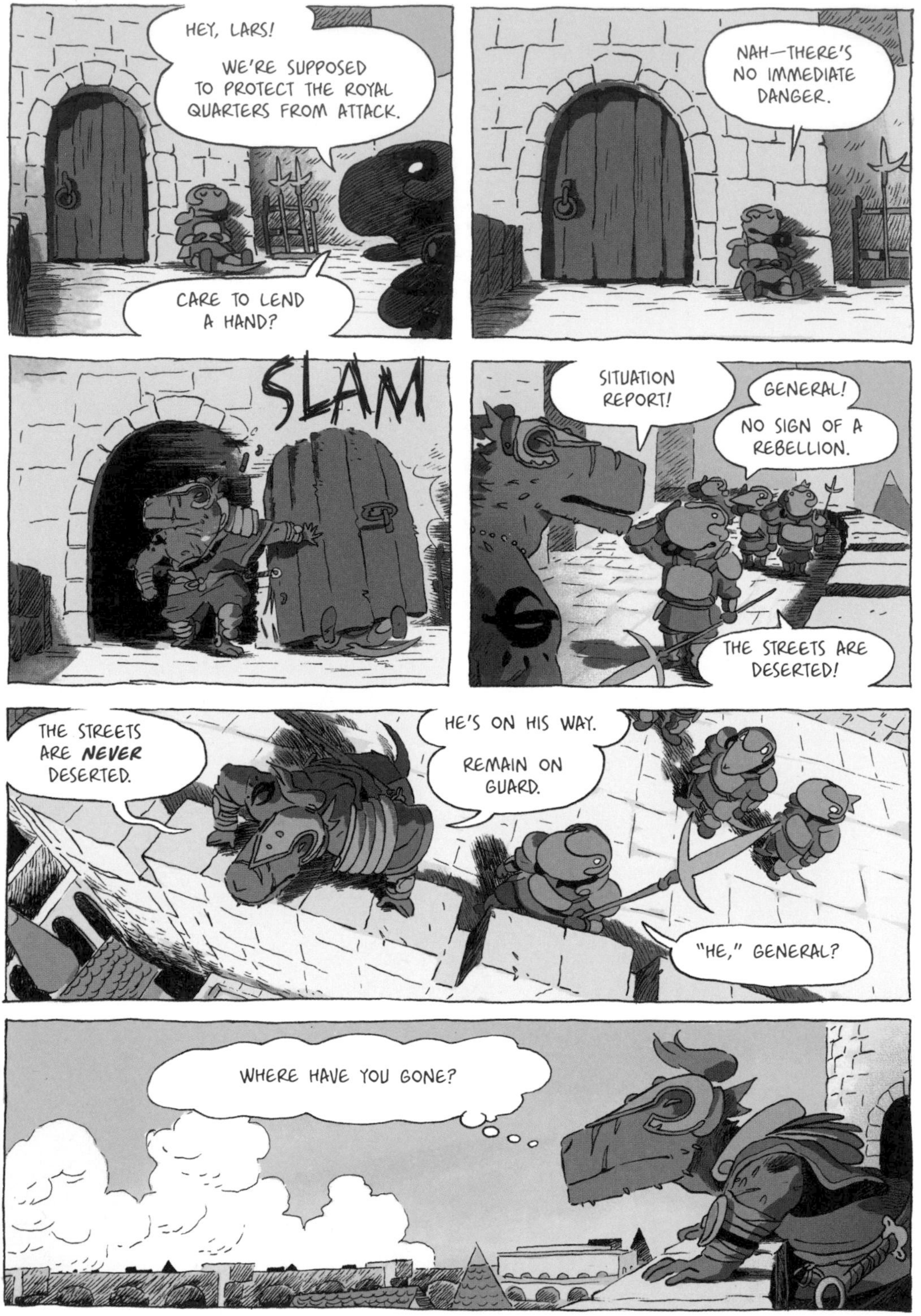
HEY, LARS!
WE'RE SUPPOSED TO PROTECT THE ROYAL QUARTERS FROM ATTACK.
CARE TO LEND A HAND?
NAH—THERE'S NO IMMEDIATE DANGER.
SLAM
SITUATION REPORT!
GENERAL!
NO SIGN OF A REBELLION.
THE STREETS ARE DESERTED!
THE STREETS ARE **NEVER** DESERTED.
HE'S ON HIS WAY.
REMAIN ON GUARD.
"HE," GENERAL?
WHERE HAVE YOU GONE?

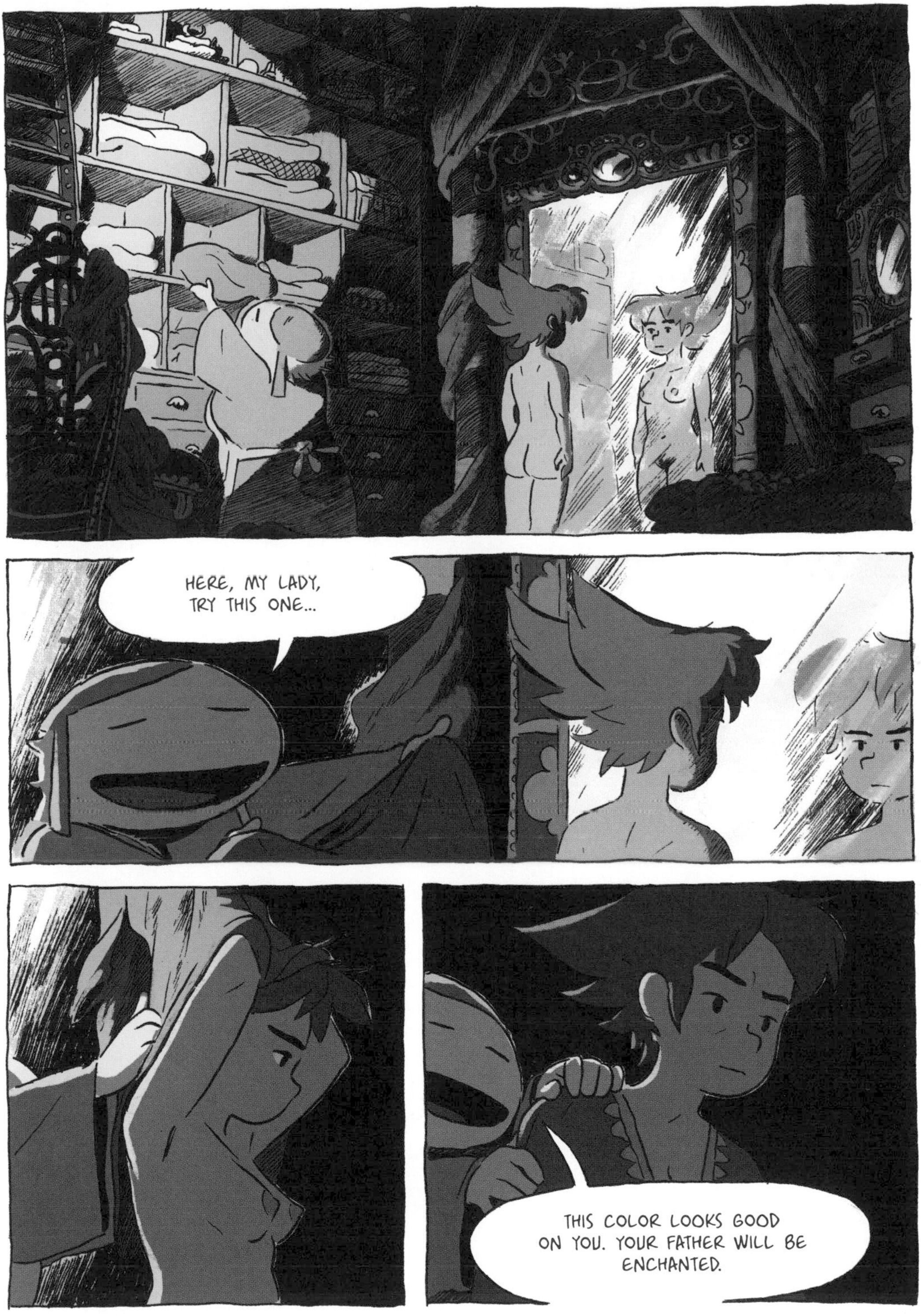
HERE, MY LADY,
TRY THIS ONE...
THIS COLOR LOOKS GOOD
ON YOU. YOUR FATHER WILL BE
ENCHANTED.

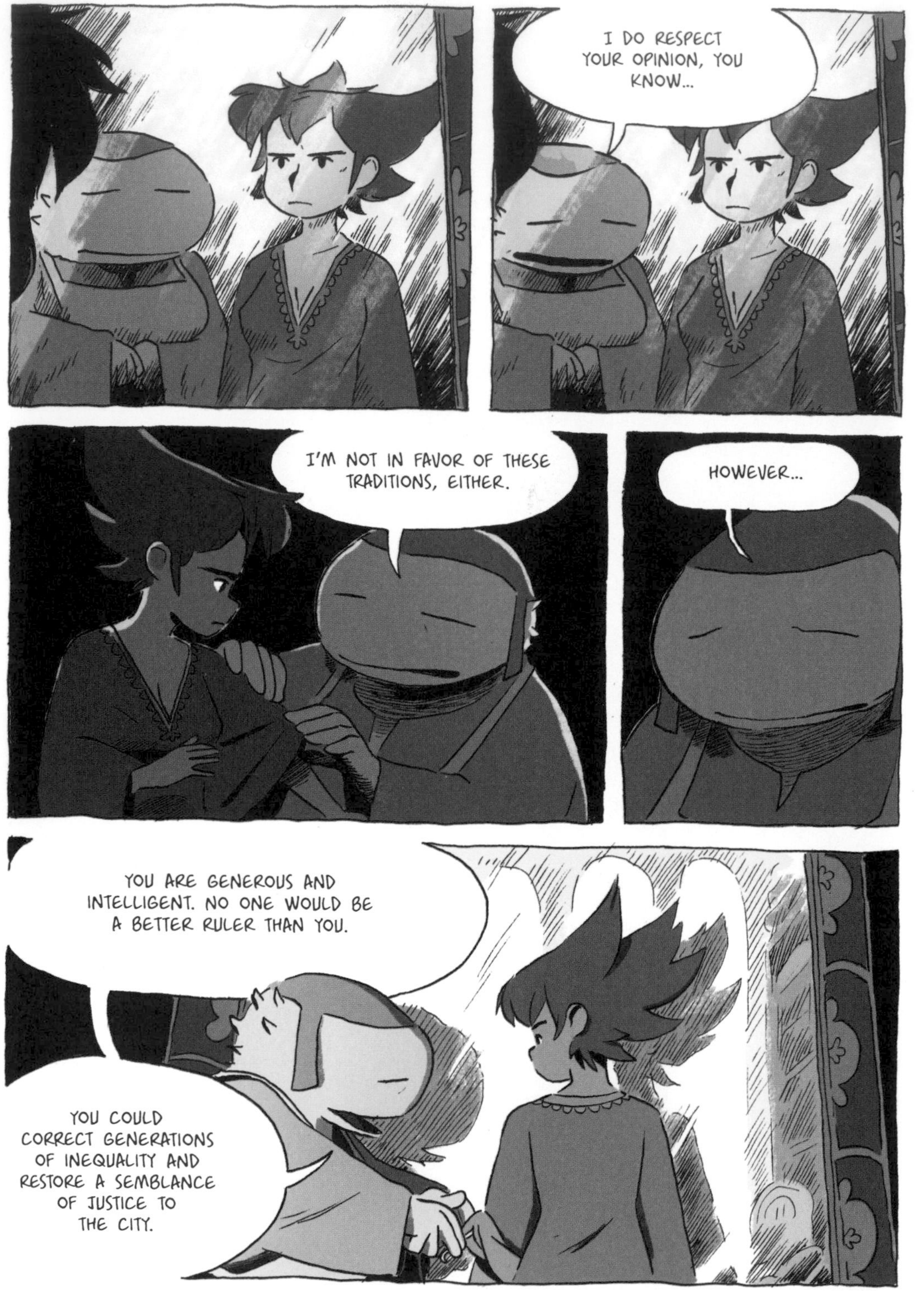
I DO RESPECT YOUR OPINION, YOU KNOW...
I'M NOT IN FAVOR OF THESE TRADITIONS, EITHER.
HOWEVER...
YOU ARE GENEROUS AND INTELLIGENT. NO ONE WOULD BE A BETTER RULER THAN YOU.
YOU COULD CORRECT GENERATIONS OF INEQUALITY AND RESTORE A SEMBLANCE OF JUSTICE TO THE CITY.

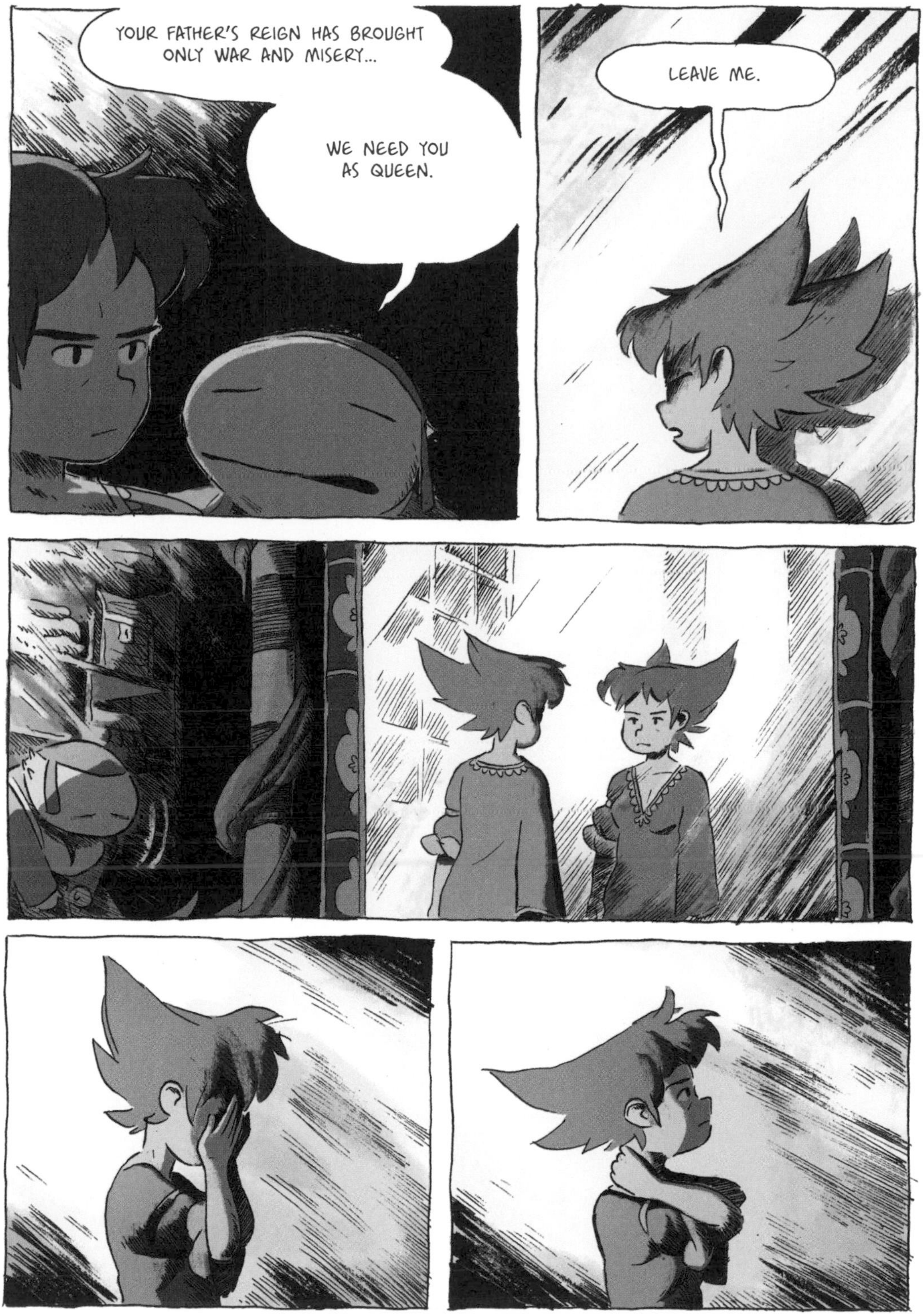
YOUR FATHER'S REIGN HAS BROUGHT ONLY WAR AND MISERY...
WE NEED YOU AS QUEEN.
LEAVE ME.

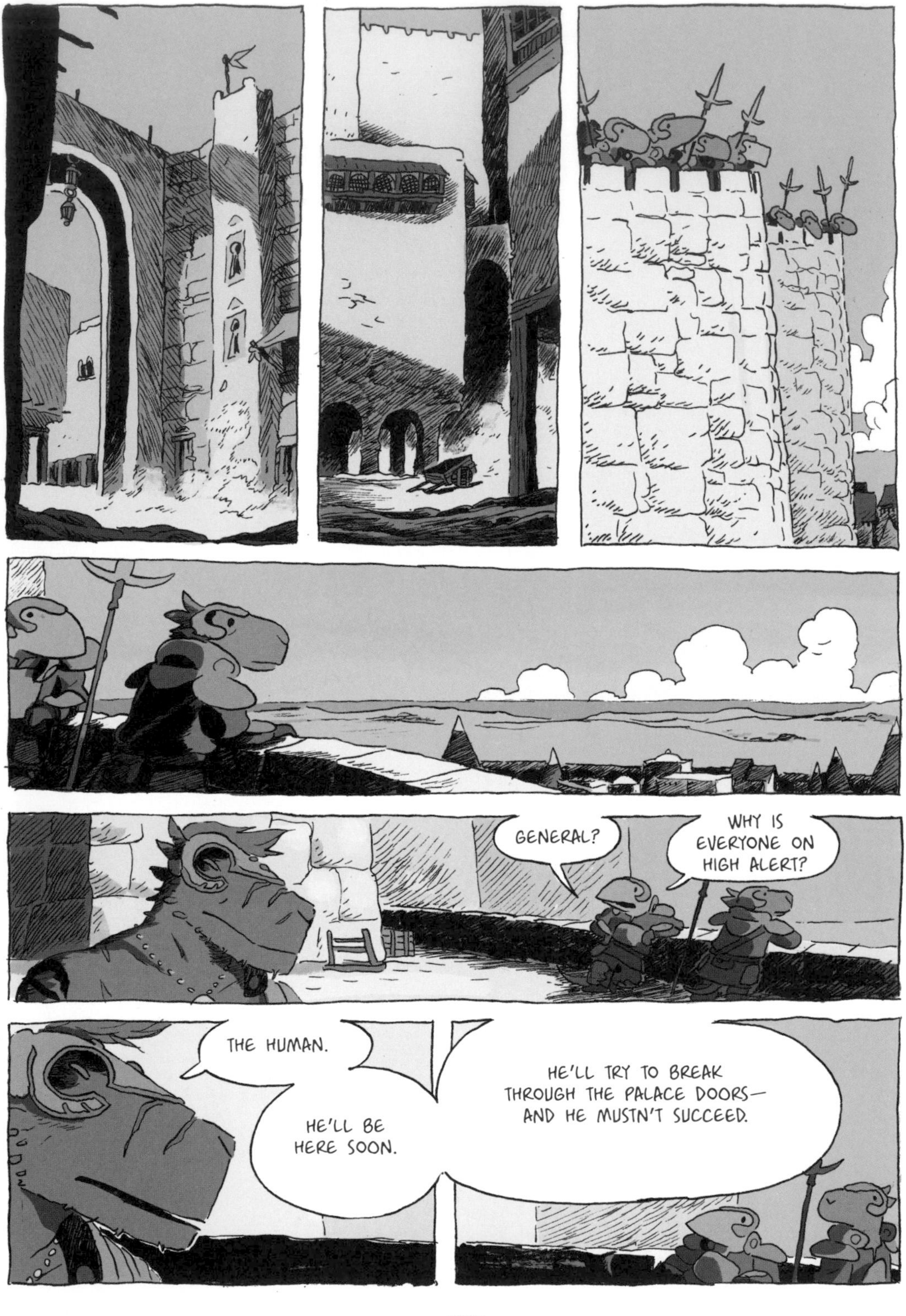
GENERAL?
WHY IS EVERYONE ON HIGH ALERT?
THE HUMAN.
HE'LL BE HERE SOON.
HE'LL TRY TO BREAK THROUGH THE PALACE DOORS— AND HE MUSTN'T SUCCEED.

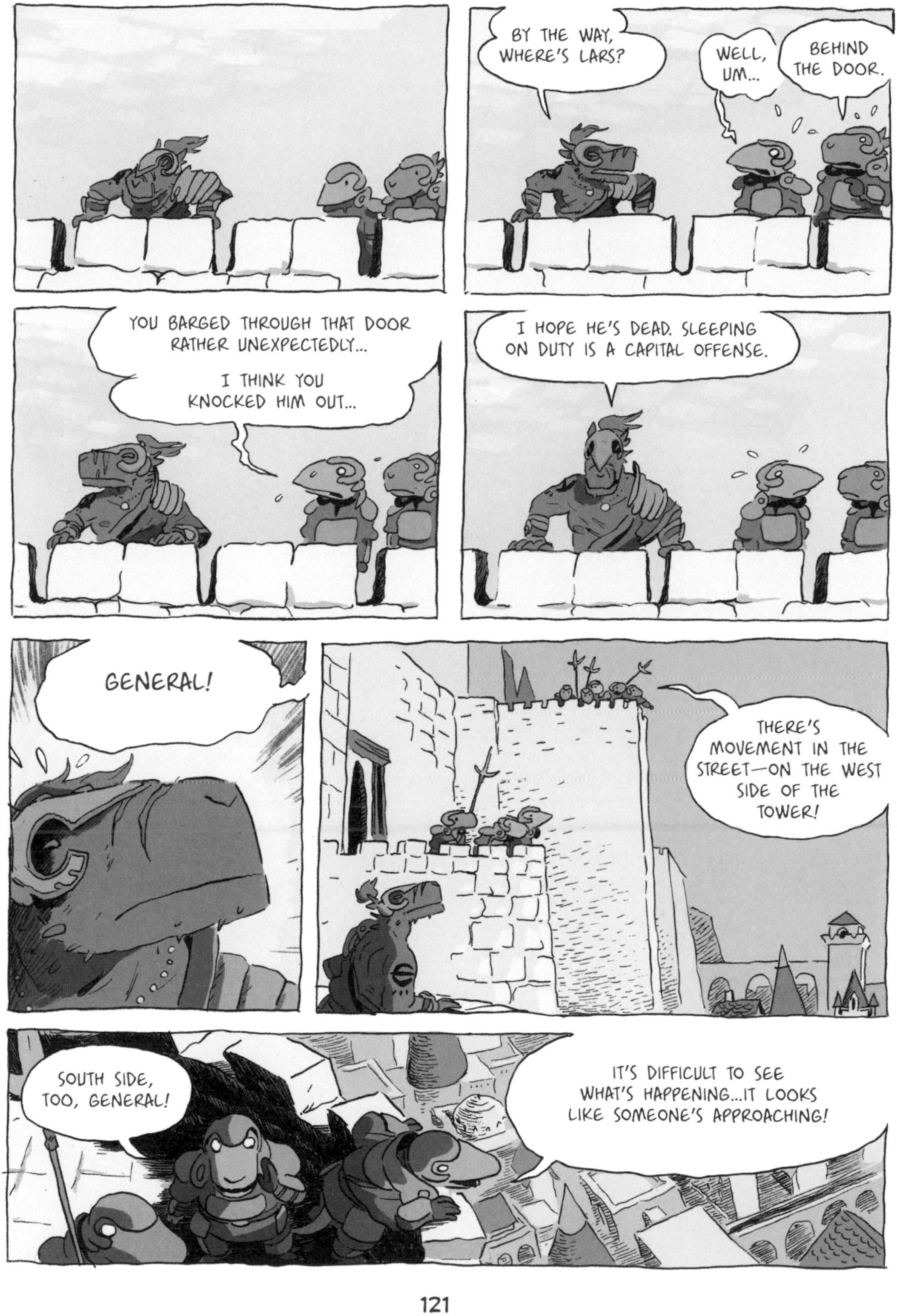
BY THE WAY, WHERE'S LARS?
WELL, UM...
BEHIND THE DOOR.
YOU BARGED THROUGH THAT DOOR RATHER UNEXPECTEDLY...
I THINK YOU KNOCKED HIM OUT...
I HOPE HE'S DEAD. SLEEPING ON DUTY IS A CAPITAL OFFENSE.
GENERAL!
THERE'S MOVEMENT IN THE STREET—ON THE WEST SIDE OF THE TOWER!
SOUTH SIDE, TOO, GENERAL!
IT'S DIFFICULT TO SEE WHAT'S HAPPENING...IT LOOKS LIKE SOMEONE'S APPROACHING!

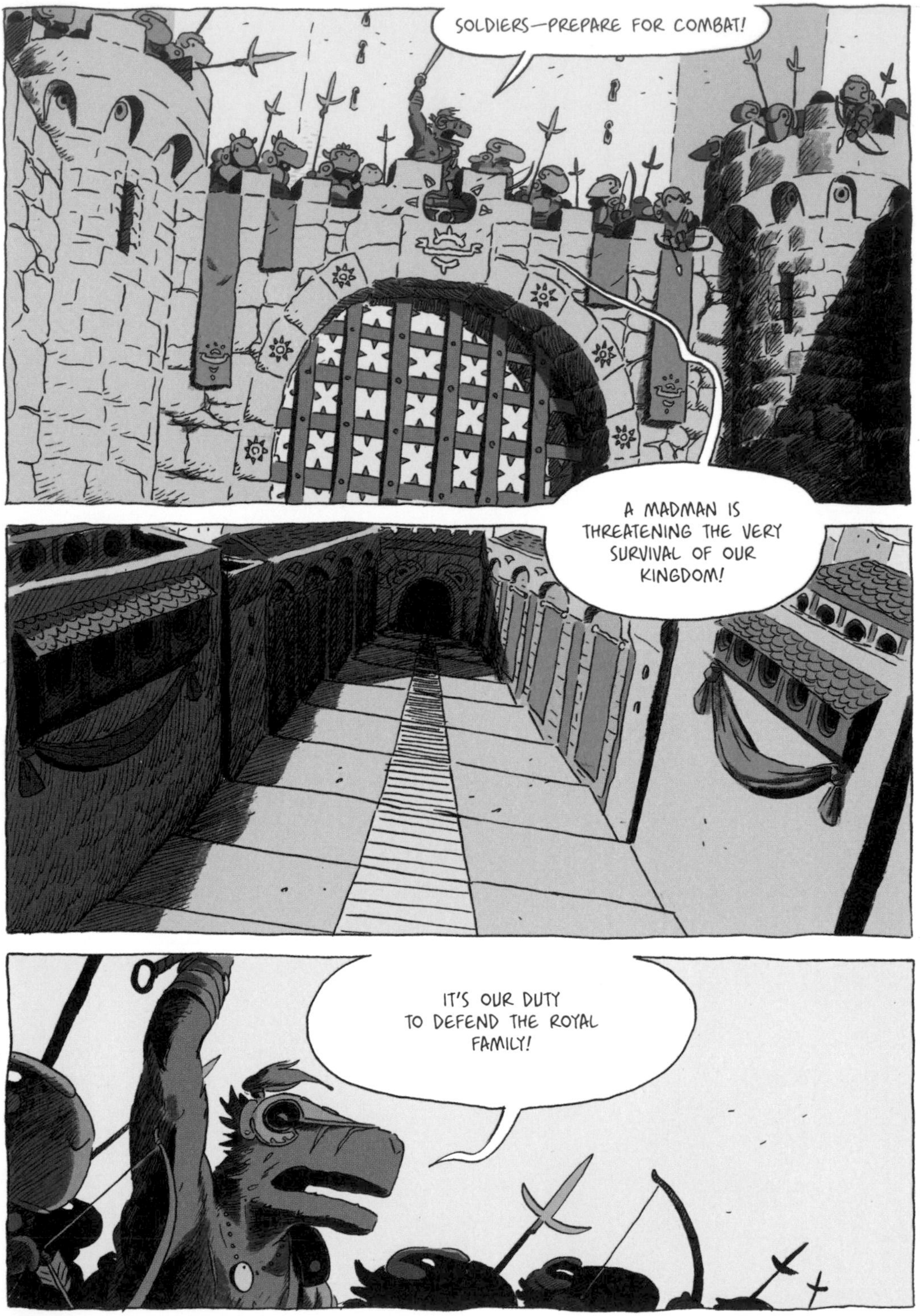
SOLDIERS—PREPARE FOR COMBAT!
A MADMAN IS THREATENING THE VERY SURVIVAL OF OUR KINGDOM!
IT'S OUR DUTY TO DEFEND THE ROYAL FAMILY!

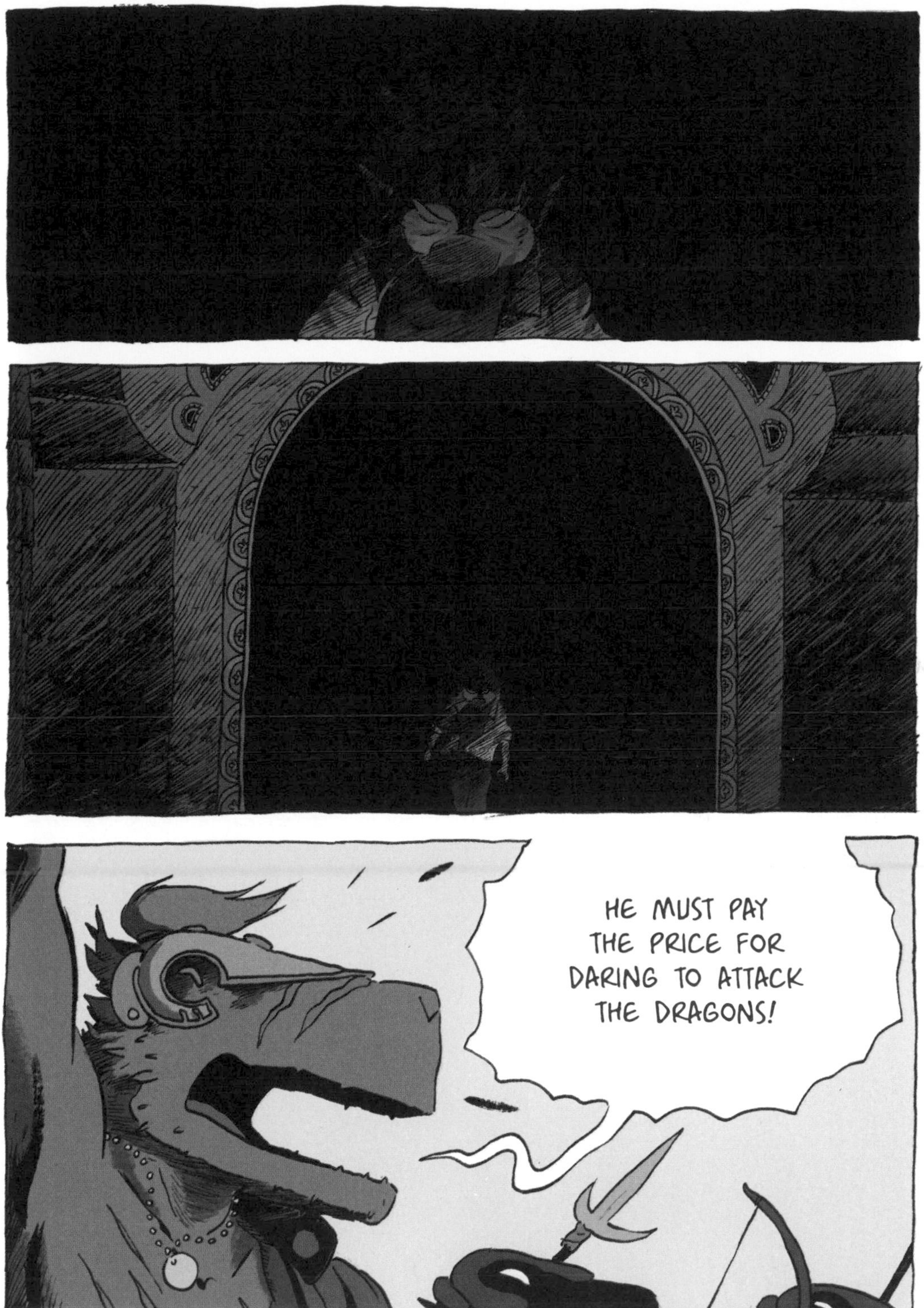
HE MUST PAY THE PRICE FOR DARING TO ATTACK THE DRAGONS!

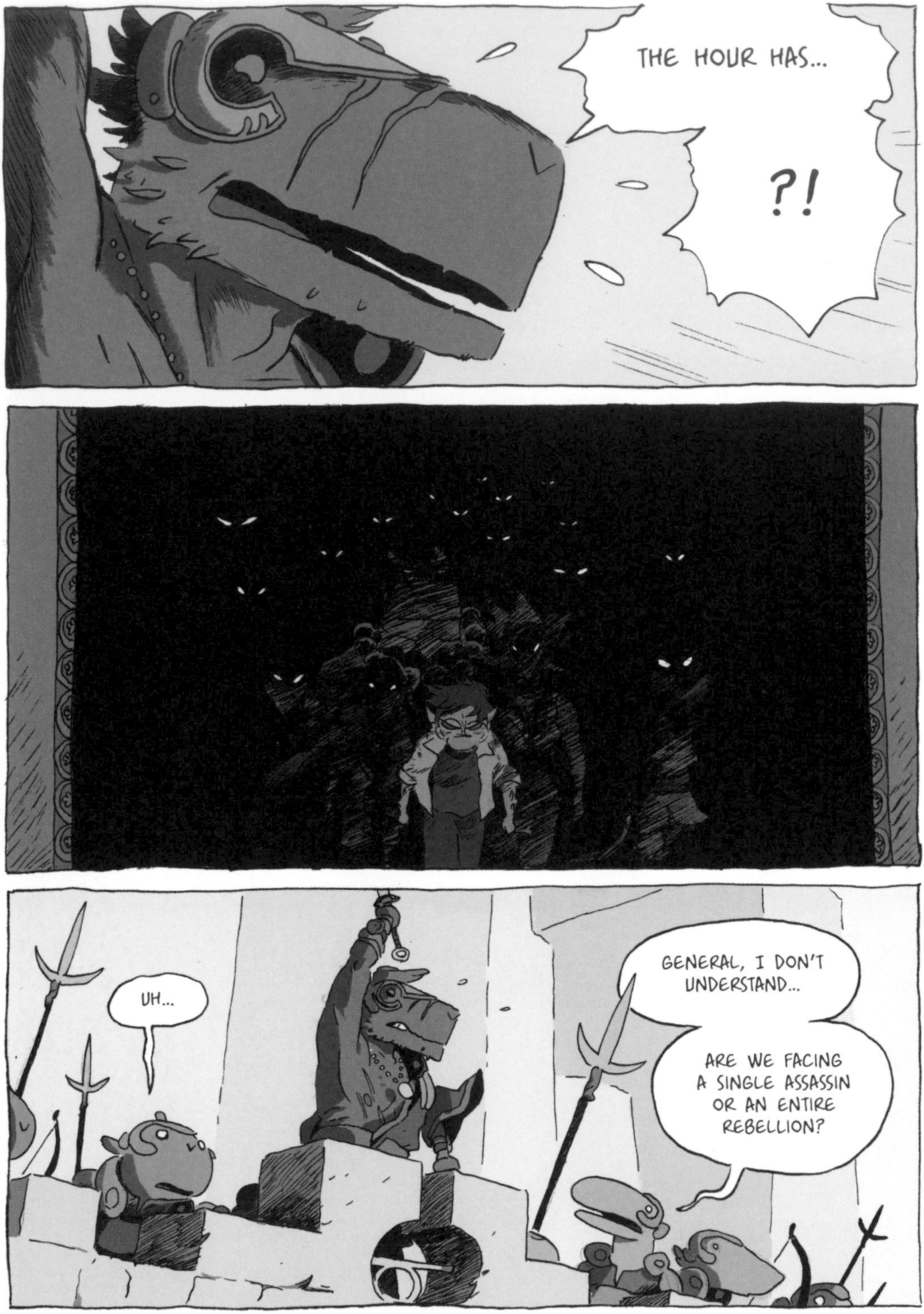
THE HOUR HAS...
?!
UH...
GENERAL, I DON'T UNDERSTAND...
ARE WE FACING A SINGLE ASSASSIN OR AN ENTIRE REBELLION?

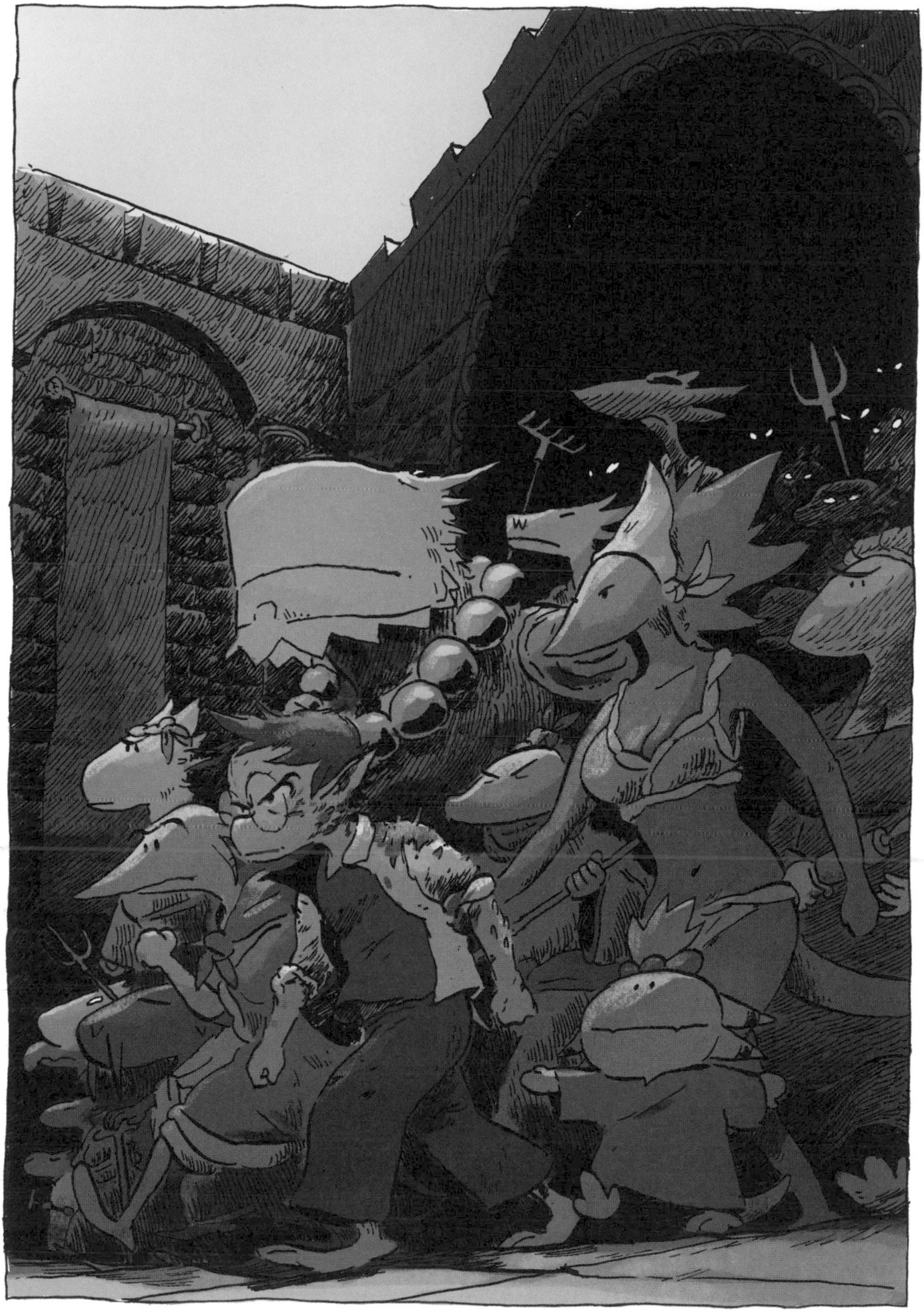

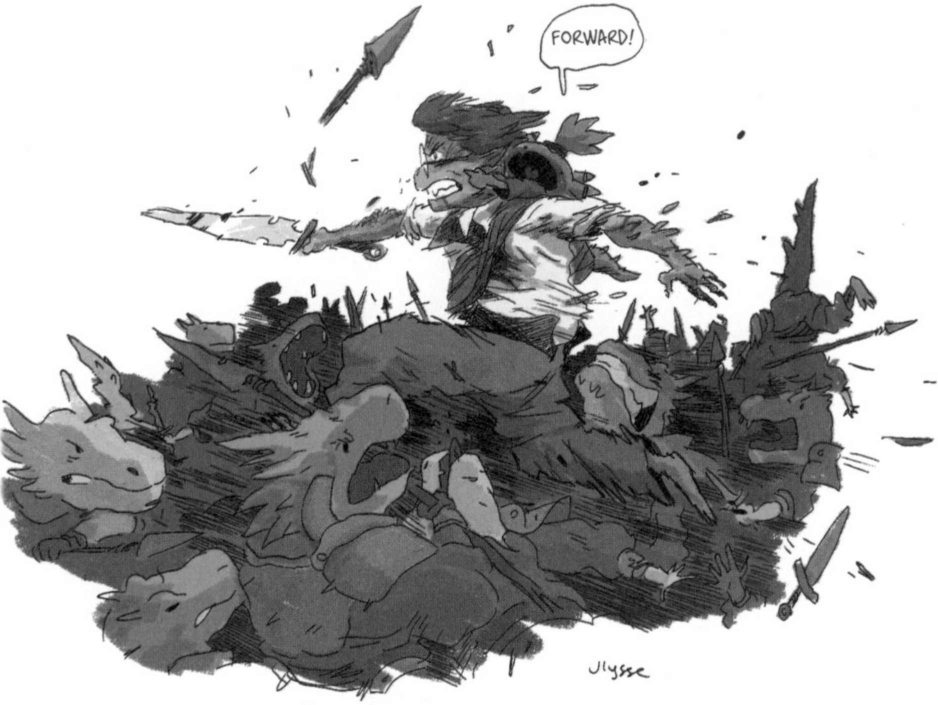
FORWARD!
Ulysse

PART THREE

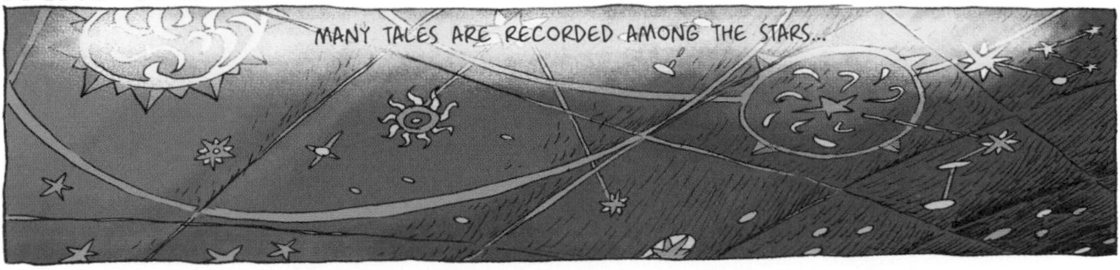
MANY TALES ARE RECORDED AMONG THE STARS...

SEARCH THE CONSTELLATIONS AND YOU WILL FIND AN ECHO OF YOUR OWN STORY.

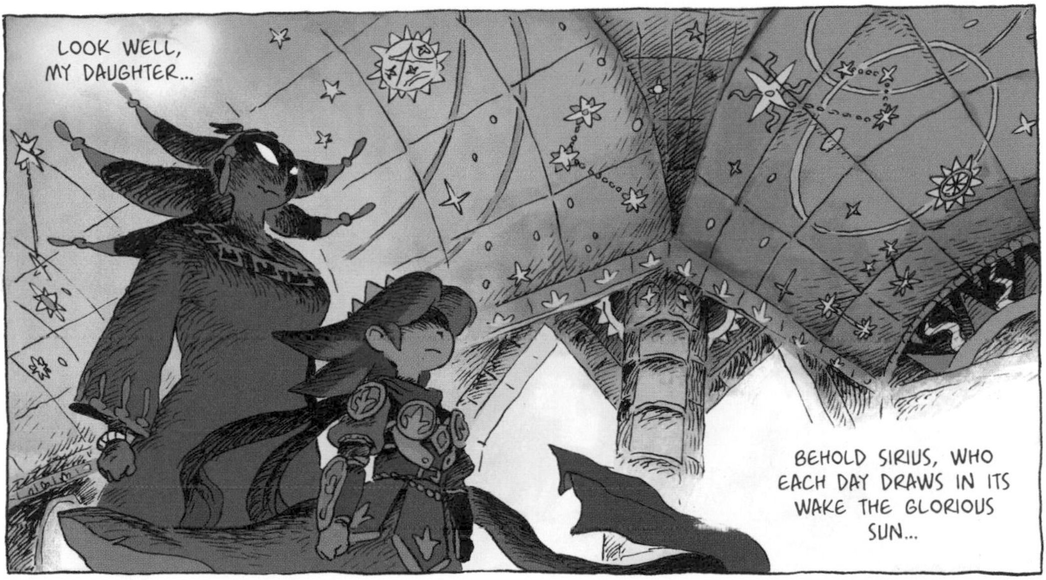
LOOK WELL, MY DAUGHTER...
BEHOLD SIRIUS, WHO EACH DAY DRAWS IN ITS WAKE THE GLORIOUS SUN...

THERE, TOO, LIES HERO, WHO MOURNS HER LOST LOVE, LEANDER...

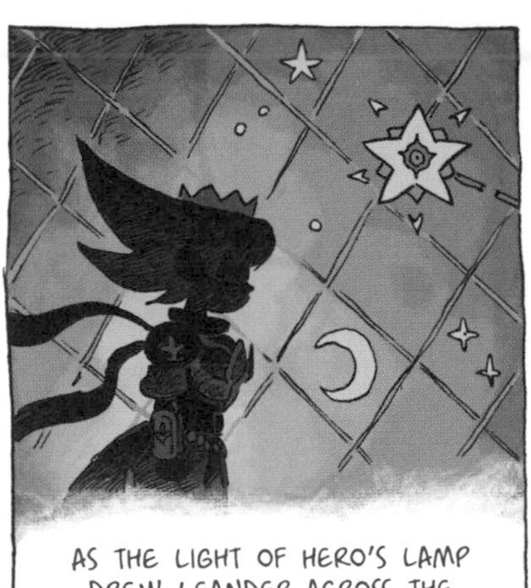
AS THE LIGHT OF HERO'S LAMP DREW LEANDER ACROSS THE TEMPESTUOUS SEA, SO, TOO, DOES THE LIGHT OF SIRIUS GUIDE THE SUN THROUGH THE TROUBLED NIGHT...

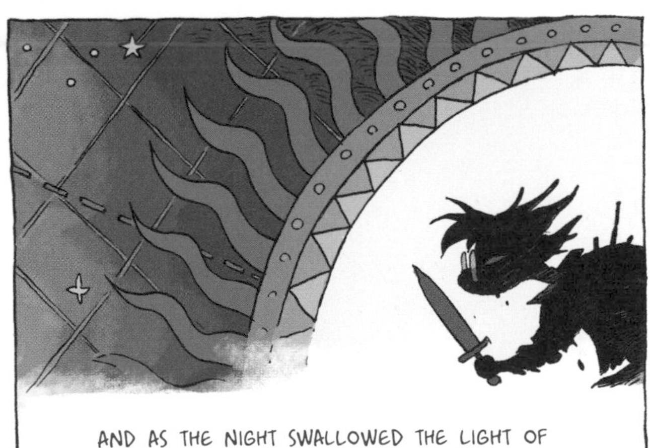
AND AS THE NIGHT SWALLOWED THE LIGHT OF HERO'S LAMP, WHEN IT FLICKERED AND DIED, SO, TOO, WILL WINTER'S DARKNESS CONCEAL THE BRIGHT GLOW OF SIRIUS...

ALAS LEANDER, BEREFT OF HIS SOLE POINT OF REFERENCE, WAS CONDEMNED TO A WATERY GRAVE...

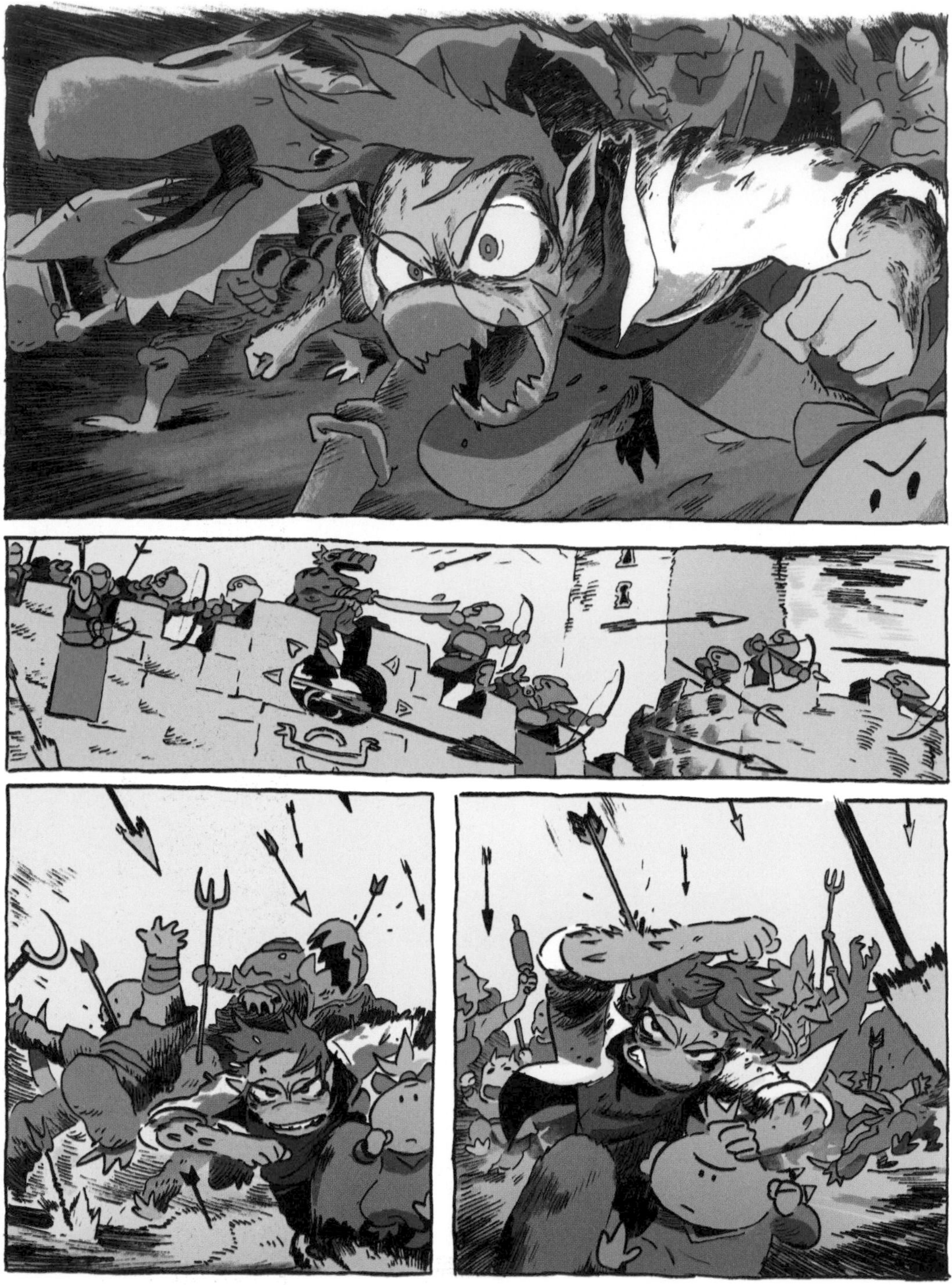

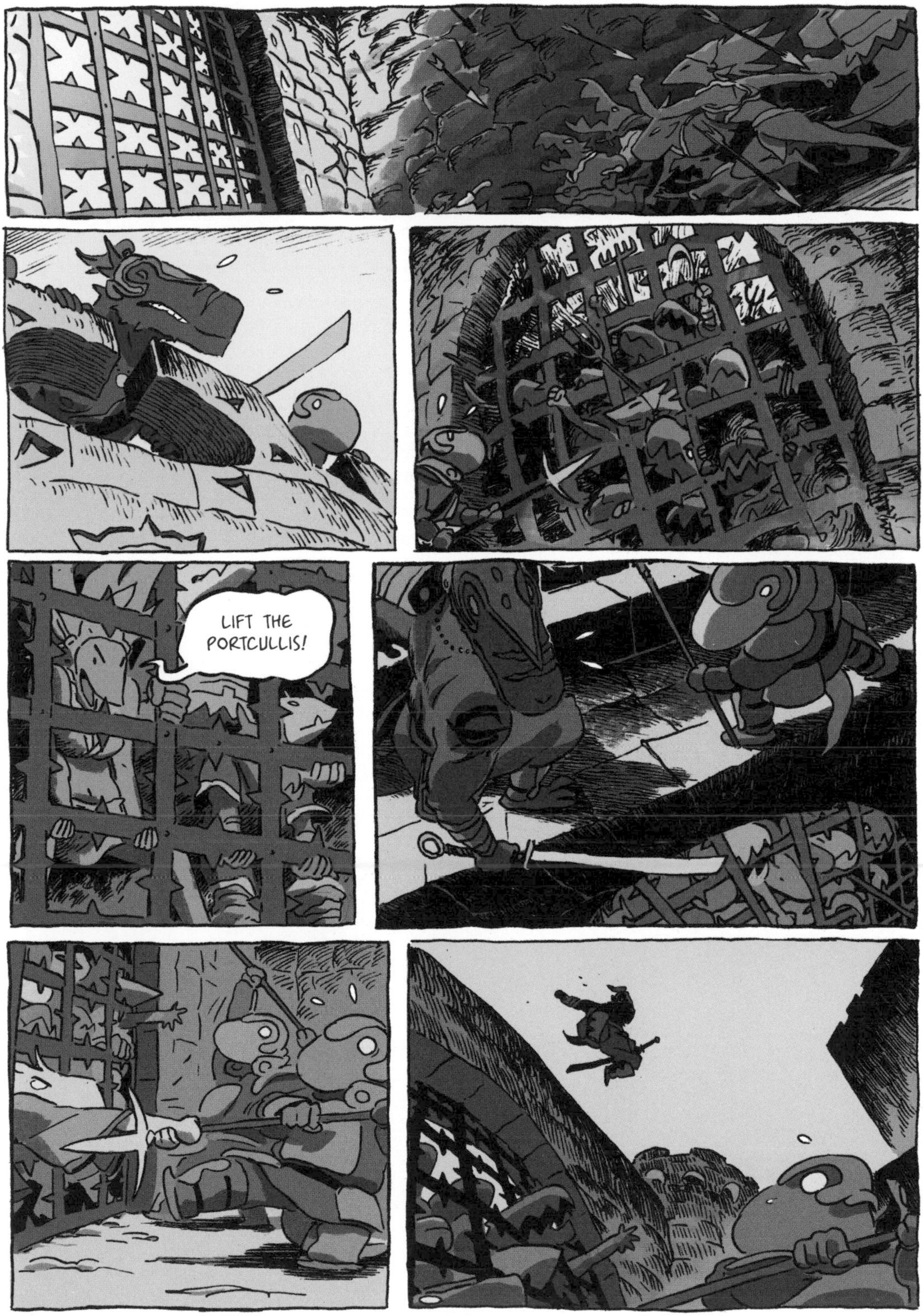
LIFT THE PORTCULLIS!

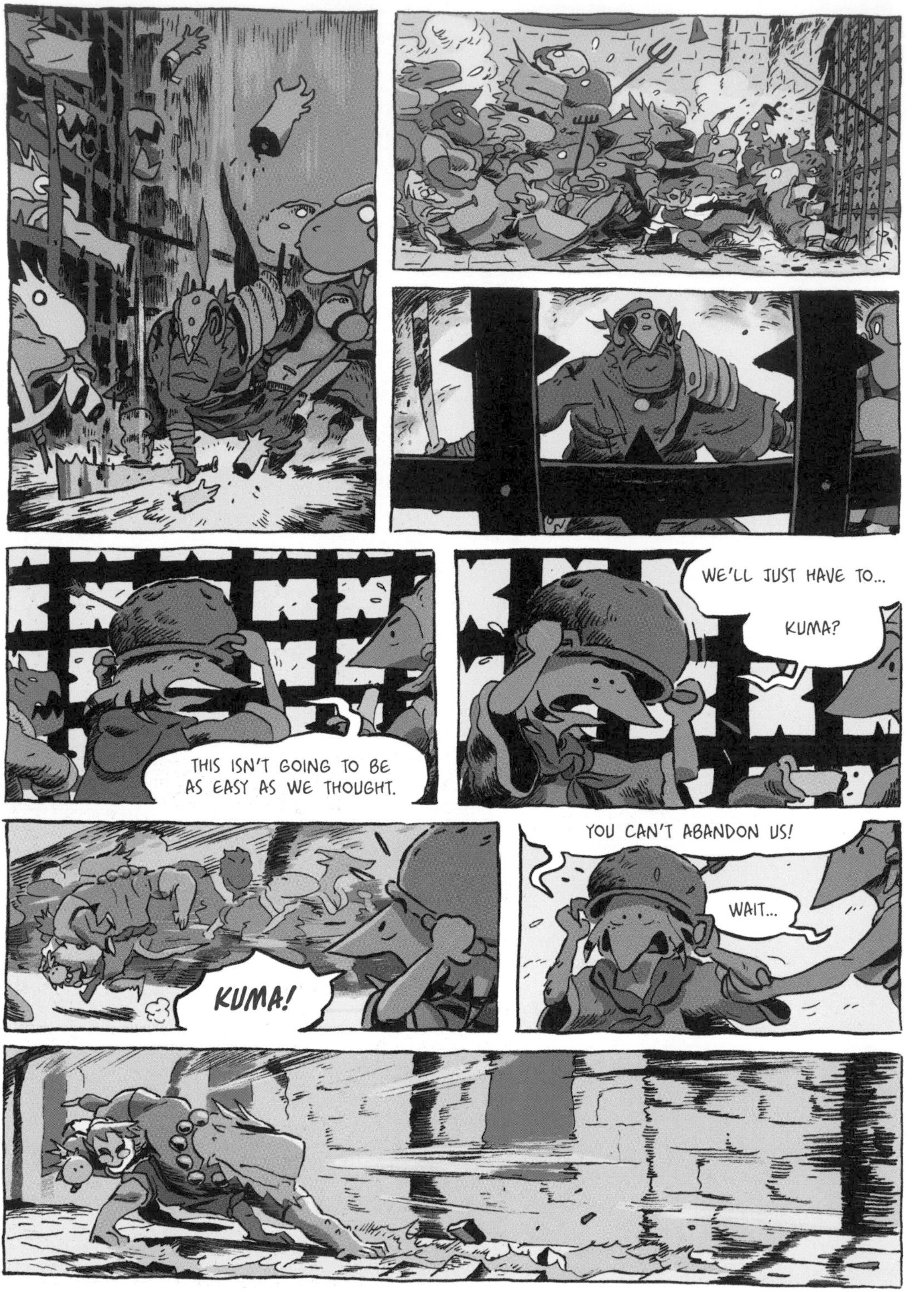
THIS ISN'T GOING TO BE AS EASY AS WE THOUGHT.
WE'LL JUST HAVE TO...
KUMA?
KUMA!
YOU CAN'T ABANDON US!
WAIT...

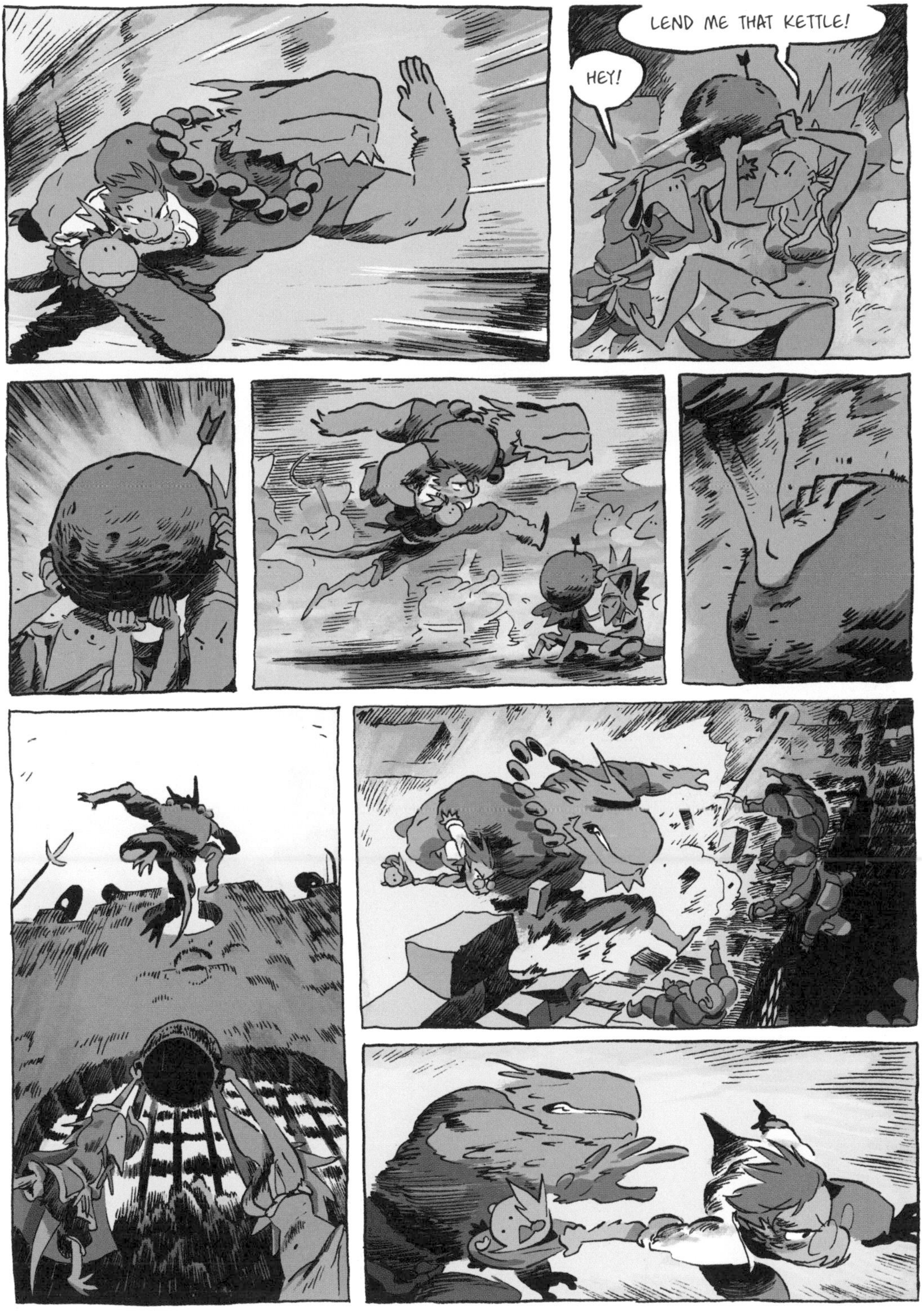
LEND ME THAT KETTLE!
HEY!

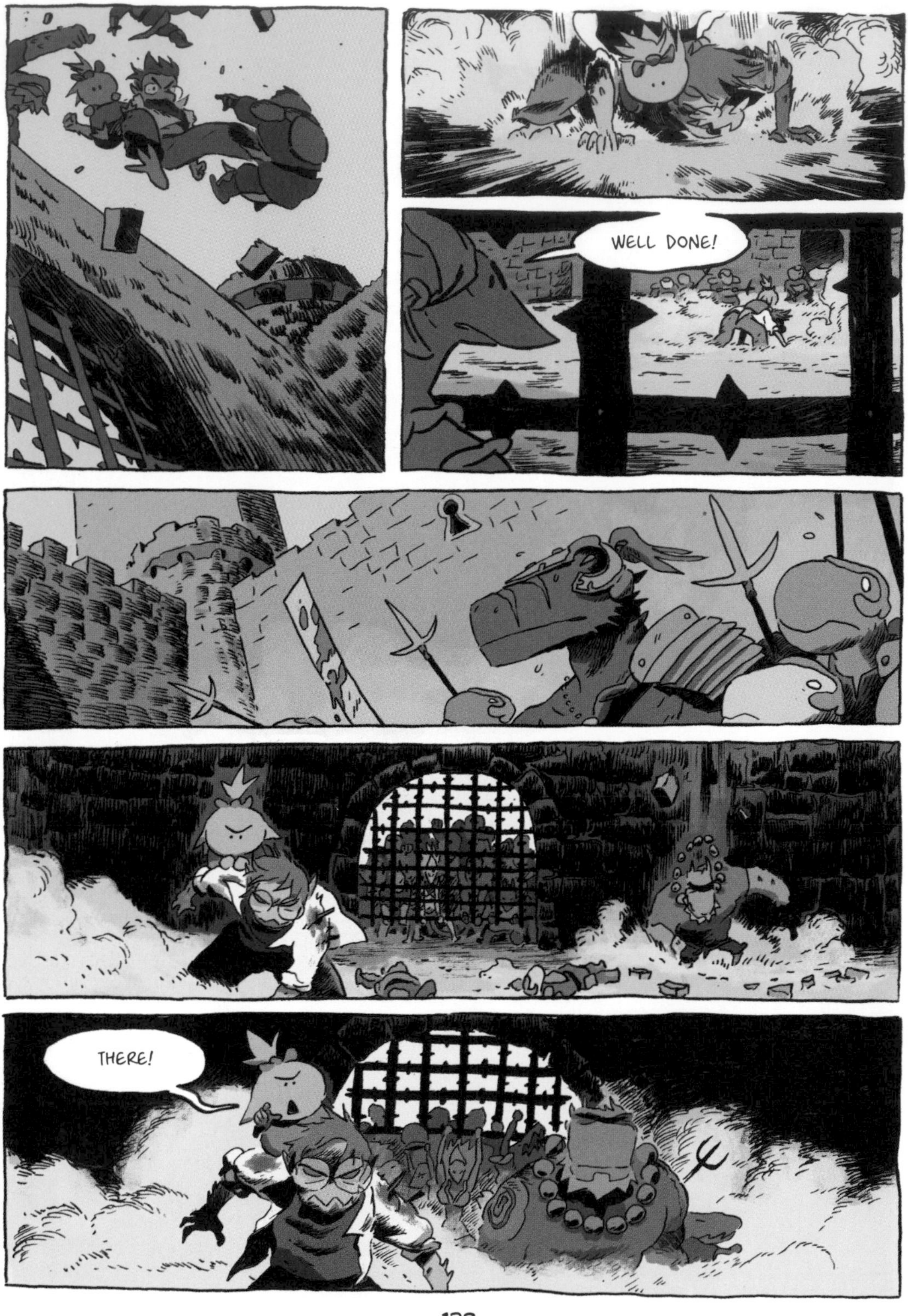
WELL DONE!
THERE!

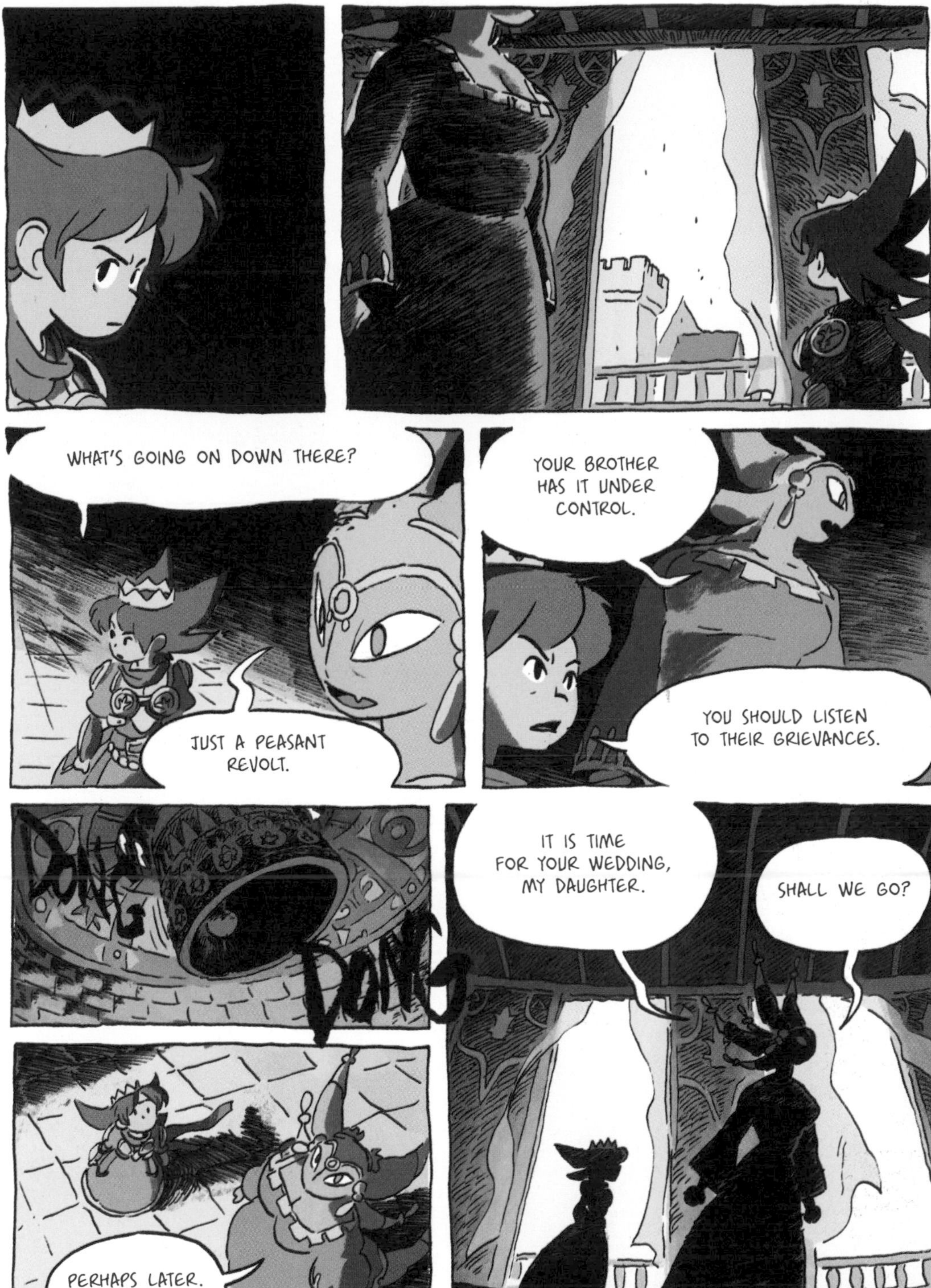
WHAT'S GOING ON DOWN THERE?
JUST A PEASANT REVOLT.
YOUR BROTHER HAS IT UNDER CONTROL.
YOU SHOULD LISTEN TO THEIR GRIEVANCES.
PERHAPS LATER.
IT IS TIME FOR YOUR WEDDING, MY DAUGHTER.
SHALL WE GO?

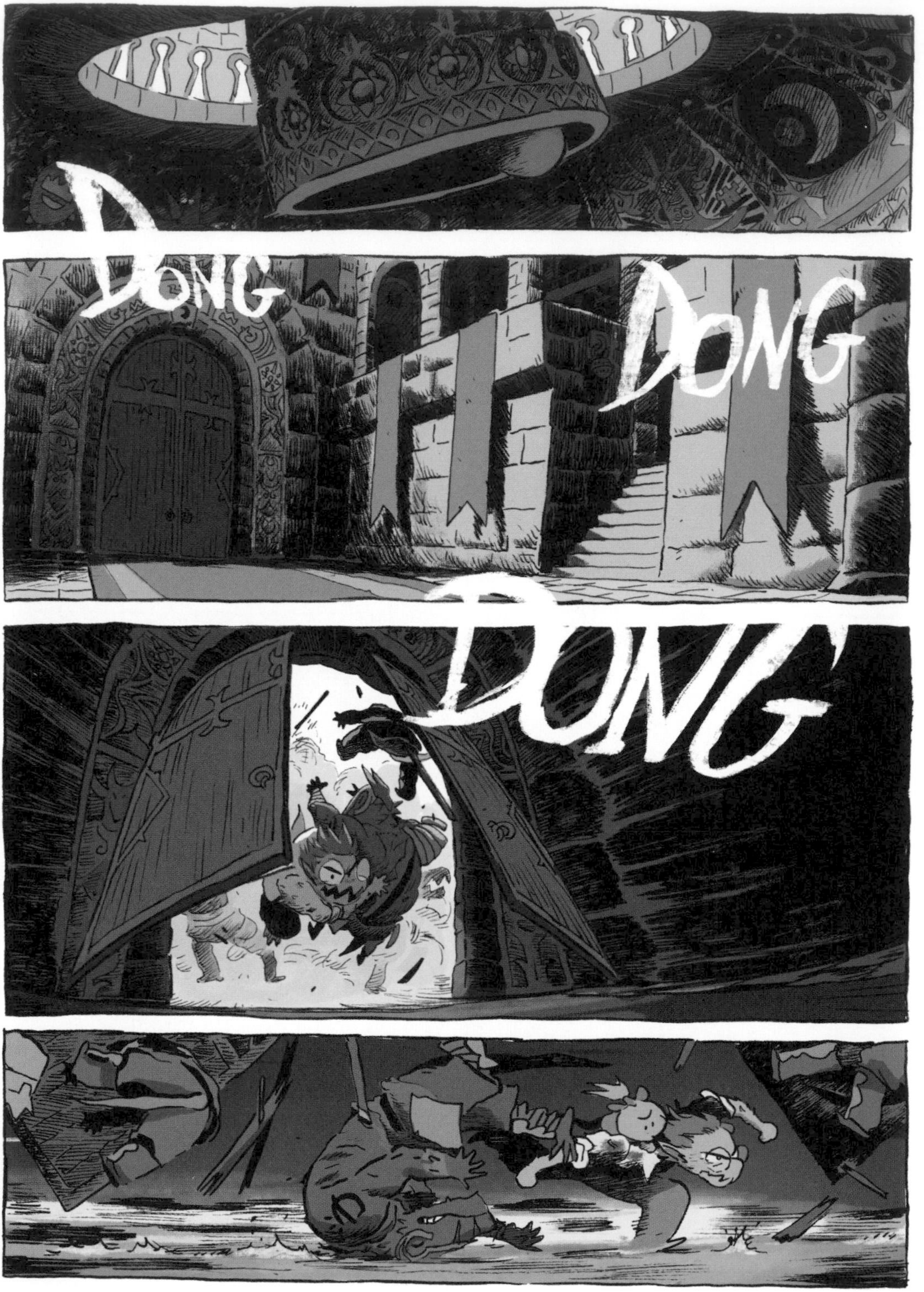
DONG
DONG
DONG

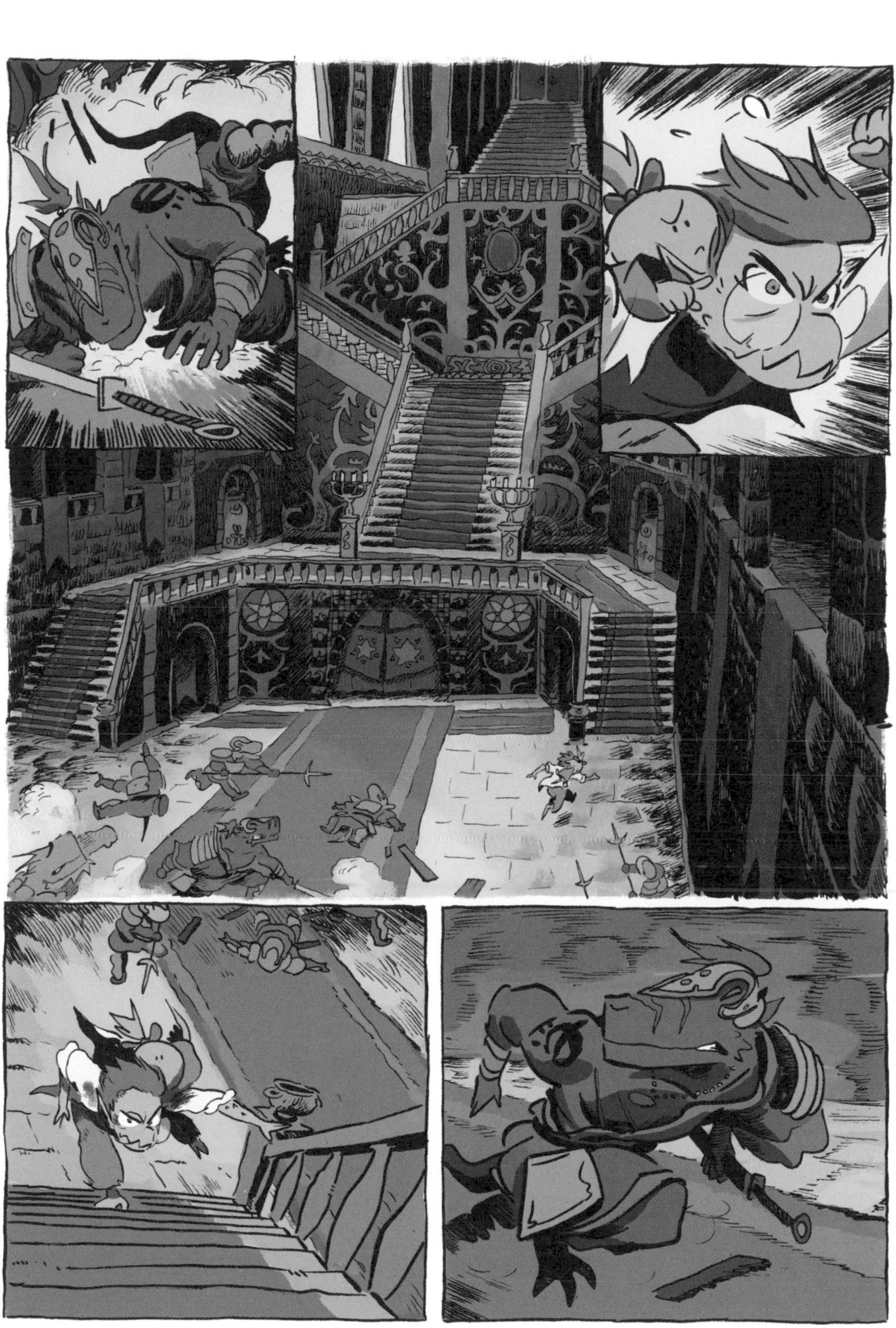

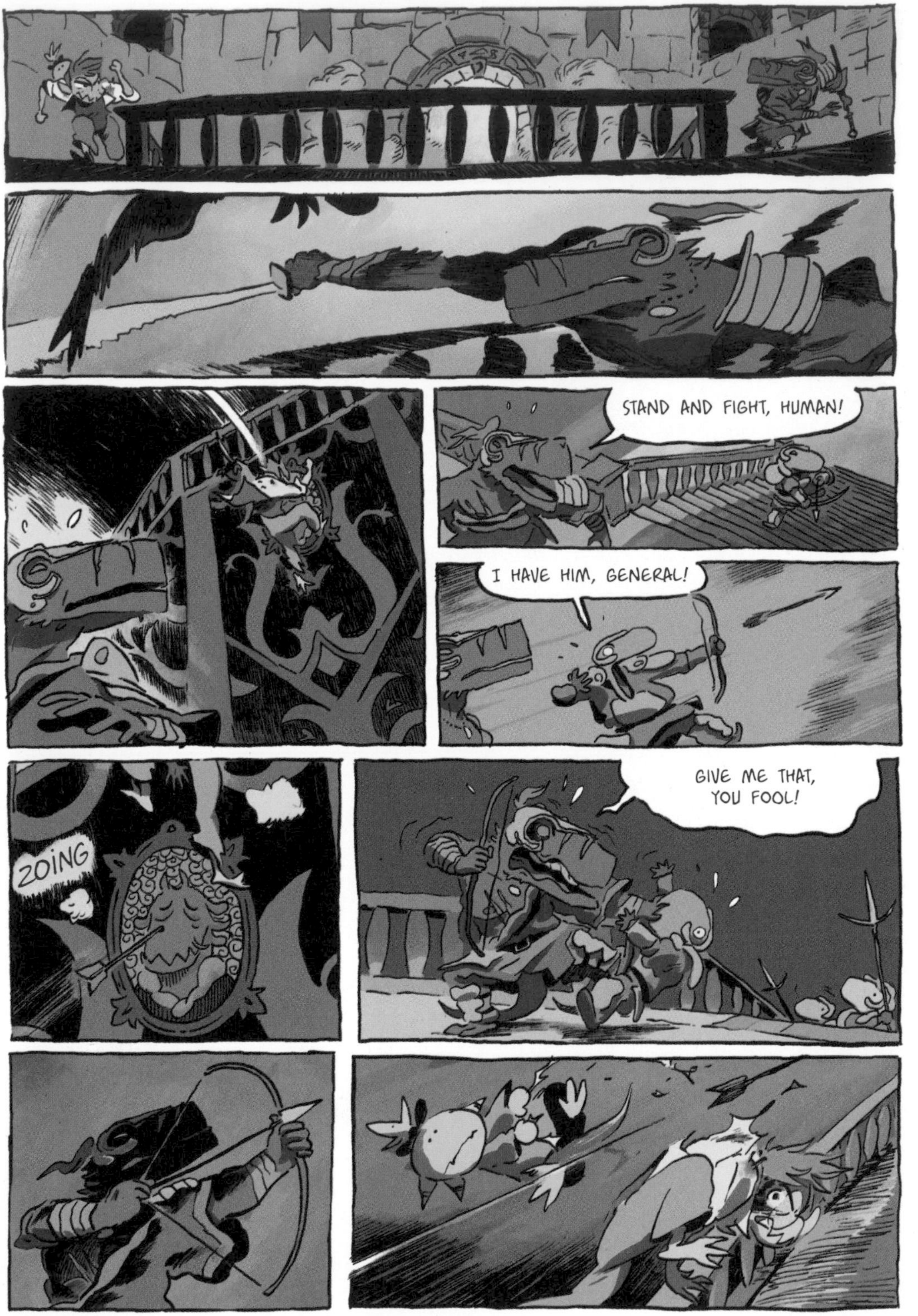
STAND AND FIGHT, HUMAN!
I HAVE HIM, GENERAL!
ZOING
GIVE ME THAT, YOU FOOL!

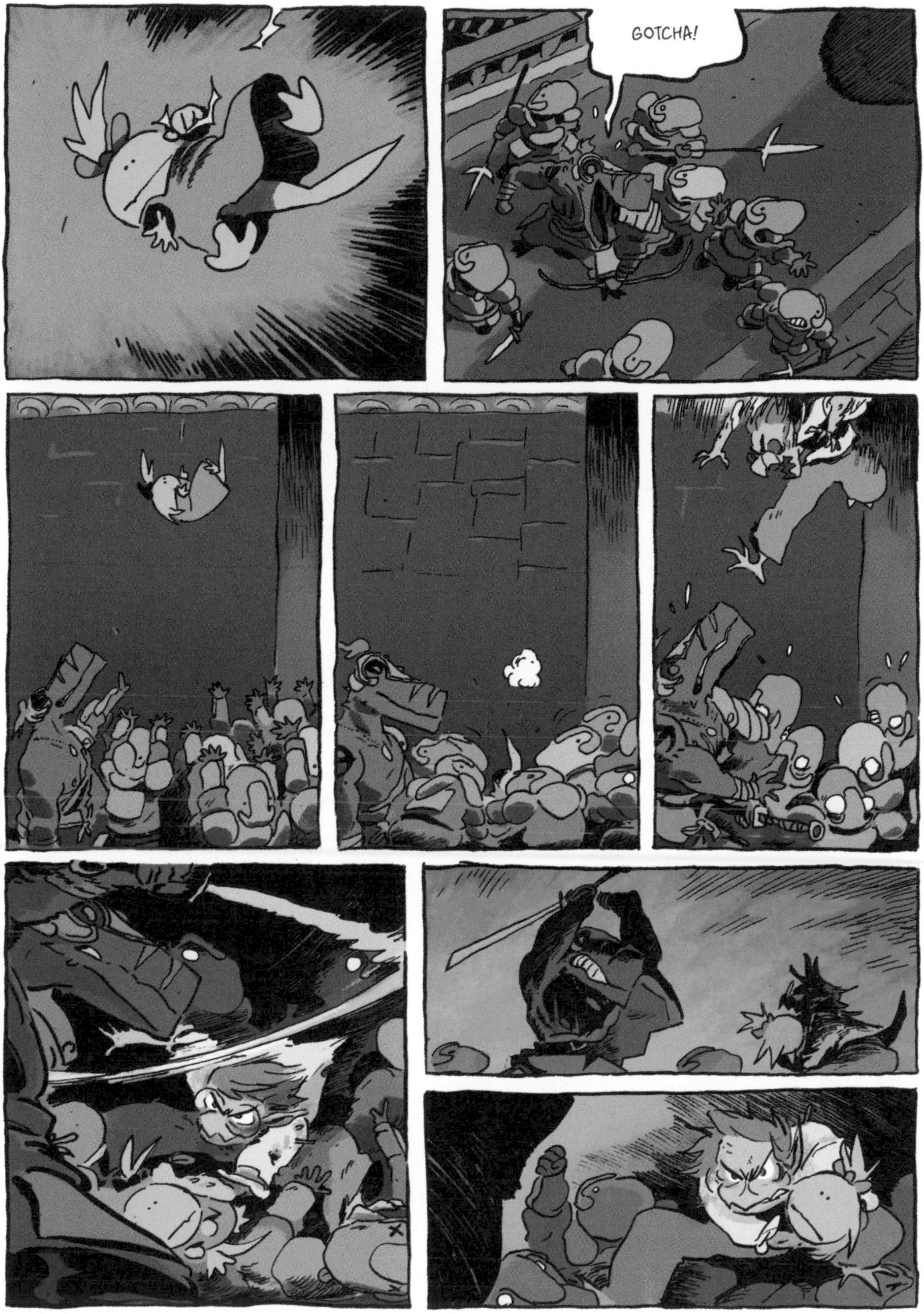
GOTCHA!

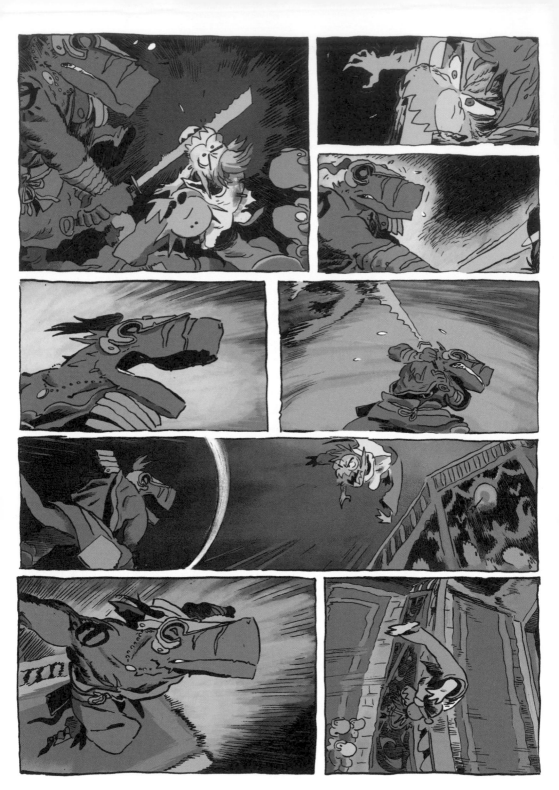

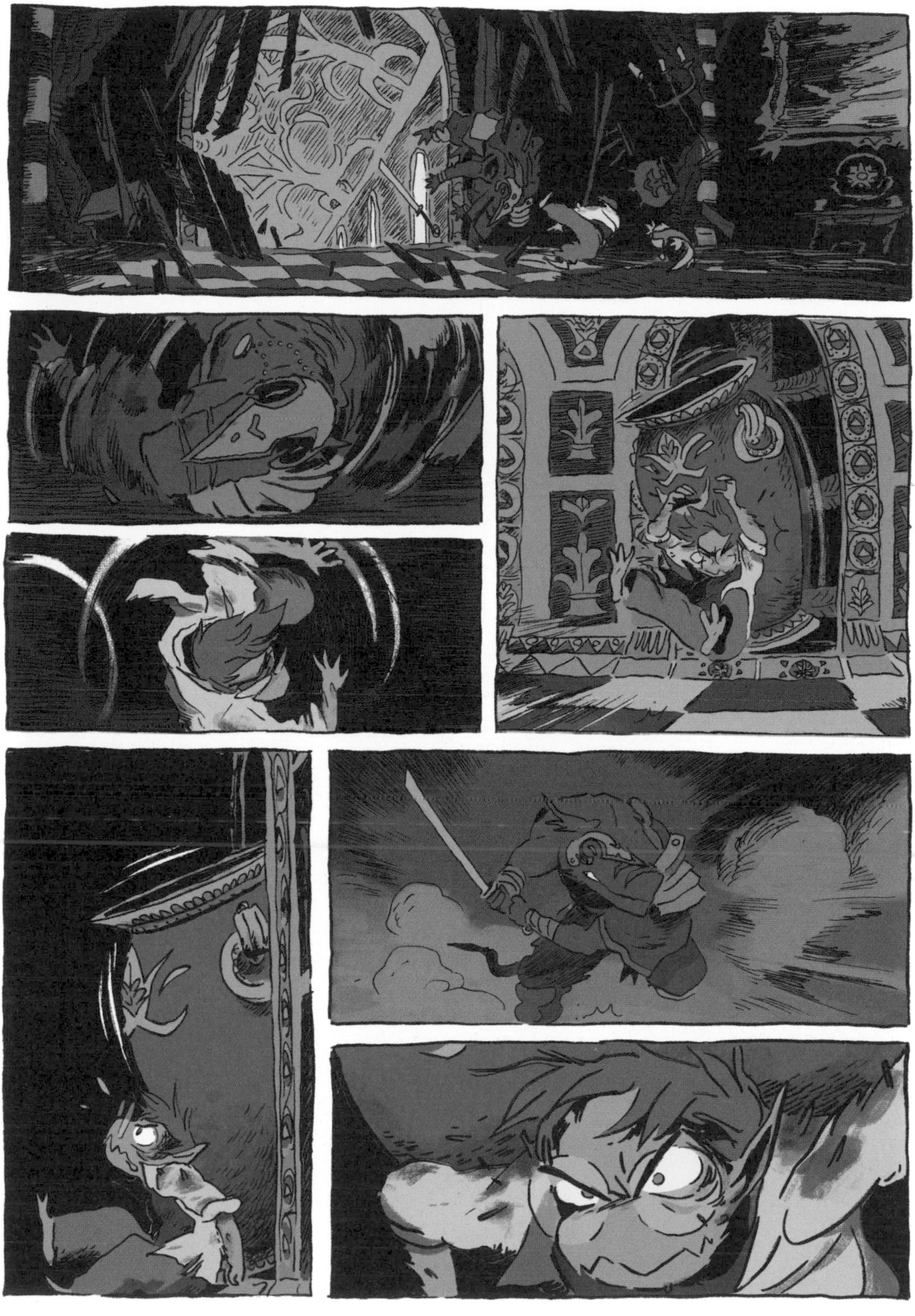

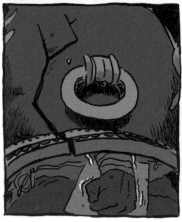

RHAAAAAAAAA

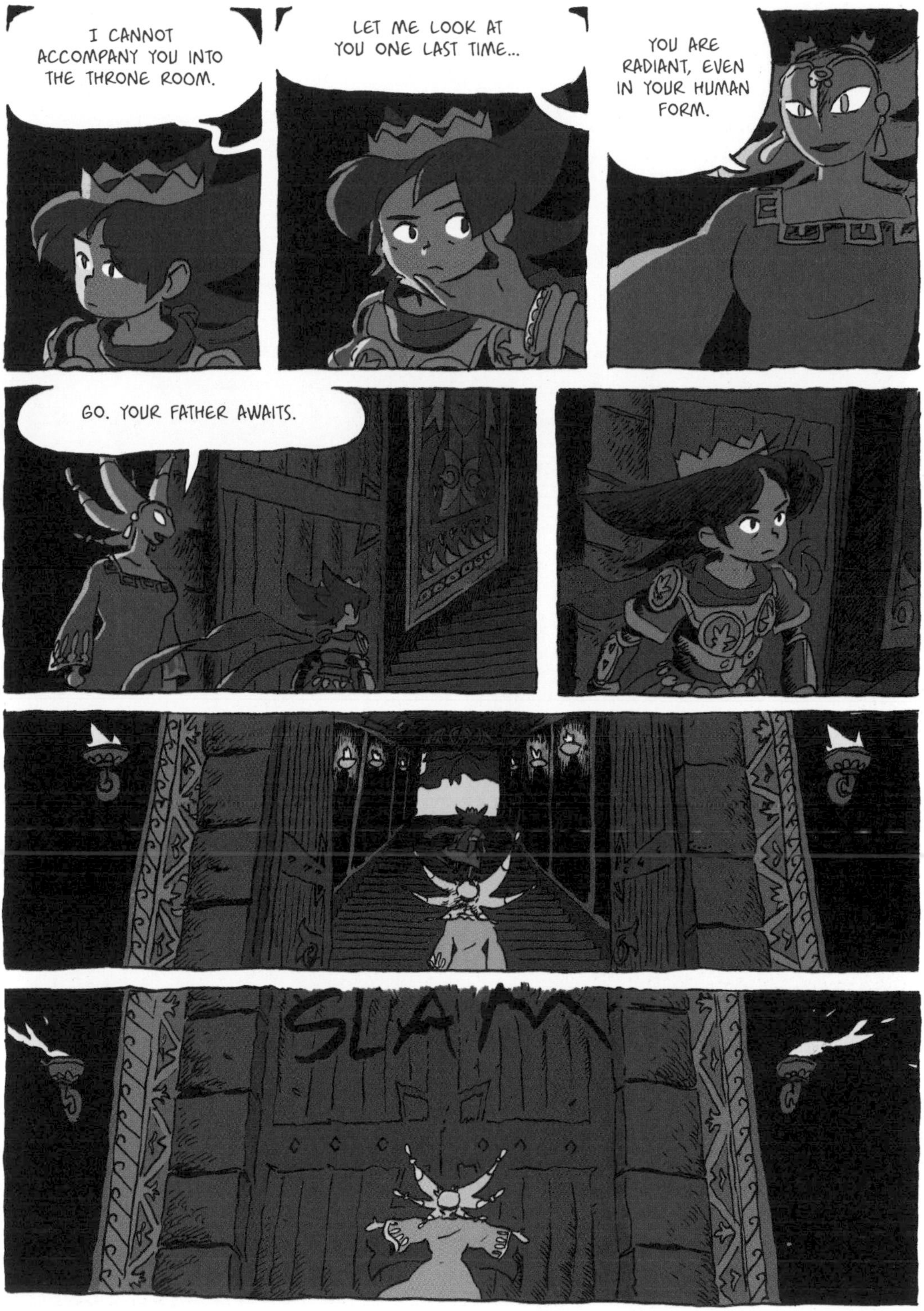
I CANNOT ACCOMPANY YOU INTO THE THRONE ROOM.
LET ME LOOK AT YOU ONE LAST TIME...
YOU ARE RADIANT, EVEN IN YOUR HUMAN FORM.
GO. YOUR FATHER AWAITS.
SLAM

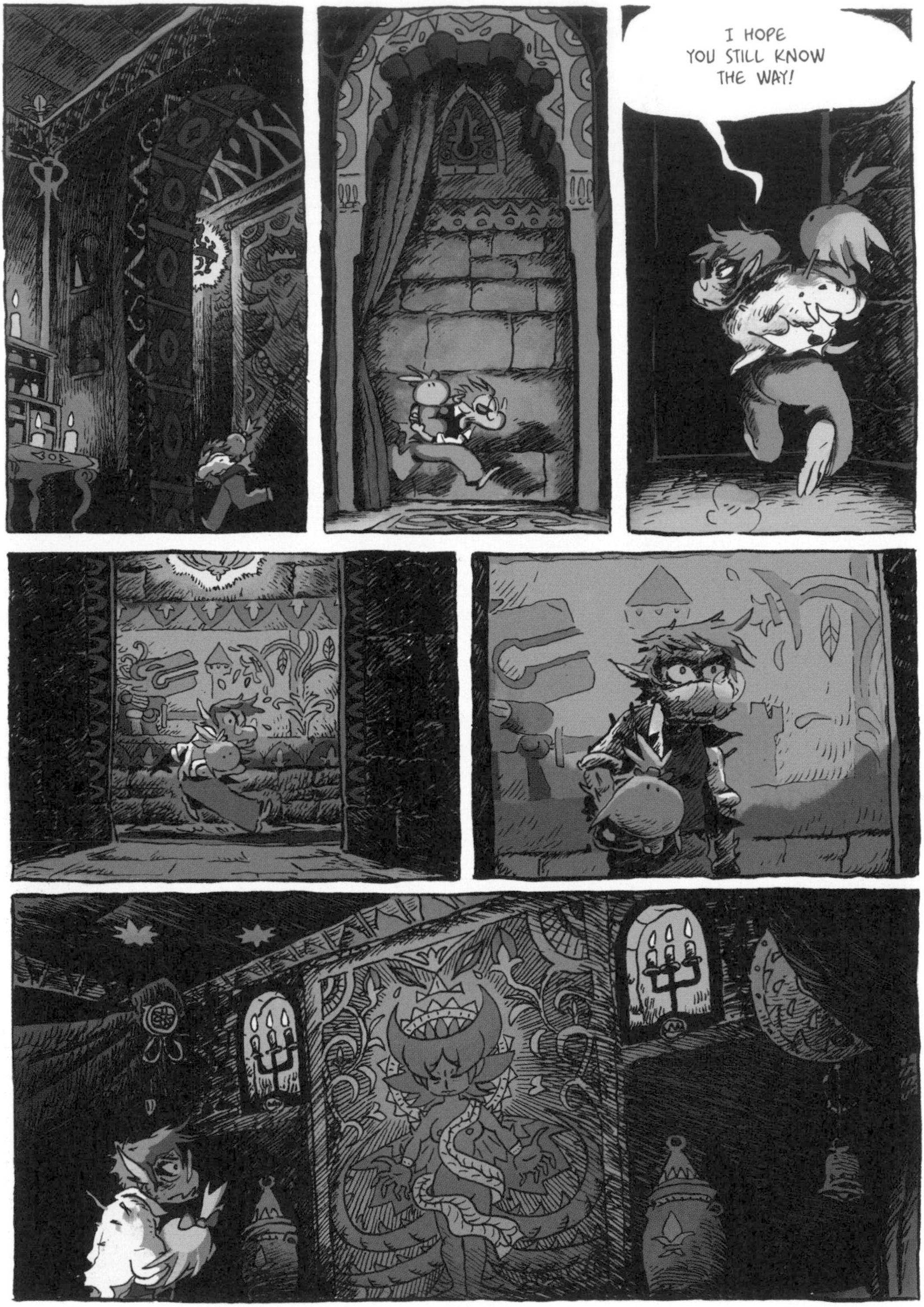
I HOPE YOU STILL KNOW THE WAY!

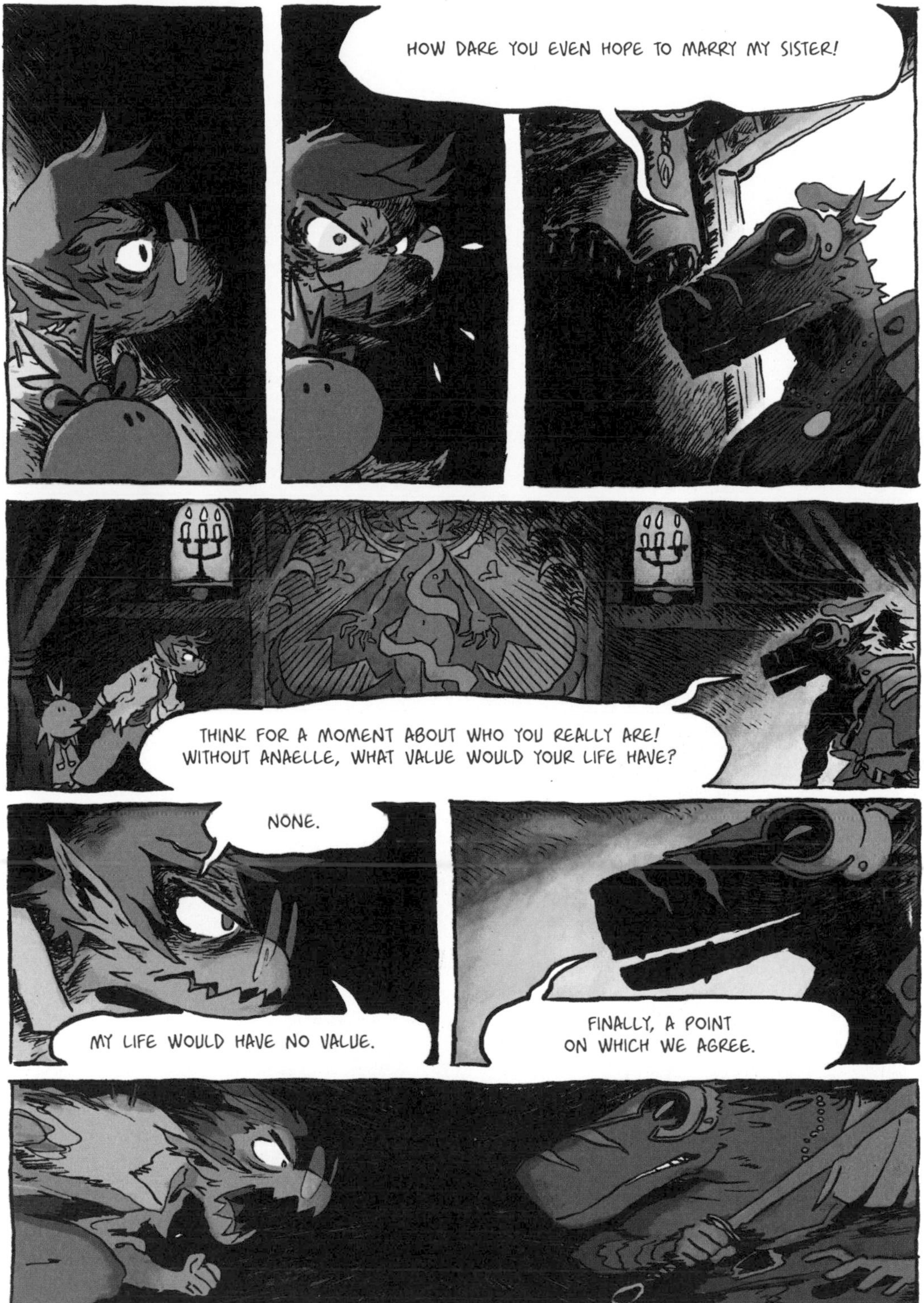
HOW DARE YOU EVEN HOPE TO MARRY MY SISTER!
THINK FOR A MOMENT ABOUT WHO YOU REALLY ARE! WITHOUT ANAELLE, WHAT VALUE WOULD YOUR LIFE HAVE?
NONE.
MY LIFE WOULD HAVE NO VALUE.
FINALLY, A POINT ON WHICH WE AGREE.

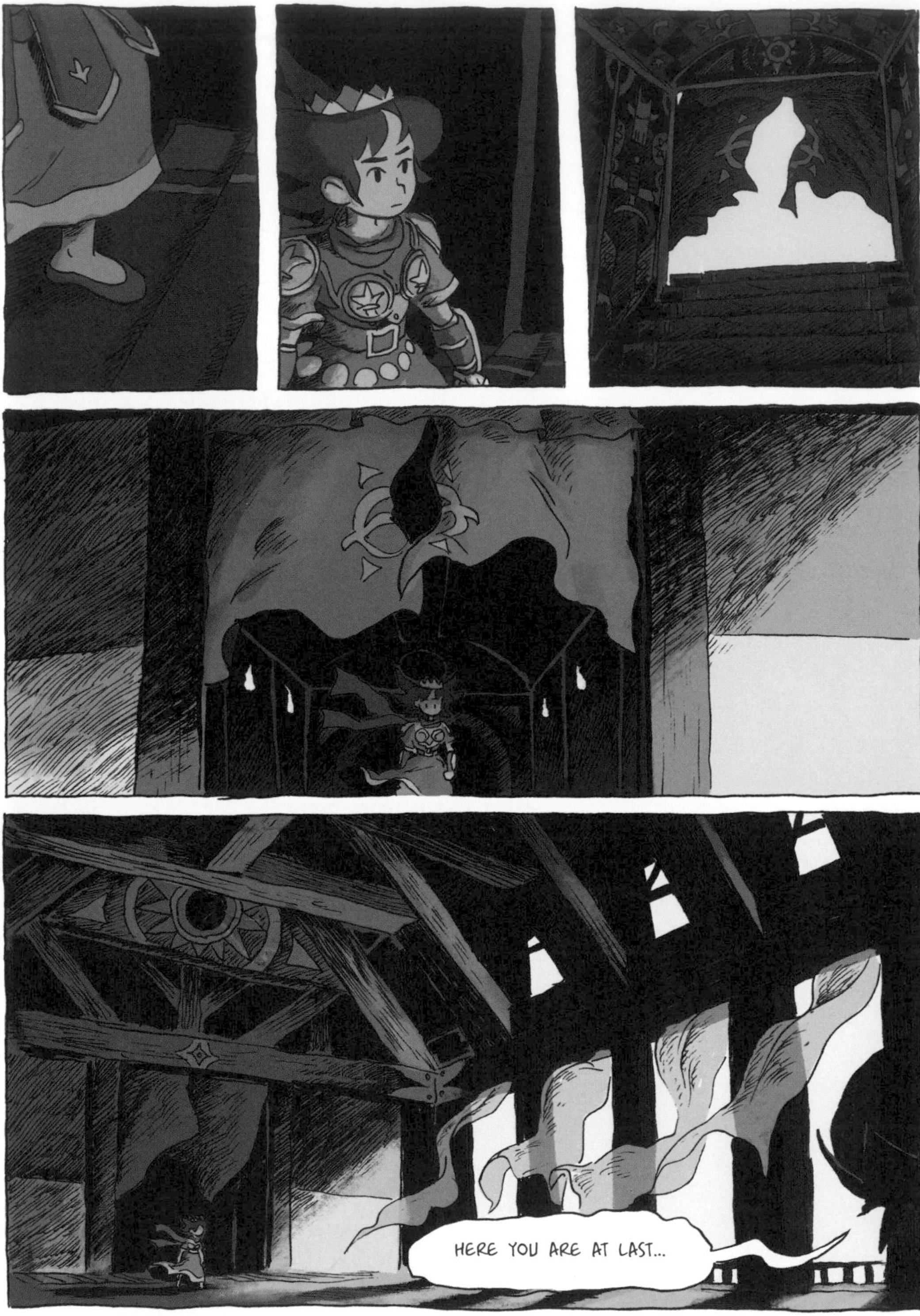
HERE YOU ARE AT LAST...

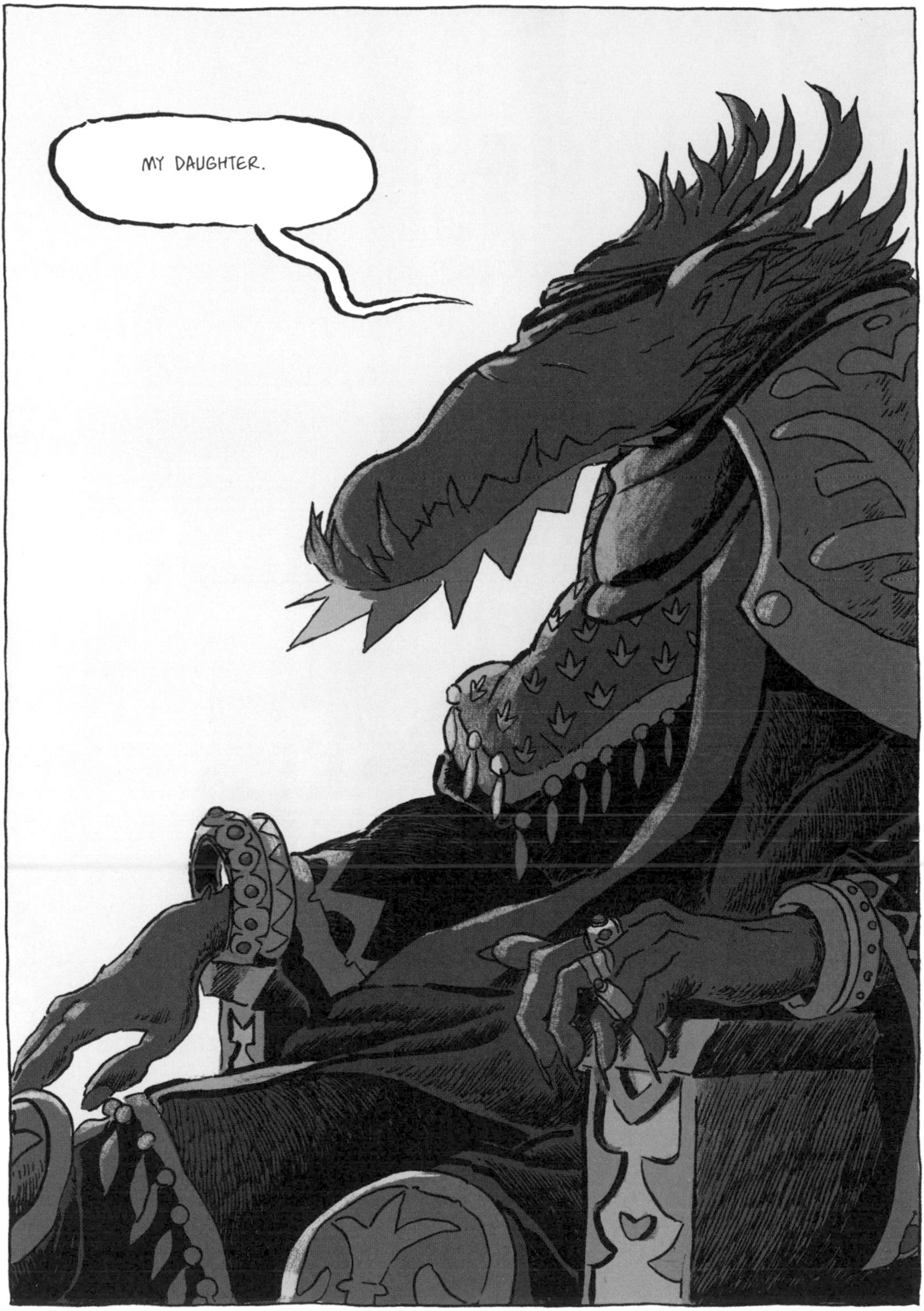
MY DAUGHTER.

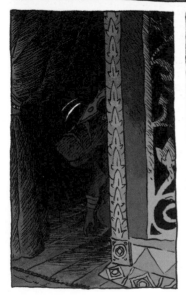

I TRUST YOU
ARE THE BEARER OF
GOOD NEWS.

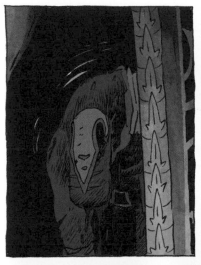

SO, YOU PLAN TO TAKE MY CHILDREN FROM ME ONE BY ONE!

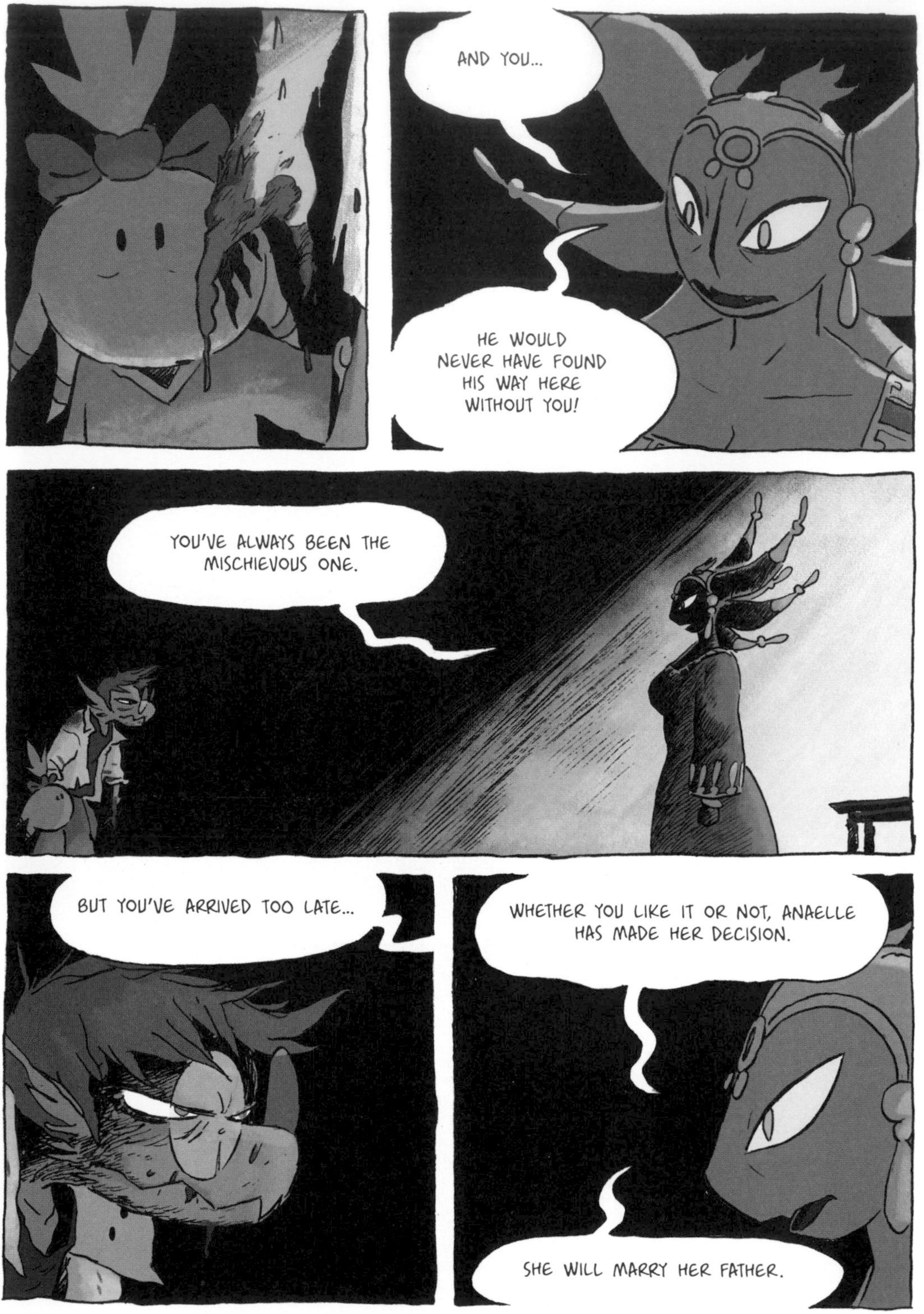
AND YOU...
HE WOULD NEVER HAVE FOUND HIS WAY HERE WITHOUT YOU!
YOU'VE ALWAYS BEEN THE MISCHIEVOUS ONE.
BUT YOU'VE ARRIVED TOO LATE...
WHETHER YOU LIKE IT OR NOT, ANAELLE HAS MADE HER DECISION.
SHE WILL MARRY HER FATHER.

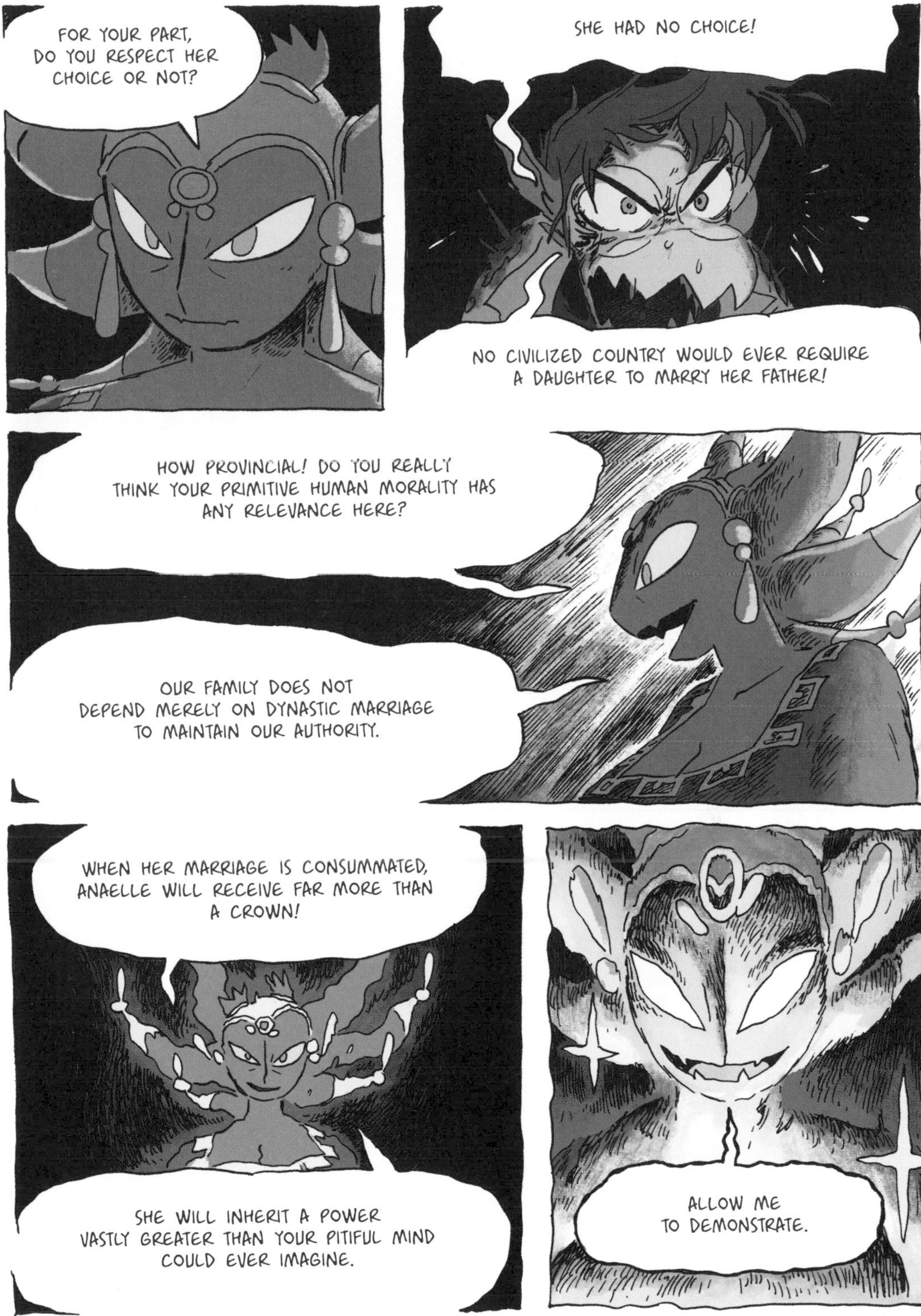
FOR YOUR PART, DO YOU RESPECT HER CHOICE OR NOT?
SHE HAD NO CHOICE!
NO CIVILIZED COUNTRY WOULD EVER REQUIRE A DAUGHTER TO MARRY HER FATHER!
HOW PROVINCIAL! DO YOU REALLY THINK YOUR PRIMITIVE HUMAN MORALITY HAS ANY RELEVANCE HERE?
OUR FAMILY DOES NOT DEPEND MERELY ON DYNASTIC MARRIAGE TO MAINTAIN OUR AUTHORITY.
WHEN HER MARRIAGE IS CONSUMMATED, ANAELLE WILL RECEIVE FAR MORE THAN A CROWN!
SHE WILL INHERIT A POWER VASTLY GREATER THAN YOUR PITIFUL MIND COULD EVER IMAGINE.
ALLOW ME TO DEMONSTRATE.

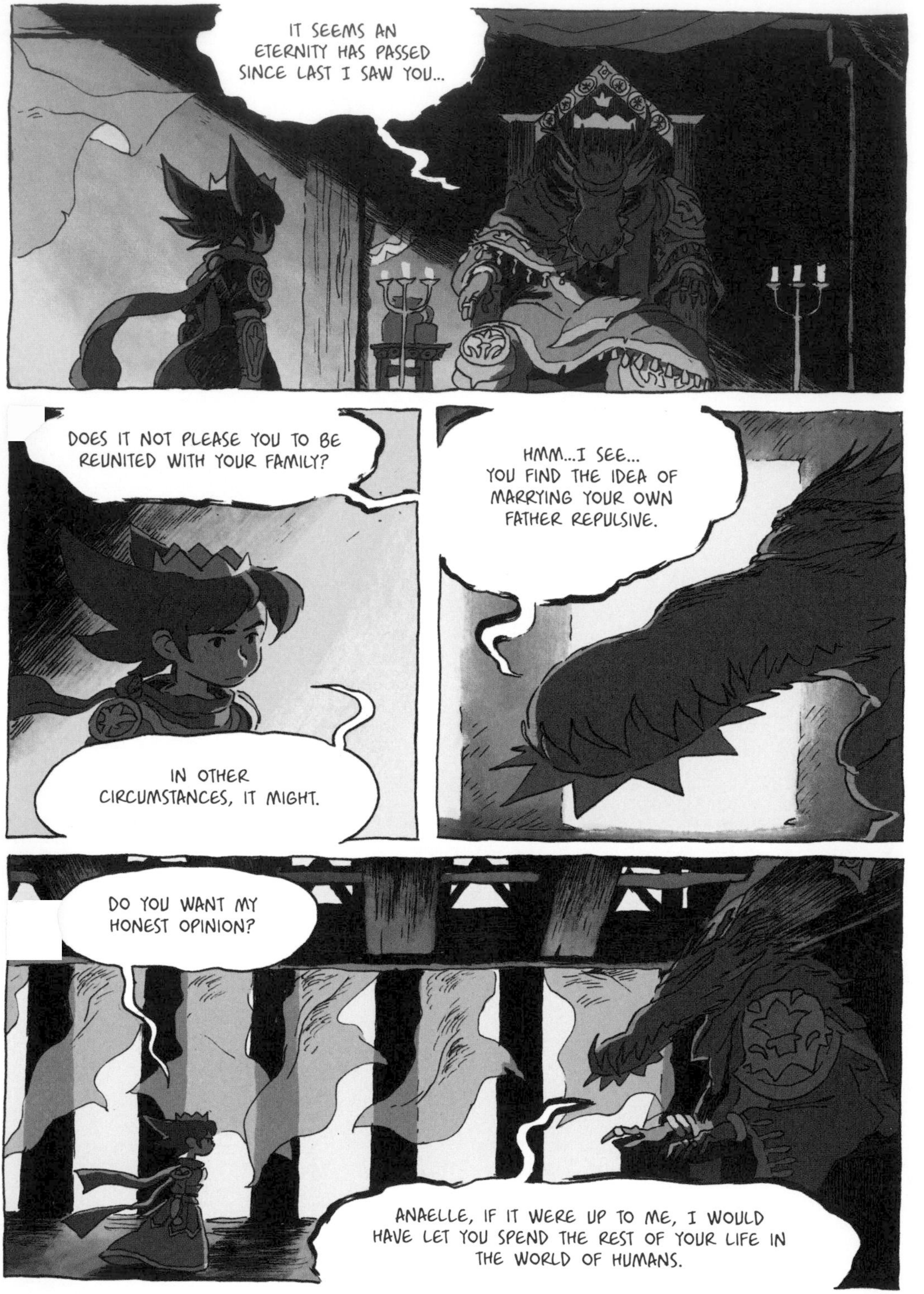
IT SEEMS AN ETERNITY HAS PASSED SINCE LAST I SAW YOU...
DOES IT NOT PLEASE YOU TO BE REUNITED WITH YOUR FAMILY?
IN OTHER CIRCUMSTANCES, IT MIGHT.
HMM...I SEE... YOU FIND THE IDEA OF MARRYING YOUR OWN FATHER REPULSIVE.
DO YOU WANT MY HONEST OPINION?
ANAELLE, IF IT WERE UP TO ME, I WOULD HAVE LET YOU SPEND THE REST OF YOUR LIFE IN THE WORLD OF HUMANS.

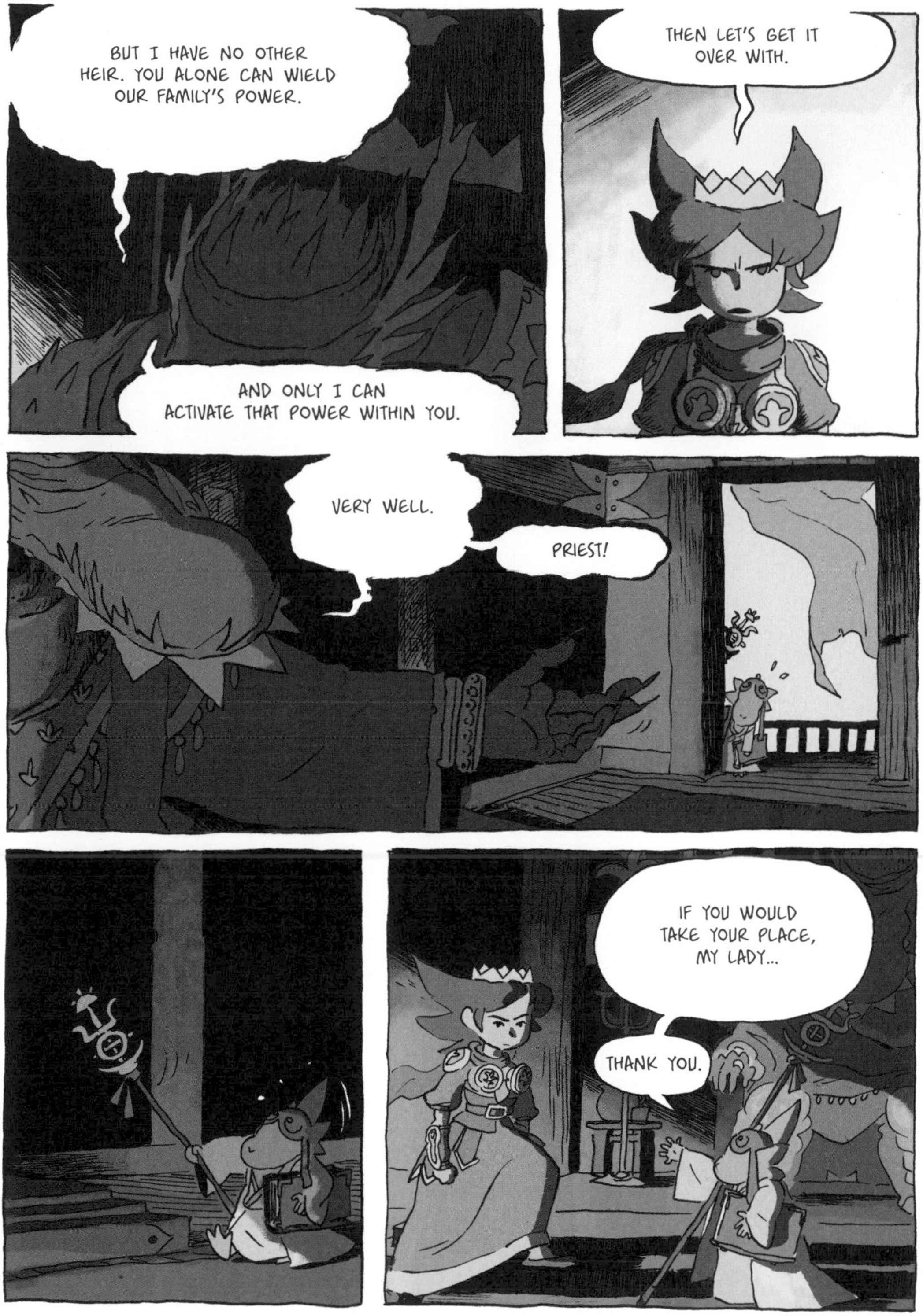
BUT I HAVE NO OTHER HEIR. YOU ALONE CAN WIELD OUR FAMILY'S POWER.
AND ONLY I CAN ACTIVATE THAT POWER WITHIN YOU.
THEN LET'S GET IT OVER WITH.
VERY WELL.
PRIEST!
IF YOU WOULD TAKE YOUR PLACE, MY LADY...
THANK YOU.

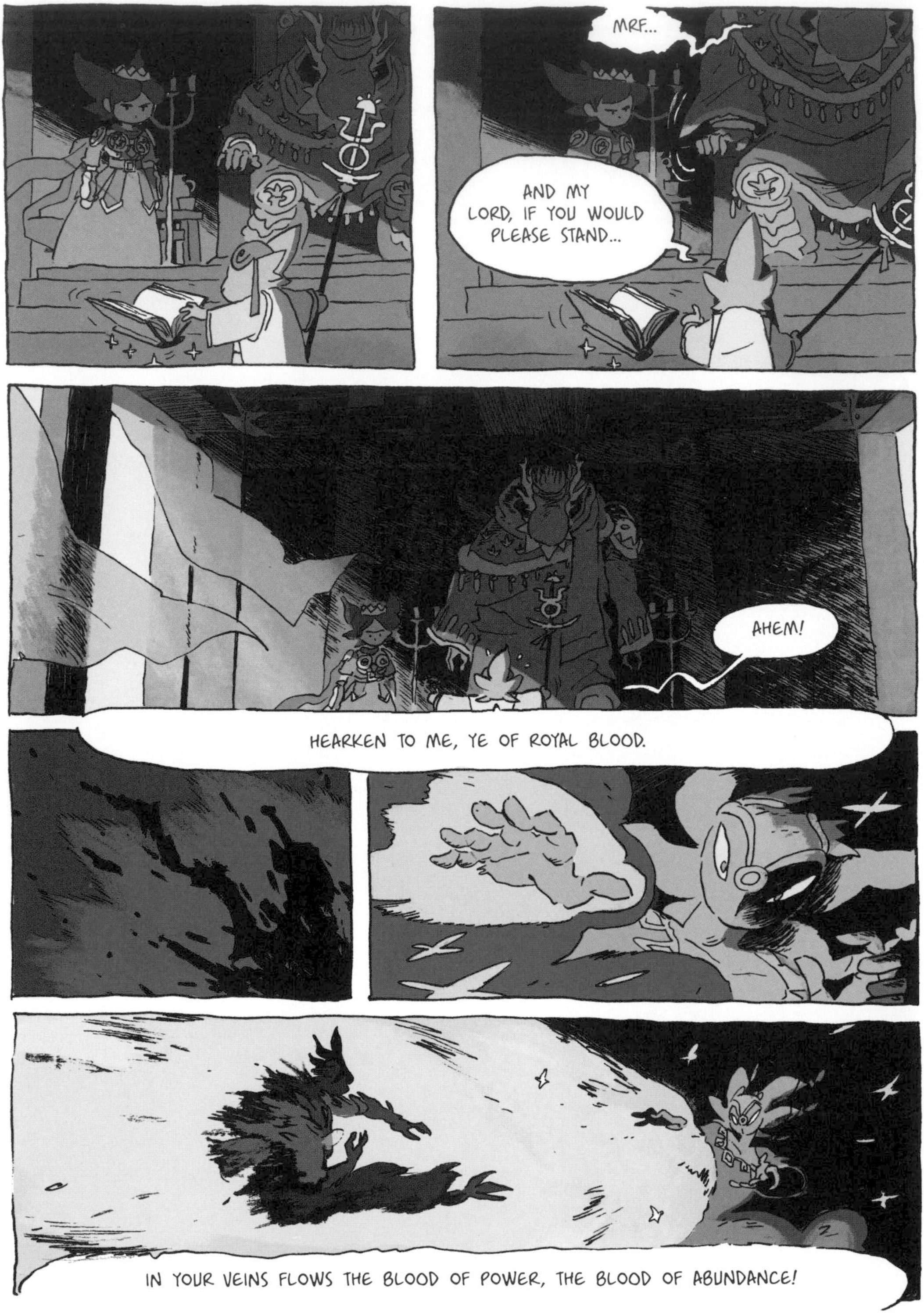

MRF...
AND MY LORD, IF YOU WOULD PLEASE STAND...
AHEM!
HEARKEN TO ME, YE OF ROYAL BLOOD.
IN YOUR VEINS FLOWS THE BLOOD OF POWER, THE BLOOD OF ABUNDANCE!

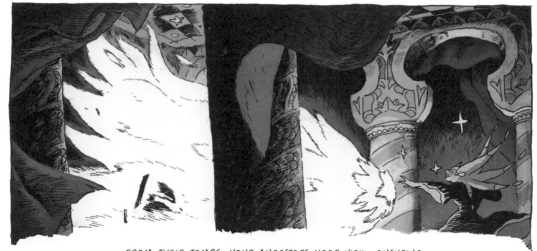

FROM THEIR TOMBS, YOUR ANCESTORS KEEP VIGIL, ENSURING THAT THEIR PRECIOUS GIFT ADVANCES UNIMPEDED AND UNDIMINISHED ALONG ITS ETERNAL COURSE.

YOU ARE KIN TO WARRIORS AND SORCERERS, SCHOLARS AND POTENTATES!

AND UPON YOU THEY BESTOW THEIR GREATEST BLESSING.

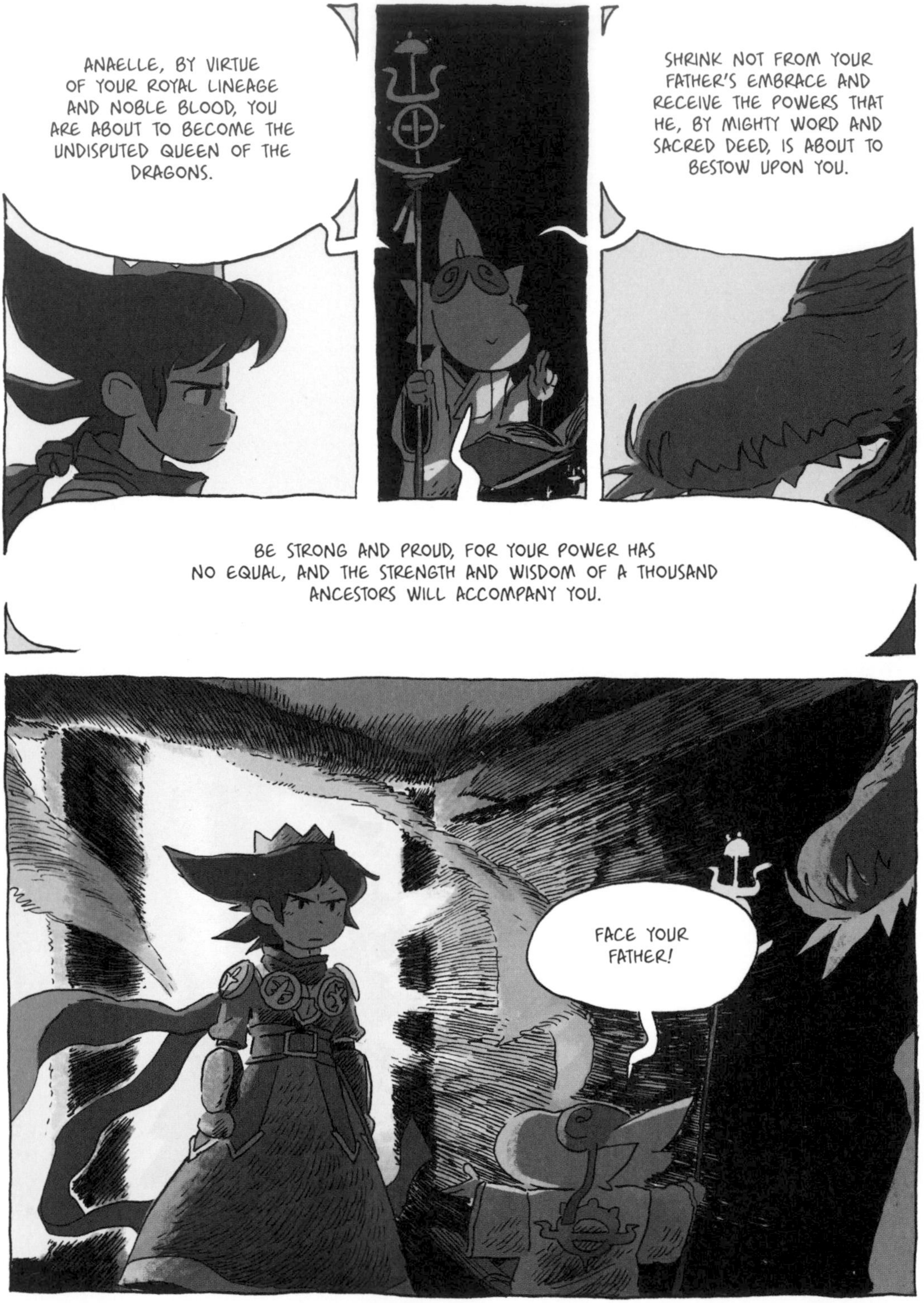
ANAELLE, BY VIRTUE OF YOUR ROYAL LINEAGE AND NOBLE BLOOD, YOU ARE ABOUT TO BECOME THE UNDISPUTED QUEEN OF THE DRAGONS.
SHRINK NOT FROM YOUR FATHER'S EMBRACE AND RECEIVE THE POWERS THAT HE, BY MIGHTY WORD AND SACRED DEED, IS ABOUT TO BESTOW UPON YOU.
BE STRONG AND PROUD, FOR YOUR POWER HAS NO EQUAL, AND THE STRENGTH AND WISDOM OF A THOUSAND ANCESTORS WILL ACCOMPANY YOU.
FACE YOUR FATHER!

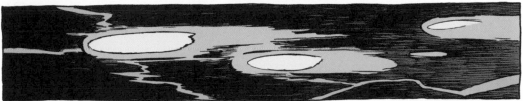

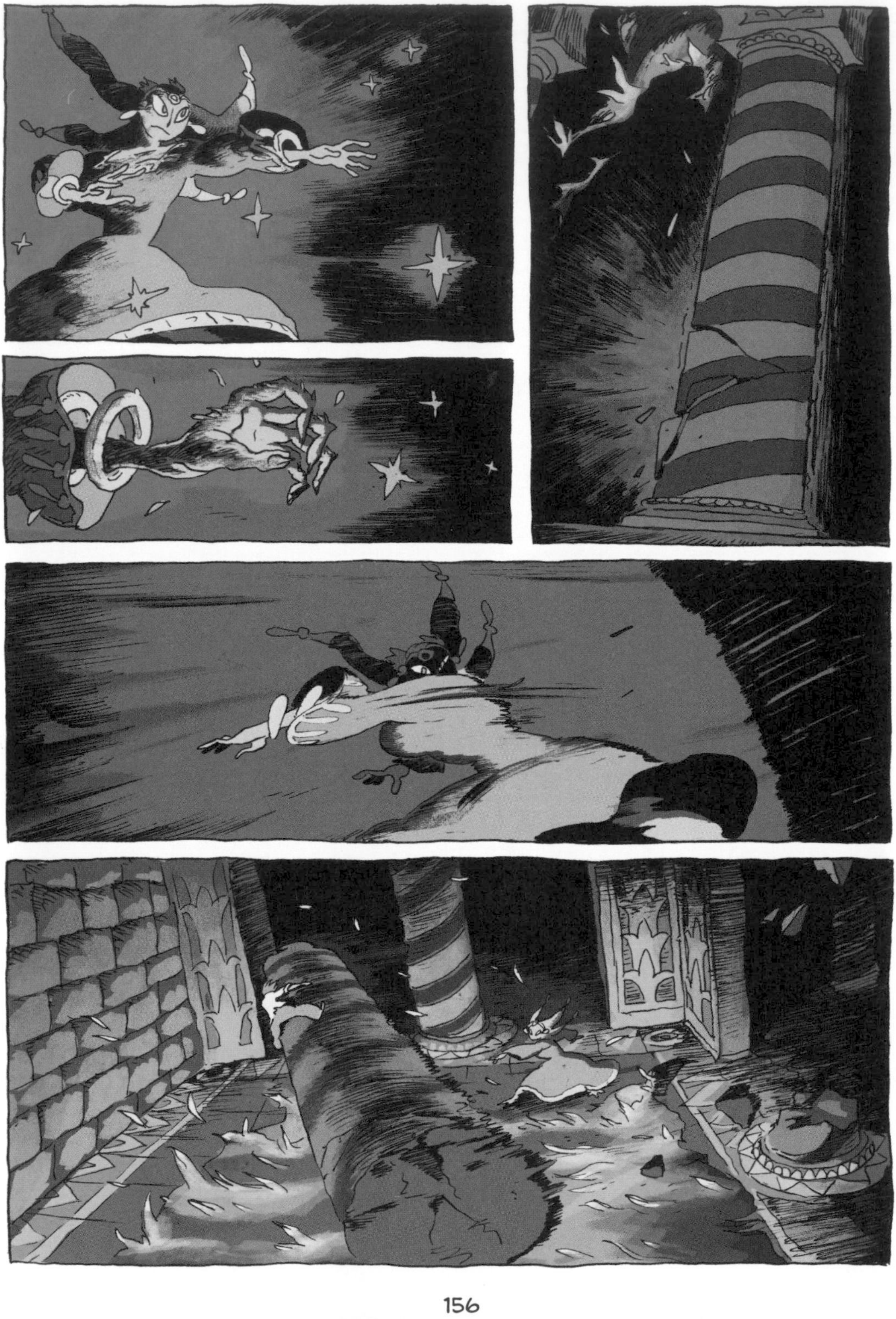

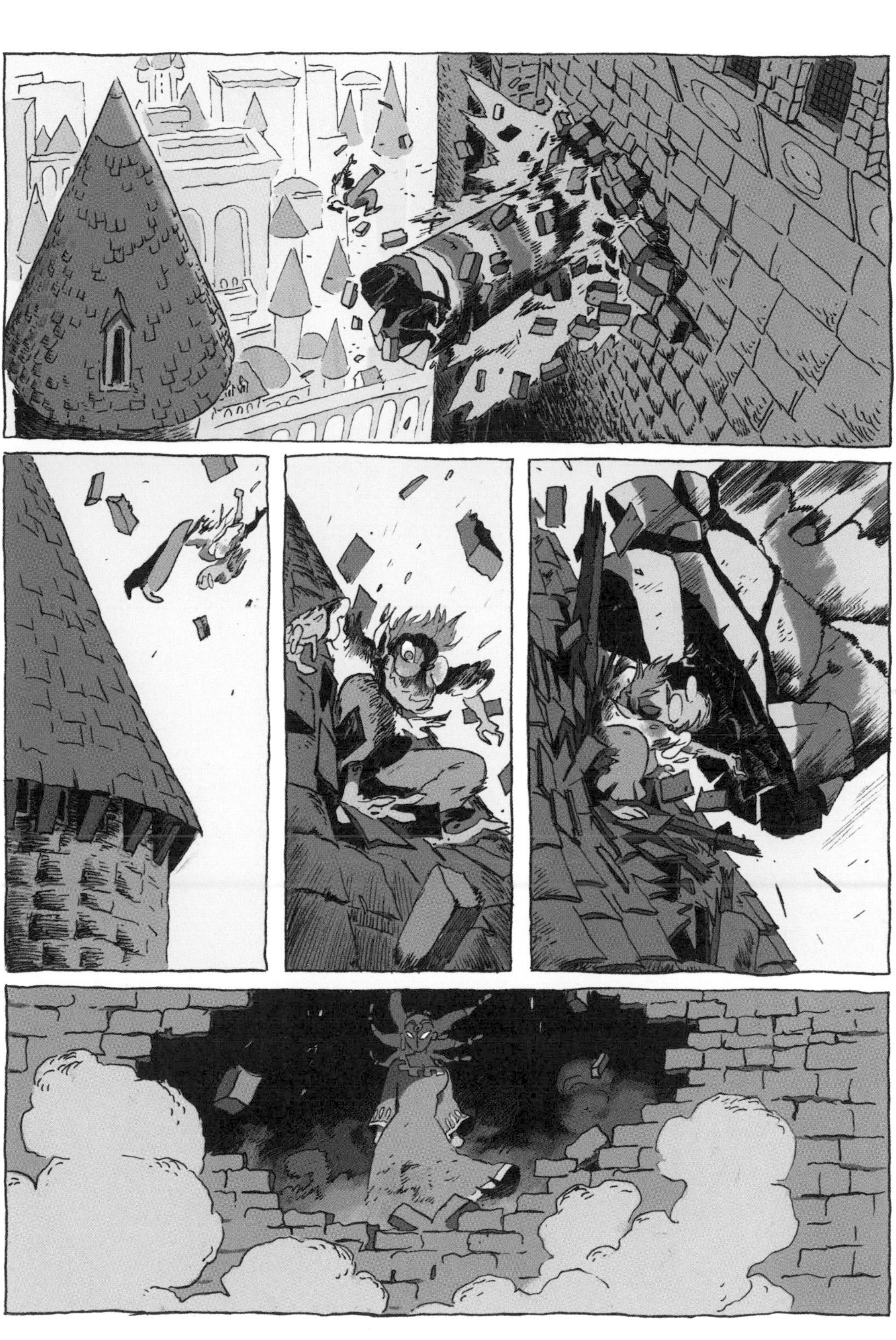

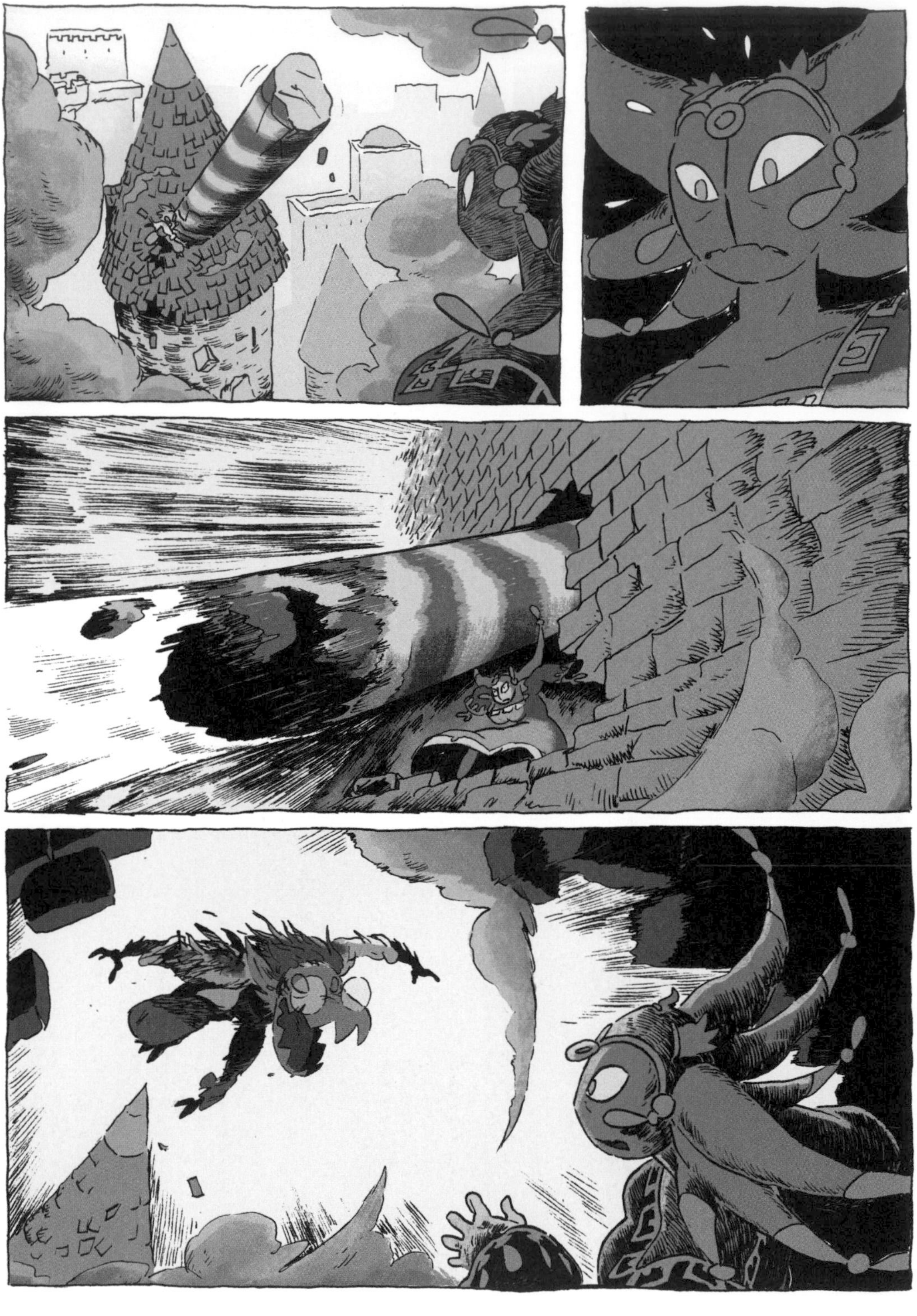

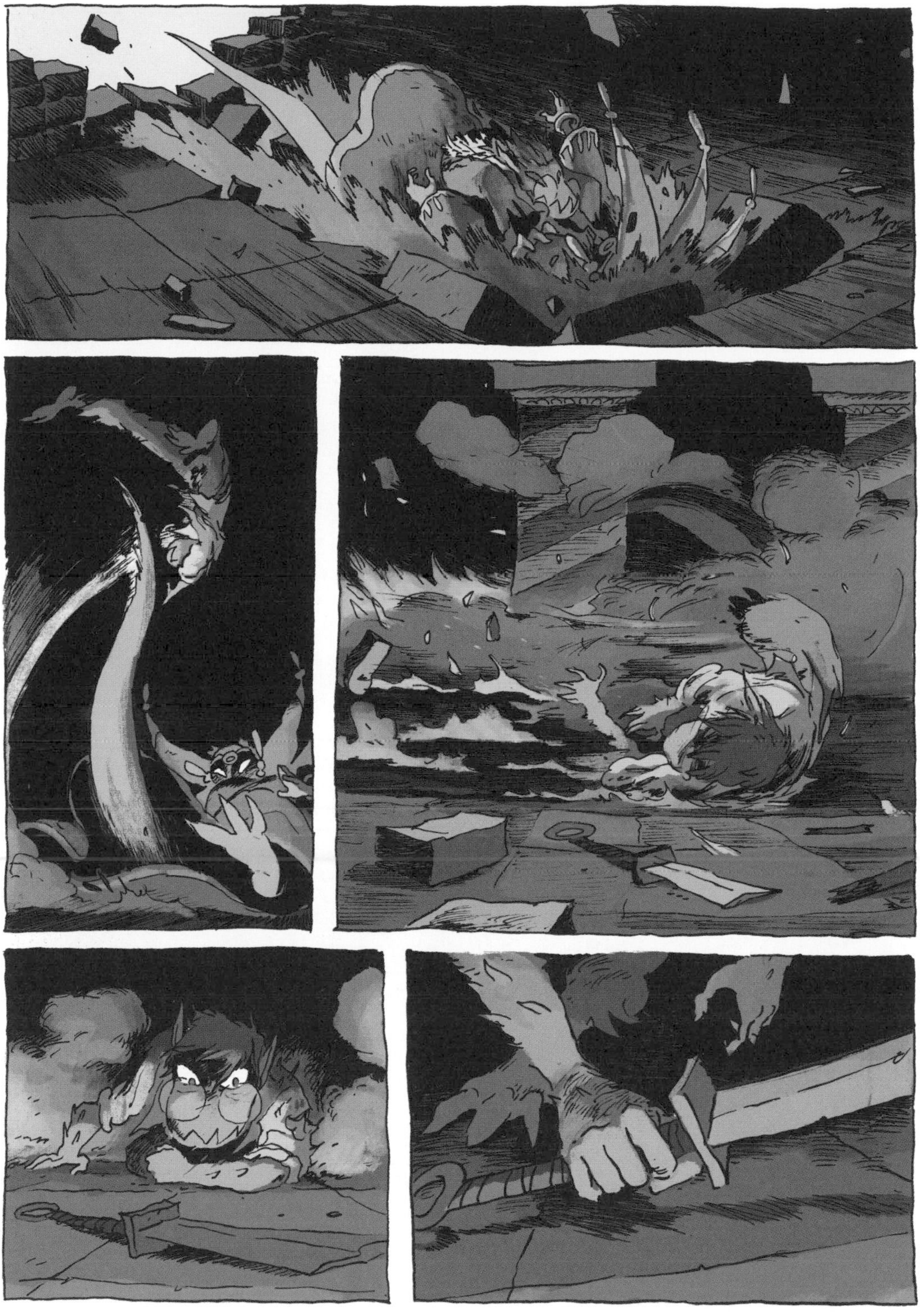

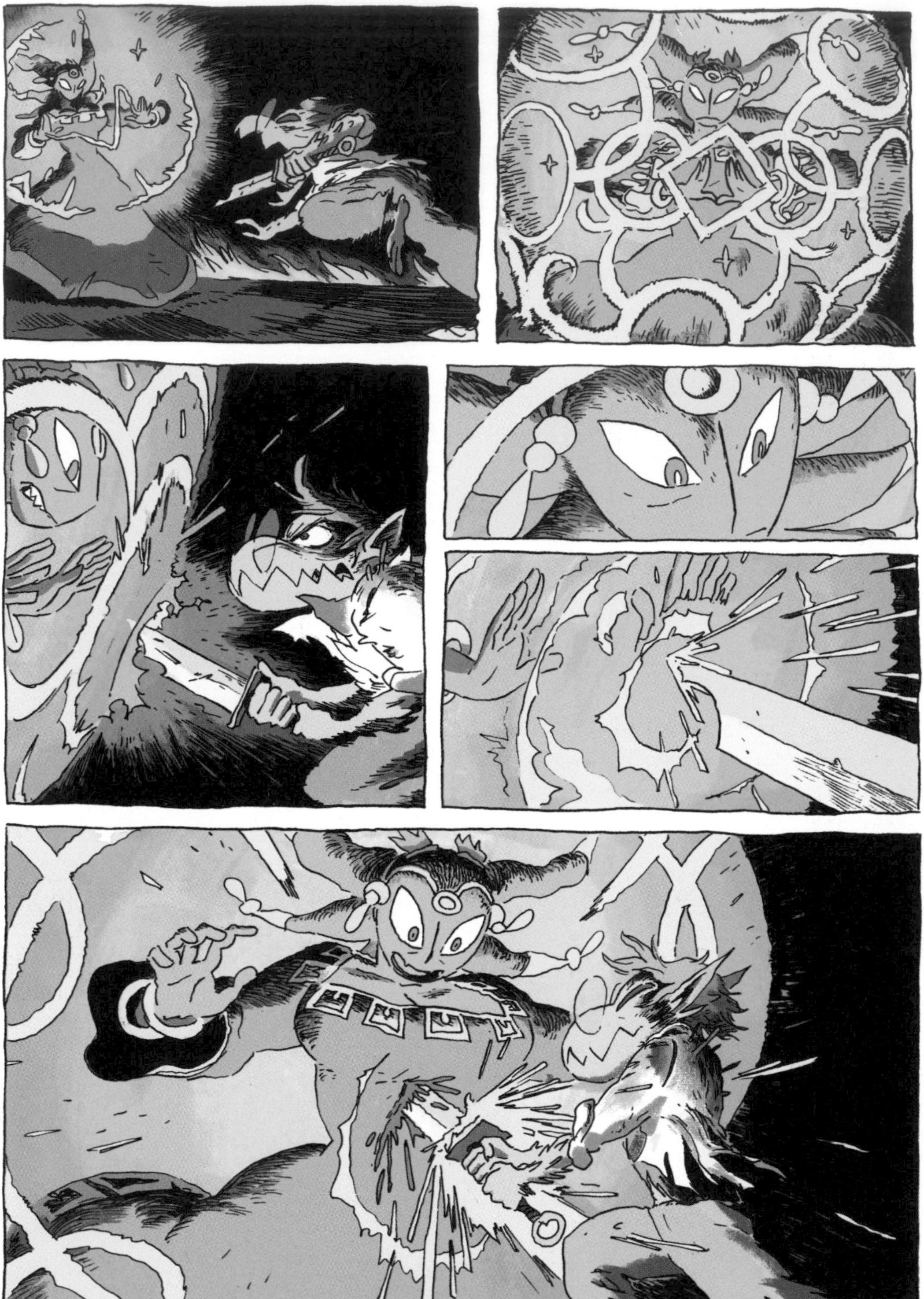

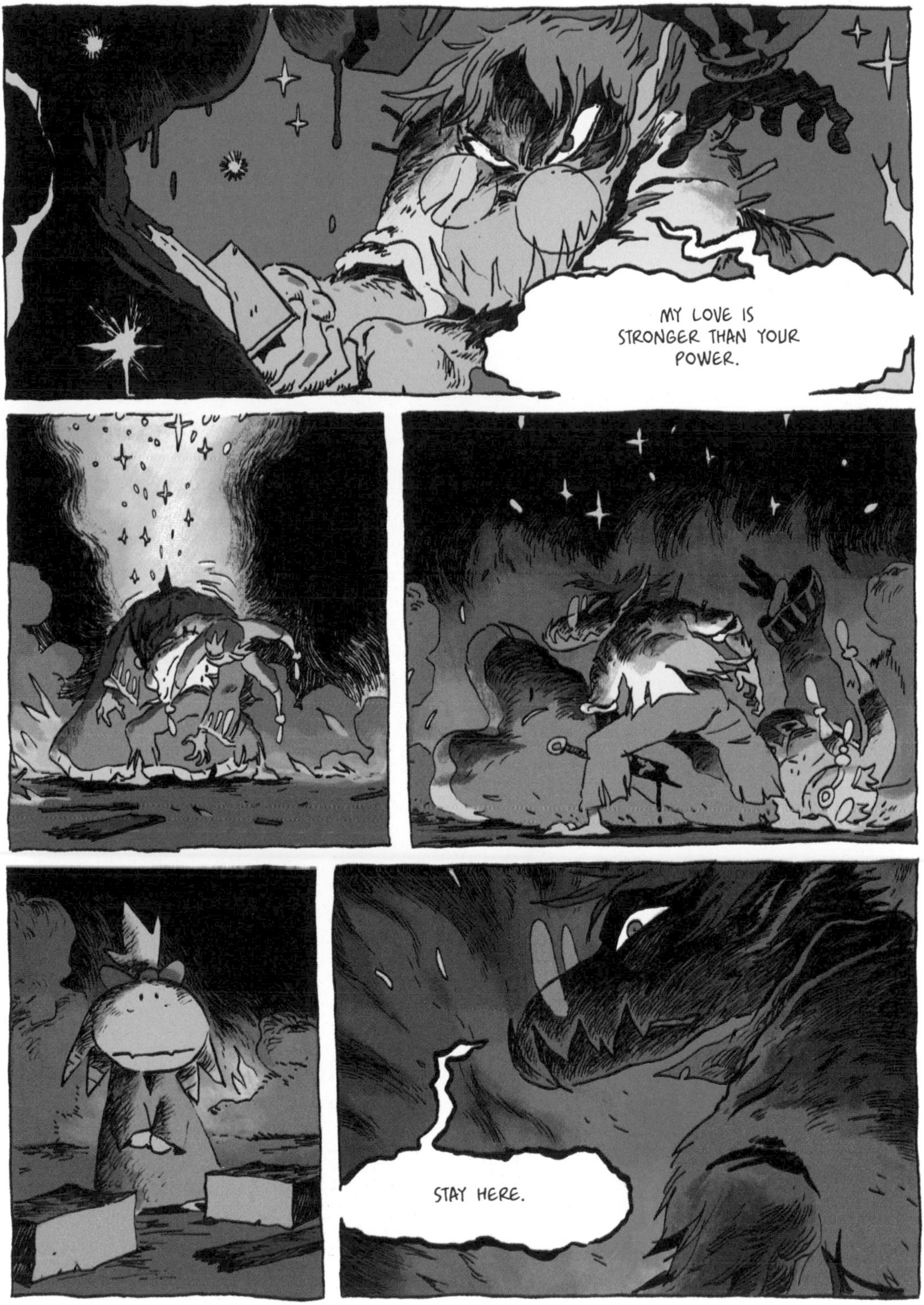
MY LOVE IS STRONGER THAN YOUR POWER.
STAY HERE.

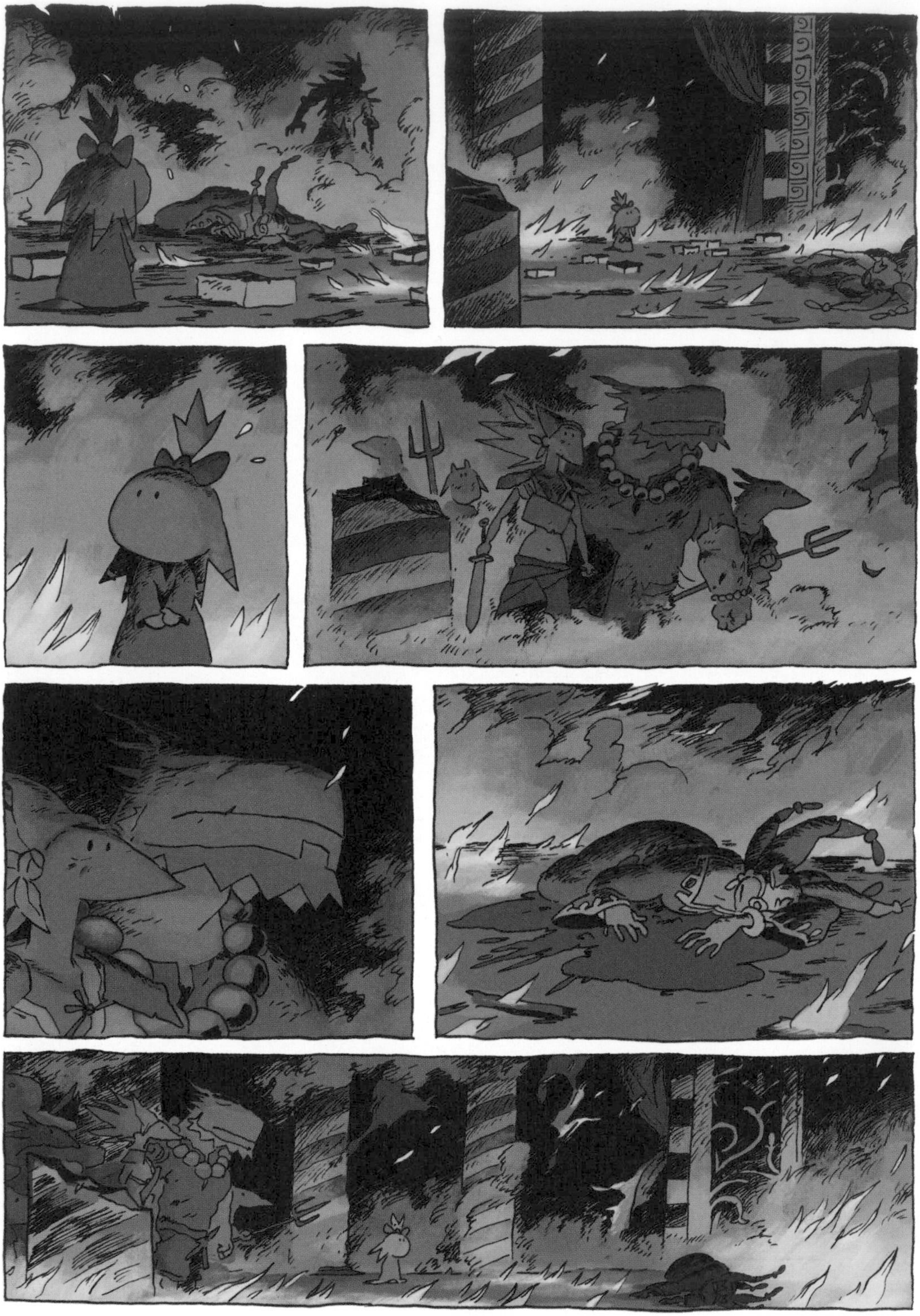

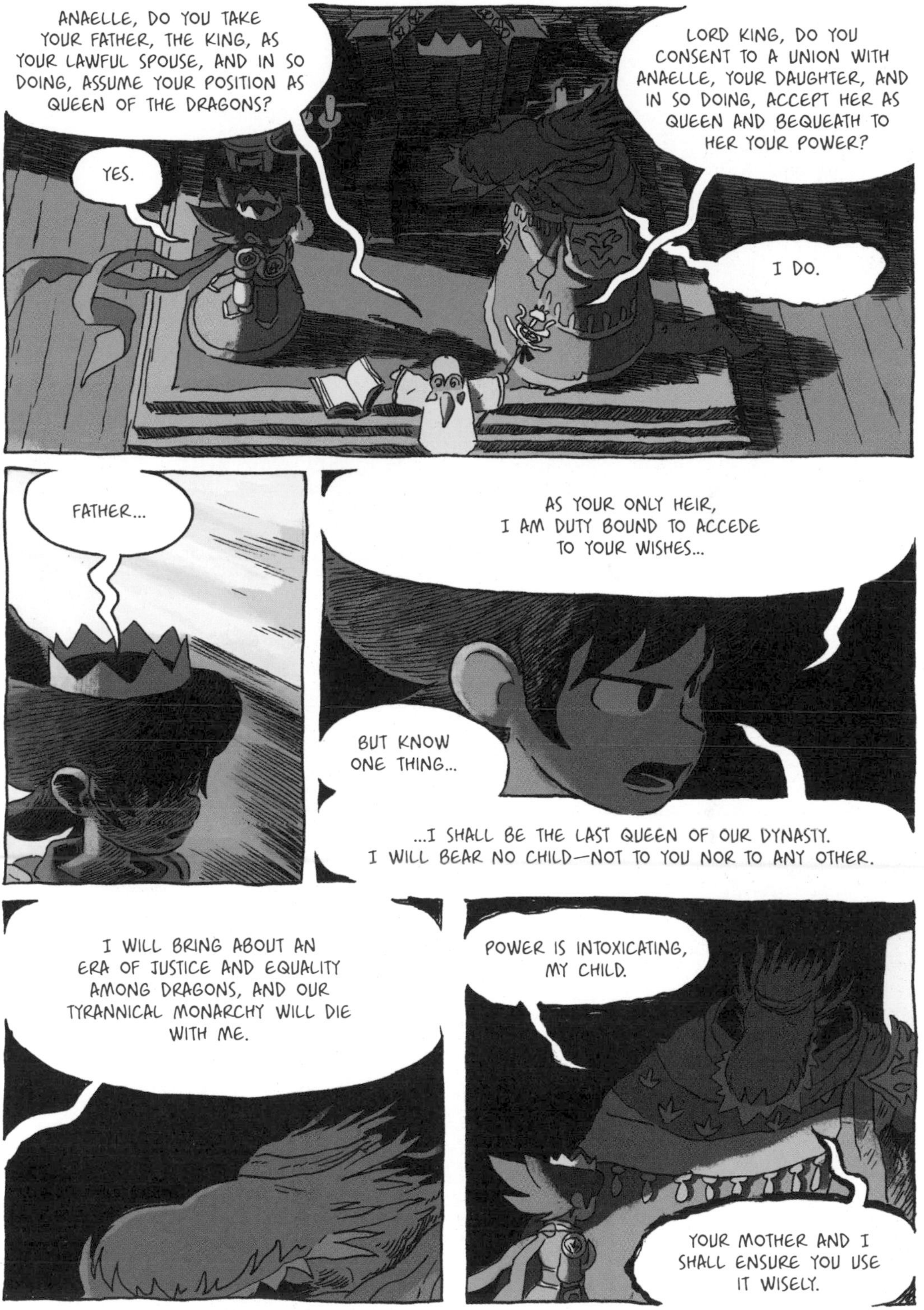
ANAELLE, DO YOU TAKE YOUR FATHER, THE KING, AS YOUR LAWFUL SPOUSE, AND IN SO DOING, ASSUME YOUR POSITION AS QUEEN OF THE DRAGONS?
YES.
LORD KING, DO YOU CONSENT TO A UNION WITH ANAELLE, YOUR DAUGHTER, AND IN SO DOING, ACCEPT HER AS QUEEN AND BEQUEATH TO HER YOUR POWER?
I DO.
FATHER...
AS YOUR ONLY HEIR, I AM DUTY BOUND TO ACCEDE TO YOUR WISHES...
BUT KNOW ONE THING...
...I SHALL BE THE LAST QUEEN OF OUR DYNASTY. I WILL BEAR NO CHILD—NOT TO YOU NOR TO ANY OTHER.
I WILL BRING ABOUT AN ERA OF JUSTICE AND EQUALITY AMONG DRAGONS, AND OUR TYRANNICAL MONARCHY WILL DIE WITH ME.
POWER IS INTOXICATING, MY CHILD.
YOUR MOTHER AND I SHALL ENSURE YOU USE IT WISELY.

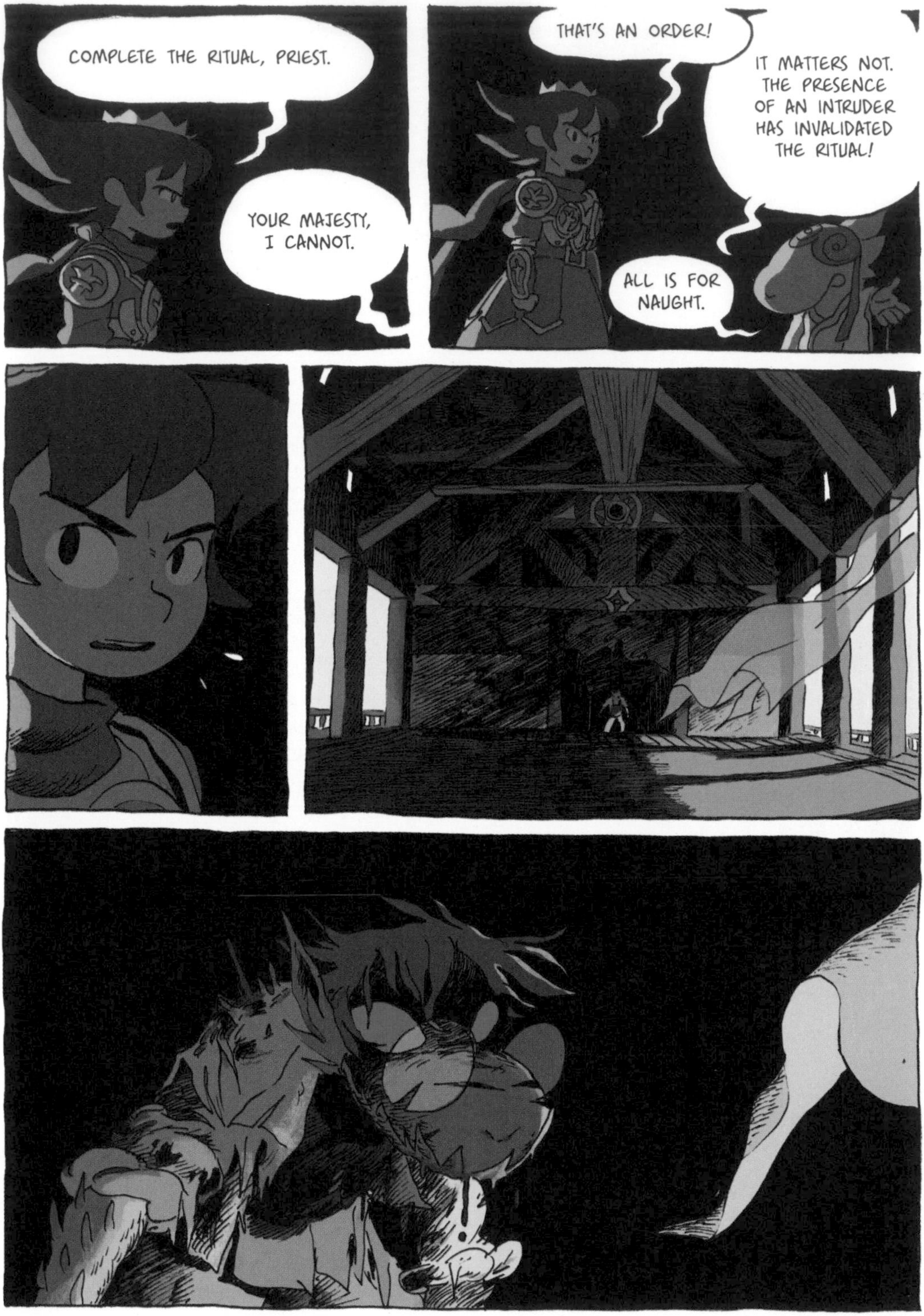
COMPLETE THE RITUAL, PRIEST.
YOUR MAJESTY, I CANNOT.
THAT'S AN ORDER!
IT MATTERS NOT. THE PRESENCE OF AN INTRUDER HAS INVALIDATED THE RITUAL!
ALL IS FOR NAUGHT.

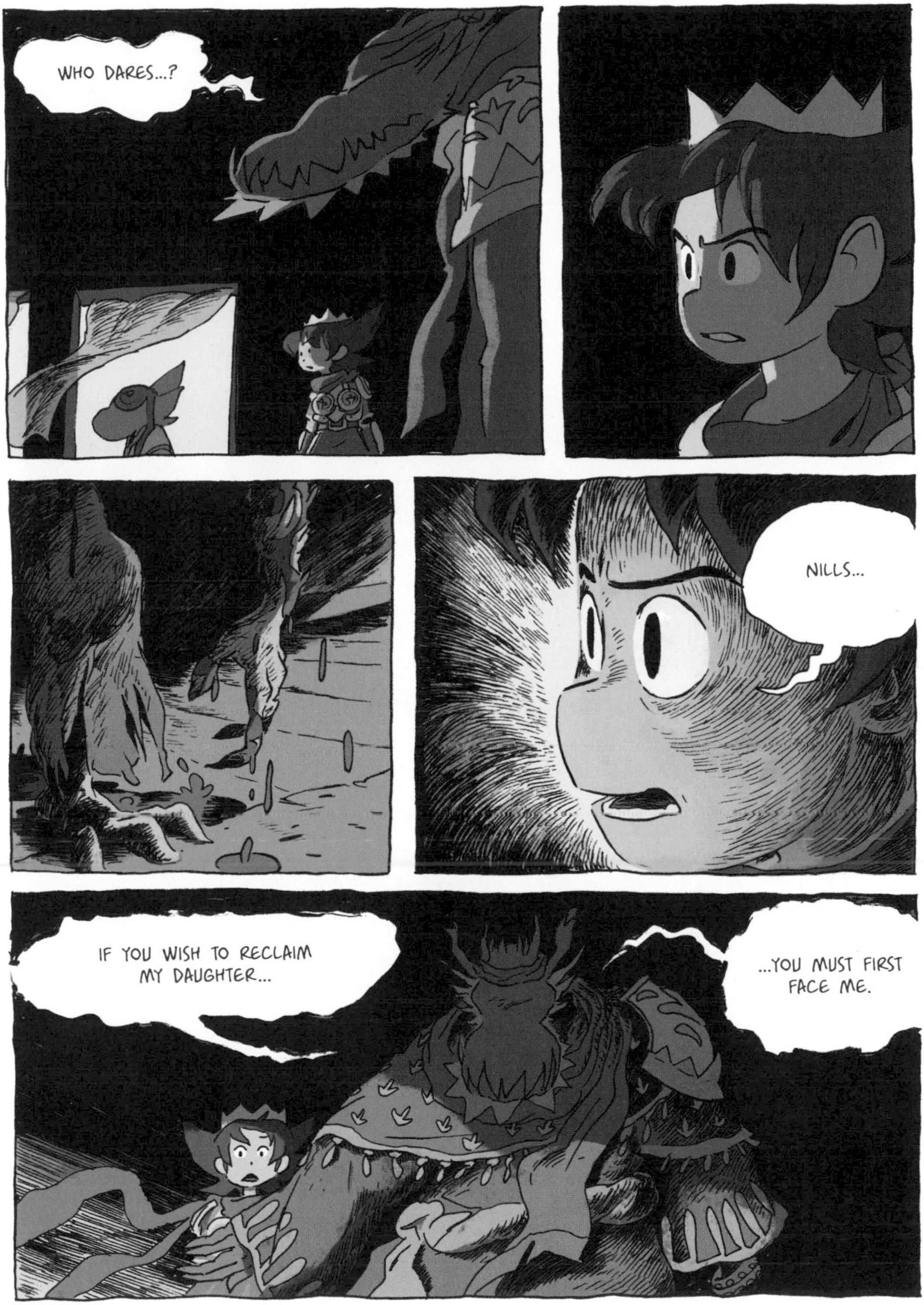
WHO DARES...?
NILLS...
IF YOU WISH TO RECLAIM MY DAUGHTER...
...YOU MUST FIRST FACE ME.

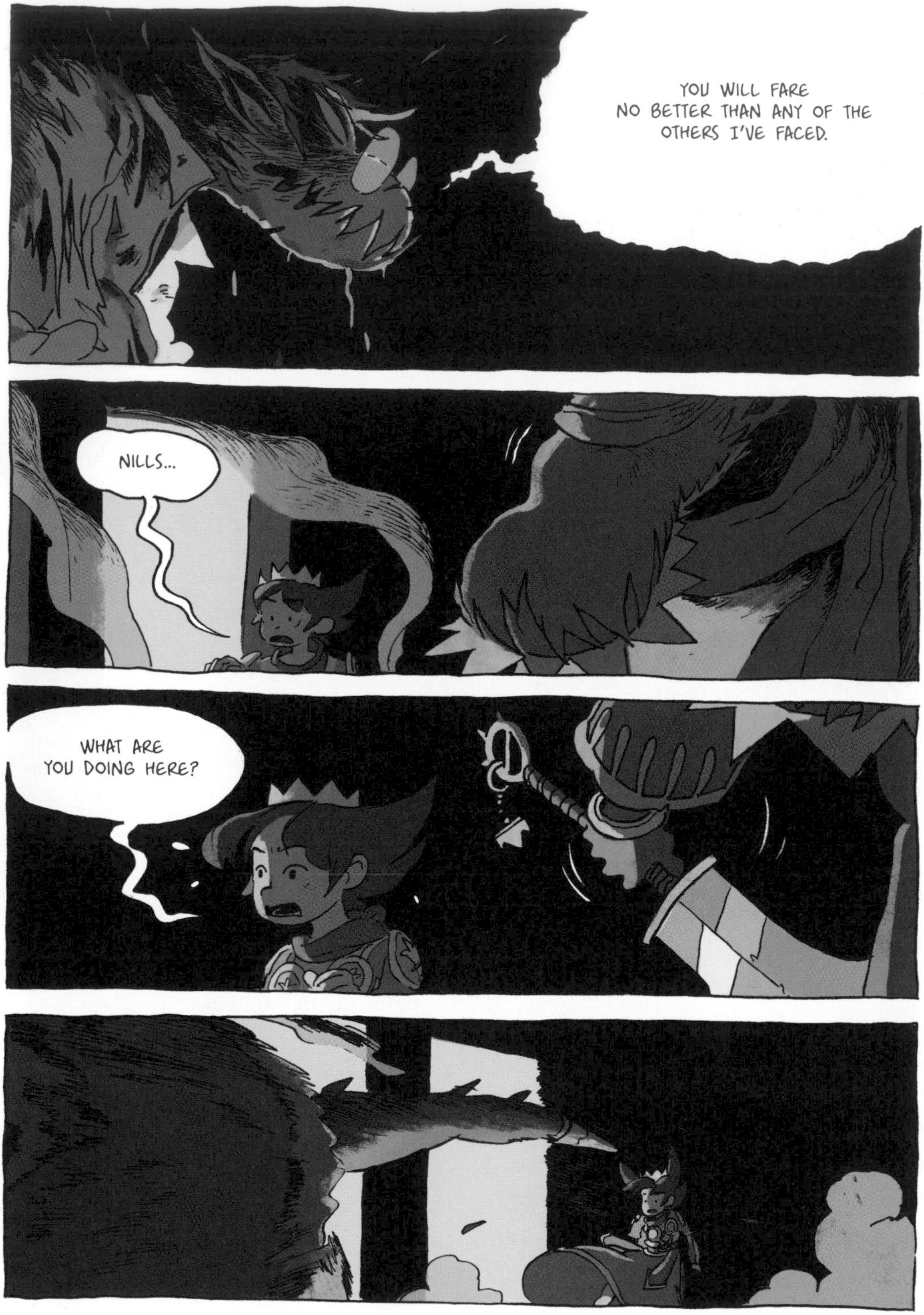
YOU WILL FARE NO BETTER THAN ANY OF THE OTHERS I'VE FACED.
NILLS...
WHAT ARE YOU DOING HERE?

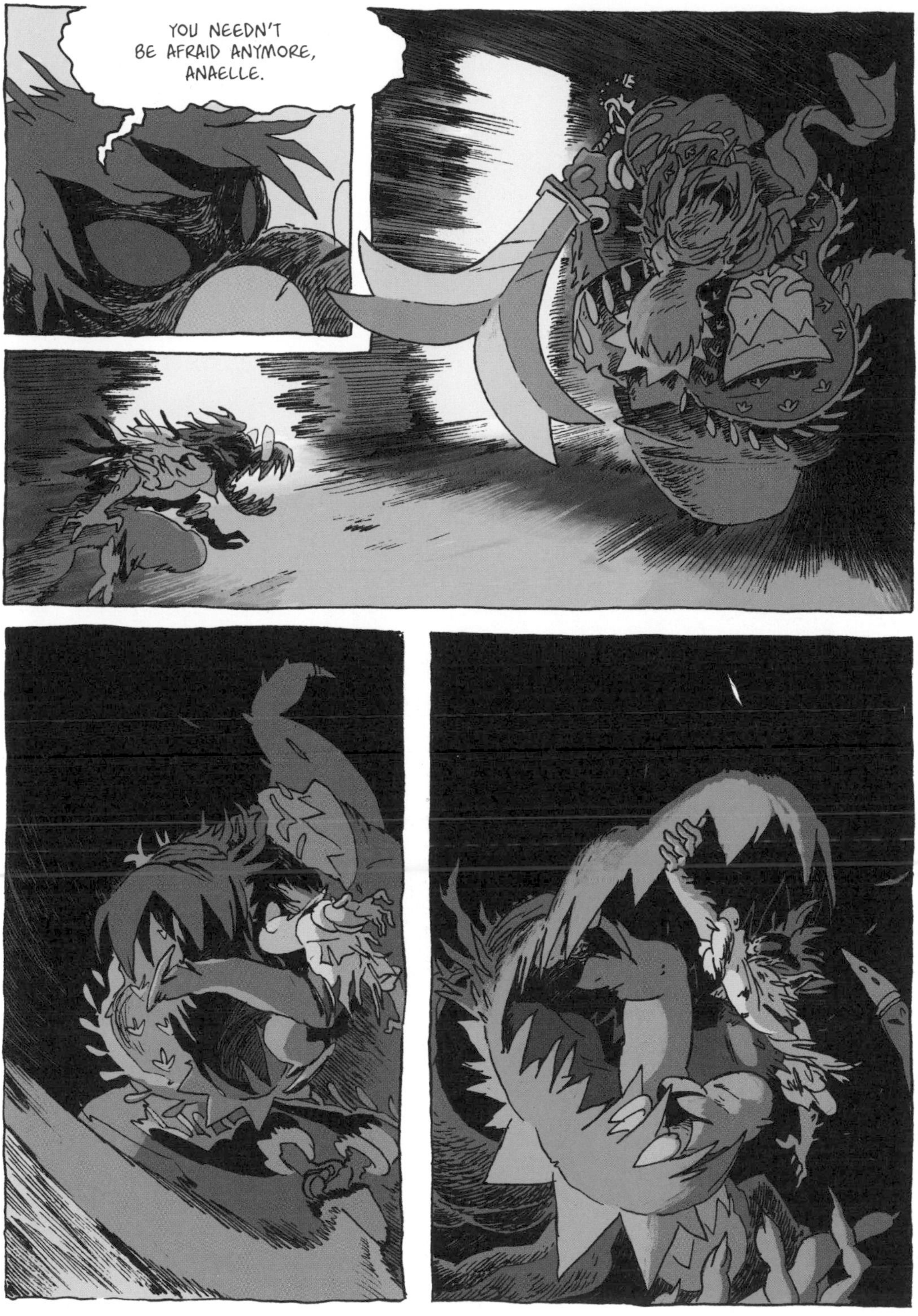
YOU NEEDN'T BE AFRAID ANYMORE, ANAELLE.

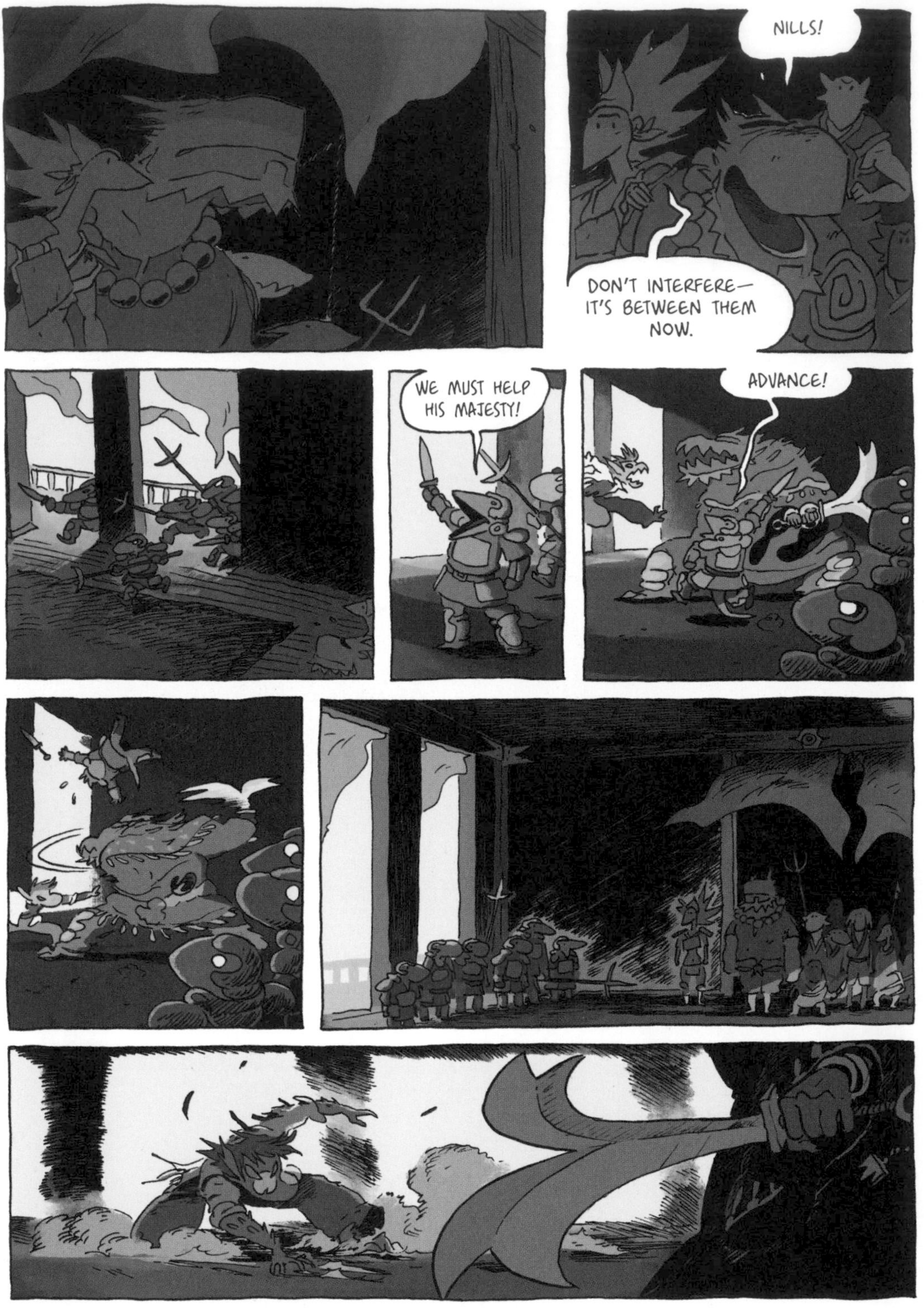
NILLS!
DON'T INTERFERE—IT'S BETWEEN THEM NOW.
WE MUST HELP HIS MAJESTY!
ADVANCE!

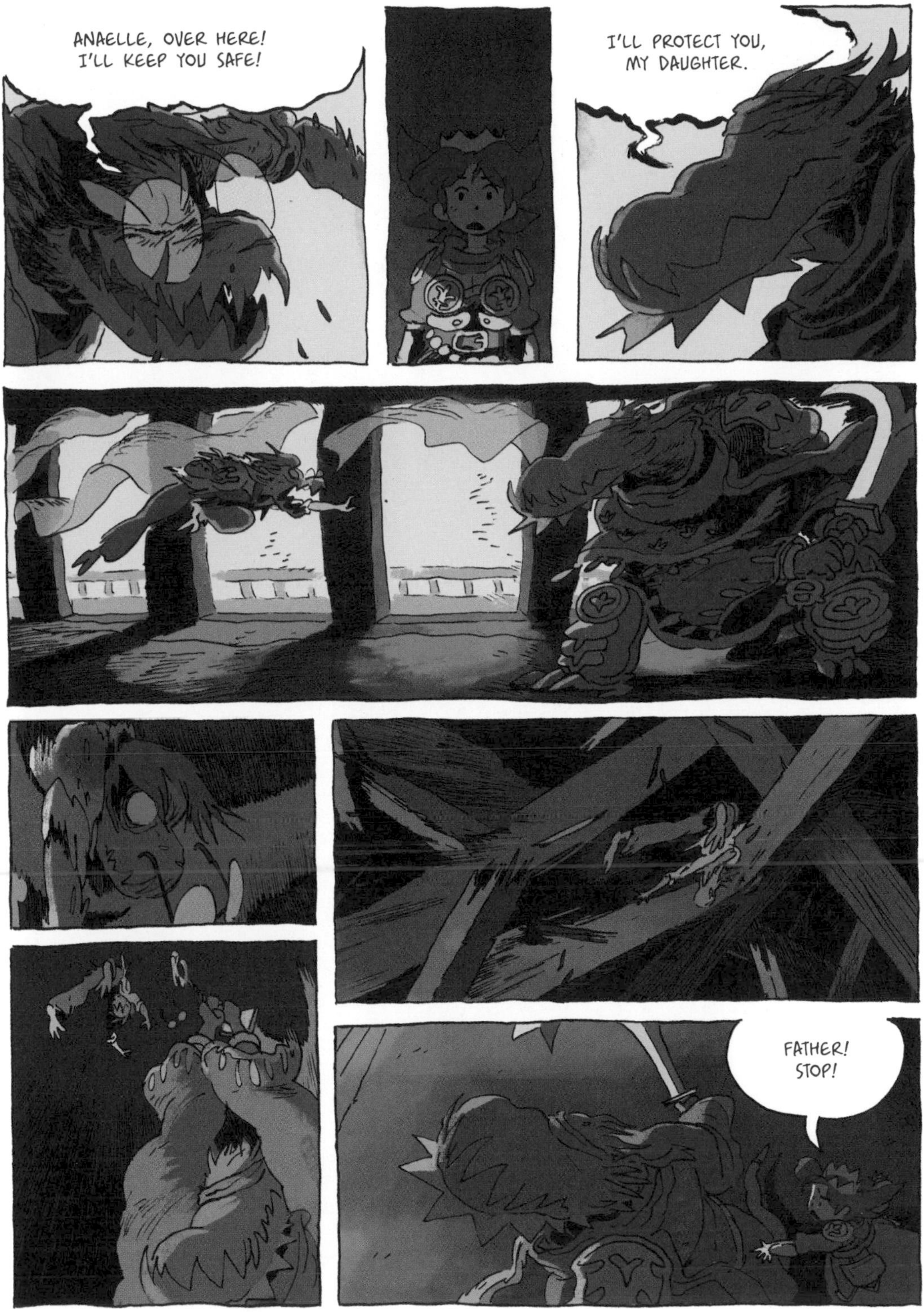
ANAELLE, OVER HERE! I'LL KEEP YOU SAFE!
I'LL PROTECT YOU, MY DAUGHTER.
FATHER! STOP!

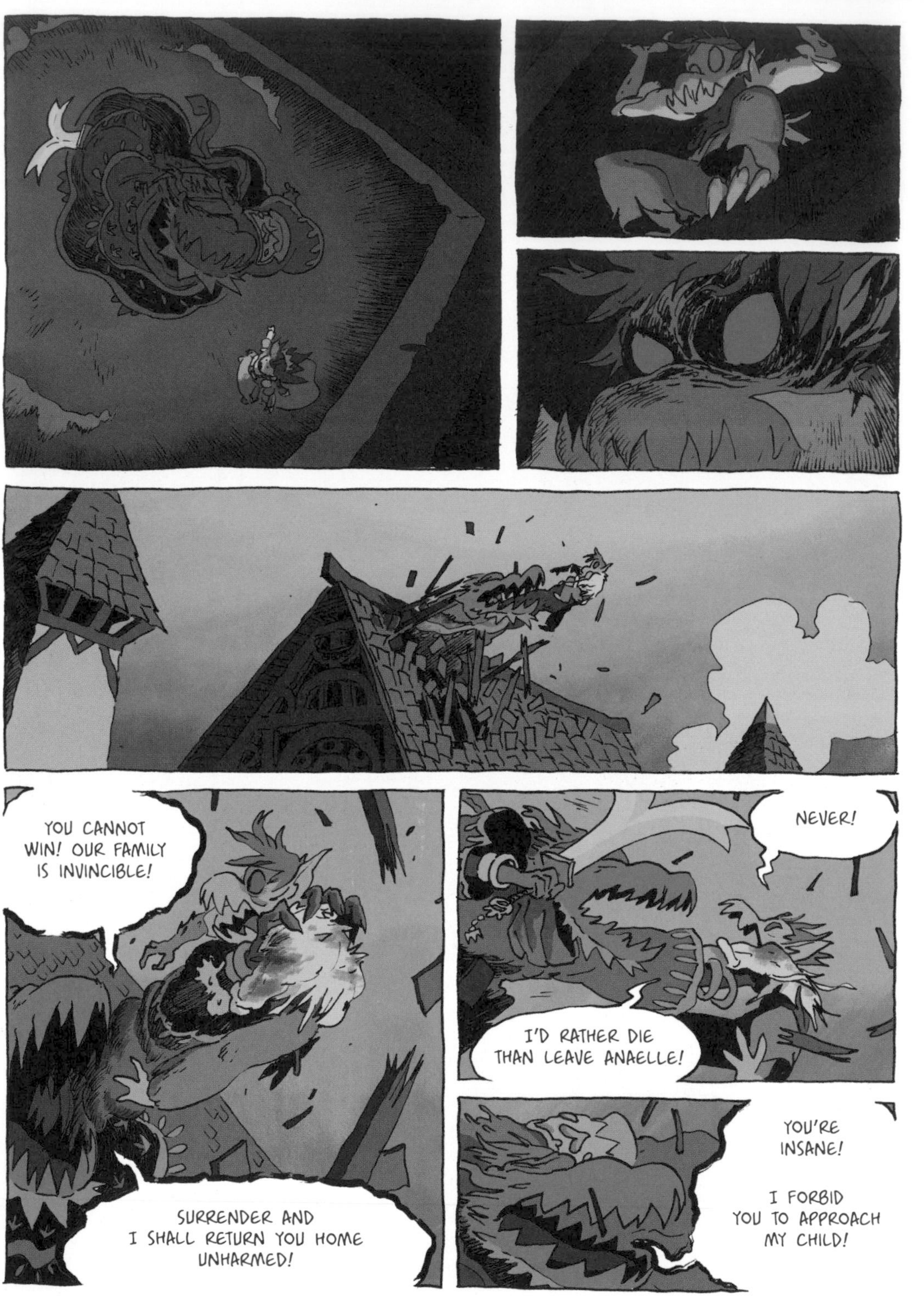
YOU CANNOT WIN! OUR FAMILY IS INVINCIBLE!
SURRENDER AND I SHALL RETURN YOU HOME UNHARMED!
NEVER!
I'D RATHER DIE THAN LEAVE ANAELLE!
YOU'RE INSANE!
I FORBID YOU TO APPROACH MY CHILD!

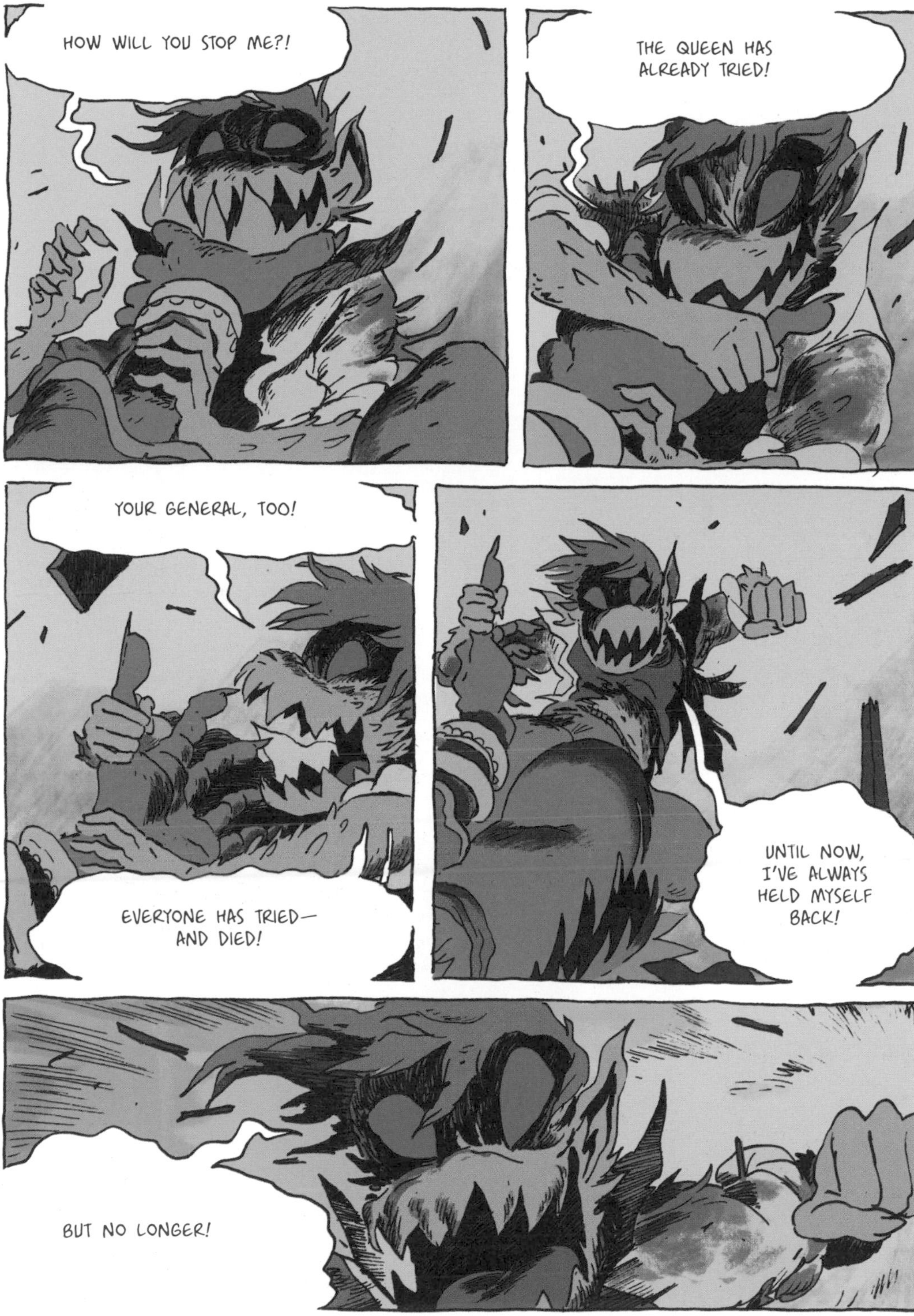
HOW WILL YOU STOP ME?!
THE QUEEN HAS ALREADY TRIED!
YOUR GENERAL, TOO!
EVERYONE HAS TRIED— AND DIED!
UNTIL NOW, I'VE ALWAYS HELD MYSELF BACK!
BUT NO LONGER!

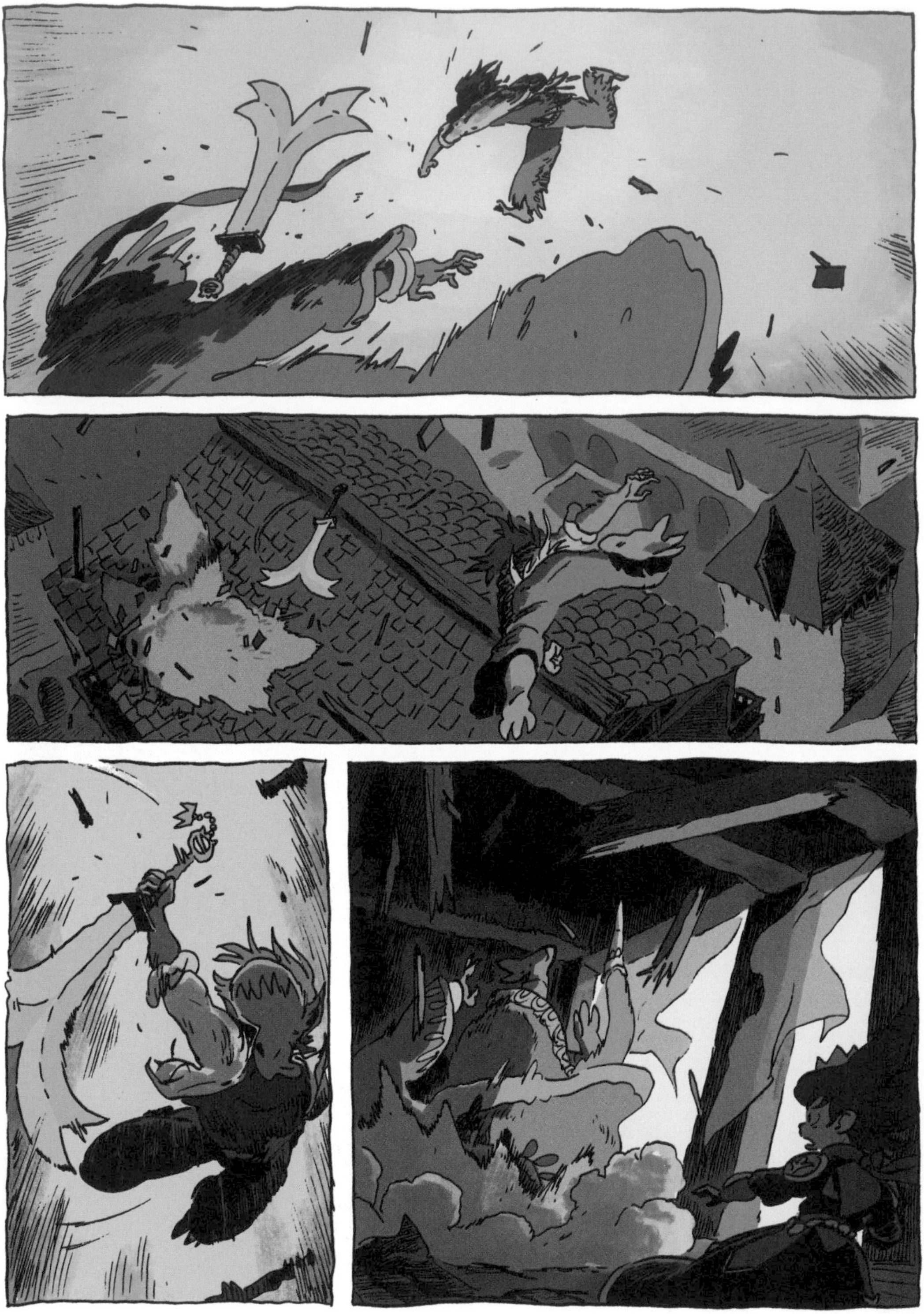

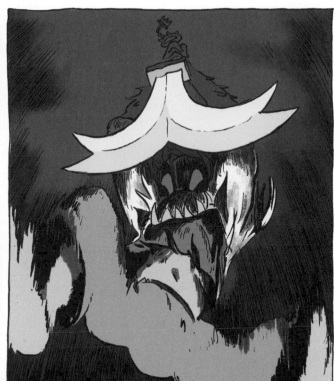

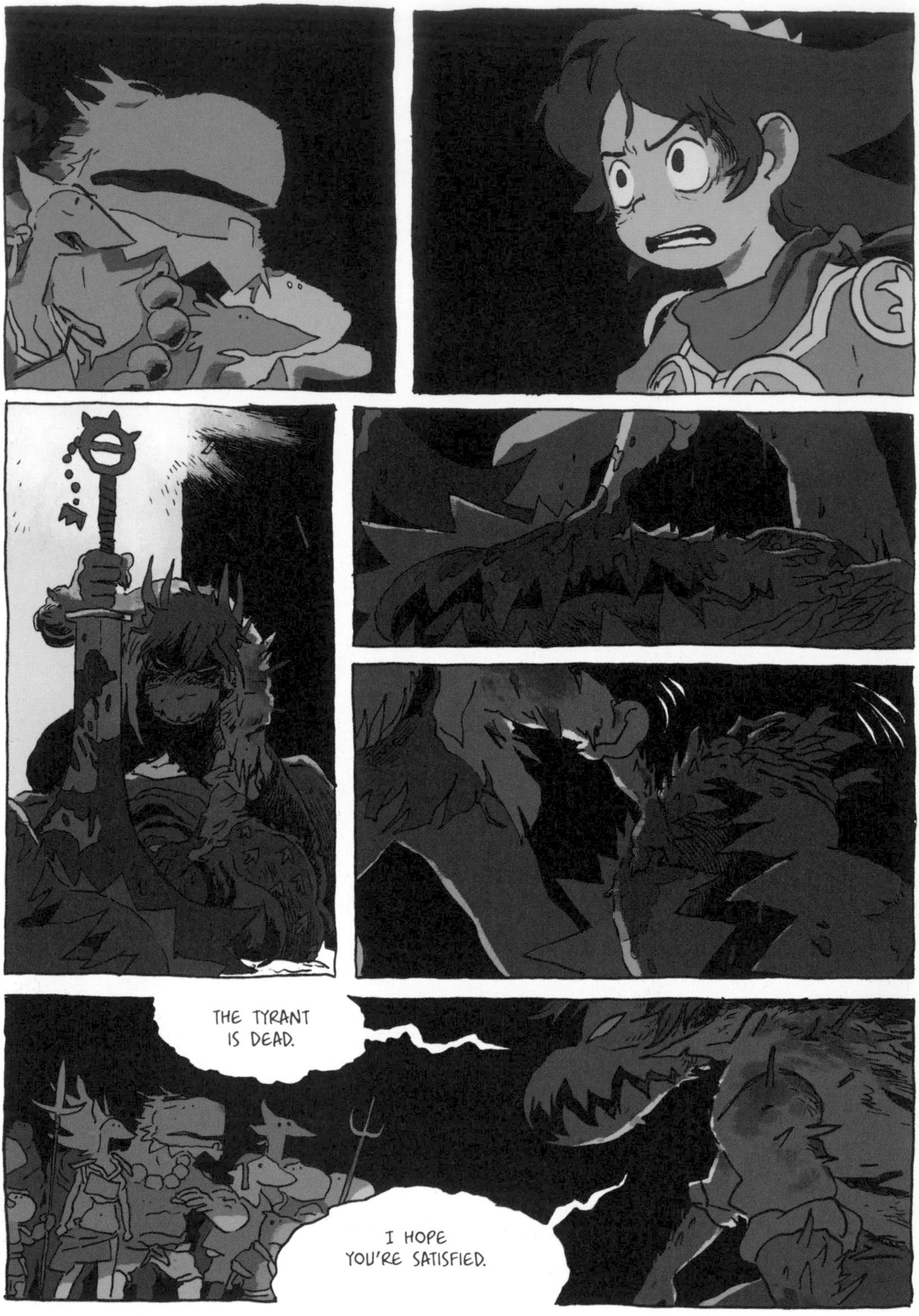
THE TYRANT IS DEAD.
I HOPE YOU'RE SATISFIED.

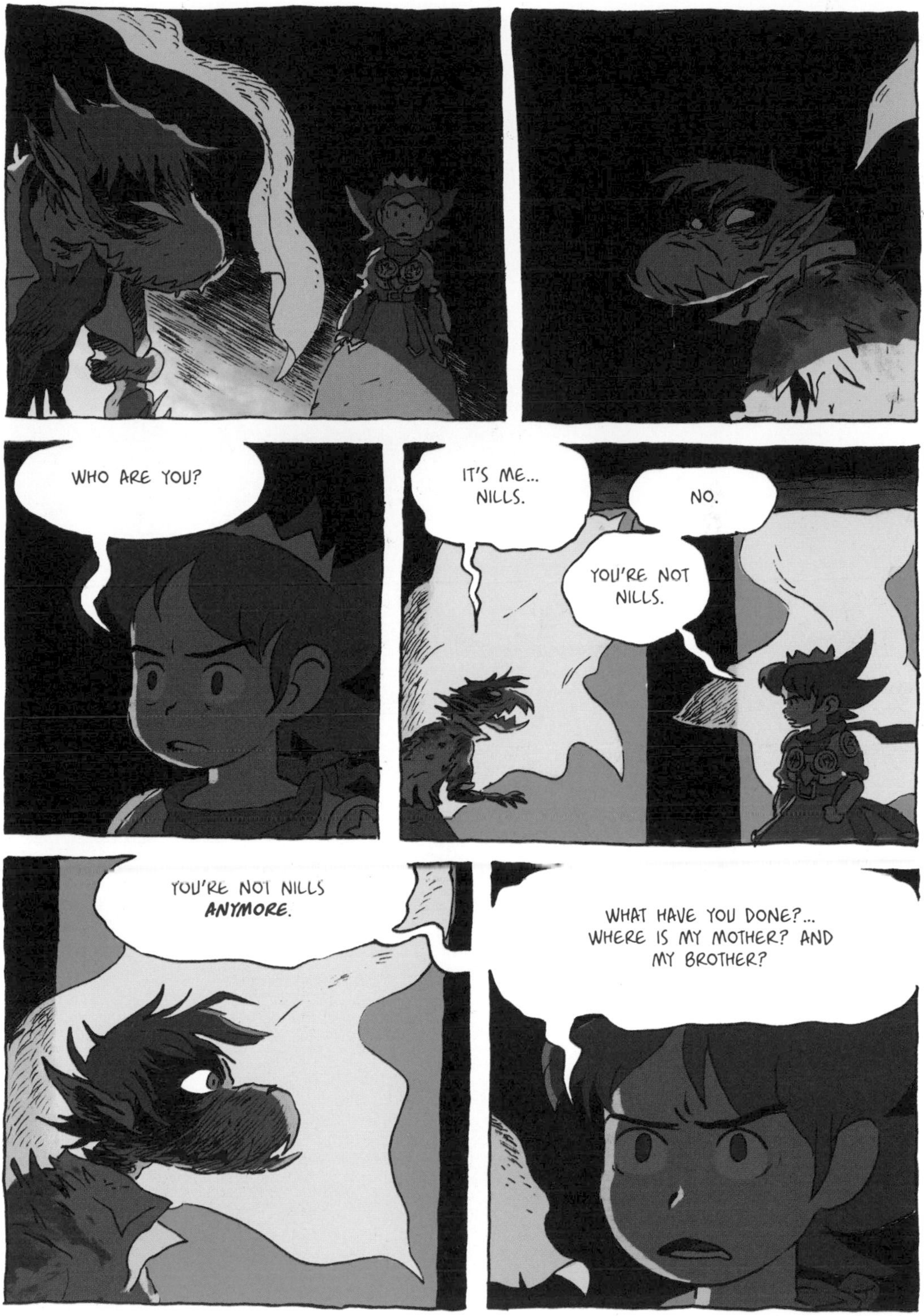
WHO ARE YOU?
IT'S ME... NILLS.
NO.
YOU'RE NOT NILLS.
YOU'RE NOT NILLS ANYMORE.
WHAT HAVE YOU DONE?... WHERE IS MY MOTHER? AND MY BROTHER?

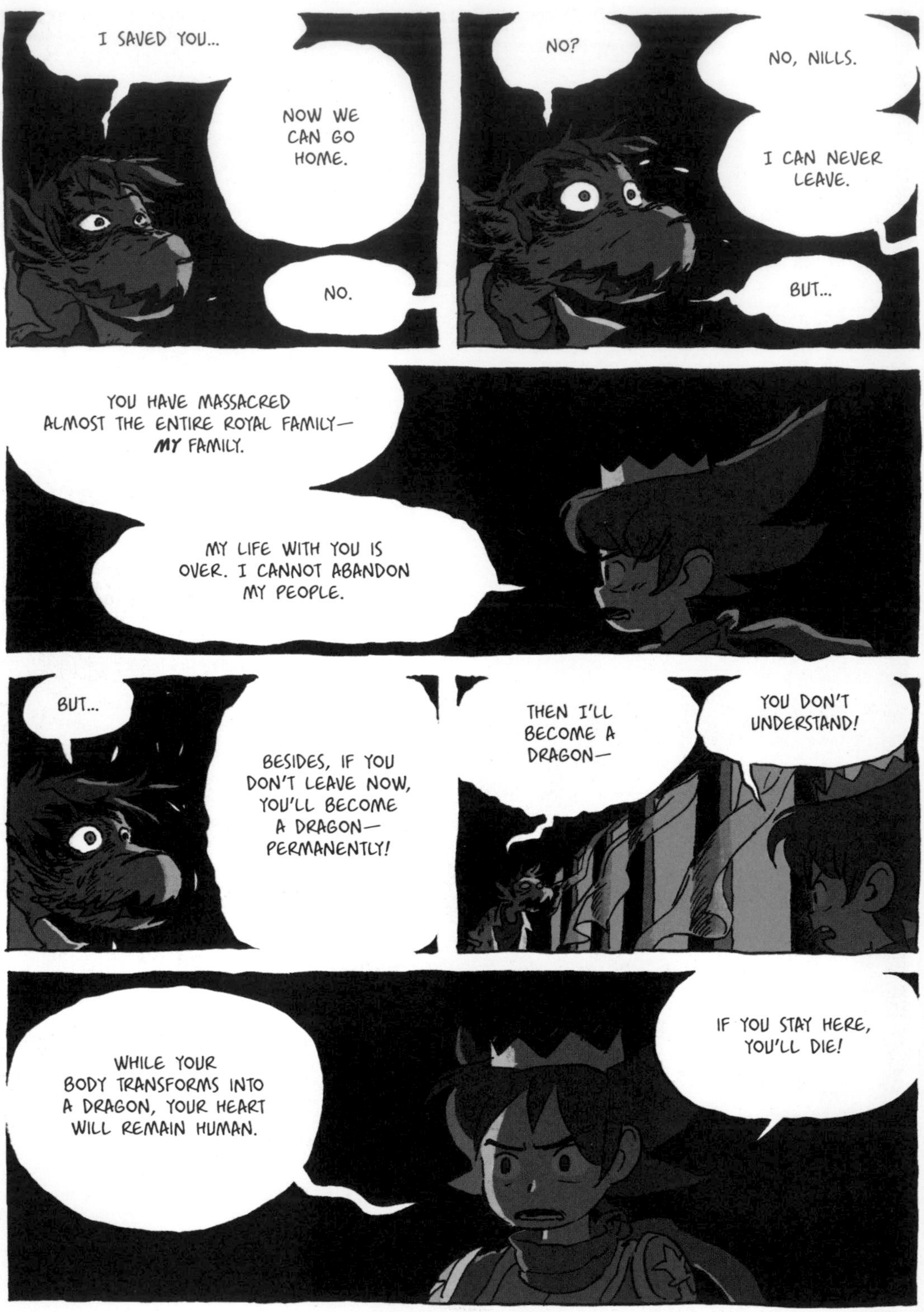
I SAVED YOU...
NOW WE CAN GO HOME.
NO.
NO?
NO, NILLS.
I CAN NEVER LEAVE.
BUT...
YOU HAVE MASSACRED ALMOST THE ENTIRE ROYAL FAMILY— *MY* FAMILY.
MY LIFE WITH YOU IS OVER. I CANNOT ABANDON MY PEOPLE.
BUT...
BESIDES, IF YOU DON'T LEAVE NOW, YOU'LL BECOME A DRAGON— PERMANENTLY!
THEN I'LL BECOME A DRAGON—
YOU DON'T UNDERSTAND!
IF YOU STAY HERE, YOU'LL DIE!
WHILE YOUR BODY TRANSFORMS INTO A DRAGON, YOUR HEART WILL REMAIN HUMAN.

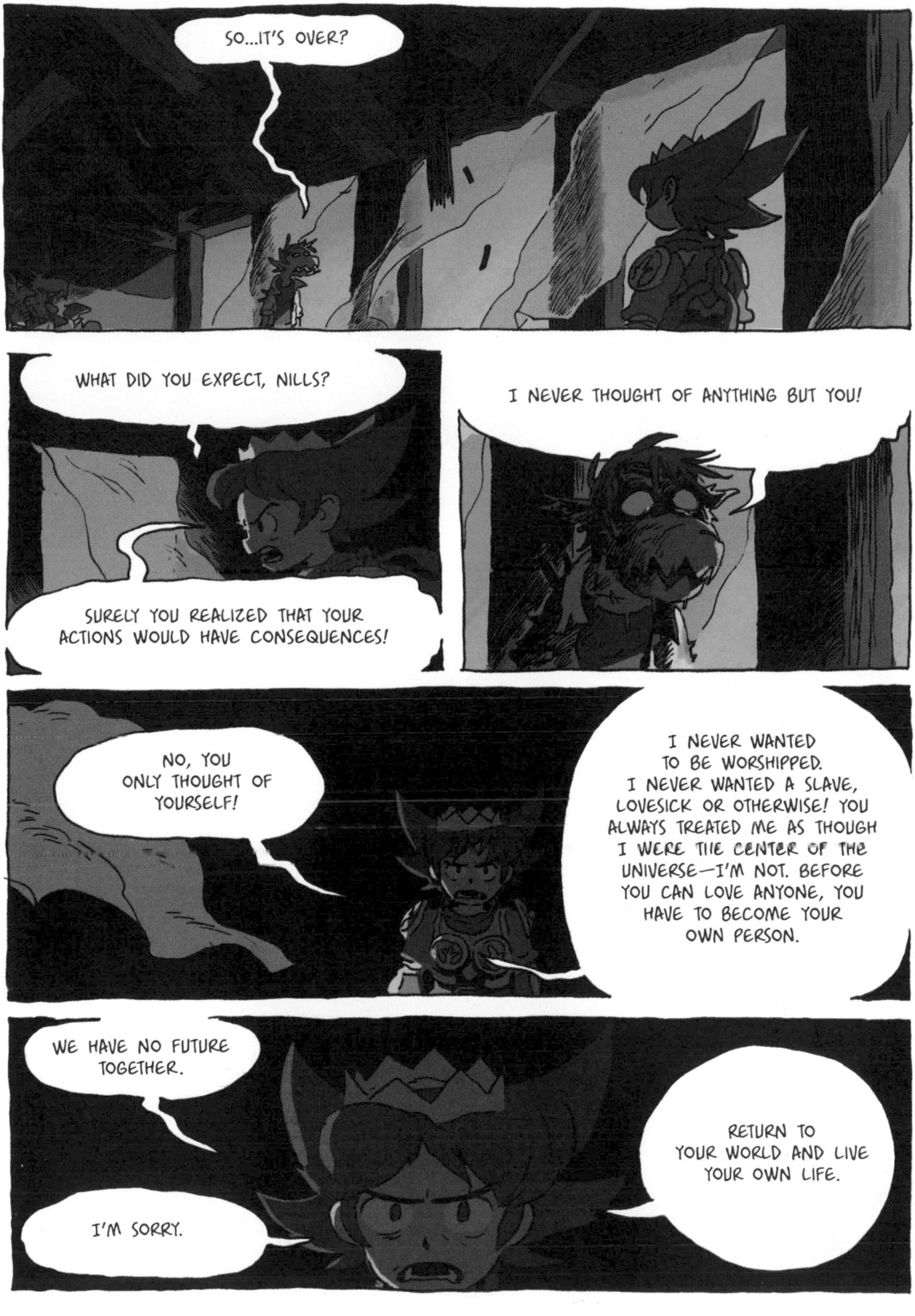

SO...IT'S OVER?
WHAT DID YOU EXPECT, NILLS?
SURELY YOU REALIZED THAT YOUR ACTIONS WOULD HAVE CONSEQUENCES!
I NEVER THOUGHT OF ANYTHING BUT YOU!
NO, YOU ONLY THOUGHT OF YOURSELF!
I NEVER WANTED TO BE WORSHIPPED. I NEVER WANTED A SLAVE, LOVESICK OR OTHERWISE! YOU ALWAYS TREATED ME AS THOUGH I WERE THE CENTER OF THE UNIVERSE—I'M NOT. BEFORE YOU CAN LOVE ANYONE, YOU HAVE TO BECOME YOUR OWN PERSON.
WE HAVE NO FUTURE TOGETHER.
I'M SORRY.
RETURN TO YOUR WORLD AND LIVE YOUR OWN LIFE.

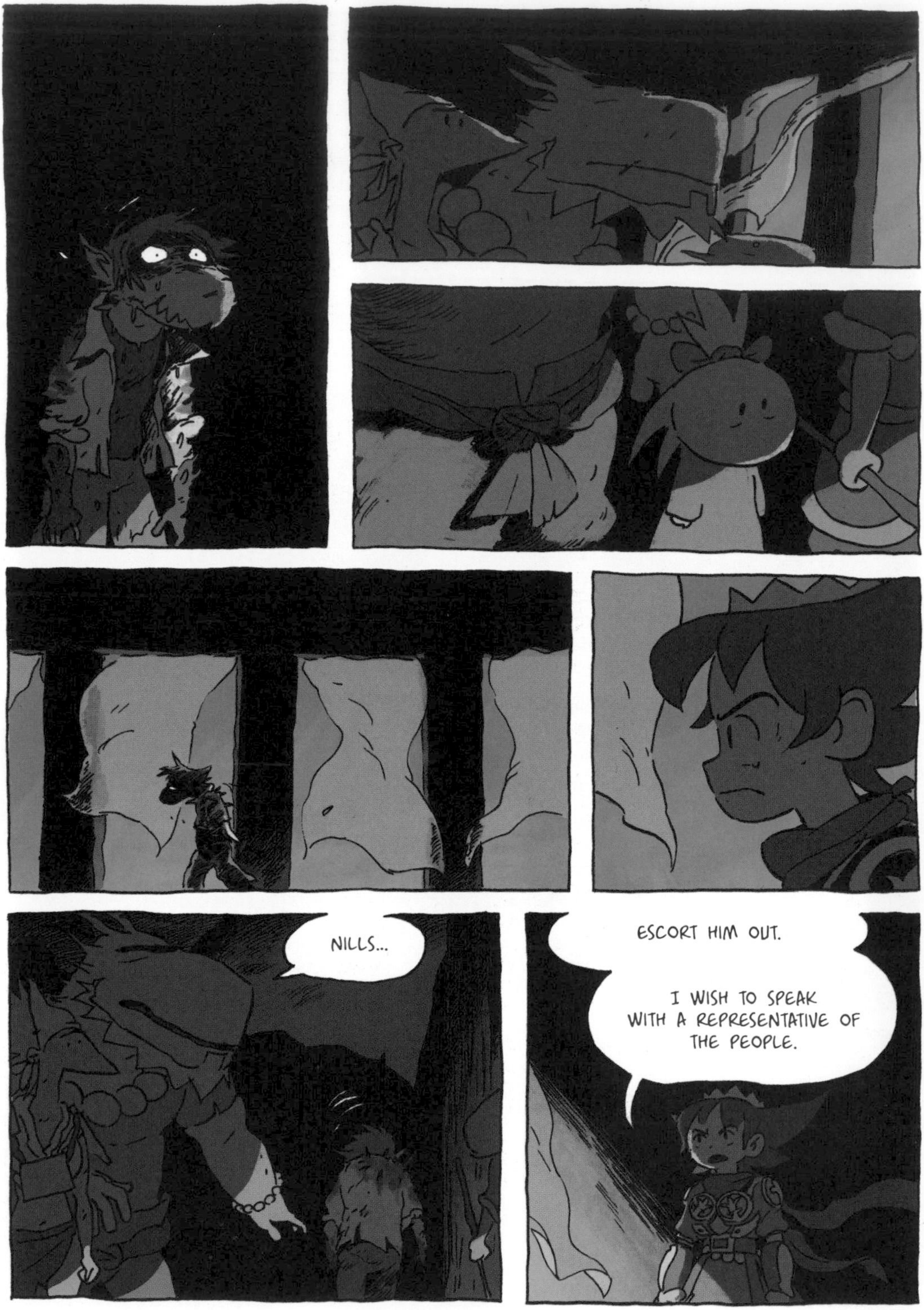
NILLS...
ESCORT HIM OUT.
I WISH TO SPEAK WITH A REPRESENTATIVE OF THE PEOPLE.

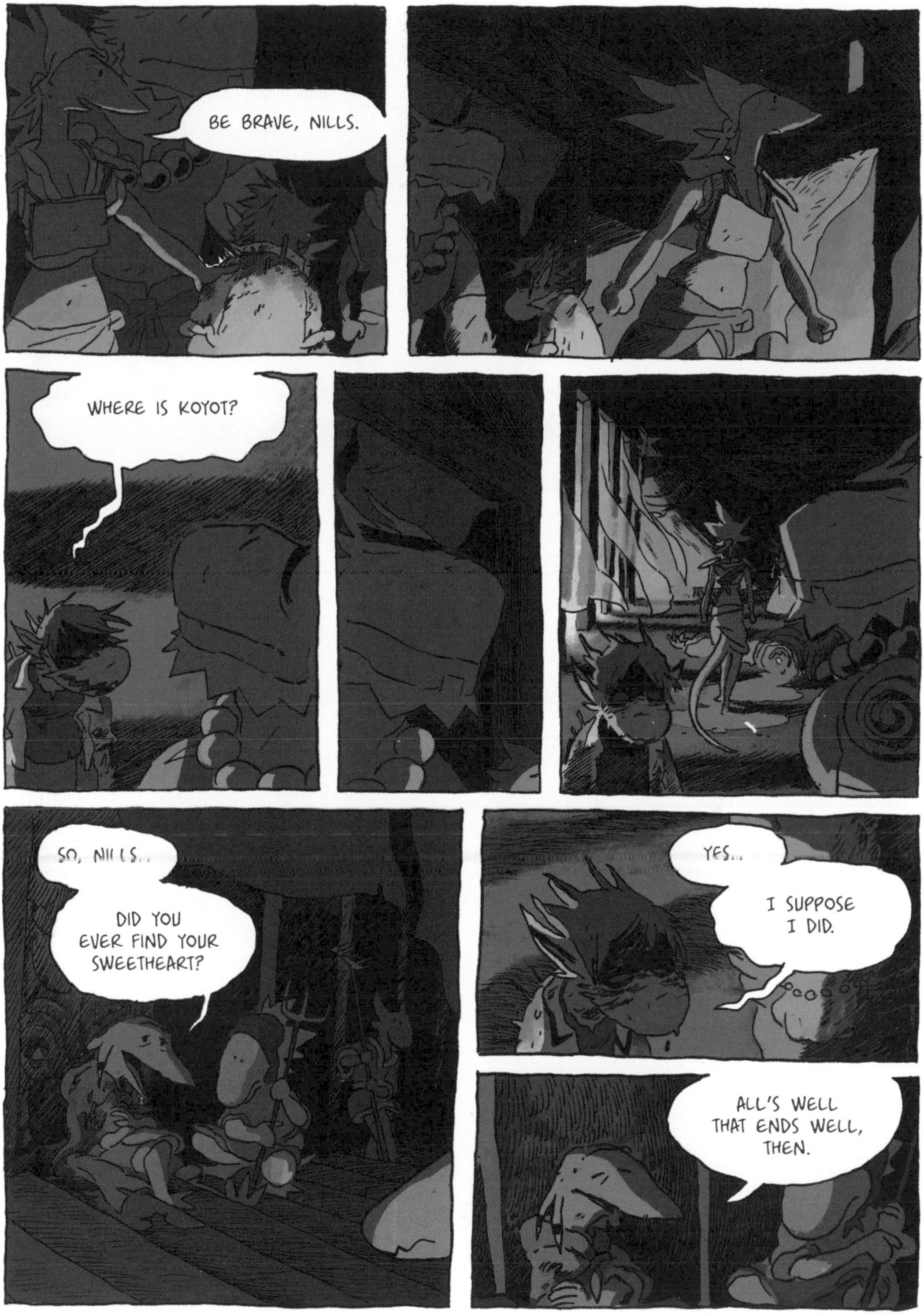
BE BRAVE, NILLS.
WHERE IS KOYOT?
SO, NILLS...
DID YOU EVER FIND YOUR SWEETHEART?
YES...
I SUPPOSE I DID.
ALL'S WELL THAT ENDS WELL, THEN.

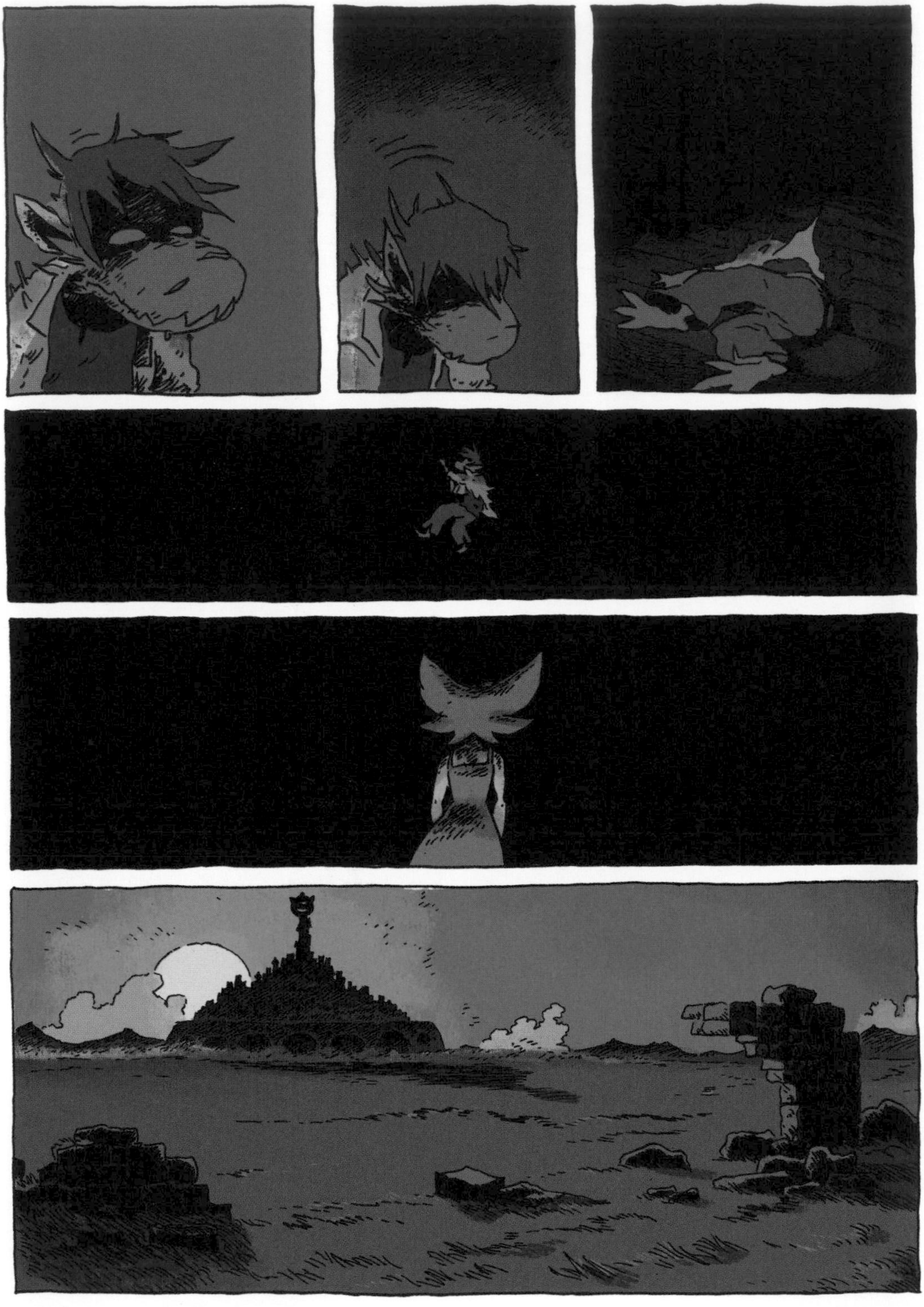

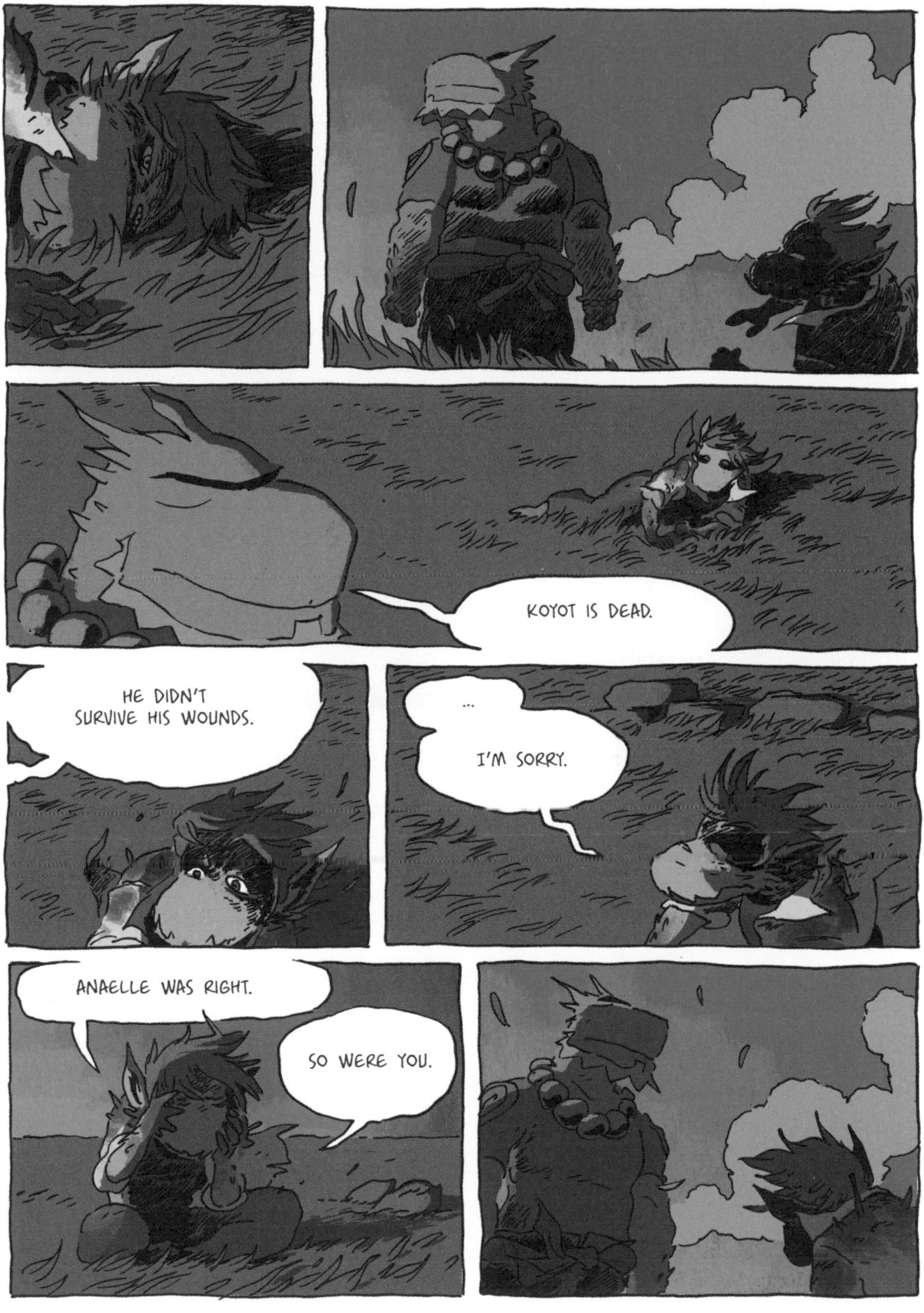
KOYOT IS DEAD.
HE DIDN'T SURVIVE HIS WOUNDS.
...
I'M SORRY.
ANAELLE WAS RIGHT.
SO WERE YOU.

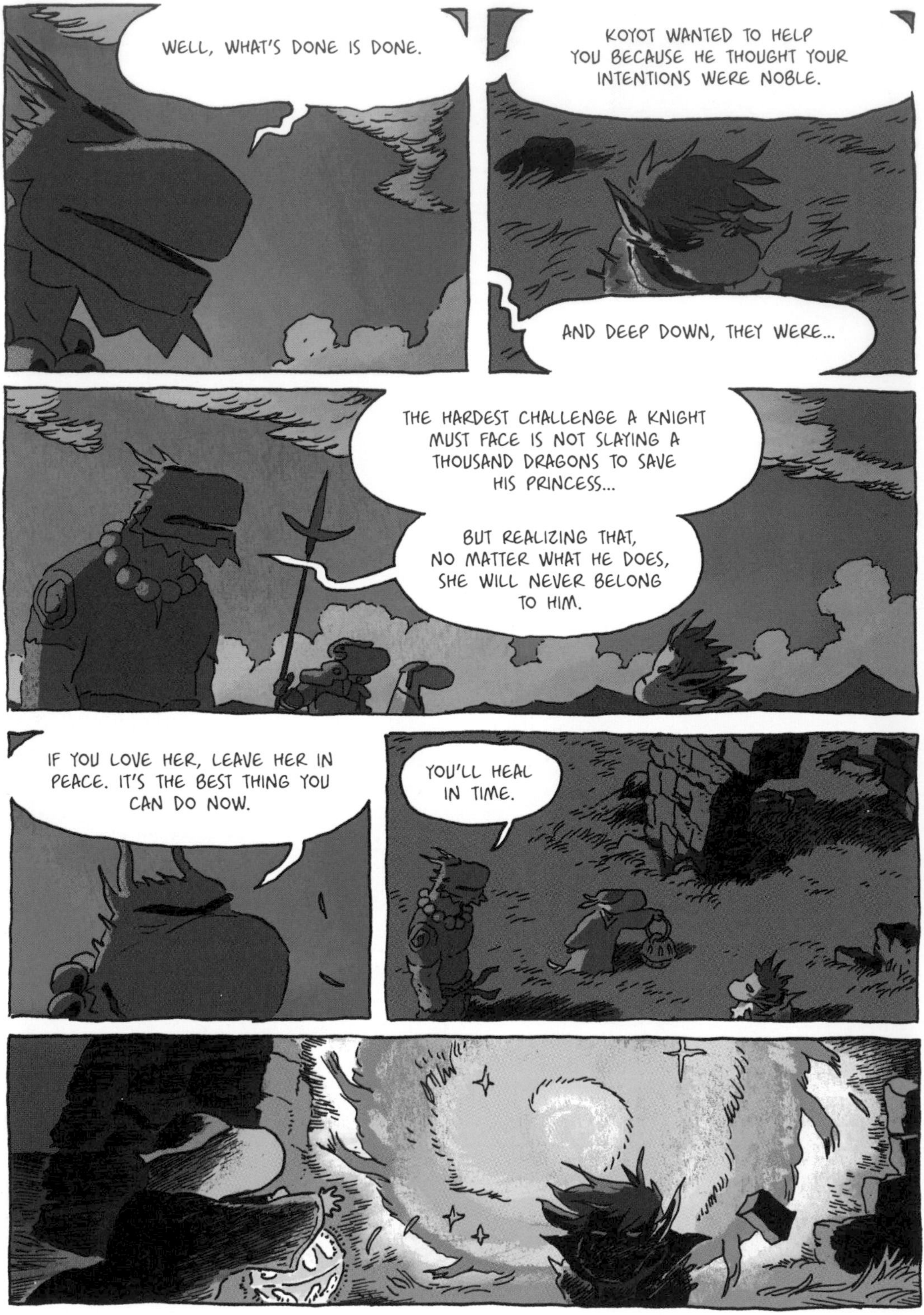
WELL, WHAT'S DONE IS DONE.
KOYOT WANTED TO HELP YOU BECAUSE HE THOUGHT YOUR INTENTIONS WERE NOBLE.
AND DEEP DOWN, THEY WERE...
THE HARDEST CHALLENGE A KNIGHT MUST FACE IS NOT SLAYING A THOUSAND DRAGONS TO SAVE HIS PRINCESS...
BUT REALIZING THAT, NO MATTER WHAT HE DOES, SHE WILL NEVER BELONG TO HIM.
IF YOU LOVE HER, LEAVE HER IN PEACE. IT'S THE BEST THING YOU CAN DO NOW.
YOU'LL HEAL IN TIME.

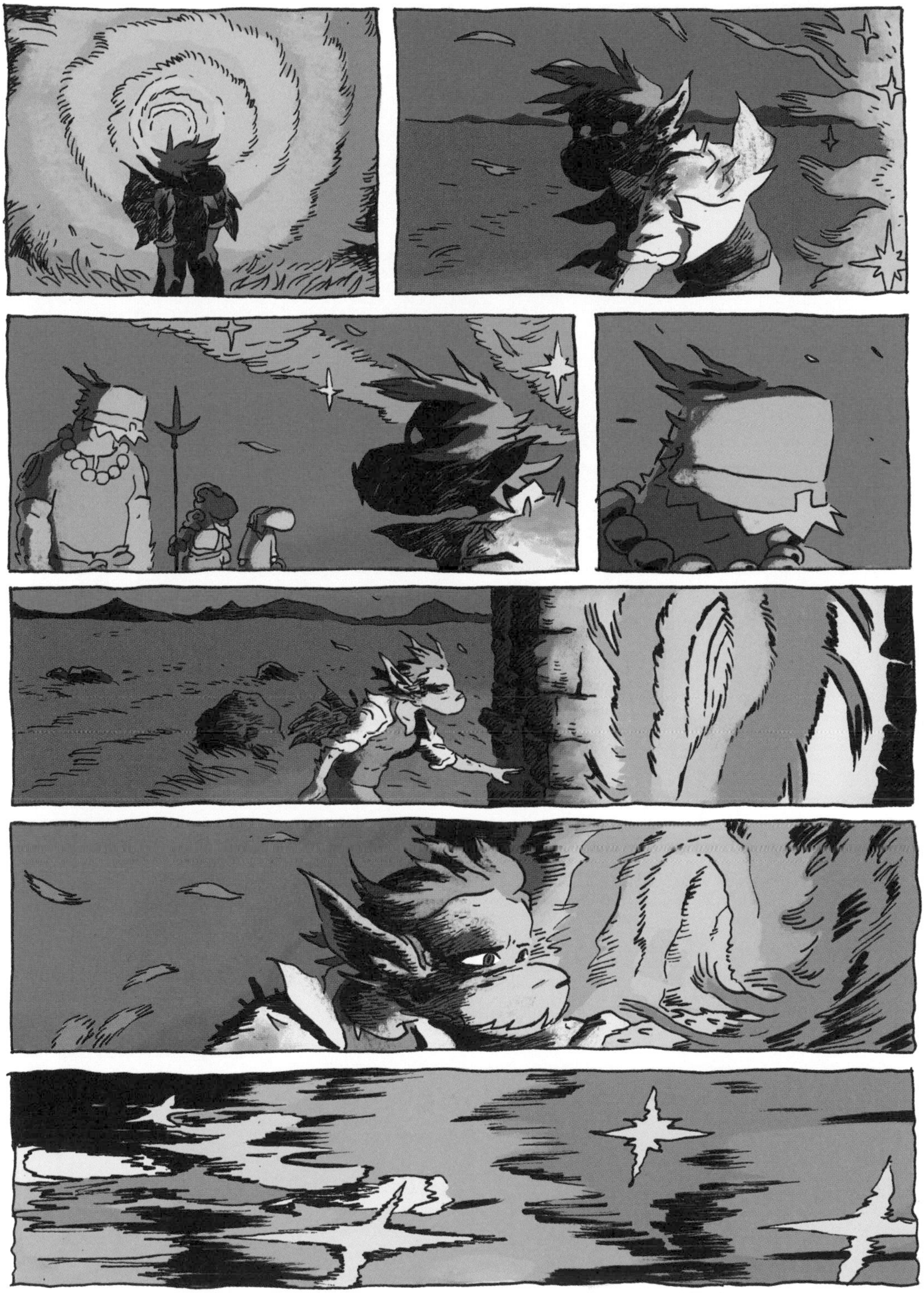

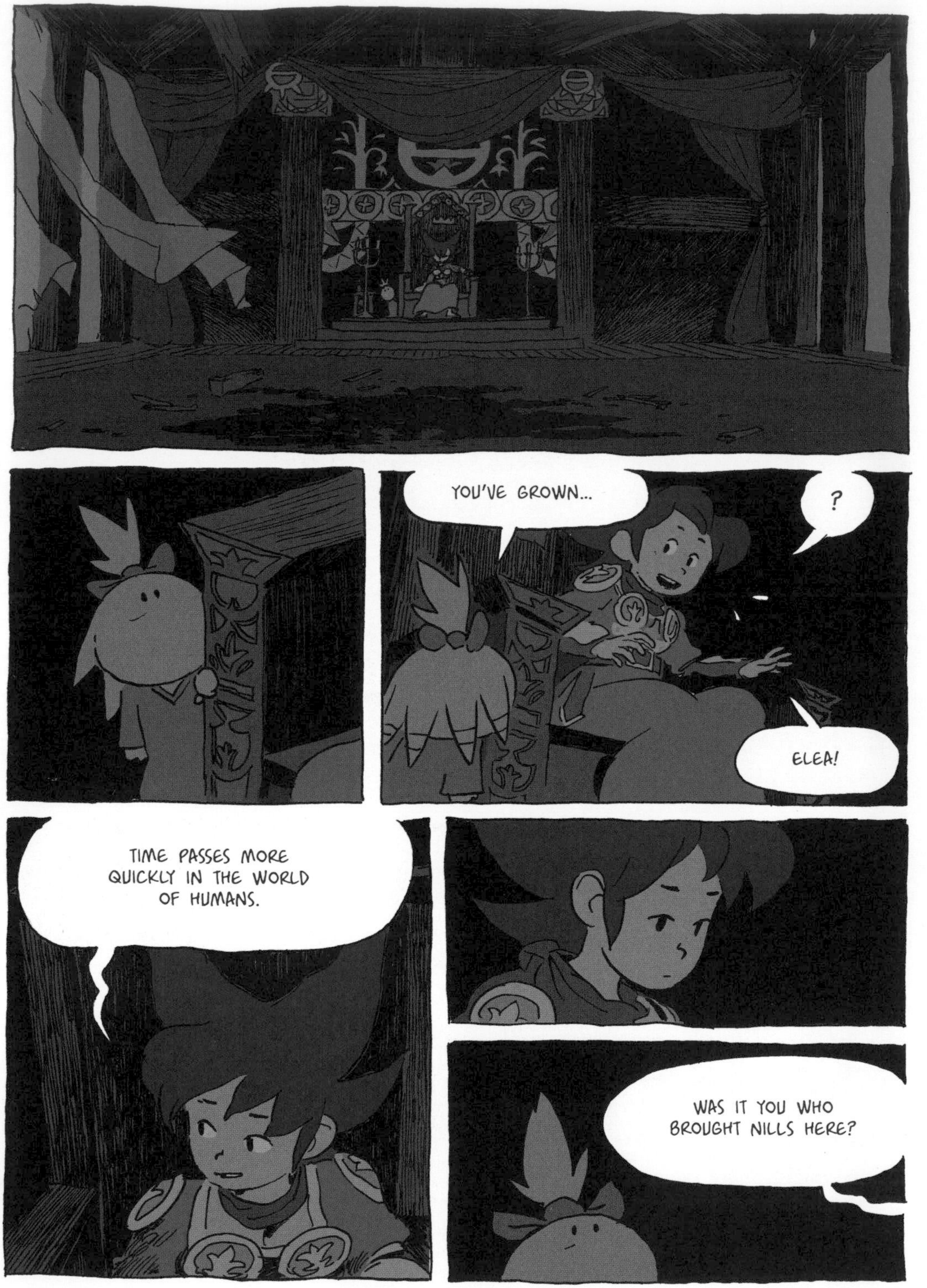
YOU'VE GROWN...
?
ELEA!
TIME PASSES MORE QUICKLY IN THE WORLD OF HUMANS.
WAS IT YOU WHO BROUGHT NILLS HERE?

YES, IT WAS ME.

WHY?

BECAUSE I COULD TELL HE REALLY MISSED YOU.

HE WOULD HAVE COME, EVEN WITHOUT MY HELP.

AND I THOUGHT YOU LOVED HIM.

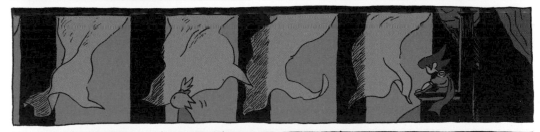

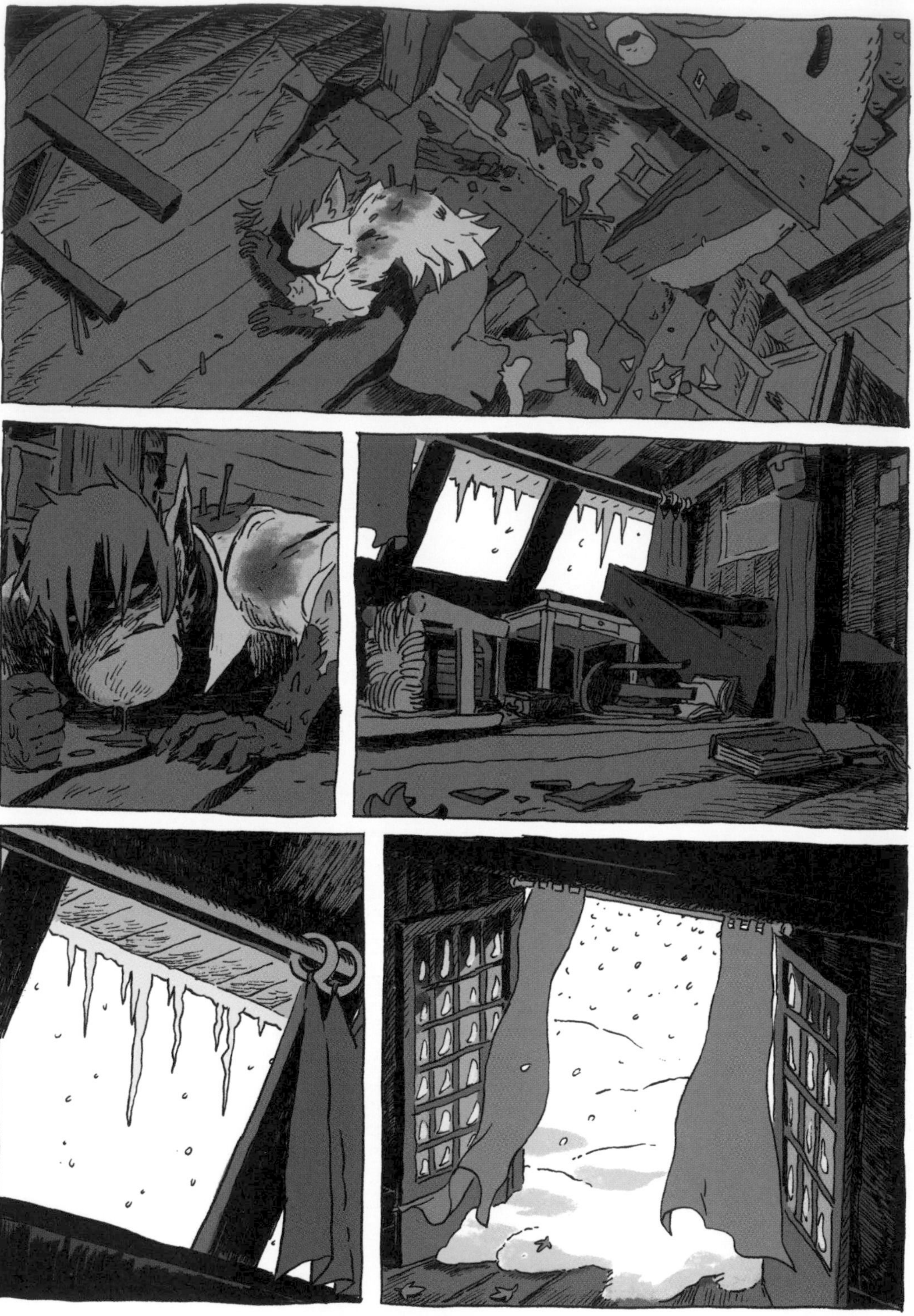

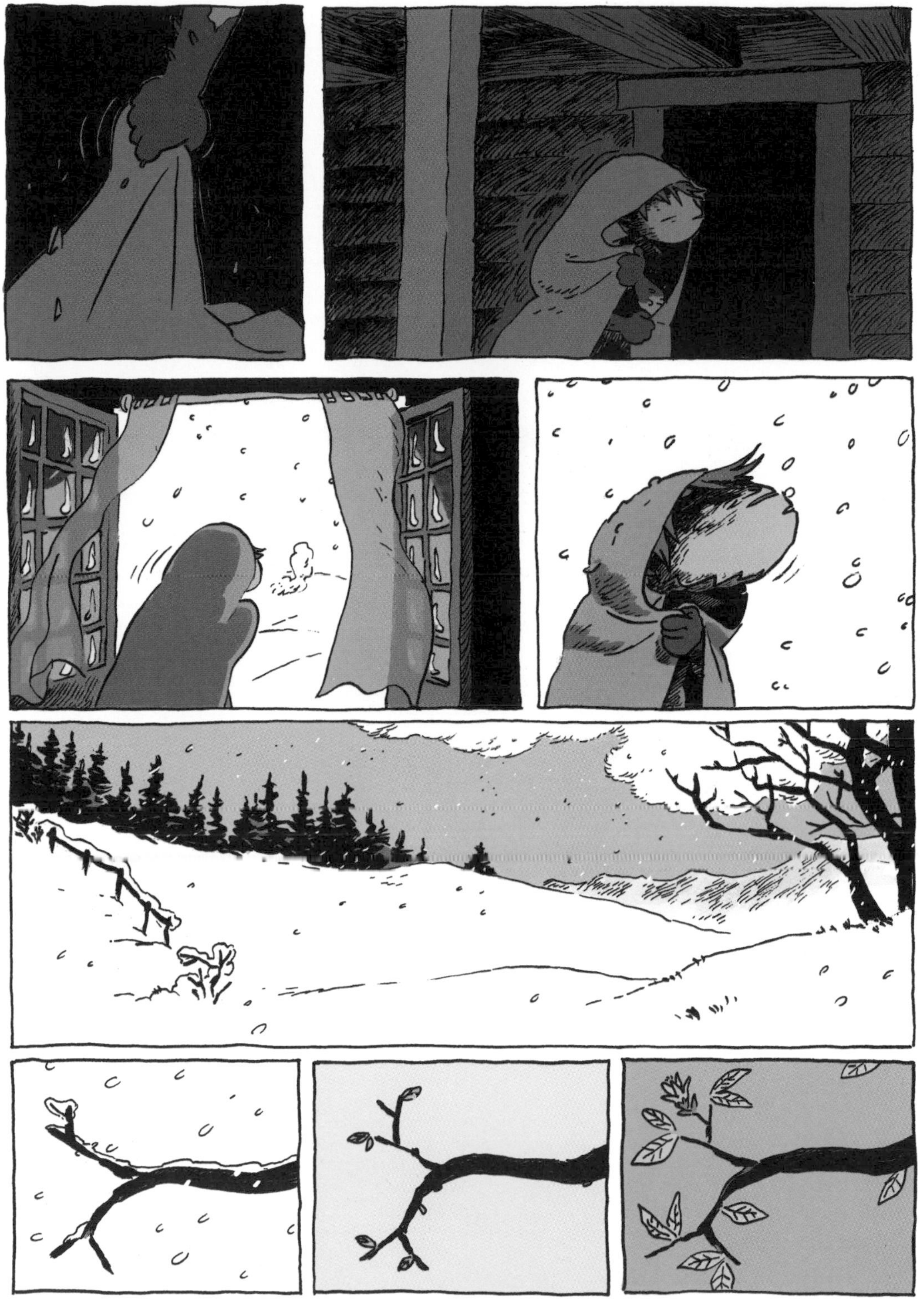

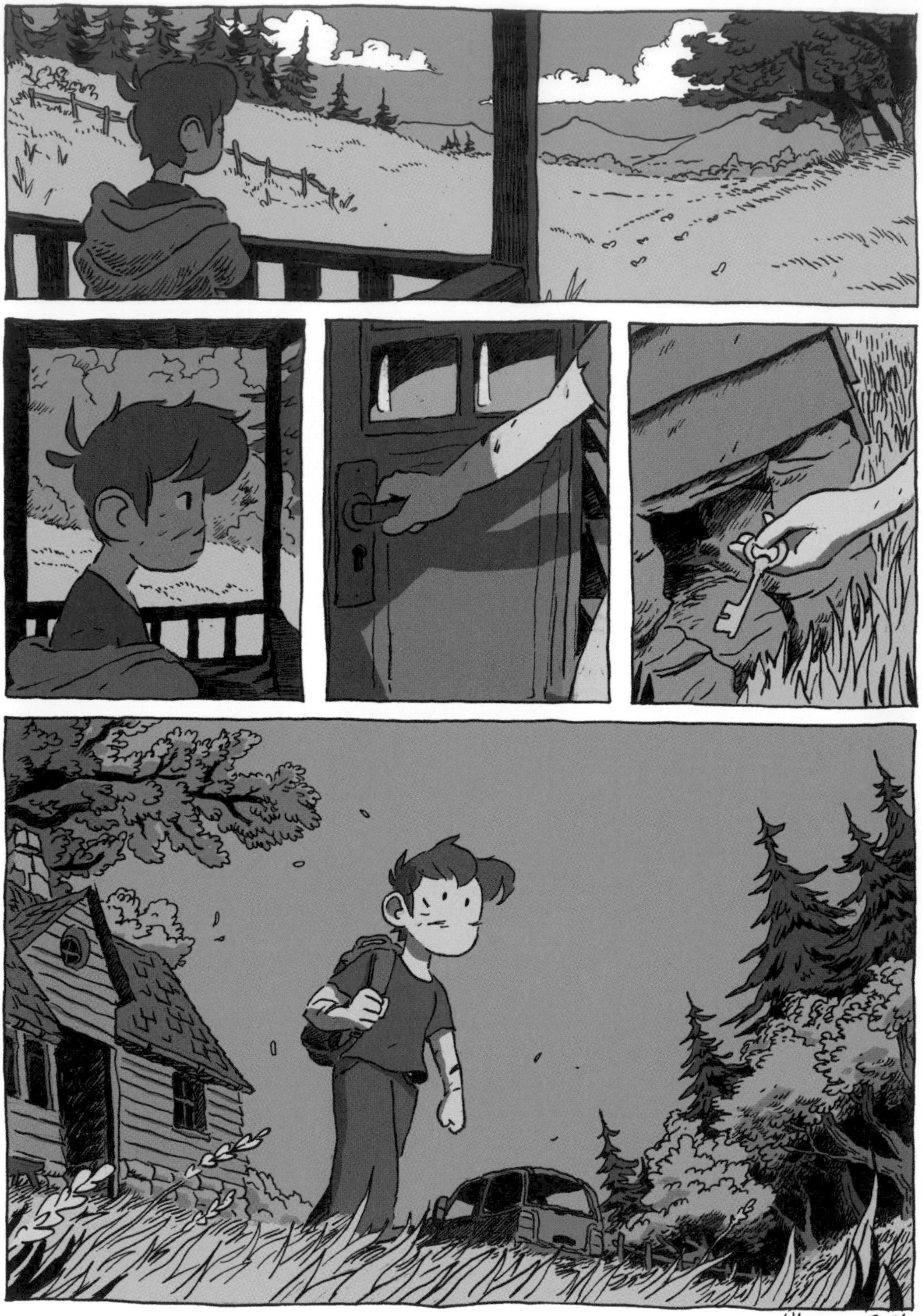

Ulysse 2014